MW00848647

D. GREG SCOTT

Trafficking U

Greg Scott

This is a work of fiction. Unless otherwise indicated, all the names, characters, businesses, places, events and incidents in this book are either the product of the author's imagination or used in a fictitious manner. Any resemblance to actual persons, living or dead, or actual events is purely coincidental.

Copyright © **2024 by D. Greg Scott. All rights reserved.**

ISBN: 978-1-962168-65-6

To the victims: may you find justice.

To the predators: may justice find you.

No person shall disclose to any other person that the Federal Bureau of Investigation has sought or obtained tangible things pursuant to an order issued or an emergency production required under this section, other than to—

(A) those persons to whom disclosure is necessary to comply with such order or such emergency production;

(B) an attorney to obtain legal advice or assistance with respect to the production of things in response to the order or the emergency production; or

(C) other persons as permitted by the Director of the Federal Bureau of Investigation or the designee of the Director.

--US Code, Title 50, Chapter 36, Subchapter IV, Section 1861 (d) (1) Access to certain business records for foreign intelligence and international terrorism investigations

Table of Contents

1. Waste Gate

Friday, November 17, 2017, 7:30 a.m.

Steve sipped his coffee and gazed at bare trees across the Little Falls, Minnesota dam over the Mississippi River while water in the closed waste gate in front of generator six drained.

The receding water exposed a large tree smashed against the steel grates protecting the generator. Which explained today's maintenance. A backhoe moved in to clear the debris. Steve stepped closer to the platform edge and peered down. Tree branches had pinned something else against the grates.

He signaled the backhoe to stop and ran to the operator cage. "Lower me down there." He pointed to the spot.

He climbed into the bucket and signaled the operator. The backhoe arm swung out and over the empty pool toward the steel grates and lowered slowly until Steve signaled to stop. He reached toward the grates and pulled a slimy branch away.

A misshapen brown head with empty eye sockets and teeth protruding from an open mouth stared back at him.

Steve yelled and staggered to the back of the bucket. He regained his composure and looked again. The head connected to a bloated body that looked like it was wrapped in wet, tattered burlap bags. A chunk of the head above one ear was missing.

He waved his arms. The bucket moved over the pool again and set down on the platform. Steve scrambled out and ran to the operator cage.

Steve shivered. "Shut it down. I'm calling 911."

2. Boardroom

Tuesday, January 16, 2018; nineteen days before
Superbowl LII in Minneapolis

Jesse Jonsen paced outside the Uncle Sam Bank
boardroom. After a career keeping the bank out of trouble by
unraveling more financial scams than she could remember,
this would take her work to a whole new level. Finally. Of
course, they'll say yes. They'd be crazy to say no.

Bottom of the hour. It's time. She stepped inside. Show
confidence. They'll notice. Senior Vice President of
Operations, Mike Swanson, stood at the front of the room.

Jesse raised her eyebrows.

Mike nodded.

Jesse strode toward the front.

Faces around the large conference table acknowledged
her. One face looked familiar. Dark hair. Black, yellow, and
red tie. With a lion design. He hinted at a smile. "Merci,
Jesse. We meet again."

Jesse smiled. "Um, hi. Nice tie." How do I know this
guy?

He smiled. "It is the emblem of my country, Belgium."
He extended his hand.

"Oh. Um, good to see you again." She shook his hand.

Mike's eyes twinkled. "I see a few of you already know
Principal Fraud Analyst Jesse Jonsen. She regularly presents

at conferences and she's a major innovator in the fraud fighting community. You also know that human trafficking is a multibillion-dollar industry, and it's coming here, to Minneapolis, with the Superbowl in a little more than two weeks. Since we're a large bank with a fiduciary duty to our community, you asked for a summary of what we're doing about it. I invited Jesse to walk you through the program she spearheaded. I think you'll find what she produced is nothing short of amazing. Jesse?"

Jesse ran a hand through her dark hair and stretched her five-foot, one inch frame to scan down the table at the people working to mate her laptop with a rat's nest of cables and connectors to the big screen system.

One looked up. "Almost ready."

Jesse adjusted her blue jeans. "Okay. As soon as they hook my laptop to the projector, I'll show you slides with details about the predictive analytics we developed. For now, the summary is, we went through transactions for people convicted of trafficking and we compared their patterns with people who have clean records. We found differences in transaction patterns. For example, traffickers tend to show charges for multiple simultaneous ride-sharing services or hotel rooms. Or rooms reserved with a credit card but paid with cash. Or maybe a pattern of cash deposits right below the legal reporting threshold. And now, just like we learned to spot fraudulent credit card transactions, we can also identify transaction patterns that point to traffickers."

One board member with a beige jacket shifted in her seat. "How did you find these patterns?"

Good sign. They're asking questions. "We went through area prison rosters and found the prisoners who did their banking with us by cross referencing names and addresses. And then we compared their transactions with an anonymized random sample of account holders not convicted of crimes to our knowledge. Once we identified the differences, we tried it with several other cities. We saw the same patterns."

A board member on the other side of the table stroked his neatly trimmed beard. "What about privacy?"

Jesse shifted to face him. "Prison rosters and the crimes they're in for are public knowledge. So, we used that and anonymized our own internal data."

"Sounds like profiling." The beard guy blinked a few times. "The police get in trouble for that."

Jesse nodded. "You're right, it's not foolproof, and so I've been working on another tactic."

A few people lifted their chins. Beard guy sat a little taller.

This is why I'm here. They'll love it. Jesse licked her lips. "When we see a pattern, I'll contact one of these pervs and pretend I'm a potential customer. When they bite, we tell the police, the police arrest them, and prosecutors have an airtight case. We nailed one last week. One less predator on the streets."

A few people squirmed.

Beard guy flopped back in his chair. "You're saying you persuade somebody you're a guy looking for a prostitute?"

Jesse chuckled. "It's all online these days. I play-act. It's similar to the tactic we use to buy fake credit cards. I just developed a different persona for this project. I call him John."

A few people smiled.

Ms. Beige jacket squinted. "Refresh my memory. You buy fake credit cards?"

Jesse turned back toward her. "Yeah. We've done it for years. I have an online persona, Teena Fay from Green Bay, and she passes herself off as a small-time wannabe credit card thief. She interacts with people in criminal underground forums and marketplaces, and she buys a few credit cards when we see fraud patterns, so we can trace them back to the point of origin."

The guy from Belgium wagged a finger. "Ah, yes. I remember when you explained your buyback program after the Bullseye Breach incident in 2013. I also sit on the Bullseye Stores' board and I believe we listened to a presentation from a contractor you hired."

Jesse smiled. "That's how I know you. Henri, right?"

"Oui, Henri Carpentier, at your service."

Yeah, now I remember. He'll be on my side. "Yep. I bought a few cards from a crook who called himself Tarman and we traced the breach back to its common point, Bullseye Stores. Jerry Barkley helped us turn that data stream against Tarman."

A woman at the end of the table looked pensive. "But doesn't that just put money in criminals' pockets?"

"Small amounts, yes. But we need to trace the transactions, and that's our only way to do it." Jesse glanced at the A/V team, still working on her laptop.

"I'm sorry." An A/V team member shook his head. "We don't have the connector we need anywhere in the building."

"Don't worry about it. I'll share the slides with details later. What's important for now is, we have a way to identify transaction patterns to help law enforcement go after these predators. And we're developing a way to catch them in the act. We can make a difference."

"Okay." The pensive woman fiddled with a pen. "You made a good case for buying credit cards. I don't like enriching criminals, but we have a fiduciary duty to protect our assets. But—" she put the pen down and sighed. "Fighting prostitution by pretending you're a customer? That's a different story."

A few heads nodded.

She leaned forward. "We're a bank, not the police. It's not our role to impose moral standards."

Jesse glanced at her supervisor, Brenda Yang, and manager, Harlan Phillips, in a back corner of the room huddled with Mike. Both nodded slightly.

"Okay, we're not going on an anti-prostitution crusade here. We're going after predators. These people use banking services to enslave others and buy and sell people like cattle. That's universally illegal, it's rampant, and it's coming here in force in a couple of weeks. We're in a position to do something about it. What would our liability picture look like if word got out that we allow predators to use our bank to conduct business?"

The pensive woman pushed herself to her feet. "I think everyone in this room wants to stamp out human trafficking, especially sex trafficking. As for our liability exposure, suspicious activity reports from the analytics program you summarized should take care of that. But your next step goes too far. What's our liability exposure when somebody sues us for entrapment, or the police lose a case and one of your predators goes free because we did something improper?" She looked around the room. "What does everyone else think?"

All eyes settled on Henri Carpentier. Henri nodded. "I applaud your passion and I am, how you say, curious. Where does this passion come from?"

Jesse pursed her lips. If he only knew. "I have my reasons."

"Oui. And I have no doubt your motives are good. But my colleague is persuasive. We are a bank, not a police agency, and our role is not to regulate behavior, no matter how dreadful. I will support your predictive analytics program, but not your program to entrap people. Similar to money laundering, you can file a suspicious activity report with appropriate law enforcement agencies when your analytics show a pattern, and then law enforcement can use its expertise to arrest and prosecute criminals."

Jesse considered climbing on top of a chair, but thought better of it. "But law enforcement won't follow through on many of these cases."

"Oui. Our society is far from perfect. But our institution will only harm itself if we try to impose our version of morality on the world. Going after sexual predators is, of course, a laudable goal, especially with the large event coming here to Minneapolis shortly. But your entrapment program sets a precedent that will distract us from our purpose as a bank, and this will eventually lead us to debate morality in our board meetings instead of overseeing the business. As a public company, our first duty is to our shareholders. We cannot take our focus away from that."

"But—"

"Thanks, Jesse." Mike Swanson stepped forward.

"Mike—"

"Jesse, thanks," Mike made his way to the front. "And I want to thank the board for hearing us out and for your guidance."

"You can't do this." The words spilled out. "These predators are sick. They groom innocent young women and turn them into slaves. They manipulate their way into these girls' heads and they ruin millions of lives. We have to do our part—"

"Jesse." It was her manager, Harlan Phillips. "Let's talk about it in my office."

Her supervisor, Brenda Yang, also worked her way to the front of the room.

Henri stood. "Perhaps it would be wise to take a ten-minute break."

The room agreed. Some people stood and stretched. Others left the room for bathroom breaks or coffee or water.

Jesse shook her head and trudged back to her chair. She packed up her laptop.

Brenda, Harlan, Mike, and Henri worked their way to Jesse.

Henri extended a hand. "Jesse, I am sorry I am not able to support your intervention program. You made a good case and this decision is painful. I cannot imagine the suffering of any parent who must endure their daughter caught in this nasty business. I will work with you to find more effective ways to fight it."

"Yeah, well, whatever." Jesse finished packing her laptop and marched out of the room. "Bureaucrats."

3. Rescue

Friday, Feb. 2, 2018, 6:30 p.m.; two days before Superbowl LII in Minneapolis.

Who's in Superbowl LII anyway? Who cares? Jesse sipped her latte at the Manitou Coffee in the Minneapolis skyway and scrolled through pictures of jeans. This horrible week of sending suspicious activity reports into a law-enforcement black hole was finally over. Let the football crazies own downtown for the weekend. Maybe she would accept Mom's standing offer to go to church in the suburbs with her Sunday morning, just to get away. Or maybe she'd sleep right through until Monday morning. She chuckled silently. Predators and perverts. This is the part of Superbowl week nobody highlights in the glossy brochures.

"Act like you know me. Please."

Jesse looked up from her tablet.

Late teens. Tall. Native American maybe? And scantily dressed, which made no sense in early February in Minneapolis. Unless...

The girl raked quivering fingers through her hair and whispered, "Quick. Tell me your name."

"Um, Jesse."

She squealed. "Jesse, it's great to see you. How long has it been?"

"Um,"

She pulled out a chair and sat. "I missed you."

"Um, yeah, I, um, I missed you too."

She glanced left and right and then whispered, "Please, help me get out of here before my boyfriend grabs me."

"What's your name?"

"Leilani."

Jesse followed Leilani's gaze to a thirty-something man dressed in a suit and scanning the room. His eyes locked onto Leilani.

Leilani peeked at Jesse's tablet. "Are you shopping for jeans? I saw some really cute ones on sale at Bullseye. Let's go try some on." Leilani's eyes pleaded.

Jesse glanced at the barrel-chested giant marching toward her table. Leilani's lower lip trembled.

Jesse nodded. "Good idea." Jesse took one last swig of her latte. They stood and stepped toward the door.

The guy grabbed Leilani's arm and spun her around. "Where do you think you're going?"

"With my friend Jesse to look at jeans. Don't worry, Kyle, I'll be right back." Leilani's arm trembled.

Jesse stepped between Kyle and Leilani. Jesse's head met the bottom of Kyle's neck. She looked up and smiled. "So, you're Leilani's mysterious boyfriend. Listen—I've always valued Leilani's fashion advice. She's gonna help me pick out a pair of jeans and we'll be back in a few minutes."

Kyle tightened his grip. "I don't think so."

Jesse reached into her purse. "Kyle, tell ya what. Here's five dollars. I want you to try one of Gloria's lattes." Jesse nodded toward a tall, red headed woman behind the counter. "That's Gloria right over there and her lattes are the best on the planet. We'll be back before you finish it."

He swore. "I don't know who you think you are—"

"I'm Jesse. And you're attracting attention you don't want to attract. Now, you can either let go of Leilani's arm right now and smile, or I'll ask Gloria to call the police. Ever heard of an old TV show, Candid Camera?" Jesse tilted her head to a video camera bubble in the middle of the store. "What's it gonna be, Kyle?"

"I could break her arm and smash your face in right now if I wanted to."

"You probably could. But I know the guy who put in those cameras. Something about a 360-degree view range with software to smooth it all out and enhance the resolution. So, if you want to try something stupid, I suggest you take your best shot because it's the last one you'll ever get."

Jesse nodded at Gloria. Gloria picked up a phone. Kyle let go of Leilani's arm.

"That's better. Ya know what? Buy your own latte." Jesse snatched her five-dollar-bill from Kyle's hands and stuffed it in her purse. "Fast hands. I used to be a thief."

Jesse put her arm around Leilani's waist and led her toward the skyway connecting most buildings in downtown Minneapolis.

"Thank you." Leilani's whole body trembled.

"Just keep walking. I know a safe place." Jesse guided Leilani onto the skyway.

Leilani looked back. "He's following us."

"Good thing it's crowded."

Leilani stumbled after several steps. Almost as tall as Kyle, she nearly collapsed on top of Jesse. Jesse tightened her grip. "Almost there."

"Where are we going?"

"My office for now. We need to ride down this escalator." Jesse guided Leilani onto the escalator in the middle of a crowd. She supported Leilani on the ride down.

Kyle took the stairs and landed on the ground floor as Jesse and Leilani stepped off the escalator. He fell in directly behind them.

Jesse scanned left and right and found what she was looking for. She slowed. Most of the crowd passed through the revolving door and outside.

Jesse whispered, "Lean on this" and guided Leilani to the security stand. Jesse turned and stepped into Kyle. "Listen, creep. Stop following us."

A security guard looked up. Jesse made eye contact. "May I help you?" A couple of other security guards also approached.

"Yeah. This creep tried to grab my friend at the Manitou Coffee. He won't leave us alone."

Kyle backed away. "Hey, I didn't grab anyone. Just tried to grab a coffee after work."

"It's on video. And now he's trying to follow us outside."

The security guards surrounded Kyle. "Listen, buddy, why don't you just wait here and give these ladies some space?" Another guard spoke into his radio.

Jesse went back to Leilani.

One of the security guards followed her. "Ma'am, do you want us to go back to the coffee shop with you and sort this all out?"

"No, I just want to go home. Can we leave?"

The security guard spoke into his radio again. "Apparently, the store owner called security while you guys were there. She saw the whole thing. We have an officer in the store right now talking to her."

"Thanks. We just want to get away from this creep."

"It would be helpful if you and your friend came back with us."

Leilani slid to the floor and whimpered.

Jesse studied the commotion around her. Five security guards surrounding a creep, onlookers craning their necks, and Leilani crumpled on the floor. This guy must be bad news. She turned to the security guard. "Give me a sec."

Jesse squatted next to Leilani and put her arm around her. "Leilani, let's go back to Manitou and finish what you started. What's the deal with this guy anyway?"

13

"He's," Leilani wiped tears. "He's my boyfriend and we had a fight. That's all. I'm sorry."

Leilani sobbed.

Jesse cupped her hands around Leilani's face. "Are you sure that's all…"

Leilani winced and pulled back.

"What's wrong?"

"Nothing."

Something didn't look right under her hair. Leilani looked down. Jesse gently pushed Leilani's hair away. A swollen purple and yellow blotch covered Leilani's jaw line below her ear.

"Did he do this?"

Leilani hugged her knees. "It was my fault."

Jesse helped Leilani to her feet and faced the security guard. "Yeah, we're going back. Call the police."

4. Sorting it Out

The police officers waiting at Manitou Coffee took names and asked everyone what they were doing in the Skyway. And then they individually interviewed Gloria, Kyle, Leilani, and Jesse in private.

"Why were you involved?" one grey-haired officer asked Jesse.

Jesse sipped a cup of coffee. "Good question. I just met Leilani a few minutes ago. But when I saw that creep trying to intimidate her—and then he threatened me—I had to do something."

"So, you're just a Good Samaritan, and that's it?"

"Yeah, that's pretty much it. But this guy is a creep. He's sucking her in, and I can't just sit back and watch."

"Can I offer you some advice from a cop who's seen it all?"

"Sure, why not?"

"Don't let yourself get sucked in."

"What's that supposed to mean?"

"It means, well, you look like a successful woman. You don't want to get sucked into a mess with people you don't know."

Jesse leaned back in her chair and pursed her lips. She leaned in and looked the officer in the eye. "I made a lot of money stealing back in high school and I almost ended up where she's going. That's why I've been fighting lowlifes like him for a long time now. This guy is a creep and if he harms one hair on her head, I'll make sure he regrets it."

"Miss Jonsen, are you making a threat?"

"No, I'm making a promise. If I can bring down a Russian credit card kingpin, I can handle this creep. So, don't worry about me."

"I'm not worried about you. I'm worried about him."

Jesse laughed. "Leilani is my friend now and I take care of my friends. Are we done?"

"Yeah. Listen, I'm sorry if I offended you."

"Don't worry about it. I can take care of myself. And I won't do anything stupid."

While police officers continued questioning Kyle, Jesse and Leilani headed into the Skyway again.

"So, Kyle is your boyfriend?"

"He's mostly a nice guy. And he treats me like a goddess."

"He didn't treat you like a goddess tonight."

"That was my fault. I guess I messed up a deal he was working on."

Jesse shook her head. "How do you know this guy?"

"We met online."

"Let me guess, he found you and told you how beautiful you are."

"Nobody else ever treated me like that. It was like he lived inside my head. He knew when I was hurting, when I was happy, my favorite colors, the clothes I liked, the food I liked to eat and when I had trouble, he helped me."

"How?"

"My dad liked his liquor better than my mom and me. So he took me in. He treated me like a princess."

"When did all this happen?"

"Three years ago."

Leilani stopped at the glass door entrance to the Downtown Patterson Hotel. "This is where I work."

Jesse gestured toward the door. "You work here?"

"Overnight, yeah."

"What do you do?"

Leilani blushed. "What do you think I do?"

"And, so Kyle is your—"

"He's my boyfriend. He's saving the money we make so we can have a life together."

"Leilani, I thought you wanted me to help get you away from that guy."

"I did. I needed a break. But I love him."

"How can you love this guy after he hit you?"

"He's under a lot of pressure right now. But after we make some money this weekend, things will be fine."

Jesse reached for Leilani's hands. "No, they won't. This guy is a creep and he's been grooming you."

Leilani pulled her hands back. "What does that even mean?"

"It means he manipulates you into doing what he wants."

"No. He loves me. And I love him."

Jesse nodded and fumbled in her purse. "Okay. But here, at least take a business card. Call me if you get in trouble and I'll help."

Leilani took the card and disappeared into the crowd.

Jesse watched the crowd. Women and men of all ages and appearances mingled and hustled to wherever they were going. Some were probably on their way to a Superbowl party. Some men in business suits in the hotel lobby on the other side of the glass doors talked about something important. Leilani approached one of them, a red-head. He recognized her. She gestured. He craned his neck toward the hotel glass doors. Jesse turned away, watching from the corner of her eye. Red-head stepped away from Leilani and the others and moved toward the hotel door. Looking for Kyle, no doubt. Jesse positioned herself farther away from the glass doors, behind groups coming and going in the skyway. Inside the hotel, Leilani headed toward an elevator.

A few seconds later, Kyle hustled down the skyway toward the hotel glass doors. Jesse ducked behind a support column. Kyle entered the hotel. Red-head chastised him and gestured toward the elevator bank. Red-head turned back to his friends. Kyle shuffled to the elevator bank and pressed a button.

Jesse turned away. Couples strolled past, arm-in-arm. Were they really couples? Or just coupling for the weekend? How many were victims and how many were real wives or girlfriends? Or boyfriends? She stepped away from the support column. A sea of humanity flowed around her as if Jesse were a boulder in the middle of a stream. Alone. At least Leilani would have plenty of company tonight.

Jesse sighed. Keep on seeking, and you will find. I am with you always, even to the end of the age. I wish that would stop popping into my head. For the zillionth time, what am I supposed to look for? And jealous of a brainwashed abuse victim? What's wrong with me? But another latte at Gloria's coffee shop would be nice. Gloria had become a friend since Jerry Barkley introduced them back in 2013. And Jesse could use a friend right now.

~

Jesse put down her coffee cup. She put her hands on the table and leaned forward. "Gloria, that guy hit her. You should have seen her crumple at the bottom of the escalator."

Gloria leaned back in her chair across from Jesse. "You mean, he hit her right in front of you?"

"No. It must have been earlier. She had a huge bruise under her ear. She tried to cover it up with makeup."

Gloria shook her head. "He teaches Literature at North Prairie University."

"Who?"

"The boyfriend. Kyle. I'll bet he's one of her professors."

"How do you know that?"

Gloria's eyes twinkled. "Baristas are better listeners than bartenders. His last name is Van Buren."

Jesse smiled.

"Now that you know how to find this guy, what do you want to do about it?"

Jesse leaned back in her chair. She took a breath. "I want to take him down. Hard."

Gloria laughed. "You know they're in the oldest profession, right?"

"I wasn't born last night."

"So, you know everyone has to earn a living, right?"

"I know all that. But that guy beat her."

"Maybe. Or maybe she had a car accident or something."

"No way. You should have seen how scared she was. That guy keeps her as a slave."

Gloria sipped her coffee. "Jesse, you're making a bunch of assumptions here. All I'm saying is, make sure they're true. Don't go off half-cocked."

"I won't—and thanks."

Both sipped their coffee.

"She got to you, didn't she?"

"No." Jesse took another sip. "Maybe."

"Everyone chooses their path in life. Just because you see someone that could be you doesn't mean you need to run off on a rescue mission."

Jesse looked down. Her cheeks flushed.

Gloria smiled. "You're getting red-faced. I hit home, didn't I?"

Jesse shook her head. "I'm not planning any rescue mission. I'm a fraud analyst, not Wonder Woman."

"Keep that in mind. These are dangerous people."

5. 1995—Busted

July, 1995. Edina, Minnesota.

Row after row of blouses in the Bullseye Store women's aisle called teenaged Jesse Jonsen. The movie theater would be packed tonight, and she needed to look good for Dylan. But not so fast. She was still at work. Job first. Isn't that what her parents taught her?

Mom and Dad thought work was at Dairy Queen. Seriously, does anyone enjoy scooping ice cream for hours on end? In a Dairy Queen uniform? Eew. Dylan had offered her a job exploring a different high school career. In business.

Tonight's movie choices were *Apollo 13*, *Batman Forever*, or *Die Hard with a Vengeance*. The new *Die Hard* movie would probably be the most fun. Which meant she needed an outfit that said adventure.

The way Dylan explained it, they did retailers a favor by finding buyers for samples of their merchandise. And today, Bullseye Stores would compensate her with clothes. Or whatever else she wanted. Having Dylan as a boyfriend was just another fringe benefit of the job, especially on date nights.

She found a black blouse. V-neck with bell sleeves. Yeah, that would look nice. She tilted the hanger. Easy to spot later.

Now for some jeans. She needed a pair to show off her almost-seventeen-year-old curves. But not too much skin. That would be gross. She spotted a nice pair and picked it up. Size six.

"May I help you?" The clerk must have been in her fifties.

"No, just looking, thanks." Jesse put the jeans back.

That made things more challenging. This clerk was new, but none of them were worth beans. It was almost laughable, how easy they made it. She browsed around the store, watching for followers. That clerk didn't bother her. The other clerks didn't seem to care.

She needed some lipstick. She zigzagged through the aisles, glancing at the ceiling for video cameras whenever she turned down a new aisle. The cameras were usually above the cash registers. Yup, there was a bubble. The angle could work.

She walked past the lipstick shelves and found a color she liked. Problem was, it was on an upper shelf. That would make it more challenging to block the camera. But not insurmountable. Still, just a dry run this time. Can't be too careful.

One more trip around the perimeter to make sure nobody was watching. And to look for anyone undercover. They were so easy to spot.

She made her way back to the lipstick shelves and picked up two lipstick packages, lightning-fast, just like she'd practiced. She turned her body away from the camera and dropped one in her purse. Now turning back where the camera could see her hands, she examined the remaining package, and then put it back on the shelf.

The trick was, don't get greedy.

Now, back to the blouse and jeans. She picked three blouses and three pairs of jeans and made her way to a dressing room.

Inside the dressing room, she pulled off her floor-length dress and long-sleeved black shirt, and then took off her sweat pants and stuffed them into her purse.

She chuckled. Even when it's hot, always wear a dark shirt. Dark covers light, but light doesn't cover dark. It was a lesson she'd taught herself months ago.

She cut the tags off the pants and shirt she liked and put them on. Next, she put on her own dress and shirt over those and adjusted herself in the mirror. "Jesse Jonsen, you look hot." She licked her finger and touched her butt. "Bssssh." She smiled.

Back on the store floor, she put the extra clothes back on their racks and headed down the main aisle toward the row of cash registers and the exit. Just another day at work. Except, this time she would sample the merchandise.

Something felt wrong. Two guys stood by the door, trying to blend in. She ducked into the lady's room. Two other women were inside. She headed to a stall and closed the door. Just stay calm. If those guys are cops, I can always go to plan B. Trouble was, she had never tried plan B for real. That's why it was plan B. But wait a minute; there was nothing wrong with wearing an outfit under her dress. After all, she came in wearing sweatpants. Sure. There's a party tonight, she knew she wouldn't have time to change clothes, and so she dressed this morning before school. Flutter the eyelashes, give her best charming look. Yeah, it could work. She took a deep breath. She was ready.

She emerged from the ladies room and strode through the door. The two guys made eye contact and exited behind her.

One raced in front of her and blocked her path. "We need you to come with us back into the store."

"Why?"

"Because you're wearing stolen pants and a blouse."

"I am not. Who do you guys think you are?"

"We're with store security and we observed you take three sets of clothes off the racks. You only put two back and left nothing behind in the dressing room."

"I did no such thing."

"I'll give you two choices and five seconds to make your decision. Either you walk with us back into the store or we wait right here for the police."

"Maybe I'll run."

"We'd rather not tackle you. Might damage the stuff you stole."

Jesse shook her head. "Fine. But I didn't steal anything."

They escorted her to an upstairs room near the front of the store. A woman was waiting at a table. "Please, sit down."

Jesse sat. The two guys sat on either side of her, across from the woman.

"My name is Lynette Richards and I'm in charge of store security here. We are recording everything that happens in this meeting on video." She pointed to a video camera on a tripod, connected to a VCR in a corner. "Please empty the contents of your purse on this table."

"I will not. And you don't have any right to make me."

"You're correct. I'm not a police officer. But the police are on their way, and I suspect after we show the video of you in the store, they'll find probable cause to search you."

Lynette stared at her. Jesse looked away. "Fine." She turned her purse over and dumped it on the table.

Lynette fumbled through Jesse's sweat pants and other items. "It's not here. We need to search your purse."

"What is this, communism or something? Is this how you guys treat all your customers?"

Lynette smiled. "Do we do it or do the police do it?"

"What difference does it make?"

"If we do it without the police getting a warrant, it might help your case."

Jesse shook her head and handed Lynette her purse.

Lynette examined Jesse's purse. "You've been here before. Today, we watched you more closely than usual. You cased the store like a pro." She opened a zipper pocket in the purse. "Ah, here it is." She showed Jesse the lipstick tube, still in its shrink wrap. "You have fast hands. We watched you take two tubes of lipstick off the shelf and only put one back. Is a five-dollar tube of lipstick worth going to jail over?"

"Wait – I must have forgotten all about that. I'll certainly pay for it. I have a credit card in my wallet."

"You do?"

"Yeah."

"How old are you?"

"Sixteen."

"How does a sixteen-year-old get her own credit card?"

"My parents got me one for emergencies."

Lynette smiled. "Well, this certainly qualifies as an emergency. What's the name on your credit card?"

"Um, I don't know. See, um, my parents have different credit cards in different names, you know, for my dad's business and stuff."

"Uh, huh. And what's your dad's name?"

"Ted. Ted Jonsen."

"And what's your name?"

"Jesse."

"And your mom?"

"Stephanie."

"So, when you show me the card, it should have one of your parents' names or your name on it. Otherwise, it belongs to somebody else. So, why don't you show me this credit card."

Sweat drops ran down Jesse's neck. "I don't think so."

"Fine. We have more to discuss. I need you take off your shirt and dress."

"No. Not with these creeps in here. And I'm not taking off my clothes in front of that camera."

"No, I wouldn't expect you to."

The phone on the wall rang. Lynette answered. "Thank you." She paused. "Yes, please send them up." She hung up. "The police are here."

~

The Honorable Judge Latisha Williams looked over her bench out into the courtroom. "Ms. Jonsen, the reports on you say you're an experienced shoplifter. You lied to your parents and faked a W2 statement from Dairy Queen. You were found with a counterfeit driver's license, Social Security card, three credit cards, and even a fake passport. Planning on leaving the country?"

Jesse's attorney stood. She gestured for Jesse to also stand. Her parents looked on next to her at the defendant table. "No, ma'am."

"What do you have to say for yourself?"

"I'm sorry for taking those clothes. I don't know what came over me. I, I guess I just wanted to fit in with some nice clothes for the party that night, and I guess I made a bad choice."

"Well, you're an enigma, I'll give you that. Do you know what an enigma is, Ms. Jonsen?"

"No, ma'am."

"An enigma is something or somebody difficult to understand. You're a practiced thief with a line of BS as long as my judge's robes, but you also get good grades. That shows you're intelligent. You also pulled the wool over lots of people's eyes. Including, as I understand it, your parents. And even here in my court, you're trying to BS your way out of trouble. That suggests courage, even if misplaced." Judge Williams reclined in her chair. "What would you do if you were me, Ms. Jonsen?"

Jesse thought about it for a few seconds. "Um, well, um, I guess I'd make you, I mean, me, pay for the dress and the shirt. And the lipstick. I should pay for the lipstick too. And, then, maybe, make me enroll in some anti-shoplifting classes. And, um, maybe make me sign a statement that I don't do it again."

Judge Williams leaned forward. "As I understand it, your parents already paid for what you got caught stealing. And they're voluntarily working out a plan to pay for what you didn't get caught stealing. Let me ask you one more question. Are you repentant?"

"I don't know what that means."

"Do you believe you were wrong?"

"Oh. Yes, I do see that now."

"Uh, huh. And there's green cheese on the moon too."

"I'm sorry?"

"Ms. Jonsen, I've been a Juvenile judge for more than ten years, and I've seen some whoppers, but yours might be the best yet. A clean looking kid with nice parents. And a criminal with a line of BS a mile long. If I put you back out on the street with a slap on the wrist, you'll be stealing again within a week. But you'll be on your own this time and when you get caught – and you will get caught – you'll end up in prison. Or dead if you get in with the wrong people."

"No. I promise. I'm done stealing. I want to reform."

"I'm glad to hear that, Ms. Jonsen. And here's how I'm going to help you. I'm offering you a choice. I can accept the prosecution recommendation that you spend the next six months incarcerated at the County Juvenile detention center. You'll have to make up your senior year of high school in the future or get a GED. You might get into a college, but you'll have to explain why you didn't graduate from high school with your peers. Or you can finish high school on time by spending your upcoming senior year at the Itasca County Group Home for Girls in Bigfork, Minnesota. It's not incarceration, but it's two hundred miles north from here and you will be closely supervised. Hopefully you'll learn a few things. Talk it over with your parents and your attorney and we'll meet back here at 2 p.m. today with your choice."

6. Monday Morning

Monday, Feb. 5, 2018

Jesse hung her sweater in a makeshift closet in the basement office of the Uncle Sam Bank building where the antifraud group operated. The outside mid-winter temperature in Minneapolis was barely above zero. Inside, it was mid-eighties. Another Monday morning at work.

"Morning, Brenda."

Brenda Yang was always in early. "Morning, Jesse. I already called about the AC. Again."

They both chuckled. Part of the morning ritual.

Brenda was already logged in and checking the usual eastern European carder forums. Jesse poured a cup of coffee and looked over Brenda's shoulder.

Brenda looked up. "Looks like Hornet's been busy." She clicked into a different screen.

Jesse whistled. "Fifty thousand CVVs, ten million dumps."

"Yep. He's asking twenty apiece for the dumps, ten for the CVVs. I already IMed Harlan."

"I'll get Teena ready."

The IM response from Harlan Phillips, Fraud Department manager, popped up on Brenda's screen. "Why are real credit card numbers more expensive than the electronic ones again?"

Brenda responded. "Until all cards have chips, dumps are more versatile. CVVs are only useful online or over the phone."

Harlan replied immediately. "Makes sense. Go ahead. Buy 100 of each. Make sure they're our BINs."

Jesse shook her head. "Remember when this was a big deal?"

"It's still a big deal. We just don't get as excited as we used to."

"Still makes me mad. We took down Tarman. Roscoe and MotleyCru disappeared. And now Hornet and his buddies."

Brenda chuckled. "Yes ma'am. We stand for truth, justice, and the American way. We enjoy walking on the beach and playing Whack-a-Mole."

Jesse smiled. "I think Teena will try to get under Hornet's skin today."

Jesse logged into the dark web credit card forum using her Teena Fay from Green Bay persona and started a private chat session with Hornet.

```
               Hey Hornet, I hear u have
               some good dumps and CVVs 4
               sale."

I luv wen u talk to me. How much
u want?

               dunno. Watcha got for BINs?

Why do u care?

               Cuz I only do business with
               certain banks that did me
               dirty.

I luv when u talk dirty. What
BINs u want?
```

Jesse responded with a few Bank Identification Numbers that matched credit cards issued by Uncle Sam Bank. Hornet replied right away.

Lemme check and get back 2 u.

> Don't take too long. I want 2 no u better. Where u live?

Why?

> Cuz it's cold here in Green Bay and I want 2 go to Hawaii with someone.

Brenda laughed. "You do have a flair."

"Who knows. Maybe he'll show up and somebody can shoot him."

Hornet responded after a few minutes.

Gotcha covered with those BINs. Got a couple thousand of each. CVVs are $10, dumps $20. Pay the usual way.

> Gimme a bulk discount. I'll give you 7 for the CVVs and 15 for the dumps. I want 100 of each.

Bulk is good. CVVs $8, Dumps $18. Qty 100 each. Final offer.

> Deal. Throw in one extra CVV and I'll use it for a plane ticket to Hawaii. You bring a couple of your dumps and dinner's on u.

Maybe later. Mixing business and
pleasure, bad 4 business.

Your loss.

Jesse paid in the usual manner. Spreadsheets with the
physical and online credit card numbers appeared in her
forum inbox a few seconds later, ready for download.

Satisfied?

Pleasure doing business with
u.

Jesse logged off and pounded her desk. "I just put $2600
in this guy's pocket and we still don't even know what
country he's from."

"Nope."

"How can you not be mad?"

"They don't get under my skin anymore."

Jesse shook her head.

"Send me the spreadsheets and I'll feed them to
Merchant-Trace. And I'll have the call center contact the
cardholders."

"For what little good that does. We put money in these
guys' pockets, we use a piece of software to find the
merchants they stole from, we warn the consumers, we send
out new credit cards, and then we do it all over again. We do
this every day and we never win."

"You won back in 2013 with the Bullseye Stores
breach."

"We need to win every time."

Brenda walked back to her desk. "Patience is a virtue,
young Padawan."

Jesse laughed. "Yes, Obi Won."

"So, what's bugging you?"

"I ran into a pimp over the weekend."

"Jesse, I didn't know you needed more money."

"Not funny. He had a girl with him named Leilani and she was traumatized."

"How do you know he was a pimp?"

"I know. He beat her up. And she called him her boyfriend. The guy is a no-good, scumbag, trafficker. But get this—he's a professor at North Prairie University."

"No. The ones doing the endowment campaign?"

"Yeah."

"And we're doing a career day there, right?"

"Yeah, we are."

"Hmm. Maybe a crusader I know needs to do some onsite due diligence."

"I'm not a crusader."

"You are, but that's what we love about you. And it gets you out of the office for a couple days. Might do you some good."

~

The winter grey outside the tenth-floor windows of the Uncle Sam Bank headquarters building in Minneapolis gave the rows of cubicles in front of Harlan Phillips's office a closed-in feel.

Harlan always reminded Jesse of Lou Grant in the old TV show. He leaned back in his office chair and crossed his hands behind his head. "It's just not like you, that's all."

"Why not?"

Harlan leaned forward. "Because fraud analysts don't head up college Career Day events."

"Well, maybe I want to broaden my horizons."

"This is community outreach. If you want to go represent our department, I can probably swing that. But I couldn't put you in charge of the whole event even if I wanted to."

"Why not?"

Harlan stroked his chin and leaned back. "Why do you want to lead it this year"

"I just do, that's all."

31

Harlan pursed his lips. "What's going on, Jesse?"

"There's nothing going on."

"Yeah, there is."

Jesse grinned. "Why does something have to be going on?"

Harlan stared. "You want my help? I need to know what's going on."

Jesse leaned back in her chair and sighed. "I think there's some ugly stuff going on at North Prairie U, and I want to find out more."

"What ugly stuff?"

"I think they're abusing students."

"Why?"

Jesse told Harlan about Leilani.

"And so, from that, you think there's some sort of conspiracy?"

"I did some research after that."

"Why am I not surprised?"

Jesse smiled. "That's why you like me, remember?"

"What did you do and what did you find out?"

"Well, first of all, forget about what I think is going on for a minute. We're the lead fund manager with NPU's endowment. Doesn't it make sense for us to do our due diligence about this organization? If there's even a hint of something ugly going on, don't we want to find out about it first?"

Harlan put his hands behind his head. "How long did you practice this pitch?"

"It just makes sense, doesn't it? And who better to find out than one of this bank's top fraud analysts? We want to get a feel for their academic standards and what they're teaching because we want to support NPU's mission and hire from there. Which is the truth, isn't it? We *do* want to make sure our partners are on the up and up, right? Just like we'd expect them to make sure we're on the up and up. Right?"

Harlan stared at Jesse and narrowed his eyes. Jesse met his gaze.

"I'll see what I can do. But you know it's not my call. And if I find out you're on some grand society improvement project—"

"You know me better than that. I'll put together an email you can forward to the department heads about their entry-level job openings."

"You don't know if you're leading this yet."

"Actually, I already talked to Sharon Wallace in HR. She said she was fine with me leading it this year if you're okay with it."

Harlan shook his head. "I should have known."

Jesse smiled and walked out of Harlan's office.

7. Career Day

Thursday, March 15, 2018

Niigaanii Hall looked like a typical university academic building. Jesse entered and looked for Kyle Van Buren's office in the English department directory. She had looked for his name on the school website, but it wasn't listed.

Kyle wasn't listed on the directory, but department chair Earl Townsend's office was in room B426. Jesse trudged up the stairs.

A greying, African American man looked up from behind his desk. "May I help you?"

Jesse stepped back. "Um, yeah, I'm, um, I'm looking for Kyle Van Buren."

The man frowned. "I'm sorry, Professor Van Buren is no longer associated with this university."

Paydirt. "Oh, I see. Do you know where I can find him?"

"I'm afraid I'm unable to help you with that." The man turned back to his desk.

Jesse stared for a second. "I'm sorry, I met him about a month ago and was under the impression he was a professor in the English department."

"Well, as I said, young lady, he is no longer associated with this university."

Jesse smiled. "Oh—does that make you old, then? Jesse Jonsen." She extended her hand.

"Earl Townsend." They shook hands. "May I ask, what was your business with Professor Van Buren?"

"May I come in?"

"I'm very busy."

"I just need a few minutes. I work for Uncle Sam Bank and I'm supposed to talk to a few department heads and get a feel for what NPU is all about."

"For the endowment campaign?"

"That's right."

"Come in. I'll give you a few minutes."

"Thanks." Jesse entered and sat in a chair next to Earl's desk.

"If you wanted to talk to me, why ask for Professor Van Buren?"

"I wanted to talk to him too, but for a different reason."

Earl reclined in his office chair and waited.

"Um. Well, I met Kyle, Professor Van Buren, on the Friday before the Superbowl in the Minneapolis skyway near where I work. He was, um, well, he looked like a pimp."

Earl stroked his lips. "A pimp."

"Yeah. I was drinking a latte when this girl approached me and asked me to pretend we knew each other. And then Kyle showed up and tried to intimidate us. The police eventually got involved, and then Leilani went to work at a hotel."

"As a prostitute?"

"I assume that's what she was doing, yeah."

"And so, you think Professor Van Buren is a pimp?"

"Sure looked that way to me, yeah."

Earl contemplated for a few seconds. "Interesting."

"So, why doesn't he work here anymore?"

"You'll need to talk to HR about that."

"You were his boss, right? And you knew him?"

"Yes."

"So, why does a college professor moonlight as a pimp?"

"I don't know. But I'm curious. What did he look like?"

"Twenties. Early 30s, maybe. Dark hair. Tall. But everyone's tall next to me. The top of my head was about at his neck. He had on a business suit."

"How was he built? Fat, thin, average?"

"He wasn't fat. When I got between Leilani and him, I was right up under his face."

"Then that wasn't Kyle Van Buren. Kyle had a weight problem. And light brown hair."

~

Corporate interviewers from Uncle Sam Bank and others had transformed the gymnasium into an exhibit floor, complete with interview spaces and basketball nets above each end. Jesse worked her way to the Uncle Sam Bank tables. Jesse's coworker, Matthew, finished hanging a banner and stepped down from a ladder.

"Ah, Jesse, there you are. A couple people from the Development Office are looking for you."

"Thanks Matthew. What were their names?"

"Harry and Meaghan. Which I thought was hilarious. Oh – there they are." Matthew gestured toward the gymnasium entrance. A man and woman headed toward the door.

Jesse trotted toward them. "Hey Meaghan. Harry."

They stopped and turned.

The dark-haired woman looked like she was on her way to a corporate board meeting. So did the guy. The man flashed a smile.

Jesse froze in her tracks. Harry and Meaghan, huh. Yeah, and I'm the queen of England. The man was Red-head from the Skyway.

"Oh—hello. You must be Jesse." She had a British accent. Meaghan, or whatever her real name was, stepped toward Jesse and extended her hand. The guy followed. Both smiled. All nice and professional.

What's the best way to play this? He didn't see me back in the skyway. Play it cool. Jesse extended her hand. "Nice to meet you. Yes, I'm Jesse."

Red-head extended his hand. "I'm Harold Rocklind."

"And I'm Meaghan Maxwell. We work in the Development Office, and we're supposed to make sure you get everything you need for the endowment campaign."

Jesse looked both of them up and down. Don't give away anything. "Thanks. I appreciate that. Why don't you show me around?"

Meaghan gestured a direction and started strolling. Harold followed.

Jesse fell in with them. "Why do an endowment campaign now?"

Meaghan said, "We reach out to poorly represented groups, and especially the Native American population in northern Minnesota, and earnings from an endowment could fund scholarships. And that could help lift those reservations out of poverty."

A few students walked toward the group, but averted their eyes and changed direction.

"And you want to raise ten million dollars?"

"Yeah. If it earns five percent, that would pay for ten scholarships of fifty thousand dollars each."

"How do you plan to raise it?"

"Part of the plan involves your help." Meaghan gestured toward the Development office building.

Harold continued. "The idea is, we invite your business customers and wealthy individuals to a meeting where we'll give our pitch. You'll invest what we raise and we'll set an earnings target after your fees."

Another group of students saw the group, averted their eyes, and changed direction.

What are they afraid of? Jesse surveyed the campus. Students walking to classes. A group talking and moving away. Another group laughing and gesturing. But a few glancing toward Harold and Meaghan and quickly looking away. Meaghan and Harold seemed oblivious – or did they? Meaghan's eyes darted. Meaghan wanted them inside. Why?

"...and we'll also lend our name to any marketing campaigns your business customers might want to run, so they can show their customers how they're helping the community."

"Jesse?" Meaghan looked concerned.

"Yes, sorry, I was admiring your campus. Helping with marketing. Yes, that's a good idea."

"Let's go inside and we'll show you details." Meaghan gestured toward the door. "Our office is on the second floor."

"Sure. But let me snap some pictures first." Jesse tapped her phone and took a few campus pictures. She turned toward Meaghan and Harold. "Let me get a couple of you guys in front of this background. She directed them to a spot with the best light. "Smile." She snapped a few, including closeups of both faces.

Meaghan pulled out her phone. "Great idea. Can I take a selfie with you?"

"Sure."

Meaghan adjusted her phone. "Harold, why don't you get in behind us."

"That's okay. I'll just take your picture." Harold took Meaghan's phone. Meaghan and Jesse posed.

"Smile."

Jesse's skin crawled. But she smiled anyway.

~

Back at the Uncle Sam Bank booth, HR people and department heads formed a human assembly line, interviewing students for summer internships and future full-time positions. Jesse strolled past tables of interviewers and interviewees, picking up snatches of conversation. She stopped at the Fraud Department table, where her coworker, Brenda Yang interviewed a young Native American woman. Something looked familiar about her.

Jesse replayed the day so far in her mind. Why was this girl so familiar? She was one of the students who averted her eyes and changed direction when she saw Meaghan and Harold. Jesse edged closer.

"Why interview in the Fraud Department?" Brenda asked.

"Because I've had my identity stolen and I want to help anyone else in a similar situation."

"Tell me how it happened."

"I bought some clothes with a debit card. And then a few days after that, my account was overdrawn. I, um, made some people really mad at me. It was awful."

"Oh. I'm sorry. As a fraud analyst, I hear stories like that all the time and they make me curious." Brenda looked up. "Oh – hi, Jesse. Leilani Berg, meet Jesse Jonsen, who works with me at the bank."

Leilani stood and smiled. She reached to shake Jesse's hand.

Jesse's jaw dropped. "Leilani?"

Leilani pulled her hand back and clutched her chest.

Brenda stood. "Leilani, are you okay?"

Leilani fought to regain her composure. "Um, yeah, I'm fine. Listen, I really need to go. Are we done?"

Brenda and Jesse exchanged glances. Brenda stood. "But we were just getting started. Don't you want to finish?"

"No. Sorry. I forgot about a class this hour. I should have scheduled this at a different time." Leilani picked up her coat and hustled away.

"What just happened?" Brenda asked.

"I know her." Jessed turned toward Leilani, retreating toward the door. "Leilani, wait up."

Leilani walked faster. Jesse trotted after her. She stepped in front of Leilani at the door. "Leilani, what's going on?"

"Nothing. I just need to leave, okay?"

"Did I scare you? What's going on?"

"I told you, nothing. Please, let me leave."

"I will, but I didn't approach you that night in the Skyway, you approached me. I saw you today with Meaghan and Harold and you avoided them. Kyle or Harold or whatever his name is—what's his real name? And you're bailing on a job interview after you saw me again. Why?"

"It was a mistake to come here. That's all." Leilani tried to move past Jesse.

Jesse blocked her path. "Leilani, please, just one more minute. You're the real reason I'm here. Something is going on and you're stuck in the middle of it."

Leilani's eyes pleaded. She blinked back tears and shook her head. "No. Can I please leave?"

"Just one more second." Jesse fumbled with her purse and pulled out a business card. "I gave you one of these before. I want you to call me, anytime you feel threatened. Twenty-four-seven. I can help."

"Why do you care?"

"Because I see a bunch of me in you. These people don't need to rule your life."

Leilani took the business card and stuffed it into her pocket. "Thanks. I'll think about it."

"Why don't you come back and finish the interview."

"No."

Jesse stood aside. Leilani darted away.

Brenda walked up. "What's going on?"

"I don't know. But I'm gonna find out."

~

Jesse knocked on English Department Chair Earl Townsend's office door on the fourth floor of Niigaanii Hall.

"Why does the guy in your Development Office supervise a pimp who pretends to be a professor who doesn't work here anymore?"

Earl looked up from desk. "You again. You're back."

"Remember the guy in the Minneapolis skyway I told you about? The guy who said he was Kyle Van Buren?"

"Yeah."

"Well, today, I met Harold Rocklind in the Development Office. But I saw this same guy supervising girls and looking for Kyle Van Buren at the Patterson Hotel in the skyway that night."

"What?"

"You heard me. What's going on here?"

Earl pursed his lips. "Come in. Close the door and have a seat."

Jesse clutched her purse and felt for the can of pepper spray.

"I assure you Ms. Jonsen, I don't bite. Please, come in and close the door."

Jesse stepped inside, closed the door, and sat.

"Professor Van Buren left under, um, unusual circumstances. You asked why Harold Rocklind in the Development office is working with somebody who impersonated a disgraced professor. I don't know, but for some time, I've suspected something foul going on here. Your experience suggests Harold Rocklind is a ringleader."

Jesse loosened the grip on her purse. "Why did Professor Van Buren leave?"

"Embezzlement."

"How?"

He was accused of stealing funds from the Development Office."

"Let me guess, by Harold Rocklind?"

"That's right. A paper trail led back to Kyle. With a few twists and turns. I was in the meeting where we asked him to resign quietly or face a full investigation. He chose to leave."

"Where is he now?"

"I don't know. But I have his phone number."

"I'd like to talk to him."

"I would too. What's your position at Uncle Sam Bank?"

"I'm a principal fraud analyst."

"Ah. Then it seems, I'm in need of your services.

Jesse nodded and stood.

"I'll be in touch. And Ms. Jonsen."

"Yes?" Jesse reached for the door.

"Let's keep this between us for now. And watch your back."

Jesse smiled. "Part of the job."

8. Big Day at the Office

Friday, March 16, 2018

Kyle paced to his office window. Sunlight washed out his dark hair, making him look like an albino. He closed the curtain.

Leilani followed him with her eyes. She looked down and fought tears. "How was I supposed to know she'd be there?"

Kyle marched to her chair and slapped her.

Her ears rang as she fell to the floor. She tried rubbing away the pain.

Kyle swore. "If you hadn't talked to her that night in the skyway, we wouldn't have this problem."

Leilani cowered. "No."

"You know, I work day and night trying to make a life for you. And this is how you repay me? What's wrong with you?"

Leilani climbed back into her chair. "I'm tired, Kyle. I have to keep my grades up and work for you. It's too much."

Kyle shook his head. He towered over her and swore again. "Maybe you're not cut out for this. Maybe I should send you back to your reservation and find somebody else."

Leilani buried her head in her hands and sobbed.

"You're pathetic." Kyle kicked the chair out from under Leilani. She sprawled on the floor. He took out his phone and started dialing.

"Who are you calling?"

"I'm calling somebody else to take your place. You don't deserve to be here."

"No." Leilani staggered to her feet.

"Why not?"

"I can do this."

"You can do what?"

"I can service customers and keep up my grades. I can make you proud of me."

"Why should I believe you?"

"Because I need to be here."

"And you don't want to end up eating dirt like your mom, right?"

"Yes."

"That's what you told me a long time ago, remember?"

"Yes."

Kyle got in her face. "So how do I know you mean it?"

Leilani stepped back. "I need this education."

Kyle softened. "I know you do. And I love you and want you to have it. We're trying to build a future together, remember?"

"Yes."

Kyle stared at her. "And who takes care of you? Who makes sure you get what you need?"

Leilani looked down. "You do."

"And who else?"

Leilani fought tears. "Nobody else. Just you."

Kyle paced around her, ending in front of her face. Leilani stared at her feet. Kyle lifted her chin. "That's what I wanted to hear. Don't let me down again."

"I won't."

"Good. Because I have a special job for you. We have a premium business group tonight and I need you at your best. No more acting like a baby, okay?"

"Okay."

"Good. Now, go to your dorm room and get your clothes. Meet me in the parking lot."

Leilani tried to compose herself.

"Go. Now. Get yourself together and meet me in ten minutes."

Leilani bolted out the door. Fighting to stay calm, she half walked, half ran across campus to her dorm room, where she rarely slept anymore. *What's wrong with me? Kyle has a plan and I'm part of it. Everyone has to sacrifice to make a future.*

She made it to her dorm room and packed. Jesse's business card caught her eye. *Maybe, after college, I can get a job like Jesse's. But Jesse is White. She probably had it easy getting into college. But nobody pushes Jesse around. Kyle could have hurt her badly back at that coffee shop. But that was in public. If they were alone, it would be different. But what about servicing dozens of men all night? Jesse wouldn't do that. But how else do I pay for college and get out of poverty? No. It has to be this way. Kyle picked me and I'll get through it. Somehow.*

She put Jesse's card into a drawer, zipped her overnight bag, and hustled out the door.

9. Hot Water

"You did what?" Harlan Phillips, sitting behind his desk, was about to explode. The top of his bald head and his ears turned red. The veins in his neck pulsated. He swore.

Jesse leaned forward in her chair across Harlan's desk. "What was I supposed to do, Harlan? Leilani recognized me and I recognized her. The second she saw me, she wanted to run."

"So, let her run. It's not your job to right all the wrongs in the world."

"Somebody is taking advantage of that girl and I can't just sit back and watch."

Harlan chewed his lip for a second. "As of right now, you're not to have any further contact with NPU or anyone who works or attends NPU."

Jesse slapped Harlan's desk. "You can't do that."

"I just did."

"Why?"

"There are a few vice-presidents with about ten million reasons to fire you after the stunt you pulled."

"What?"

"There's a lot of money and scholarships riding on this. And there's pressure to get it done."

"Harlan, there's something ugly going on there."

"Maybe there is. But I'm trying to look out for you."

"I'm a big girl."

"I know you are. And I know what you're like when you get on one of your save the world missions."

"Is that what you think I'm doing?"

"Yeah."

"Harlan, that girl is somebody's daughter."

"Every girl is somebody's daughter. You scared her away from a job interview."

"She saw me and bolted."

"And then you chased her across the gymnasium and badgered her."

"I did not. I followed her and talked to her."

"Well, stay away from her. And from NPU. They don't want you back."

Jesse shook her head and glared.

"Why are you still in my office?"

"I don't know." Jesse stood to leave.

"Jesse."

She turned.

"Get NPU out of your head."

Jesse rolled her eyes.

"I'm serious."

Jesse left the office.

"Don't do something stupid." Harlan's voice shouted at her back.

10.   Hot Coffee

Gloria sipped her coffee across the table from Jesse. "So, what are you gonna do?"

Jesse stared at her own coffee. "Don't you have a store to run?"

Gloria scanned her skyway Manitou Coffee shop. "I have a good crew." She took another sip. "Well?"

Jesse shook her head. "I don't know."

"What's the worst that can happen if you show up at NPU again?"

"I could lose my job."

Gloria laughed. "Jobs are overrated."

Jesse smiled. "Says the lady who works twenty-four-seven on her business."

"That's different. It's not a job when your name's on the door."

Jesse sighed.

"If they fire you, you can always get a different job. You worked at Bullseye when we first met, right?"

"Yeah. That was right before I started with Uncle Sam Bank."

"Why'd you leave Bullseye?"

"They outsourced everything I did. I couldn't stay."

"So, the conditions where you worked became unacceptable, and you found somewhere that was acceptable?"

"Yeah, that's a good way to say it."

"Are the conditions at Uncle Sam Bank still acceptable?"

"Don't know. They've never told me to back away from anything before."

"What about when you and Jerry went after that credit card thief?"

"Harlan finally gave the go-ahead."

"What you did was a little unorthodox, wasn't it?"

Jesse laughed. "Yeah, it was. But we shut Tarman down. Never heard from him again after that. I wonder what happened to him."

"Maybe he crawled back under whatever rock he came out of. Good riddance."

Jesse took another sip.

Gloria also took a sip. "It occurs to me, you have a knack for thinking outside the box."

"What do you mean?"

"Well, that persona of yours. Teena Fay from Green Bay?"

"I just do that so I can get in with carders. That's how I found Tarman."

"They all have nicknames. They think they're dealing with a two-bit crook from somewhere in Wisconsin. They have no clue who they're really dealing with, do they?"

"Of course not. But I can't very well approach them as me and find out what I need to find out."

"You're right."

Jesse stared at her cup. After a few seconds, she looked up and met Gloria's eyes. Gloria smiled.

So did Jesse. "Yeah. That could work."

Gloria's eyes twinkled. "What could work?"

"Teena Fay from Green Bay can't do this. But maybe Brooke Macalester could."

Gloria nodded. "I like Brooke. But I don't like Macalester. Too fancy sounding. How about something native? Google some names on your laptop."

Jesse and Gloria shifted so they could both see Jesse's laptop screen and searched.

After a few minutes, Jesse stopped. "Wait a minute. I'm White. Why take on a Native persona?"

"Isn't that where that school draws its students?"

"Not all. What if Brooke were White – like me – but maybe her family lives up North somewhere."

"Why?"

"This is different than carder forums. This persona will need a social media account, and if the right people find her and try to groom her, she'll probably need to meet the guy over a video chat. I can disguise myself to look like I'm early twenties, but I'm White. So, Brooke has to be White."

"Makes sense. Maybe she comes from a broken home and so she's vulnerable."

That familiar adrenaline rush tingled Jesse's fingers. "Yeah, maybe. But wait—Indian casinos are a big deal in Minnesota, right? This is better. Brooke has a mom and dad, but her dad fixes gaming machines across Minnesota, Wisconsin, and maybe the Dakotas, and he's gone all the time. Maybe he drinks too much, and maybe her mom is a waitress somewhere. They both have to work all the time to make ends meet. and so they don't pay enough attention to Brooke."

Gloria nodded. "Leaving her vulnerable to grooming. I like it."

"She needs a last name. How about Hampton? Brooke Hampton. How's that sound?"

"Brooke Hampton. Yeah. Sounds like money, but her family doesn't have any."

Jesse smiled. "Thanks, Gloria. And since I'm not approaching anyone at NPU, I'm not going against my manager."

"He might wonder why you're playing social media at work."

Jesse laughed. "True. I'll probably have to do this from home."

"Or here. You're welcome to my office if you need it."

"Thanks."

11.   Social Media

Friday, March 30, 2018

Demand was through the roof, especially on weekends. It was an amazing business model, even if *Harvard Business Review* would never write it up. The problem was supply. And supervision. The girls were all high-maintenance and he could never keep enough in stock.

And that's why he needed supervisors like the new Kyle Van Buren. Some tasks are better delegated. A businessman has to be careful. And the real Kyle wouldn't care anymore that somebody was impersonating him. All in all, a win for everyone.

How did anyone find workers before social media came along and girls told the world about their whole lives? But it was tedious finding the right one. Maybe someday, a computer genius somewhere would come up with an automated way to do it. But until then, start with "A" names, work through the alphabet, and hand promising candidates to somebody to process.

Alicia Callahan had a boyfriend. April Hanson loved her stupid cat. Ariel Morris was Officer Morris's daughter. Right here in Little Falls. Definitely hands-off. Belinda Dagmar—well, wait a minute, Belinda was fifty years old. Why is a fifty-year-old named Belinda? And why couldn't they just say they were old up front instead of making him wade through their profile?

Who names their kid Bellatrix? The name alone would turn off clients. But Brooke. Yeah, Brooke was a nice name. He searched the social media platform for girls named Brooke. There were a few in Duluth, but nothing exciting.

Here was one in Onamia. Brooke Hampton. Why does a White girl named Brooke Hampton live in a town in the middle of an Indian reservation? He skimmed through a few posts. Fought with her dad. Parents didn't like her friends. Dad was out of town in another post. Another fight. Here was a post where she said she was lonely. Bad poetry. Wants somebody to love her. Bla bla bla. It's worth having Kyle check her out.

12.   Reverse Grooming

Saturday, March 31, 2018

Jesse logged into Brooke's social media account and checked for notifications. A few more friend requests were waiting. Amazing how many creeps picked up on public messages about problems with Brooke's parents. Dad was gone most of the time fixing slot machines and mostly drunk when he was home. Mom spent her evenings as a waitress, leaving Brooke to take care of the family trailer and mostly fend for herself. Brooke wanted to go to college, but her family had no money and her parents made no effort to search for financial aid.

Jesse chuckled. Inventing Brooke's backstory was almost as fun as playing Teena Fay from Green Bay. Almost. But the creeps she was after this time were nastier, closer to home, and more dangerous than the worst credit-card hustlers on the planet. The adrenaline rush was amazing. Even better than when she was a teenage thief. But this time, she was fighting a good fight. It felt good. Almost euphoric.

Brooke accepted the friend requests and skimmed a few private messages. All from lowlifes.

```
Hey baby, I would love to get
together with you.
```

And

Yur cute. Let's go on a date.

And more. Jesse seethed. Scumbags. She wanted to twist their family jewels with industrial pliers.

Another friend request popped in. From a guy who called himself Kyle Van Buren. She looked at his profile picture. It was the same skyway creep from Superbowl weekend. Paydirt. This idiot posted his own picture on a public social media platform. Overconfidence, Kyle. Or whatever your real name is. That will bring you down. She accepted his friend request. His first PM came quickly.

Hi. I couldn't help but notice
your troubles with your parents.
I want you to know, you don't
have to live like that.

Jesse smiled. Time to get deep into character.

Hi Kyle. How did you find me?

Pretty much by accident. My
cousin is named Brooke and I was
looking for her and you came up
in the search results. You're
beautiful.

Oh, this guy is smooth.

I'll bet you say that to all
the girls you meet.

No, not all, just the beautiful
ones.

LOL - how do I know you're
not some creep?

I'm not. Just a guy chatting
with a beautiful girl.

> OK. So what do you wanna chat
> about?

I do have an ulterior motive.
Sort-of. I noticed you mentioned
you want to go to college. Part
of what I do is help people in
your position.

> How?

I work for North Prairie
University, and we're always
looking for students. See, we
get federal help, and the more
students we bring in, the more
federal $$ we get. So yeah, it's
a money thing, but you're still
beautiful too.

> Wow. This sounds too good to
> be true. Maybe you're some
> creep who wants to kidnap me
> and sell me to Chinese pimps.

LOL – I like your imagination.
I'll paste in a website link for
you to look over. If you like
it, PM me back. How's that
sound?

> That sounds pretty good.

Good. Maybe tomorrow then?

> Maybe. We'll see.

OK, I look forward to it.

Kyle sent the URL link. The web page was filled with pictures of smiling students on the NPU campus, with a "Click here to apply for financial aid" button. The application asked all the typical questions about parents' income and expenses. Tomorrow would be time to offer the hook.

Kyle messaged the next evening.

```
Hello Brooke. Did you get a
chance to look at the
application?
```

> ```
> I did. But I can't fill it
> out.
> ```

```
Why not?
```

> ```
> It wants a bunch of numbers
> from my parents and they
> won't do it.
> ```

```
Don't they care about you?
```

Don't be too fast. Brooke will need to think about this. Jesse stood and stretched. After a few minutes, it was fingers to the keyboard again.

> ```
> I don't know.
> ```

```
Tell me more.
```

> ```
> Well, they're worried about
> putting down numbers on that
> form.
> ```

```
Why are they worried?
```

> ```
> Something about taxes. I
> don't understand it all.
> ```

You can tell them the IRS never
sees these forms. And maybe they
can get you into college without
paying anything.

> I already told them. I'm
> sorry, but they won't help.

That's a shame. But don't lose
heart. There might be other
programs. In the meantime, would
it be okay if I send you a card?

Oh boy, there's a twist. He wants Brooke's address.

> Wow. That's so nice. But my
> parents would kill me. They
> don't want anyone to know our
> address. They say nothing
> good comes in the mail.

I completely understand. Let me
look into what else we can do.
Is it okay to chat tomorrow
night?

> Yes.

Great. I have a good feeling
you'll do great things with your
life. I want to help.

> Thanks

Good night.

Jesse let him stew for next three days. Kyle left messages.

Hi Brooke. How are you tonight?

Hi Brooke. Are you ok?

Hi Brooke. I hope you're ok.

Hi Brooke. I miss you. Are you
ok?

Jesse responded Friday evening.

> Hi Kyle. Sorry. My dad was
> home and I couldn't get on
> the computer.

I'm glad you're ok. I was
scared.

> I'm sorry. I didn't mean to
> scare you.

I have great news. I think we
have a program that could work
for you.

> Really?

Yes. It's a work-study
opportunity. And the best part
is, you can start right away and
accumulate credit toward college
expenses.

> That sounds great!

I thought you'd like it. Are
your parents ok with you working
at a job?

> I think they're mad I don't
> have a job. There just isn't
> much here.

I know. Jobs are hard to find.
But NPU has some influence and
there are a few slots for
students that show promise. I
pulled some strings and one of
them is yours if you want it.

> Wow. What do I have to do
> next?

Can you get away next Saturday?

> I think so.

Why don't I meet you somewhere
and we can talk about it. Do you
have a favorite place?

> Sometimes my mom lets me eat
> at the casino where she
> works. The food is pretty
> good.

Maybe I could pick you up and
show you the college here in
Little Falls. We could eat
somewhere here and make a day
out of it. I'll drop you off at
home.

> That sounds nice.

What am I thinking? Brooke can't meet this guy face to
face. Can she? Maybe I could rig up a disguise. Lots of
makeup and a wig maybe. No. He'd recognize my voice.
And why meet with him at all? Just lead him on.

> But I usually fix dinner for
> my dad on weekends when he's
> home.

No pressure. But we need to talk
about the work study
opportunity. They won't hold the
slot open indefinitely.

        Let me think about it, ok?

Ok. When should I call you?

        I'll message you in a couple
        days.

I look forward to it. Listen, I
know it's a big step, but I
can't wait to meet you face to
face. Our work-study program
will open up whole new worlds
for you.

        Thanks.

13.   Planting Seeds

Monday, April 16, 2018

The outside temperature in Minneapolis was in the mid-forties. Inside the cramped basement office, the air conditioners struggled even more. As usual, Brenda was in early.

"Morning, Brenda."

"Morning, Jesse. I already called about the AC. Again."

They both chuckled.

"Brenda, I need your advice on something. Got a second?"

In her late-forties with greying hair, Brenda looked over her glasses at Jesse and offered her usual motherly smile.

Jesse grinned back. "What?"

"What did you do?"

"Well nothing, really. I invented another character. That's all."

Brenda sighed. "You're on another mission."

"No. Well, maybe. There's a whole class of crooks we haven't paid any attention to."

"Are we cleaning up the planet again?"

"We're about to get in bed with some really nasty people on this NPU thing. So, no, I'm not trying to save the world. It's part of our job, right?"

"You're wavering."

"We can do better than Whack-a-mole."

Brenda chuckled and shook her head. "What'cha got?"

Jesse showed Brenda the chat log with Kyle. "Do I have enough to nail this guy? And how do I draw him out in the real world?"

"Okay, wait a minute. The real Kyle Van Buren is missing, right? And the fake Kyle is the pimp for that girl I interviewed at the Career Day event?"

"Yeah."

"So, how do you know this Kyle is the same guy?"

"His profile picture looks just like the guy I saw in the Skyway back in February."

"You do know that people post fake pictures, right?"

Jesse laughed. "I am a fraud analyst, aren't I? What are the odds that some guy at random would post a fake picture of himself that looks just like the guy I saw in the skyway?"

"Okay, you have a point."

"Think there's enough here to take to the police?"

"Don't know. But given the context, you probably have enough to raise a red flag about underwriting their campaign."

"I was thinking the same thing. But I want to nail this guy. He's exploiting girls. Leilani could have been me a few years ago."

Brenda sipped her coffee. "One step at a time. Show Harlan what you found out, make a recommendation, and maybe you won't have to do this in your spare time."

"Think he'll be mad?"

"Why?"

"He told me to stay away from NPU."

"Well, did you?"

"I didn't drive up there or call anyone if that's what you mean."

"You set up a fictitious social media profile and lured in a pervert. Wherever he happens to be from. No different than what Teena Fay from Green Bay does with carders."

"Thanks."

Brenda smiled that special smile. Again.

"What?"

"You already knew all this. Why ask me?"

Jesse smiled. "Because it's good to bounce this off a friend."

Brenda nodded. "So, when do you talk to Harlan?"

"I'll get on his schedule this afternoon."

~

Harlan finished reading the chat log and faced Jesse across his desk. "And this is the same guy you met in the skyway back on Superbowl weekend?"

"Yeah. His picture is on his profile. We need to take this to the police."

"But you don't really have anything here. He invited Brooke to see his college campus. That's hardly a crime."

"He's grooming her. And he's trafficking that girl, Leilani."

"You don't know that."

"Harlan, I was there. This guy is bad news and we're about to partner with him."

Harlan leaned forward. "Let's say you're right. This guy is dirty. He works for NPU. That doesn't mean NPU is dirty."

Jesse also leaned forward. "He's impersonating a missing professor. Hello?"

Harlan leaned back. He stroked his chin and nodded. "All right. Let's take this upstairs."

~

"Thank you for bringing this to my attention." Senior Vice President of Operations Mike Swanson leaned back in his office chair.

Harlan and Jesse watched from across his desk.

"But I recall giving instruction to stay away from NPU after hearing complaints. Why didn't you stay away?" Mike's eyes bored into Jesse.

Jesse stiffened. "I did stay away. This guy came to me."

"You baited him."

"And he took it. So now, what are we gonna do about it?"

Mike pursed his lips. "I'll take it from here."

Jesse stood. "And that's it?"

Harlan stood. "C'mon Jesse, let's go."

Mike stood. "Harlan, Jesse, thanks for coming up. And Jesse, a word of advice?"

"Yeah?"

"You have a great reputation around here. We all appreciate your passion. But one of these days, one of your crusades will get you in big trouble. Don't cross the line."

Jesse rolled her eyes.

"C'mon, Jesse, let's go." Harlan gently took her elbow.

Jesse and Harlan made their way down the hall and stepped into the elevator.

Jesse pressed the tenth floor and basement buttons. "Why did he blow us off?"

"He didn't blow us off. He said he'd handle it."

Jesse shook her head. "No. He blew us off."

"Did it ever occur to you that top managers might have other things on their mind than your latest save-the-world ideas?"

"Harlan, the guy who's grooming Brooke – his buddies will drag this bank through the mud."

"And Mike said he'd handle it."

The elevator stopped at the tenth floor. Harlan exited and put his hand in the door. "You did your job. Give Mike a chance to do his. Okay?"

Jesse rolled her eyes.

"You heard me."

"Okay."

"Good."

14.   Neck Deep

Mike Swanson swore under his breath. It started as just a little bit of racy fun, helping a few girls pay for college. And then it morphed into a moneymaking opportunity while helping a college raise money. And what was wrong with that? After all, he had expenses too. Kids in college, a mortgage, country club memberships. Weren't senior managers expected to maintain a certain lifestyle?

Harold at NPU answered after a couple rings.

"Harold, this is Mike. We have a problem."

Mike brought Harold up to speed on what he had just heard from Jesse. "Who is this Kyle anyway?"

"He works for me. He helps with recruiting."

"Why are you recruiting underage girls?"

"I don't know. I'll look into it."

"Listen. This thing is getting out of hand. If you want me to keep supporting you, you'd better do more than look into it. Do you have any idea how much trouble we could both get into if something like this got out?"

"So, make sure nothing gets out."

"And how am I supposed to do that?"

Harold swore. "You're a senior vice-president, aren't you? Make her stand down."

"I tried. But I can't push too hard. That just paints a red flag on your operation. And me."

"Hmm. You do have a problem."

Mike sighed. "You mean, we have a problem. I can't force her to stop, especially not when she's doing this on her own time. And if I know Jesse, the harder I push for her to let go, the more she'll dig in her heels."

"Fire her."

"What?"

"Find some excuse and get rid of her."

"I can't do that."

"Why not?"

"It would look suspicious."

"Set her up."

"What are you talking about?"

"Do I have to put the pieces together for you? Didn't you catch this Jesse embezzling from your bank? I wonder where she stashed the money."

"I can't do that. We have controls in place to prohibit such behavior."

"Are all managers as stupid as you? Is she smart?"

Mike nodded. "She's the best."

"Well then, use that against her. Make it look like she found a way around your fancy controls."

"You want me to destroy somebody's career for this? I won't do it."

"Mike, what would happen to your career if word got out you were seeing prostitutes and soliciting bribes?"

Mike jumped to his feet. His chair nearly toppled over. "What?"

"C'mon, Mike. You know how this works. When it leaks—and it will if this Jesse gets in our way—when the press calls, we'll say, 'We're just a small college trying to raise money. We were shocked when a senior vice-president at Uncle Sam Bank wanted to put some of that money in his pocket in exchange for helping us.'"

Mike squeezed the phone harder. "This is your way to deal with problems? Threaten your partners?"

"You should see your video. It's really good. It would be a shame if it ended up on Youtube."

"You try anything like that and I'll sue you to eternity."

"Yes, I expect you would. And an army of analysts would look for problems because it just has to be fake. But after seeing your still pictures with a few of our girls, they wouldn't look very hard. And we both know that video is not fake."

Mike's knuckles hurt. He loosened his grip on the phone. "You asked me to get involved with this deal. Who do you think you're dealing with anyway? Some two-bit hustler?"

"No. You're a senior vice-president with a lot to lose. It really would be a shame if you had to resign in disgrace. Maybe you could go live on an Indian reservation. I hear housing is pretty cheap."

Sweat beaded on Mike's forehead. "I could report you to the police."

"You could. And maybe they'd believe you. What is it they call stuff like that? Going nuclear?"

Mike paced. "You told me this is all innocent fun; nobody gets hurt. I would never have agreed to this otherwise."

"Listen, things don't need to get ugly. Make your girl— Jesse go away and everyone wins. Go buy an island with your share."

Mike stopped pacing. "And what about Jesse?"

"Your girl shouldn't poke around where she doesn't belong."

"I don't have any leverage," Mike shouted in the phone.

"Sure, you do. Plant some money somewhere in her name and let her hang herself."

Mike squeezed his eyes shut. "I don't have any money."

"Yes, you do. I've seen what you spend it on, remember?"

Mike sighed. "Okay. I need a few days to set it up."

"Sounds good. And Mike—"

"Yeah."

"No more panic calls."

15.   Earth Day

Sunday, April 22, 2018

The camera operator counted down with his fingers. Three, two, one, and then pointed to the interviewer. She looked into the camera and smiled. "In honor of Earth Day, we're here, somewhere in northern Minnesota, talking to entrepreneur, financier, and ecologist, Anders, 'Uncle Andy' Nordqvist about the Marceau experimental forest."

She waved her arm. The camera followed and recorded a sea of pine and birch trees as far as the eye could see. The camera panned back to Anders, standing next to the interviewer in front of a large, round glass structure.

"Anders—", she started.

"Please, just call me Andy. Or 'Uncle Andy' if you prefer."

The interviewer laughed. "How did you get the nickname, 'Uncle Andy?'"

"I do not remember how I acquired that nickname. It was a long time ago. All I know is, I love giving back to my adopted country."

"And you're certainly giving back. Tell us about, well, this." She looked back at the glass structure.

"We have several of these cylindrical models in the area. They are each roughly thirteen meters in diameter and nine meters tall, open to the sky. We pump heat into each one, to model what happens at different average temperatures relative to the natural temperature. They range from two degrees Fahrenheit to sixteen degrees Fahrenheit above normal. We use these models to predict the effect of climate change."

"I see. And so, what's this one?"

"This one is the warmest, sixteen degrees above normal." He opened the door. "Shall we step inside?"

Inside, the foliage looked mostly brown and dead. "As you can see, warmer temperatures make a large difference."

"Wow."

"Yes. Our modern industry pumps large quantities of greenhouse gasses into our atmosphere, and soon, the arboreal forests at this latitude around the world will start expelling carbon instead of absorbing carbon. This will accelerate greenhouse gas volume in our atmosphere, which will further accelerate global warming. It's a vicious cycle which will lead to catastrophe."

"And you help fund all this?"

"I do what I can in my own small way. I dedicate a percentage of our Lekplats resort profits to ecological projects."

"Tell us about your resorts."

"Our first resort, Norra lekplatsen, is near Mille Lacs Lake. People enjoy a luxury stay with opportunities to admire the beauty of northern Minnesota. We staff it with a work-study program in partnership with North Prairie University. This allows us to operate in both an ecologically and economically sound manner. We recently opened another resort in the Florida Everglades and we're expanding across the country and internationally."

"Norra lekplatsen?"

"It means, 'Northern Playground,' where there's no such thing as bad weather, only the wrong clothes."

The interviewer laughed. "I understand you're giving away ten thousand trees in honor of Earth Day."

"Yes, that's right. Come visit either of our US Lekplats resorts, and bring a tree home and plant it."

"Sounds like a great memorial to a wonderful experience."

"We hope so. Our fervent wish is for those small saplings to grow into mighty trees in a few years and absorb millions of liters of greenhouse gases."

"Very nice. And thank you for your time and the education."

16.   Setup

Monday, April 23, 2018

Junior Programmer Analyst Dennis Waverly tapped keyboard keys on the computer in his Uncle Sam Bank cubicle and ran the test program again. Do more with less. But don't break anything. And don't waste money on experiments. IT is a cost center, not a profit center, and bla bla bla. It was the constant refrain from management that didn't have the first clue about the technology that kept Uncle Same Bank running. It was a wonder any of the bank's systems worked at all.

But maybe this little innovation could save some money. Most managers' eyes would surely glaze over when he presented the tech details to them. But five hundred dollars per desktop for Microsoft Office licenses, vs. free for open-source LibreOffice, times thousands of employees, multiplied to a big number. The kind of number finance managers love to eliminate from their spreadsheets. And the kind of number that looks good on a resume. All he had to do was rework *Merchant Trace* to accept ODF formatted LibreOffice Calc spreadsheets in addition to Microsoft Office Excel spreadsheets. It would save millions.

And then maybe somebody would notice badge number 225307, Dennis Waverly, invisible superhero, currently bringing home an annual salary adequate for poverty.

His computer chirped. It was an IM from some guy named Mike Swanson. Dennis looked in the company directory. Wow. Mike Swanson is a director-level manager. Dennis adjusted his shirt. He laughed. Dude, it's text, not video.

```
I heard you're doing good work
on Merchant Trace.
```

Wow, he noticed. I like this guy.

```
            Thanks. I think we can save a
            bunch of money.
```

```
I need to talk to you about some
things. Can you come up to my
office?
```

I picked a bad day to wear a Grateful Dead shirt to work.

```
            Sure.
```

```
Great. Ten minutes?
```

```
            OK.
```

```
Thanks.
```

~

The twentieth floor didn't look much different than the floor where Dennis worked. But Mike Swanson had a real office, with an assistant in a cubicle in front.

Mike strode out of his office and extended his hand. "Dennis, thanks for coming up right away. Come on in. And close the door would you please?"

"Am I in trouble?"

"No, no, not at all. I need to talk to you about something, um, sensitive. And I wanted to get to know you a little. Have a seat."

"Thanks." Dennis sat.

"What are you working on?" Mike asked.

"Well, a few things. I'm getting deeper and deeper into *Merchant Trace*, and I have an idea that might save the bank a load of money."

"That's the program that traces fraudulent credit card transactions, right?"

"Yeah."

"How comfortable do you feel maintaining that program?"

"The code is pretty convoluted. Looks like it's been patched a few times. I was hoping to rework some of it."

"Interesting. What else are you working on?"

"That's my main focus. But I'm also the contact for *Glimpse*."

"What do you think of that program?"

"Well, it looks straightforward. But I'd rather somebody else own it."

"Why?"

"I don't feel comfortable spying on people."

Mike nodded. "I don't like it either. But we're a big bank and sometimes we have to watch people interact with their computers."

Dennis leaned back. "But recording every keystroke and mouse click? I turned it on for myself the other day. It's scary. And it's a bandwidth hog."

"I wish we didn't need it. But auditors would crucify us if we didn't have it."

Dennis looked down and sighed. "I'll do the best I can with it."

"I know you will." Mike leaned forward. "That's what I wanted to talk to you about. But before we go any further, you are not to talk about this to anyone, not your coworkers, not your family, nobody."

Dennis swallowed. "Um, okay. What's going on?"

"Ever heard of FISA?"

"No. What is it?"

"The Foreign Intelligence Surveillance Act."

"Okay—"

"I've been served with a FISA warrant. FISA warrants are special because I can only talk about them with people I need to service them. Which means, if you tell anyone about this, we could both go to prison."

Dennis moved to the edge of his seat. "What? You're kidding, right?"

"No, I'm not. You can look it up. The FISA court meets in secret and it issues warrants when the FBI or other agencies ask them to. The warrants go to individual people, and those people have to return the information the government wants. If they talk about it with anyone else, they can go to prison."

"Seriously?"

"Yeah. As I said, we can look it up right here if you want."

"So Big Brother really is watching."

"Something like that, yeah. But terrorists really do want to kill us, and so the government needs to do some of this stuff in secret."

"I still don't like it."

"Neither do I. But it's the law and we need to obey it."

"What does that have to do with me?"

Mike leaned back. "You know our Fraud Department buys samples of stolen credit cards, right?"

"I figured that's how they got 'em. And they feed those to *Merchant Trace* to find the merchants they were stolen from."

Mike leaned forward. "Right. Well, apparently, they didn't cancel some of those credit card numbers."

"What? That doesn't make sense."

"I know. And that's why I need your help. The government thinks somebody here is working with overseas bad actors and they want me to help find them."

"What do you want me to do?"

"I need you to install *Glimpse* on every computer in the Fraud Department and send the results to me."

"What?"

"I need you to set it up quietly. Don't talk to your manager or anyone else about it. Do it tonight if possible and report back to me when it's done."

"Wait a minute. I don't even know how many policies this violates. And some government order says I have to do this?"

"Yes. If anyone questions you, tell them you're working on an assignment for me."

"Can I have a copy of this order?"

"No. But I can show it to you." Mike pressed a button on his phone. "Karen, would you print that PDF I saved yesterday and bring the copy in here please?"

17.   Embezzler

Friday, May 25, 2018

Jesse hung her sweater in its usual spot and poured a cup of coffee.

"Morning, Brenda. Want a refill?"

"Happy Friday, Jesse. I'm good. Thanks. I already called about the AC."

"One of these days, I want to make that call."

"You'll have to get here at seven for that."

Jesse laughed. "Oh. Well, okay then. What are you doing for Memorial Day?"

"Sleeping."

They settled into their morning routine. Jesse's desk phone rang. It was Harlan.

"Jesse, I need to talk to you in my office. Can you come up?"

"Sure. Be right there." Jesse finished her call.

Brenda looked up. "What was that about?"

"Dunno. I don't think he's ever called me into his office."

"Almost like a trip to the principal's office."

"Yeah. Maybe."

On the elevator, the rest of the work day swirled in Jesse's mind. That thief, Hornet was up to no good. Again. She had bought batches of dumps and CVVs every week for the past six weeks. Somehow, she would find a way to trap him. Most galling, he tutored junior crooks in that forum. Maybe Teena could become one of his students and find out more about him. Fake Kyle had gone silent. But so had Brooke, and Kyle was waiting for Brooke to respond to his offer. She would need to address that. Maybe tonight.

The elevator dinged. Tenth floor. She headed toward Harlan's office.

Harlan and Mike Swanson were waiting.

Harlan gestured. "Jesse, please have a seat."

Harlan moved behind his desk and sat. Jesse sat in front of the desk, facing Harlan. Mike remained standing between Jesse and the door.

This looked serious. "What's going on?"

Mike spoke. "I'll get right to the point. It's come to my attention there was some unusual activity in your carder forum fund. When was the last time you used that account?"

"Last week. Hornet keeps posting new batches and we need to keep buying samples. It's infuriating. Why?"

"How many cards do you usually buy?"

"I don't buy any cards. I buy information to produce card-not-present transactions, and information to produce physical cards. Usually around a hundred at a time."

"Do you rent a post office box?"

"No, why?"

"Are you sure?"

"I think I'd know if I had a post office box. What's going on?"

"After you buy those credit card numbers, what happens to them?"

"You already know what we do."

"Humor me."

Jesse rolled her eyes and shook her head. "We feed a spreadsheet with the card numbers into *Merchant Trace*. The software finds merchants common to all the cards and then we alert the merchants. And then we retire the card numbers."

"If you retire the card numbers, then why did somebody buy thousands of dollars of merchandise online with bad credit card numbers and ship it all to a post office box you control?"

"What?"

"You heard me. You rented a post office box, you used those credit cards to buy merchandise, and you sold it to the highest bidder."

Jesse's world went into slow motion. "What are you talking about? Brenda and I always retire those card numbers right after we buy them. It's standard procedure." Thoughts ping-ponged inside her head. Have we ever had a reason to not retire a stolen card number? This doesn't add up.

She tuned into Harlan's voice. "...Mike and I both agree, you've done some great things for us during your time here, and so we're not calling the police. But we have to terminate you, effective immediately. We'll give you three months to provide restitution, but I don't know how you're going to find fifty thousand dollars."

This is not happening. "Wait a minute. What?"

Harlan slid a document across his desk. "We need you to sign this document acknowledging what you did and agreeing to reimburse the bank." Harlan handed Jesse a pen.

Jesse took the pen and picked up the document. "Is this some kind of joke or what?"

Mike shook his head. "It's no joke."

"You don't mind if I read this first."

"Of course."

Jesse skimmed it. "The undersigned hereby acknowledges and affirms (1) I purchased at least $50,000 in merchandise using stolen credit card numbers issued by Uncle Sam Bank, and (2) I will reimburse Uncle Sam Bank (hereafter called, 'the bank') the sum of $50,000, no later than ninety days from the date of the aforementioned signature." And more legalese.

Jesse looked up. "I think I need to talk to an attorney."

Mike towered over her, "We're not the police. This is between you and the bank."

"What happens if I don't sign?"

"Then we'll have no choice but to refer this to the police and charge you. But we'd rather keep it quiet."

Jesse looked over the document more carefully. It had a list of transaction dates, merchants, and amounts. Which could prove useful. "Would you print me another copy of this?"

"We were planning on making a copy after you sign."

"Well, this way you'll have two originals, right?"

Harlan and Mike made eye contact. Mike nodded. Harlan printed a second copy and laid them on his desk in front of Jesse.

Jesse stood and stuffed one copy in her pocket. She turned toward Mike and tore the other copy in half. She set the torn papers on Harlan's desk. "You do what you want. I didn't steal anything."

This is where they smile and congratulate me for passing their stupid test. And why are they testing me anyway? These mind games are crazy. That has to be what this is.

Harlan said something.

"Sorry, what?"

"I said, wait outside please."

Mike opened the office door and gestured. Jesse stood. A uniformed security guard waited. Jesse walked out. Mike shut the door.

The security guard looked like an NFL linebacker.

Jesse glanced at the elevator. "What would happen if I ran into the elevator?"

The guard smiled. "It would be best if you didn't try to find out."

Jesse nodded. "Just curious. Are the cops on the way?"

"I wouldn't know."

"Well, then, I'm going to make some phone calls. Do you have a problem with that?"

"I do, but I don't have authority to stop you."

"Well, good. When your managers ask who I called, tell them I'm calling all my accomplices to bury the evidence."

The guard's lips turned up. He nodded.

Jesse took out her phone and dialed.

"Dad, it's Jesse. I'm about to be arrested." She looked the security guard in the eye. She raised her voice so everyone in the office could hear. "I wanted you to hear it from me first. I didn't steal anything, but there are some managers who say I did. I don't know what's going on, but I'm gonna get to the bottom of it. But I might need your help getting out of jail. Again."

A few heads popped up over cubicle panels.

Her next call was to Brenda. "Brenda, they're arresting me for stealing that last batch of CVVs. Or dumps, I'm not sure which."

"What?"

"Listen, I don't know when they'll take my phone away, but I need a favor. Would you gather up the logs of when the call center contacted all those consumers and forward to my home email?"

"Jesse, did you —"

"No, I didn't. But I promise I'm gonna find out who did. That's why I need those logs. They say we never retired the numbers. But why would we warn consumers without retiring the numbers?"

"Right. Jesse, I'm still processing this. They're arresting you?"

"They probably disabled my company email. That's why I need you to forward the logs to my home email."

"Um, there are probably processing logs from retiring those numbers. Want me to get those too?"

"Yeah, thanks. Great idea." Jesse fought tears. "Listen, I need one more favor."

"Name it."

"I don't know where they're taking me. I left a voicemail for my Dad, but he won't know where to find me. Would you, um, would you make sure you know what jail they're taking me to and let my dad know?"

"Yeah. What's his number?"

Jesse gave Brenda her parents' home and cell numbers. "Thanks. Let Gloria know, too."

Four uniformed police officers arrived at 3:30 p.m.

"Jessica Jonsen?"

"What took you so long? He's the one you want." Jesse gestured toward the security guard.

The guard's face turned red.

Jesse laughed. "That's what I'm gonna remember about this day when this is all over. The expression on your face." She turned to the lead officer. "I'm Jesse Jonsen."

The officer nodded. "We have to cuff you."

"Of course, you do. Want a tour of the bank?"

"That won't be necessary."

18.   1995—Trip North

September, 1995. Highway 169, near Mille Lacs Lake, Minnesota.

The trip north in the police van stretched for mile after mile after mile, with nothing to see but birch trees, lakes, and asphalt. Jesse looked out the back window again. Her parents' car was right there behind the van.

"Turn back around." The beefy deputy blocking her from the van door looked like a no-nonsense army commander. "If I have to ask you again, I'll put you in handcuffs."

Jesse rolled her eyes.

"What's your deal anyway?" The girl on her other side looked like a crackhead, with frizzy hair and wild eyes.

"Huh?"

"Workin' on some project to learn how the other half lives?"

"No. Just a big misunderstanding."

"Yeah, I'll bet. Lemme guess. You thought your parents were sending you to summer camp."

Jesse shook her head. "What's your deal?"

"Me? Oh, let's see. I was mistreated when I was younger. Yeah, a priest tried to nail me, but I wouldn't let him. My dad's a drug dealer and my mom runs an escort service."

"You're lying."

Frizzy arched her eyebrows. "What if I am?"

"Well, then I won't believe anything you tell me."

"Why do I care?"

Jesse shook her head. "Forget it."

"That your mommy and daddy behind us?"

Jesse stopped herself from turning. "What if it is?"

"Are they gonna tuck you in tonight and make you all comfortable?"

"I doubt it."

"Then why are they following us?"

"They want to find out what Itasca's like."

Frizzy nodded and laughed. "So, they *are* gonna tuck you in tonight. Maybe they'll get a hotel in Bigfork so they can dry-clean your cheerleader outfit every day."

Jesse laughed. "Are there any dry-cleaners in Bigfork?"

"Guess we'll find out. What's your name, Preppy?"

"Jesse. What's yours?"

"Africanishaniqua ."

"No it's not."

"Why not?"

" 'Cause you're as white as I am."

"That's just because my parents made me take a drug that bleached my skin."

Jesse rolled her eyes. "What's your real name? Or do I just call you Frizzy."

"If you call me Frizzy, I'll call you Preppy."

"I don't care what you call me."

"Okay, Preppy it is, then."

Jesse shook her head. "Nice to meet you, Frizzy."

Birch and pine trees along US Highway 169 raced by. And after a few minutes, a sign: "Grand Rapids 20 miles."

"Hey Preppy—think your parents might tuck me in tonight too?"

Jesse laughed. "Shut up."

"Or maybe they'll adopt me. They'll get rid if you 'cause you're a preppy who had everything handed to her and chose a life of crime. But me--I'm a poor, disadvantaged youth and they'll want to rescue me. So they'll dump you and adopt me."

The smell of pine filled the air on State Highway 38, north of Grand Rapids.

Jesse studied Frizzy.

"What'cha lookin' at, Preppy?"

Jesse shook her head. "You don't look disadvantaged to me."

"Well, I am. One leg's shorter than the other. It's from the accident."

Jesse chuckled. "What accident?"

"My boyfriend hot-wired a car. But the cops chased us and he wrapped it around a telephone pole. It killed him and maimed me horribly. After I got out of the hospital, the police sent me to Itasca, and that's why I'm here."

Jesse chuckled. "Why do I even ask you questions?"

" 'Cause you're curious about me. You probably live a sheltered life and your parents are sending you up here for a week to learn how bad girls live. What did you do anyway, apply the wrong-colored makeup?"

"Yeah, something like that."

"You did not. I'll bet you wrecked your mama's Mercedes."

"Nope. I told you, the whole thing's a misunderstanding."

Ten more miles passed.

"Hey Preppy, wanna know why I'm really here?"

Jesse took the bait again. "Sure."

"You first."

"Fine," Jesse said. "The cops at Bullseye Stores said I tried to steal some clothes."

"Well, did you?"

"No."

"So, why did they think you did?"

"I had some makeup in my bag I forgot to pay for. I offered to pay, but they'd already called the cops, and now here I am."

"You said they caught you stealing clothes."

"I had an outfit on under my dress and it looked like one of theirs."

"Uh huh."

"Okay, your turn. And what's your real name?"

"I told you. Sha'Quonda."

"You said it was Africa something earlier."

"Well, I was putting you on then. My real name is Harlemisha."

"But you just said – oh, forget it."

Frizzy laughed. "Okay, truth. I'm here because a security guard at the Mall of America wanted me and I told him no."

Jesse laughed. "One of these days, you'll tell me the truth and your real name."

"Maybe I already did."

Jesse rolled her eyes. "Really, why are you here?"

"I'm making lemonade."

"Huh?"

"You know. When life gives you lemons?"

Jesse rolled her eyes again.

The van turned onto a narrow side street, took a left and then a right, and then another left turn onto a dirt road. Two miles of empty fields later, they stopped in front of a large house that looked like it came from an old Western movie set.

"We're here, ladies. Allow us to escort you inside."

~

Jesse and her parents waited in an adjacent room while Frizzy went through her intake meeting in the director's office.

"Mom, let's just go home. I don't like this place. It's in the middle of nowhere."

"You heard the judge. It's either finish high school here or jail."

"Dad, can't you do something?"

"Even if I could, I wouldn't. You let a lot of people down, Jesse."

"Mom, why is he so grumpy? Just take me home."

The office door opened. Somebody escorted Frizzy out of the office and farther into the house. A fortyish woman appeared in the office door. "Please. Come in."

Jesse stepped inside with her parents.

"My name is Karen Adams and I'm the director here. Let's cover a few ground rules. First is running away. We have security at the door twenty-four by seven, but we don't lock the building at night. If you want to leave, nobody will stop you. But we'll know and we will call your parents or other responsible party.

"The nearest house is a mile away, and we're in northern Minnesota. You'll want to dress warmly in the winter. The bears hibernate in winter, but watch out for wolves year around. You can hear them howl; they're beautiful. Overall, it's a bad idea to leave this house at night. But sometimes our residents need to learn lessons about consequences, and this house is not a prison. I hope you make the right choices."

Jesse rolled her eyes.

"She doesn't believe me." Karen looked out a window behind her. "Ah. Lovely. Jesse, come here, I want to show you something."

Jesse and her parents walked to the window.

Karen pointed to a couple of moving dots. "I love the view from this window." She picked up a pair of binoculars. "Here, take a look." She handed the binoculars to Jesse.

Jesse looked and then handed the binoculars to her mom. Mom and Dad both looked. Dad handed the binoculars back to Karen. "What are those?"

"Black bears. They weigh about four hundred pounds. You don't want to surprise them and you want to stay away from any momma bear with her cubs."

Jesse moved back around Karen's desk and slumped in her chair. Mom and Dad also sat. Dad smiled.

"Jesse, if you don't learn anything else from your time with us, I hope you learn there are consequences for your actions."

Jesse shook her head.

"We also restrict your access to the telephone and we watch your mail. Cell phones are becoming popular, but we don't allow them. And, even if we did, coverage is spotty at best. The only interaction any resident has with the outside world is with your responsible party. For you, that means your parents. And, of course, your teachers at school."

Jesse shook her head.

Karen shuffled some papers. "The next order of business is school. Let's see." She found the paper she wanted. "Yes, here we are. You're a senior. We'll enroll you in our local high school for your senior year and you and your classmates here will have a nice graduation party next June."

Karen explained the rest of the rules and went through an overview of the property. Jesse's parents signed papers and asked a few questions. Jesse's mood grew blacker as the minutes passed.

Karen stood and walked around her desk. "Jesse, I know you don't believe this now, but we're trying to help you. Your life will have nothing but sorrow if you continue on your present path. And now, let me show you your room. I believe you met your roommate, Nadine Ladysmith, in the van on the way up here."

~

"Your real name is Nadine Ladysmith?" Jesse and Frizzy sat alone in their room. Jesse's parents had said their goodbyes and left.

"I'm gonna change it as soon as I turn eighteen."

"Why"

"Do I look like a Nadine?"

"I dunno. It's your name."

"You look more like a Nadine, Preppy."

"My name's Jesse. It's my real name. And I'm not preppy."

"Yeah you are."

Jesse rolled her eyes. "So, whaddya like to do, Nadine?"

"Do me a favor, okay? Don't call me Nadine."

"Well, what should I call you?"

"I was thinking of maybe Chastity. Or maybe Serenity. Those sound like good names."

"Nah, too long. Maybe something simple, like Candy."

"Candy. Yeah, I like that. Candy Smith. That'll be my name." Candy's eyes lit up. "Thanks, Preppy."

"Okay, Candy, whaddya like to do?"

"I like to party. And guys like to party with me. And I turn lemons into lemonade. How about you, Preppy, what do you like to do?"

"If you want me to call you Candy, then you can call me Jesse. That's my name, Jesse. Like Jesse James."

"Fair enough. Jesse it is, then. Let's shake on it."

Jesse shook her hand. "Deal. Guess you could call me a businesswoman."

"Sounds exotic. What kind of business?"

"Clothes mostly. I sell designer clothes at a discount. And IDs. And other stuff sometimes."

"Ooh, cool! So, could I buy a driver's license from you?"

"Maybe. It's a little more complicated than usual while I'm here."

"How about a dress?"

"Those are tougher. Hard to get inventory."

Candy laughed. "'Cause you were busted for shoplifting, right?"

"It was a misunderstanding."

Candy shrugged. "Huh. You like Vodka?"

"No."

"Too bad. It makes the parties better. Goes good with lemonade, too."

19.   Jail

The last time Jesse was on the wrong side of the legal system, she was a teenaged thief. But she had gotten her life together, at least until now. She sat on her cell bunk, put her head in her hands, and bawled.

Somebody banged on her door. "Shut up in there."

Jesse jumped. An officer's head passed the window on her cell door.

"What if I don't want to shut up? What if I want to scream at the top of my lungs?"

"Suit yourself."

A camera in the corner opposite the stainless-steel toilet and sink caught her eye.

"Hey, what if I have to pee?"

The officer laughed. "Welcome to the Hennepin County five-star hotel."

Jesse scrambled to the door. "Hey, when do I see a judge?"

"Happy Memorial Day weekend. Probably not 'till Tuesday. Enjoy your stay." The officer walked away, laughing.

A thousand bricks fell on Jesse's shoulders. She staggered back to the crappy bed on a concrete shelf and sat. Four overnights in this place. And what about after that? What about bail? What about mail? A line from an old TV show. Jail without bail in case you fail. What about, well, everything? Where did she fail? The world would continue but she was stuck in here. For stealing credit cards. She chuckled. After more than twenty years of putting away crooks and fighting for victims, here she was again. Full circle.

Those old sentences bubbled up again. Keep on seeking, and you will find. I am with you always, even to the end of the age. No. I'm not going there. This situation is absurd. I'm not a crook. I didn't steal anything. Not this time. She wiped her wet cheeks. Cut this out, Jesse. Let's make lemonade. Just like Candy used to do.

Jesse teared up again. But this was different. So long ago, but now more like yesterday.

What would Candy do now? Probably try to seduce any male officer she could find. Jesse laughed. Good luck with that in here. But somehow, Candy would find a way to turn this lemon into lemonade. And now Jesse would do it. For Candy. Just like she'd done with every situation since Candy died.

Jesse wiped her eyes. Again. She splashed water on her face. Makeup must have smeared everywhere. It probably clashed with prison-jumpsuit-orange. She wiped around her eyes with toilet paper until no more makeup came off. No mirror, but hey, use what you have. That's how we make lemonade.

Now, why was she stuck in here? Looks like I have three days to figure it out.

~

Her cell door opened. A woman in an officer's uniform who could pass for Paul Bunyan's twin sister filled the doorway, holding a baton. "Come with me."

Jesse stood as tall as she could stretch. "Worried I'll use a Kung-Fu move or something?"

The officer chuckled. "I'm taking you to overnight guest accommodations in our housing unit upstairs. I'm afraid room service won't be available. Enjoy your weekend with us."

Jesse laughed. "You can put that baton away. I don't bite."

~

"Assemble for breakfast in five minutes. Breakfast will be available for the next half-hour. If you choose not to eat breakfast, please inform a staff member immediately."

Jesse sat up and rubbed her eyes. What time is it anyway? Happy Saturday morning. She followed people to the cafeteria and found a table that looked peaceful. She sat and took a bite of food. The place looked like any cafeteria. Well, except for uniformed corrections officers patrolling the area. And two floors of closed rooms.

A Hispanic girl sat across from her. Early twenties. Short. "Hi. I'm Maribel."

Jesse took a sip of orange juice. "Jesse."

"You're new here."

"Stuck over the weekend."

"Why are you here?"

"I was set up. People say I bought a bunch of merchandise with stolen credit cards."

Maribel smiled. "Not bad. A lady with class."

"Is this where you tell me everyone here is innocent and who to watch out for?"

Maribel laughed. "No. You're innocent until proven guilty. Most everyone else in here has already been proven guilty."

"Ah." Jesse put her fork down. "So, what are you guilty of?"

"Prostitution."

"Mmm."

"It's not as glamorous as stealing credit cards. But my boyfriend and me, we have a future."

"Why are you telling me this?"

"You looked like you could use a friend."

Jesse smiled. "Well, thanks."

Maribel stood. "See ya around." She turned to leave.

"Wait. How do you and your boyfriend have a future?"

Maribel sat again. "Because when I get outta here in three more months, we're gonna make some more money and then go live somewhere nice."

"How long have you been here?"

"Three months."

Jesse nodded. "Halfway through. Where do you want to live?"

"Dunno. Maybe Florida. Hawaii maybe. Or Vegas."

"How old are you?"

"Nineteen. I'm legal."

"You remind me of me when I was seventeen."

Maribel laughed. "Now that's funny. You and me the same."

"Well, we look different. But I was on the same path you're on. What's your boyfriend's name?"

"Connor."

"My boyfriend was Dylan."

"Did he care about you?"

"I thought he did."

"Well, that's not my Connor. He really cares about me. And I care about him."

"Sounds nice. How did you guys meet?"

"Online. I forget where. See, I'm a singer and I liked to post videos of me singing songs. Connor saw one of them and we started talking. He's trying to break in as an agent. And I'm trying to break in as a singer. And we hit it off."

"How does prostitution fit in?"

"That's how we meet people. We just need somebody to give us a chance in a club and then we're on our way. And maybe one of our customers is a club manager."

Jesse shook her head.

"What?"

96

"I'd love to hear a song. Anything you want."

Maribel smiled. "Anything?"

"Yeah. Well, not just anything, I guess. Something nice."

"You like 'Amazing Grace?'"

"Yeah. That's a great song."

"All right." Maribel cleared her throat and took a breath. "A-ah-mazing Grace, how sweet the sound."

Jesse's jaw dropped. A few heads turned.

"That saved a wretch like me." More heads turned.

Maribel stood. "I once was lost, but now am found." The room went quiet.

"Was blind, but now I see."

Jesse wiped tears. Somebody shouted, "Do some more." Several people clapped, including a couple of officers.

Maribel sat. Her face was red.

"That was incredible. You have an unbelievable voice."

Maribel looked down. "Thanks. People tell me that all the time. That's why I want to sing in front of audiences."

Jesse shook her head and wiped another tear. "Maribel, you don't need to sell yourself. Just go audition at 'First Avenue.'"

"Oh, no – that guy is a jerk. He'd throw me out if I ever tried to talk to him."

"How do you know that?"

"He just is, okay?"

"Is Connor talking to him?"

"We don't need 'First Avenue.' Connor and me, we're gonna go bigger than that."

The PA boomed. "Please bring your plates and trays to the counter."

Jesse stood. "Maribel, it was nice meeting you."

"You too. Hey, next time, tell me about your boyfriend. I'll bet you have some pretty good stories."

Jesse nodded. "Yeah. I do. Lunch, right here?"

"Sure."

"Hey Maribel—where can I find something to read? And maybe a pad of paper and a pen or a pencil?"

"There's a commissary right down there. Not sure if they sell paper and pencils. Why, are you a writer?"

Jesse laughed. "No. I just need to collect some thoughts. And since I have a free weekend—"

Maribel smiled. "Maybe the COs will let you have some paper and a pen."

"COs?"

"They like to call themselves corrections officers. Not guards."

"Oh. Good to know, thanks."

"And magazines are on the tables over there. I like *People*."

~

Jesse picked at her lunch. "What is this stuff?"

Maribel laughed. "Mystery meat. Just like high school."

They both tried a bite.

Maribel put her fork down. "So, tell me about your boyfriend when you were in high school."

"Oh, you mean Dylan? I stole things for him. It was 1995. I was a Hanson fan. Ever heard of Hanson?"

"Weren't they a country band or something?"

"No, not quite. They were the number one band for teenage girls when I was a teenager. Now, nobody remembers who they are. Anyway, I didn't like my dad, and Dylan and I were going to do things differently. We were gonna make a ton of money and live happily ever after somewhere else. Sound familiar?"

"What happened?"

"I got caught."

"Then what happened?"

"We broke up. And I decided I didn't like where my life was going. I finished high school, went to college, and then grad school, and now I'm a principal fraud analyst. Well, at least I was."

"Until you got caught again, huh?"

"Yeah, something like that. But, innocent until proven guilty, right?"

"Yeah, sure."

"Ya know, I've spent most of the past twenty years trying to put crooks away. And now, some crook who wears nice suits is trying to put me away. I promise you this, I'm gonna put him away. I didn't steal anything from anyone and I'm gonna figure out how he framed me and make him pay."

They both ate a few bites of food.

Jesse sipped her water. "How do you stomach this stuff?"

Maribel laughed. "You get used to it."

They chewed a few more bites.

Maribel put her fork down. "You think Connor is like Dylan, don't you?"

Jesse sighed. "Yeah, I do. I see guys like that groom vulnerable teenagers all the time."

"Groom?"

"It's where they promise you whatever you're looking for. Maybe you have a bad family life, maybe you want to be a movie star, maybe you're just spoiled like I was and want some adventure. Whatever it is, they convince you they can get you what you want if you sell yourself. And then you're trapped."

"It's just that, well, Connor is good at talking to people, ya know?"

"I'll bet he is. But while you're stuck in here, what's he doing?"

"Dunno. I feel bad because I should be helping him, but I can't from inside here."

"Has he been by to visit?"

"A couple times. But he says it's best to stay clear of jailhouses. Bad karma. But he'll be waiting for me when I get out."

Jesse took another sip of water. "How'd you get caught?"

"We made a date with some guy and he turned out to be a vice cop. I offered him free service but he wasn't interested."

"How much money have you made?"

"I don't even know. It's a lot. You would not believe how much guys pay. Connor's putting it away for later."

"Why don't you ask him how much there is."

"Oh, no, he doesn't like to talk about money. I asked him about it a few days before I got caught and he got really mad."

Jesse nodded. "Did he hit you?"

Maribel looked down. "Yeah."

"Hard?"

"It left a bruise. He said he was sorry later. He's under a lot of stress."

Jesse fought tears. "You keep making me cry."

"I'm sorry."

"No. Don't be sorry. Connor should not have hit you. That's not how you treat a girlfriend."

"He said he was sorry."

"Nobody deserves to be treated that way. If this guy really were your boyfriend—" A thought exploded in Jesse's mind. "Wait a minute—that all happened a few days before you got caught?"

"Yeah."

"Who made the date?"

"Connor makes all the dates."

"Does he, now."

"Are you saying he set me up?"

"You're in here, aren't you?"

"I need to go." Maribel chugged the rest of her water and marched away.

"Maribel, wait." Jesse tried to follow her.

An officer blocked Jesse's path. "Word of advice. Mind your own business while you're in here."

"I didn't mean to upset her."

"Sit down and finish your lunch. Unless you want to spend the rest of your time here in a cell."

20.   Rule Five

Tuesday morning finally came. By now, the routine was second-nature. The person behind the counter dished out another blop of oatmeal. Jesse took a glass of orange juice and wandered away.

Maribel sat at a table. Alone. Jesse hesitated.

"Are you gonna stand there all day or what?" Somebody behind her. A couple of officers looked at her. Jesse strode to Maribel's table and sat.

"Maribel, I'm sorry I upset you."

"Just go away."

"I will. I'm on my way to court today. I was hoping you'd wish me luck."

"Okay. Good luck."

"Hopefully, I get out on bail today. I was wondering, after I'm out, is it okay to come visit you?"

"Why do you want to visit me?"

"I was hoping we could be friends."

"I'm a prostitute and you work in some fancy bank. Why do you want to be friends?"

Jesse laughed. "I don't work in a fancy bank anymore. But even if I did, I was thinking, maybe we could go talk to people at 'First Avenue' when you get out."

Maribel looked down. And then looked Jesse in the eye and nodded. 'Yeah. I'd like that."

"Okay. But I have a condition." Jesse smiled.

"What condition?"

"After they hear you sing and offer you a gig, I want a free backstage pass to one of your shows."

Maribel smiled. "Deal."

~

"Where's your attorney?" From his bench, Judge Brandon Lundergan peered over his glasses at Jesse.

Jesse smoothed her hair. "They're hard to find over a holiday weekend, Your Honor. Looks like I'm it for right now."

"This charging document says you stole over fifty thousand dollars. Which means you must not be indigent."

"I didn't steal anything. And I'm not indigent. But I'm not rich either."

"I suggest you find an attorney, Ms. Jonsen."

"I'd love to. Got any recommendations?"

"Do you understand the charges against you?"

"Not really."

"I'm going to continue this Rule Five hearing until later today and ask a public defender to counsel you. The charging documents set your bail at ten thousand dollars—"

"Your Honor, we would move to increase bail to fifty thousand dollars." Somebody in a suit on Jesse's left.

"Why? And where am I supposed to find that kind of money?"

"I'll ask the questions, Ms. Jonsen." Judge Lundergan turned to the prosecutor. "But it's a valid question. Why didn't you work this out when you got the arrest warrant?"

"We did, Your Honor, but since then, we found additional information on her background. She has a criminal history and some of her accomplices are foreign nationals in hostile countries. She is a flight risk."

Jesse shook her head. "You've got to be kidding"

"Ms. Jonsen, I won't ask you again. I'm in a good mood this morning. Don't spoil it. We'll continue this after Ms. Jonsen has a chance to discuss her situation with a public defender. Ms. Jonsen, I suggest you use this time wisely. When I see you again, I'll expect you to have an attorney who knows how I run my court. Do I make myself clear?"

"Yes, sir." She looked up at the judge, who stared down at her. She massaged the back of her neck. "Um, what do I do now?"

"A bailiff will escort you to a public defender with access to a telephone. I suggest you use it."

~

"Wow." Public Defender Lisa Mitchell looked up from a pile of documents.

"Is that a good wow or a bad wow?" Jesse leaned forward against the conference room table.

Lisa leaned back. "Well, they went to a lot of trouble to build a case against you. You buy stolen credit cards as part of your job?"

"Yeah."

"Well, this says you bought several credit cards with the bank's money and then used those to buy merchandise online, delivered to a post-office box. It doesn't say what you did with the merchandise. Sold it I guess?"

"No, I didn't sell it."

"What'd you do with it?"

"Wait a minute. I didn't steal anything."

"And you just fell into a trap. Watch out for that when they ask you questions. In their eyes, you're guilty, no matter what, and if they put you away for ten years, they'll get a good job review at their next performance appraisal. So, they'll ask you questions with the unstated assumption you're guilty and then they'll twist whatever answer you give to look like an admission. Don't fall for it. If they ask you what you did with the merchandise, tell them you never stole the credit cards and you don't know about any merchandise. That *is* the truth, right?"

"Well, yeah."

"I believe you."

Curiosity invaded Jesse's brain. "Why?"

"Because this thing smells funny. Why would you buy a bunch of merchandise with stolen credit cards and then sell it all online. You're too smart for that. You work all the time, right?"

"Yeah."

"So where did you stash all the money?"

Jesse smiled. "There wasn't any money to stash. I didn't steal anything."

Lisa smiled back. "Good. You're learning. Here's another thing. Don't let them throw you off balance. They want you scared, and they'll try every rhetorical trick in the book to intimidate you. Don't play into it."

"Well, I am scared."

"You should be. They will put you in prison for a long time if they can. And then they'll have dinner at a nice restaurant to celebrate."

Jesse buried her head in her hands. "I can't believe this is happening."

"Believe it. And get ready to fight."

Jesse nodded.

"Let's look at the case they have against you. You have a persona named Teena Fay from Green Bay, right?"

"Yeah."

"And you deceive people with that persona to buy stolen credit cards, isn't that right?"

"Yeah."

"So, you lie for a living."

"I can't very well tell criminals I'm buying samples to figure out where they were stolen from."

"No, probably not. And that's how I want you to answer when they ask if you lie for a living. Because they will. So, how does Teena Fay from Green Bay operate?"

"Well, she logs into various carder forums and banters. Most of the players think she's a small-time operator from somewhere in Wisconsin. Sometimes she buys CVVs and dumps. She always pays on time. Her spelling and grammar are awful."

"What stops you from going off on your own?"

"Two-factor authentication?"

"Two what?"

"I can't buy on my own. The carder shop sends a confirming email to an address I registered with them to make sure I'm me. But Brenda has the email password."

"Wait – you're telling me you couldn't buy one of these alone even if you wanted to?"

"That's right."

"What if you logged in as somebody else?"

"I suppose I could set up another identity. But using the bank's money takes approvals."

"Don't you have some discretionary power?"

"I can do two hundred dollars without approval."

"So, ten batches of ten credit cards for twenty dollars each. Buy $500 in merchandise with each one, for fifty thousand. Spend two hundred for credit cards, you can sell fifty thousand in stolen merchandise for four cents on the dollar and break even. But you probably get close to fifty cents on the dollar. It's a great gig. Especially when the bank fronts it."

Jesse dropped her jaw.

"That's what they say you did. They got you because of your post office box."

Jesse took a couple breaths. "I don't have a post office box."

"Well, yes you do. They have a record of it. It's in your name. And they say they have video of people picking up packages."

"When they fired me last week in Mike Swanson's office, they said something about a post office box. But it didn't register until now."

Lisa nodded. "That's how this works. The more off-balance you are, the easier for them to railroad you. You'll want a copy of every video they have. Here's the next thing we need to talk about. Apparently, you were quite an operator when you were younger."

"I was. Until I got caught. Spent my senior year in a girls' group home up north. And I put it all behind me. I went to college and grad school and I spent my adult life trying to stop people like me when I was younger."

"Well, your past is coming back to bite you. The prosecution wants bail set at fifty thousand."

"I heard. How am I supposed to find that kind of money?"

"They don't care. You can stay in jail if you want. But I wouldn't recommend it."

Jesse swallowed.

"Do you have family, friends, anyone willing to mortgage their house for you?"

"I don't know."

"The court gives it back when you show up for your trial."

"How long does that take?"

"Could be a few months. Maybe longer. Depending on the complexity of the case. Or maybe you'll take a plea bargain and get on with your life."

Jesse shook her head.

"When we go back in, I'll ask that they release you on O R."

"O R?"

"Your own recognizance. Meaning you're trustworthy enough to show up without them holding monetary leverage over you."

"What if the judge says no?"

"He probably will say no. They'll probably offer to split the difference, at twenty-five thousand. I'll have a good shot at persuading them to use the original amount on the warrant, ten thousand."

"But somebody still needs to put up a lot of money because of me."

"There's another option. You could use a bail bond company. You pay those guys ten percent and they guarantee the full amount of the bail. But they keep the ten percent."

"So I pay a thousand dollars to get out of jail and then it's gone?"

"Assuming we can reduce the bail to ten-thousand, yes."

"That's extortion."

"Well, technically it's not." Lisa laughed. "It's the law."

Jesse rubbed her eyes. "And how much do I pay you?"

"Those taxes that came out of your paycheck pay for me. But I can't defend you after today."

"Why not?"

"Because you're not indigent. Which means you can afford an attorney."

Jesse sighed. "This keeps getting better."

"I have somebody in mind for you, though. Dominic Levenson."

"Why do you like him?"

"We grew up together. He taught me everything I know after I got out of law school."

"Okay."

"I'll call him and get you on his calendar."

"Thanks. I also have some other people I'd like you to call, if that's okay."

~

Judge Brandon Lundergan looked down at Jesse from his bench again. Lisa stood next to her this time. "Are you a flight risk?"

Lisa smiled. "No, Your Honor, my client is not a flight risk. Her family lives here and she intends to vigorously defend herself."

Judge Lundergan nodded. "Bail set at ten thousand dollars. Don't destroy my trust, Ms. Jonsen."

~

Jesse's cell door opened. It was Paul Bunyan's twin sister again. Holding the same baton. "Come with me."

Jesse laughed. "Still worried about my Kung-Fu skills?"

"Somebody posted bail. Bring your stuff. You're not coming back."

~

Jesse climbed into Gloria's minivan. "I'll never drink enough coffee to pay you back."

Gloria started the car. "It was worth it just to see the looks on their faces."

"Why?"

"They wouldn't take my business check or credit card. It had to be cash. So I came back with ten-thousand, one-dollar bills. The wheelbarrow is in back."

Jesse laughed.

"And I'll get it all back after you beat this thing, right?"

Jesse nodded. "Yeah."

"Good. We've got work to do."

"We?"

"Hey, I invested good money here. I need to protect it."

21. Ashley

Friday, June 15, 2018

Five-foot, six Ashley Dunbar wanted to scream. She pushed her long dark hair out of her eyes, stormed outside her parents' immaculate house, and slammed the door. The walls vibrated. Something crashed to the floor. *I'm sixteen years old and I can go out anytime I want.*

She stomped to the end of the driveway and called her friend, Carissa.

"Everything's cool. Meet me at the park entrance."

"Did you have another fight with your parents?"

"It's so stupid. I just want to go out tonight and celebrate a little."

"So, what's wrong?"

"Their stupid religion. They think we're gonna go smoke weed and get drunk and get pregnant."

Carissa laughed. "Oh, is that all? I guess they wouldn't like the male strippers, then."

Ashley laughed. "Could you imagine the scandal that would cause?"

"I'll meet you at the park in ten minutes. If it's any help, you can stay at our house a couple days. I'll ask my parents to talk to your parents later."

"Thanks."

~

Carissa took another bite of pizza. "So, what's the deal with you and your parents anyway?"

Ashley sipped her pop. "I don't want to think about it right now." She stretched her arms and stared out over Lake Nokomis. Several rental canoes lined one side of the beach. A few toddlers made sandcastles in the wet sand near the water.

"Maybe next time, we can plan better and you can bring a swimsuit."

"That's okay. I don't want to get wet."

"Seriously, what are we gonna do about your parents?"

Ashley picked up another pizza slice. "I just couldn't take another night in that house. Thanks for letting me sleep over."

Carissa looked out toward the parking lot.

"What?"

Carissa's eyes widened. "It's a gold Mercedes."

Ashley turned.

"No. Don't look. They're parking. And a lady is staring at us."

"Why can't I look?"

Carissa shook her head. "Just don't look. I don't know who she is."

"Is she alone?"

"No. Geez, the driver is opening her door."

"You mean, like a chauffeur?"

"Yeah. She's in the back seat."

"What does she look like?"

"Dark hair. She looks rich. She's walking toward us."

"Excuse me." It was a woman's voice, behind Ashley. She had a British accent.

Ashley turned. "Hi. Were you talking to us?"

"Yes, I was. Specifically, you."

Ashley laughed and gestured toward Carissa. "Whatever it was, she made me do it."

Carissa blushed.

The woman smiled.

"My name is Meaghan and I noticed you from the parkway. I'm a model scout and I am looking for nubile young women to help us present a resort property in northern Minnesota to corporate clients. I may also need assistance modeling a clothing line."

"Umm, wow."

"May I chat with you for a moment?"

"Sure. Have a seat."

Carissa slid the pizza box toward Meaghan. "Want a slice?"

Ashley laughed. "I'm Ashley."

"Carissa. Nice to meet you, Meaghan. What does nubile mean?"

"It means your friend Ashley has a certain attractive quality that works in photographs."

Meaghan handed a business card to Ashley. "Please contact me if you're interested and we can discuss it further." She stood to leave.

"Wait a minute." Ashley swung around. "Tell us more."

Meaghan smiled. "Of course. As I said, my agency has been hired to promote a resort on the shore of Mille Lacs Lake. You may have seen some of our television adverts for Norra lekplatsen, which means Northern Playground in Swedish. For our next series of ads, we want to photograph the rooms with nubile young women in various poses, wearing clothing from a line we represent."

Carissa shook her head. "What kind of poses?"

"Sensual, but tasteful," Meaghan said.

Ashley pursed her lips. "But nothing that would get me kicked out of school, right?"

"Of course not."

"What would I have to do?"

"The process is quite simple, really. We have a location where the lighting is optimal in the early evening. You'll wear our clothing and we photograph you."

Carissa scowled.

Ashley laughed. "Sounds like fun. And you're a woman, so there's no funny stuff, right?"

"I'm unsure what you mean by 'funny stuff,' but of course I personally help supervise all aspects of the work. Are you interested?"

"Yeah."

"Wait a minute," Carissa said. "You can't just run off up north and take a bunch of pictures. How far away is this place?"

"About two hours by car. We were ready to return when we noticed you. We would have you back by late this evening or tomorrow morning."

Ashley smiled, "Sounds like fun. So, I'd just get in the car with you and take off?"

"It would be slightly more complicated. You are a minor child, so we would, of course, need permission from your parents or other responsible party to protect us all from future liability issues."

"C'mon Ashley. Let's go." Carissa reached for Ashley's elbow.

Ashley pulled her elbow away. "Wait a minute. Here's the thing, Meaghan. My parents and I, well, we don't get along so well. I'm not sure they'd say yes."

"Ah, yes, that could be a bit of a problem. I don't wish to come between you and your parents, but if you believe it to be helpful, I would be willing to talk to them. I have a sixth sense about these things and I believe we may be able to offer you a bright future. And possibly you, too, Carissa."

Carissa chuckled. "No, thanks."

"Well, then, Ashley, if you wish, we can visit with your parents straightaway. Perhaps our chance meeting will turn out well for all of us."

"You mean, like, right now?"

"Yes."

Ashley laughed. "Wow. Carissa, let's do this. Come with me."

Carissa shook her head. "No. I don't like this. And I'm not leaving my car here."

Meaghan smiled. "Carissa, you are, of course, free to choose. Ashley, if you are interested in my offer, then let's talk to your parents. And then we'll introduce you to Norra lekplatsen."

22.   Strategy

Defense attorney Dominic Levenson took a sip of whatever it was he was drinking. "So, you say you can't buy credit cards on your own, right?" He set the cup back on his desk. Dominic looked Jewish. Right down to the yarmulke on the back of his head. His office looked functional and tidy except for the folders and papers that covered his desk and spilled onto the floor.

Jesse scrunched her nose. "What is that you're drinking?"

Dominic glanced at his cup. "This? Just some tea I like to brew. Want some?"

"No, thanks. It's, um, pungent."

Dominic laughed, "Yes, it is. But it got me through law school. These days, I brew it when I'm faced with perplexing cases. Helps me focus."

"Is this case perplexing?"

"Yes. If you can't buy cards on your own, how did anyone buy cards on your behalf?"

"Somebody impersonated me."

"But Brenda has to respond to the confirming email, right?"

"Yeah."

"So is Brenda in on it?"

An elephant hit Jesse's chest and knocked her back in her chair. "No. She can't be."

"Because you guys are friends?"

"We're more than friends. She mentored me when I first started my job at the bank. She's like a big sister to me."

"So, how did she confirm it?"

"I don't know."

"We need to talk to Brenda." Dominic wrote on his notepad. "Another mystery. How do they know you bought the cards?"

"I didn't buy any cards."

"Yes, you did. You buy cards all the time. But how do they know you bought *these* cards?"

"I told you. Somebody must have impersonated me."

"Right. But how?"

"What difference does it make?"

"For you, it's the difference between prison and freedom."

"How?"

Dominic chuckled. "This is why nobody should defend themselves. Your attorney can see things you miss because I have fresh eyes."

Jesse leaned forward. "Keep going."

"They have to prove you bought *these* cards. Not just *any* cards. *These* cards. Because somebody used these cards to buy that merchandise. But they don't have anything. Their case is, you buy cards all the time, therefore you bought these specific cards. That's it. It's drek. Any first-year law student should easily destroy this."

"Well, that's good then, right?"

Dominic stroked his chin. "Maybe. Lisa's correct. They're hiding something." Dominic took another sip. "There's more. The post office box has problems."

"How?"

"It's in your name, but that doesn't mean anything. I could go rent a post office box in anyone's name. The post office doesn't care. You rent a box, they give you a key. It's that simple."

"So—"

"So, they framed you. That's what the evidence we have says. No prosecutor in their right mind would take this to trial."

"Well, that sounds good."

"It does, but—"

"But I don't have a career anymore."

Dominic finished his beverage. "Maybe we can do something about that."

23.   Plea Offer

Friday afternoon, June 15, 2018

The caller ID was so familiar, Dominic had never bothered to put it in his contacts. But still, let her sweat just a little bit. He answered on the third ring.

"Good afternoon, Marissa, you know I'm very busy." Bantering with prosecutors was always fun. Bantering with this prosecutor was especially enjoyable.

"I'll bet you are, Dom, but today is a lucky day for you and your client."

"Which client? And how so?"

"Your new client, Jesse Jonsen, the one who stole those credit cards. And probably your only client."

"I enjoy it when you try to get my goat. But I really do have several documents to finish. Why is today our lucky day?"

"Because we decided to reduce the charge to embezzling five hundred dollars. She pleads guilty, we'll recommend a minimal sentence with restitution, she's probably out scot-free in thirty days."

Dominic adjusted his yarmulke. If she thought she had a decent case, she would not make this offer. Something else is going on.

"Dom, you still there?"

"Yes. Sorry. You left me speechless. Why such a generous offer?"

"It has strings attached."

Dominic smiled. "Of course it does. What are they?"

"The offer expires at close of business today. After that, we go to trial. And you know the penalty for a fifty-thousand-dollar theft charge."

"Only if you win. And you just telegraphed you have a weak case."

"Maybe I do and maybe I don't. Do you want to gamble years in prison versus a recommendation for time served?"

"Well, aren't you generous? I'll pass your offer to her. Close of business today doesn't give her much time to decide."

"That's the offer. Take it or leave it."

Dominic laughed. "Well, at least you still have some pride. I'll get back to you."

~

Jesse spoke into her phone. "That's the offer? I plead guilty to stealing five hundred dollars and it's all done?"

"Yes," Dominic said. "And a prosecutorial recommendation for a sentence of time served. Plus, restitution. You pay five-hundred to the bank."

"But I have a theft on my record. And I don't have a career anymore because my reputation is ruined."

"Yes, that's true."

"Dominic, what do you think?"

"I'm interested in your thoughts first."

"Okay." Jesse squeezed her phone. "Tell her to put her offer where the sun doesn't shine. I didn't steal anything from anyone and I'll go to prison for the rest of my life before I admit to something I didn't do." Wait a minute, he just wants my reaction.

Her fingers relaxed. She took a breath. "You're smiling, aren't you. You knew that's what I'd say."

Dominic laughed. "I suspected. But I wanted to hear your thoughts first before I gave you mine."

"Why? Do you think I should take the deal?"

"No. Absolutely not. For two reasons. First, you just now convinced me you didn't do it. I'm your attorney and I'm ethically bound to defend you no matter what. But since you really are not guilty, and she telegraphed her case is weak, my advice as your attorney is to decline her offer. She wants an answer by close of business today."

"Oh. Well, in that case, what if we make a counter offer?"

"What would that be?"

"They drop all charges, apologize, and make all this go away. Or else we destroy them in court."

"I like the way you think. I'll pass it along. We need to do some homework."

24. Photo Shoot

In the middle of the bed, on top of a white bedspread, Ashley lifted the front of her red nightgown to her neck. "This is embarrassing." She covered her front with her arms.

Meaghan took her hand. "You're doing very well. It's natural to be nervous your first time. The trick is to show skin, but not too much skin." She lowered Ashley's nightgown. Just a little. "What do you think, Harold?"

Harry pointed his phone at Ashley. "Needs more leg."

"Ah, yes." Meaghan exposed Ashley's leg. "Point your toes, dear. And bring one knee up."

Harry snapped a few pictures. "Getting there. Now, lean her back on some pillows. And put her arms over her head."

Meaghan slid a couple pillows behind Ashley and adjusted her arms. "Smile. Invite people into your room."

Ashley smiled. Harry snapped a few more pictures.

"Now, show me a pouty look."

"This doesn't feel right."

Meaghan stepped in "Just have fun with it, dear. Truly, it's harmless fun. You're inviting families from around the world to visit us."

"But I don't know how to make a pouty look."

"Perfectly understandable, my dear. You and I can have some fun with it later. For now, Harold, perhaps a few other poses might be in order."

Finally, the photo shoot finished. "Can I put my regular clothes back on?"

"Of course, my dear. Feel free to dress in the bathroom. When you're dressed, would you like to look at your pictures?"

"Sure." Ashley grabbed her clothes and headed into the bathroom. Harry and Meaghan spoke quietly outside. Something about give it time. It was hard to hear.

Ashley finished dressing and popped out of the bathroom.

Meaghan smiled. "Yes, dear, you look ravishing."

Harry smiled and sauntered away.

Ashley watched Harry's back. "He's cute."

Meaghan raised her eyebrows. "Let's have some dinner. Then we need to get you back home. Or would you prefer to spend the night and go home in the morning?"

"Thanks. But I didn't bring anything to sleep in. And I don't want to mess up a room."

Meaghan gestured to the red nightgown, now on a hangar. "You have a perfectly good nightgown. Sleep in it, you can wear your clothes home in the morning. Or perhaps we'll scavenge some clean clothes for you. As for the room, we have to change these sheets tomorrow anyway after our work today. Might as well reap the benefit."

Dinner in the restaurant was right out of a glamour magazine. Shadows from flickering candles on every table danced across the faces of men and women dressed in nice clothes in the dimly lit dining room. Quiet conversations buzzed.

"May I offer you a glass of wine?" the waiter asked.

"No, I can't. I'm only sixteen."

"Nonsense." Meaghan held up a hand. "Don't think of it as alcohol, dear. Think of it as sophistication."

"But I'm not sure it's legal."

"Ah—the legality. It is legal if you're in a family setting, and as far as I'm concerned, Ashley, you are a welcome part of my family. And so, if you want to try a sip of wine, that is perfectly acceptable. You may enjoy the experience."

Ashley's ears felt warm.

Meaghan laughed. "You're blushing, dear." She turned to the waiter. "Yes, please pour my guest a glass of wine. And one for me as well. You pick the vintage. And for our meal, we'll have whatever the chef deems appropriate."

"Very good, ladies." The waiter left.

Meaghan's eyes bored into Ashley's brain. "Do not be afraid to try new things, dear. That's how you learn. All those experiences and new sensations will help you in your life."

The waiter returned after a few minutes and poured wine.

Meaghan lifted her glass. "To friendship, family, and mutual success." She smiled.

Ashley lifted her glass.

Meaghan sipped her wine.

Ashley watched and then sipped hers. It was warm going down. The taste wasn't bad. She took another sip. The warmth spread. What an amazing feeling. She took more sips.

Harry wandered to their table, carrying a laptop.

"Ah, Harold. Thank you for joining us. How are the pictures?"

"They're great. I can't wait to show you. Ashley, you're a natural."

Ashley tried to suppress her smile, but it burst out like a ray of sunshine piercing the clouds. The people here appreciated her. She was special. She could do anything.

Harry opened the laptop and scrolled through a few pictures. "Ashley, you look hot."

"I do feel warm. It's probably the wine." Ashley giggled.

"I didn't mean that kind of hot. I meant you look hot in these pictures." Harry leaned forward. "And here in real life."

Ashley's heart skipped a beat. What was happening?

"Is it okay if I take a few pictures of you here at the table in this light?"

Heat rushed to Ashley's ears. "Sure."

Harry smiled. He took out his phone and snapped a few pictures. "I am so glad Meaghan found you."

How did she not notice his gorgeous smile before? "Me too." She smiled.

The food came. The waiter described what was on her plate, but the words faded. The plate looked like a work of art. At this elegant table, sitting next to Harry, who also looked like a work of art.

"It all looks excellent, as always," Meaghan said. "And for you, dear. Does your meal look appetizing?"

"Definitely. I feel like I've been transported into another world."

Harry smiled. "So do I." He took a bite.

"Shall we look at some more pictures?" Harry reached for his laptop and scrolled through the first few. They were amazing. She looked like an adult. Sultry. Yeah, that was the word. Sultry. But unavailable in her red nightgown.

Harry smiled. "Ashley, you're beautiful."

Ashley smiled back.

Meaghan spoke up. "Ashley, if you don't mind, I'll leave you with Harold to escort you back to your room when you're ready. Tomorrow morning, we'll discuss your future with us and then drop you home."

She left. Leaving Ashley alone with this man she had met only a few hours earlier.

"Are you okay?" His eyes glowed under his gorgeous red hair.

She looked down. "Yes, I'm fine. I'm sorry, this is all so overwhelming."

He nodded. "Yes, I can see how it would be. We're building a major business from the ground up here, and there's always something going on. It keeps all of us busy."

"But why pay so much attention to me?"

"Because you're special. I was skeptical when Meaghan asked me to photograph you, but now I see how special you really are. Ashley, you can go a long way. And—"

"And what?"

Harry looked down. "Well, I hope you go a long way with us, right here. We have a lot to offer."

Ashley nodded.

"But where are my manners? I want to get to know you. Tell me about your life. What do you like? Who are your friends? What about your family?"

"Not much to tell, really. I'll be a senior in high school. I'm not sure if I want to go to college, or what I'd major in. My parents and I fight. A lot. When Meaghan found me, I was hanging out with my best friend for a couple days away from my parents."

"Ah. I understand. I left home when I was seventeen, got a job, and never looked back."

"How old are you now?"

"I'm ancient, believe me. I'm twenty-three."

Ashley smiled. "Did you go to college?"

"I did eventually, yes. It helped. A lot."

"How?"

"I got an education, and that helps me with the business." Harry gestured.

"This is your business?"

"I'm one of the owners."

"Wow."

"Ashley, you can go to college too. NPU and the resort are partners. NPU students earn class credit and pay for tuition by working here."

"Cool."

~

It was after midnight. Ashley looked up. The candles were out at all the tables except this one. The restaurant was empty. "Goodness—how late is it?"

Harry looked at his watch. "About 12:30."

Ashley yawned. "They probably want to clean this table."

Harry laughed. "I'm sorry. I didn't realize it was so late. Want me to walk you to your room?"

"Yes. That would be nice."

They rose and walked toward the door. Harry reached for Ashley's hand. She took it.

~

A vacuum roared in the hallway outside the door. Last night had been a blur. But in the light of morning, dressed in that red nightgown, Ashley knew one thing—she was in love. Harry came out of the bathroom, fully dressed. He smiled and kissed her. "When you're ready, I'll drive you home. I can't wait to enroll you in our NPU work-study program."

25.   Evidence

Monday, June 18, 2018

Dominic played the next video on a computer in his office. It was similar to all the other post office security clips. In each clip, a young woman or man walked past the camera to the post office box, opened the box, retrieved a slip of paper, and then gave it to a worker behind the counter and left with a package.

Jesse pointed. "Freeze it." She stared at the image of a girl, walking out and carrying a package. "That's Leilani."

"Who's Leilani?"

"She's from NPU. That's her, carrying out a package from that post office box."

"How do you know her?"

"I met her in the skyway with her pimp. And then I met her again when we did a campus visit."

"Wait a minute—and then she shows up here? That can't be a coincidence."

Jesse's jaw dropped. "Now, it makes sense."

"What makes sense?"

"Mike Swanson is dirty. I told him everything I knew about NPU and that's why he set me up."

"I don't get it."

"Connect the dots. I told Mike everything I knew about NPU. The bank is underwriting a ten-million-dollar endowment. And now Leilani shows up on this video. Mike's the common element."

Dominic worked his jaw. "So you're saying your ex-boss's boss is part of a prostitution ring and he framed you because, what, you got too close?"

Jesse stood and paced. "There's more to it than that. The pimp with Leilani used a fake name, Kyle Van Buren, belonging to an NPU professor. But Earl Townsend told me the real Kyle Van Buren disappeared last fall. It's more than just prostitution. These girls are slaves. And somebody murdered the real Kyle Van Buren." Jesse stopped and faced Dominic. She put her hands on the table, "Mike Swanson is in the middle of it and we're gonna expose it. All of it"

Dominic crossed his hands behind his head and leaned back in his chair. "Let's not get ahead of ourselves. Right now, our goal is keeping you out of prison. We'll save the world after that, okay? Besides, your murder slavery theory is a huge leap."

Jesse sat. "That whole campus is sick. I could feel it. And I got some guy to groom a social media character I invented."

Dominic leaned forward. "Jesse, my job is to defend you. If attacking NPU is relevant to your case and helps defend you, then I'll consider it. But going on offense with your theory is a bad defense strategy because it shifts the burden of proof onto us. So, unless we have irrefutable evidence, I'm not taking that risk.

"Then I'll get the evidence."

"No, you won't. Not yet. For now, you'll stay as far away from NPU as you can and you'll help me defend you. After we hear 'not guilty,' then we'll work on proving you innocent and proving them guilty. Okay?"

Jesse sighed. "Okay."

"Don't just say it. Mean it. Don't go off half-cocked. You'll end up in prison and you won't be able to help anyone."

~

Three hours later, Dominic brought up a copy of the next piece of evidence on his computer. "Do you recognize this?"

Jesse studied it. "It looks like things I typed. There's my login and password onto the computer we use to buy credit cards. There's my login into Hornet's website.

"Hornet?"

"The latest credit card thief."

"Why are they logging keystrokes from that computer?"

Jesse looked up. "Good question."

"Maybe you can help me make sense of this." Dominic fumbled through a directory and brought up a video. It showed computer mouse movements and keystrokes from somebody logging on to a computer.

"Wait, stop." Jesse pointed to the screen. "Back up a couple seconds."

Dominic moved the pointer back and clicked the play icon."

"Freeze it, right there."

Dominick clicked the pause icon.

Jesse scooted closer. "Look." She pointed at the characters in the login box. "Those are Brenda's credentials. Somebody recorded Brenda logging into this computer."

Dominic nodded. He clicked the play icon. Brenda finished logging in. And then she opened Teena Fay's email and retrieved a confirmation code. She pasted it into a text editor, saved it, and then logged out.

Dominic paused the video. "What are we watching?"

"When I buy credit card samples from the forum where Hornet hangs out, it emails a confirmation code to the email I told it about. Brenda and I set this up a long time ago. I need to send that code back before it processes the transaction. It's a safety measure to make sure the buyer really is the buyer."

Dominic laughed. "Identity thieves worried about validating somebody's identity?"

"Yeah. Crooks usually have better security than good guys. In case a fraud analyst impersonating a small-time Wisconsin crook tries to disrupt their work."

They both chuckled.

"Wait a second. Dominic, play that back again. Start in the middle somewhere and freeze it."

Dominic moved the video back to the halfway point and paused it.

Jesse pointed to the screen. "Look at the time and date. 9:50 p.m. That couldn't have been Brenda."

"Why not?"

"She never comes into the office at night. She has a family at home. Plus, if she did, the badge readers would have a record of it. But I'll bet there's no record in any of the stuff they send you."

"You're right. There are no badge reader logs in any of this."

"Play back the one of 'me' buying a credit card again. Let's look at the date and time."

Dominic played it, pausing after the login.

Jesse smiled. "Look at that – about fifteen minutes earlier. Mike Swanson logged in as me, set up the deal, then logged in as Brenda to get the code, saved it, and then logged in as me again and grabbed the spreadsheet with the credit card numbers. And he did it after work when nobody would see him."

Jesse stretched. "But now I have more questions. We have a program called *Glimpse* that records user sessions. That's how they captured those videos. Sometimes we use it for training. But we also have a process to install it on somebody else's computer. The IT Department needs manager signoffs to set it up. You can't just install it on somebody's computer, and anyway, Mike doesn't know how."

"So, how did he get this program on this computer without your knowledge, that's your question?"

"That's one of my questions. My other question is, how did he get Brenda's and my login credentials into Hornet's forum?"

Dominic nodded. "Good questions, indeed. But how is this relevant? Obviously, they logged your keystrokes and retrieved the login information they needed. They'll claim they suspected you were a thief and that's why they had to take these measures to catch you in the act."

"But wait a minute. If they had my login credentials before making this video, then anyone could have logged in as me, right?"

"That's true. We can introduce that question to raise reasonable doubt. But how do we prove it?"

Jesse nodded. "I might know a guy."

~

Dominic handed a box of doughnuts to Brenda. "This is the least I can offer for coming in on a Saturday to help us."

Brenda took one. "Thanks." She handed the package to a bony, bald-headed Jerry Barkley, sitting next to her in Dominic's office.

Jerry passed the package to Jesse. "No, thanks. But I will have one of those oranges in that bowl."

Dominic tossed Jerry an orange. "Jesse, you invited Jerry here this morning. Jerry, you and Brenda seem acquainted. So I'm the only one here who doesn't know you. Forgive me for being blunt, but tell me why Jesse invited you here."

Jerry worked on peeling his orange. "Jesse and I first met back in 2013 when she was on her way out of Bullseye Stores and over to Uncle Sam Bank. We ran into each other again after Thanksgiving that same year when somebody stole all those credit card numbers from Bullseye. One of those credit cards was mine and I was mad. I helped figure out how the scheme worked."

Dominic nodded. "I remember that incident. Didn't the FBI shut that whole operation down?"

Jesse smiled.

Brenda laughed. "That was the official story. But Jerry, didn't you go to a store in the middle of the night and follow a few test transactions?"

Jerry nodded. "Yep. I found the attackers' FTP sites. And the program they used to grab the data right out of the POS systems."

Brenda nodded. "And weren't you involved in the MOA incident somehow too?"

Jerry's face clouded. "Yeah. I was also in the middle of that one. Lots of good people died. I lived."

Dominic nodded. "Ah – that's where I remember your name. You're a hero."

Jerry shook his head. "I'm just an IT guy trying to earn a living."

Dominic continued nodding. "Which brings up a good point. We don't have any money to offer for your help."

"Don't worry about it. Jesse is a friend. And from what I've heard so far, these guys are human traffickers and they screwed her over good."

Jesse nodded. "That sums it up."

Jerry popped an orange section in his mouth. "How can I help?"

Brenda gestured to Jesse. "We need to know if somebody installed a recording program we call *Glimpse* onto my computer, Jesse's old computer, or the virtual computer we use to buy credit cards. And if they installed it, when did they do it?

Jesse nodded. "And if they installed it, where did they send the data it captured? I thought of you because I know you built that system at Bullseye to capture network traffic. I was hoping you could do something similar for Brenda."

"A bridge? Sure, I can build one. And if the program is still on those computers, you can find it in Settings and Apps."

Jesse shook her head. "It might not be that simple. It's supposed to be hard to find."

Jerry nodded. "Maybe we should image the hard drives."

Dominic leaned forward. "Forgive me again, but I speak English. What does that mean? And what's a bridge?"

All eyes turned toward Jerry.

Jerry smiled. "You image the hard drive by connecting another blank hard drive to the computer, booting it from a memory stick I'll make for you, and then issuing a command to make a block for block copy. And then you put it back the way it was. The bridge is easy. Brenda, your computer connects to your work network, right?

Brenda raised her eyebrows. "Yeah."

"So what we do is, insert a little box between your computer and the work network. Your computer connects to my box and my box connects to the network. We call that box a bridge, and my bridge records everything back and forth. If it works right, it's all transparent. You bring it in, grab a bunch of data, and then take it out. Nobody but you knows it's there."

Brenda shifted in her seat. "Sounds simple enough."

"It pretty much is. But there's a catch. My bridge needs to take on your computer's MAC Address."

Dominic also raised an eyebrow. "A what?"

"Every network card has a unique MAC Address. Media Access Control for people who like acronyms. It's how we tell what's connected at the hardware level. It's a good bet the bank network only lets in MAC addresses the network admins allow, probably to stop the kind of stuff we're planning. And they probably keep profiles of systems connected to their network. I can make my box use the same MAC address as Brenda's computer, but I need to know her computer's MAC Address. And, Jesse's too, I guess. And also your credit card buying system."

Jesse nodded. "The system I use to buy credit cards is a virtual machine."

Jerry sighed. "Oh, well, that makes things more fun."

Brenda and Dominic exchanged glances.

Brenda's face clouded.

Jerry chuckled. "What? It's doable. I can teach you everything you need to know. Just make sure you connect the right cables to the right ports on my bridge. We can practice it right here in Dominic's office."

Jesse looked down. Brenda squirmed.

Jerry glanced around the room. "Oh. Or, I guess I could go in with Brenda and set it up."

Brenda stood. "I'm not comfortable with this. Jesse, you know I love you. But I could get fired for this. And, Jerry, you could get in big trouble too. We're talking about sneaking into a major bank's network and stealing information. This goes against everything we believe in."

Dominic nodded. "Jerry, in layman's language, you're proposing to surreptitiously tap into the bank's network and gather information, is that correct?"

"That's right. And also, to make copies of, I guess, three computers. One of which is a virtual machine."

Dominic grinned. "Technology details aside, Brenda, as a department supervisor, I presume you don't have authority to order such an action."

Brenda shook her head. "No. I don't. In fact, we have policies against that kind of stuff. We train employees to report any activity like that if they see it. I could get fired. Jerry, you could go to jail."

Dominic nodded again. "If you do gather such evidence, I am ethically bound to share it with the other side. Including how and when you gathered it. If the evidence is favorable to us, the other side will no doubt object and the judge may disallow it."

Jesse nodded. "Yeah. Brenda and Dominic are right. Jerry, I can't ask you to risk going to prison for me. And tapping into their network is ethically wrong."

Dominic took a bite from his doughnut. "However, there is a strategy we can pursue in discovery. We can ask them for hard drive images of the systems in question. We can also ask for all logs and data related to this *Glimpse* program. They will no doubt remove the offending program and strip any relevant information from those logs. And we will have tipped our hand. But it might be interesting to compare hard drive images they send us with hard drive images you, Brenda, made as a conscientious employee to make a backup of those systems."

Brenda shook her head. "No. Even bringing in a memory stick into the building, not to mention, a blank hard drive could get me fired. We have policies specifically forbidding those things."

Dominic nodded. "Very well. Then we'll find another way."

"But it also galls me." Brenda smacked her fist into her hand. "Nobody contacted me about installing that program in my department. And that's also a policy violation."

26.   Destiny

Ashley slammed her bedroom door and threw herself on her bed. How could her parents be such jerks? Especially after the amazing time she had at the resort, where they treated her like an adult and not some teenager. And, of course, where Harold, no, Harry, was waiting.

Harry. What had come over her? What was it she loved so much about him? She smiled through her tears and rolled onto her back. It had felt so good. And so right.

But it had happened so fast. Was it the wine? The wine had felt good, but it was deeper than that. Harry had unleashed something in her, something not Mom or Dad or anyone could put back. She wasn't just some high school kid. She was a young woman with an opportunity to join a team and build something great. She was destined for him and he was destined for her, and they were all destined for greatness.

But she was stuck in this stupid house with Mom and Dad going to their stupid jobs every day, and her going back to one more dreary year in her dreary high school. She sat up and pulled Meaghan's card from her pocket. Just one phone call. She could finish high school near the resort, accumulate college credits, and graduate with a head start in business. The man of her dreams was a bonus.

Or she could help Mom fold more laundry.

She turned the card over and over. Just one phone call.

She picked up her phone and dialed.

27.   1995—Independence Party

October, 1995. Itasca County Girls Group Home, Big Fork, Minnesota.

Whimpering woke Jesse in the middle of the night.

Jesse climbed out of bed and shook Candy. "Candy. You okay?"

Candy sat up. "I had the worst nightmare. It was my uncle. He tried to—I, uh, I don't want to talk about it."

Jesse sat on her bed. "He tried to what?"

Candy rubbed her eyes. "Never mind. It was just a dream." Tears formed in the corners of her eyes.

"What's wrong?"

"Nothing. Let's go back to sleep. We have to be good little girls for school in the morning. That's what my uncle used to say. After."

"After; after what?"

Candy paused. "Never mind."

"Wait — after what?"

"Jesse, they want me to come home for Thanksgiving. I, I can't."

"What did your uncle do?"

"Nothing. Let's just go back to sleep."

~

Two weeks later, Candy sat across from Jesse at lunch. "I'm leaving and I need your help."

"Why?"

"I told you. I can't go back home. How much would an ID cost?"

"You mean, like a Driver's License?"

Candy nodded. "Yeah. That says Candy Smith. Born 1974, so I'm twenty-one years old."

"When do you want your birthday?"

"How about July 4. Independence Day."

Jesse laughed. "Okay. I could probably get you one for $125. But what would you do with it?"

"Turn another lemon into lemonade. And have fun with my boyfriend."

Jesse gestured around the room. "What boyfriend?"

Candy giggled. "I'll find one. How do you get your IDs?"

It was Jesse's turn to giggle. "I know some people."

"But you can't talk to 'em from up here."

"Maybe you can find a boyfriend with a cell phone."

Candy smiled. "I like that idea."

"He'll also need a camera to take your picture. And he'll need some postage stamps."

"Why?"

"We'll have to send your picture and half the money to my guy in Minneapolis. And then, the other half when the IDs get here. Unless—"

"Unless, what?"

Jesse strummed the table. "Well, unless there's a way to open a bank account up here. Then we can do wire transfers.

"How do you know all this stuff?"

"Social studies." Jesse laughed. "You'd better find a pretty good boyfriend."

Candy's eyes twinkled. "That won't be hard."

A week later, Candy met Jesse at lunch again. "Jesse, I want you to meet my new boyfriend. Ethan, this is my best friend, Jesse."

Ethan and Candy sat. "Nice to meet you Jesse," Ethan said. "I heard you can get fake IDs."

Jesse grinned. "What do you want a fake ID for?"

"It'd make it easier for a couple buddies and me to get beer."

Jesse shrugged. "I need a phone."

"My dad lets me bring my cell phone to school. "

"You mean, like, you have one on you right now?"

"Yeah."

Jesse's grin turned into a smile. "This is gonna be a beautiful friendship. Let's go somewhere private. Ethan, I need your cell phone. Got a camera?"

"Not on me, but I can bring one tomorrow."

A week later, Jesse had a local bank account and a post office box. Ethan took care of logistics, and mailed pictures of Candy, Ethan, and five of Ethan's friends to Minneapolis. Two weeks after that, Ethan picked up the IDs from the post office box.

Jesse had just one more detail left. "Ethan, I need to borrow your cell phone again."

"What for?"

"I need to pay my partner in Minneapolis. First rule of business. Always pay your suppliers."

Jesse called the local bank and made two wire transfers. One to Dylan in Minneapolis, the other for $250 to her own bank account. The one her parents still didn't know about. The one that would be waiting when she finished here. Not bad for a couple hours' work. Even if it took more than three weeks. Maybe later, she could start a business school for Ethan and his friends, just like Dylan at home. Who says crime doesn't pay? She handed the phone back to Ethan.

~

It was Thursday night and a November chill filled the air.

Candy sat on her bed. "Hey Jesse, I wanted to say thanks."

Jesse fluffed her pillow and tossed it on her bed. "For what?"

"For the lemonade. Ethan says those IDs are great. He's taking me to Grand Rapids tomorrow after school. I'm not coming back."

Jesse sat on her bed across from Candy. "You're really going through with this?"

"I told you, I can't go back home next week for Thanksgiving."

"What will you do?"

"Ethan's parents are out of town and he has some money. We're gonna check into a hotel and party like there's no tomorrow. And then on Saturday, I'll start looking for a job and get an apartment. Ethan says he'll help."

Jesse thought for a couple seconds. "But what about finishing high school?"

"I told you, I can't go back home."

"But you never told me why."

Candy stood. "It's my uncle, okay? I was his plaything."

"You mean–"

"Yeah. And you can't tell anyone. Promise."

"But–"

"Promise. And mean it." Candy paced back and forth.

"Okay, I promise. But Candy, you have to graduate."

Candy stopped pacing. "No. I'm not going back because nobody at home believes me. I'm almost eighteen and then I'll be on my own anyway. And now that I have this ID, I won't need to."

Jesse stood. "I'll miss you."

They hugged.

"I'll miss you too, Preppy."

Jesse stood back and laughed through tears. "I'm not preppy, Frizzy."

Candy laughed. "We don't need to get sloppy. I'm not leaving 'till after school tomorrow."

28.   Casing the Bank

Monday, June 25, 2018

Brenda strode through the revolving doors and into the Uncle Sam Bank lobby.

"Morning, Brenda." The security guard, behind his desk next to the entry turnstiles, nodded at her larger-than-usual bag. "What'cha bringing for lunch today?"

"Morning, Roger. Just a few sandwiches for the department." She fumbled for her badge, buried somewhere inside the bag filled with equipment she didn't want to talk about here. A tiny sweat bead broke over her left eye. Why didn't I clip my badge to my shirt before I came in?

Roger chuckled. "Maybe I'll come back later if you have any leftovers."

Brenda found her badge and placed it against the entry turnstile. The gate swung open. She stepped through. I'm not cut out for this 007 stuff. She forced a smile. "I'll bring some up later if there's anything left." She headed to the elevator bank behind the lobby.

A sea of humanity was already waiting, most headed up to various offices. Brenda joined them and pressed the Down button. More people filed through the turnstiles.

Remember, it's just another day at work. Yeah, a day when I'm bringing in a bunch of equipment to steal data from the bank. Other than that, just a normal day.

An elevator heading to the basement finally arrived. She stepped inside. A few people followed.

The floor display flashed B2. The elevator stopped. Everyone departed and headed to their jobs. Brenda headed to the Fraud department. Her Fraud department. The group she had nurtured the past ten years. The group now under fire from crooked managers. Which was why she was breaking rules she helped write.

She opened the door and walked inside. It was sweltering. Again.

"Morning Brenda." Early risers' heads popped up along the path to her desk in back. Right next to Jesse's old cubicle.

"Has anyone called about the AC?" she asked.

~

Dennis Waverly stretched. Another half a workday gone in the blink of an eye. But he was so close. Just a couple more kinks and *Merchant Trace* would run just fine with either Excel or ODF spreadsheets. And then he could go to management with a proposal to adopt open source and save millions of dollars in licensing costs. He chuckled. Just pay me ten percent of the savings. That's not too much to ask, is it?

Another pesky calendar reminder popped up for the zillionth time. Remove *Glimpse* from the Fraud Department computers. Mike Swanson had the information he needed and Dennis had put it off for too long. The problem was, he had used PowerShell scripting outside the normal GPO structure to set up *Glimpse* on those systems, and the IT Department had no record of it because he had deleted the audit log entries. Which was risky and violated enough policies to get him fired. But was also necessary because of FISA. But it still didn't feel right. And now, removing it would need more PowerShell scripting and create more audit logs to doctor. But the longer that software stayed on those computers, the more risk to his job. He'd get it done after work today, and then put all this behind him. He headed to the cafeteria for lunch.

~

"Good night, Brenda." The last of her analysts left.

Brenda was finally alone. She shut down her computer, crawled beside her desk, and popped off the computer cover. Just like Jerry had taught her.

Peering at the motherboard, she found connectors that looked like the right ones. She fumbled in her bag and found an empty hard drive and one of the red cables. Jerry called them SATA cables. She connected one end to the motherboard. But the internal power cable was too short to reach the floor, where she would set the empty hard drive. She set an old policies and procedures binder on the floor and stacked a tissue box on top. That did the trick. She connected the empty hard drive and set it on top of the tissue box. She smiled. Rube Goldberg would be proud.

She inserted a USB flash drive, booted the computer, and entered the commands Jerry had given her to clone her hard drive. She repeated the process for Jesse's computer, powered off since they fired Jesse. And now all she could do was wait. Time to crawl inside a good book.

~

Dennis studied the PowerShell script output. The *Glimpse* removal went well on all computers except two. One belonged to Brenda Yang, a supervisor in the Fraud Department. The other was previously assigned to a Jesse Jonsen, but now was unassigned. Maybe she's the one they fired. The computers were unreachable, which meant he would have to physically find them and remove *Glimpse* manually.

~

Brenda looked up from her book for about the 137th time. It had been an hour, with no way to tell how much longer this operation would take.

A noise. Footsteps.

Brenda stood. A young man was checking every cubicle, working his way toward her. She stepped into the aisle in front of Jesse's cubicle. "Can I help you?"

The man jumped. "I'm Dennis. I need to do some maintenance on your computers, but two aren't responding, and so I need to do a house call." He poked his head over Jesse's cubicle wall. "What are you doing?"

"I'm making a backup."

"Why?"

Brenda focused on breathing. "Because we need to make sure we save some of the information on this computer."

"Why not put it on the server?"

"Because this information isn't appropriate to put on the server." That was too harsh. "Look, here in the fraud department, sometimes we take on super sensitive tasks that we can't share. And so, the information needs to stay right here. It can't go on the server."

Dennis walked around her and glanced at the monitor in Jesse's cubicle. He smiled and shook his head. "You're not running a backup. You're cloning that hard drive. Why?"

Brenda licked her lips. This can't be happening. "You need to leave. Now."

Dennis shook his head. "No. Why are you cloning this hard drive?"

"Do you want me to call Security?"

"I *am* security."

"No, you're not. Who are you?"

"I told you. My name is Dennis and I need to do some maintenance on these computers."

Brenda looked him up and down. "Are you the one who planted monitoring software on these computers?"

"I don't know what you're talking about." He blinked several times.

Brenda grinned. "You're not a good liar. Let me see your badge."

"Let me see yours."

"You're in my department. Show me your badge right now or I make a phone call."

Dennis nodded. He showed Brenda his badge.

"Badge number 225307. Dennis Waverly. Well, nice to meet you, Dennis." Brenda grabbed a piece of paper and wrote the name and badge number. "Now, tell me why you planted that software on our computers."

Dennis shook his head. "Nope. Now it's your turn. Who are you?"

"Brenda Yang. I supervise this department."

"Most supervisors I know don't clone computer hard drives."

"Somebody tampered with our computers. You can see how the Fraud Department might not like that."

"I still have to report it," Dennis said.

"As will I."

29.   Consequences

Tuesday, June 26, 2018

Harlan Phillips closed his office door and invited
Brenda to sit.

Harlan sat behind his desk. "What's the emergency?"

Brenda shifted forward in her seat. It had been a long
night. She drew a deep breath.

"Harlan, you know I've been loyal to this bank for many
years. But when I found out somebody had installed *Glimpse*
on our computers, I had to take action. And so, I made copies
of Jesse's hard drive and mine."

Harlan nodded. "I know. I had a voicemail waiting for
me when I walked in a few minutes ago. You of all people
know you violated more policies than I can count. Why did
you do it?"

"Because somebody in this bank is dirty. It all goes back
to when they fired Jesse. And I don't like people spying on
me or the people in my department."

Harlan leaned back in his chair. "Did it ever occur to
you, that maybe people in the Fraud Department might need
some accountability themselves? But for your information, I
don't have any idea about *Glimpse* on any of your systems.
I never authorized it."

"Then who did?"

"How should I know? What makes you think somebody installed it on your systems anyway?"

"Because I saw the logs."

"There are no logs. I called IT to find out. There's no record of anyone installing *Glimpse* on any of your systems, and as far as I'm concerned, you put your job and career at risk last night with that stunt. Where are the hard drives you copied?"

"I brought them home."

"You did what?"

"I'm having them analyzed."

Harlan shook his head. "You're telling me, you stole proprietary information from the bank, and now you're sharing it with somebody? You're in neck-deep, you know that?"

"Yes."

"If you bring those hard drives back in and I watch you destroy them, and I talk to whomever you shared them with, I might be able to put in a good word for you. Whether it will do any good, I don't know."

"How do I know you're not a crook?"

"You're the one in trouble here. By your own admission, you brought in unapproved media, connected it to two bank-owned systems, removed proprietary data, and shared confidential bank information with an unknown third party. Who may have shared it with others, for all I know. How do I know *you're* not a crook?"

Brenda nodded. "You don't. But you do know I helped build the best fraud analyst group in the industry, and I would not put my whole career at risk without good reason. I'll bring those hard drives back in and give them to you after I have Jerry Barkley look at them."

Harlan crossed his arms. "Not good enough. And you know it."

"Wait – there's no logs?"

"That's right. I talked to IT right before I talked to you. I told you, there's no record of anyone installing *Glimpse* on any of your systems."

"Then what did I watch with Jesse's attorney over the weekend?"

"I don't know. Movies?"

"I watched a playback of somebody on our computers using fraudulent credit cards to steal merchandise."

"What playback?"

"Jesse's attorney has it. Recorded at night."

Harlan's phone rang. "It's Mike." Harlan answered. "Mike, what's up?"

After a pause. "Yes, she's here in my office with me." Another pause. "Okay, we'll be right up."

Harlan hung up. "Mike wants to see both of us in his office."

~

Mike Swanson met them outside his office. Dennis Waverly was already inside.

"Harlan, close the door."

Everyone entered. Harlan closed the door.

"Brenda, per policy, I have no choice but to terminate you, effective immediately. You knowingly violated several bank policies last night, some of them you wrote yourself. It doesn't matter why you did it, we can't tolerate it. Imagine if everyone decided to take matters into their own hands. The bank would cease to operate. You should have come to me."

Brenda stood. "Why did you spy on my department and then try to cover it up?"

Mike leaned back in his chair. "None of this is any of your concern. Security will be up here in a few minutes to escort you to your office to gather your personal belongings and leave. Your badge has already been deactivated, and security will escort you out of the building."

"Just like that?"

"What did you expect? But you've been a loyal employee for a long time, so I'm offering you a break. If you show Dennis persuasive evidence that you destroyed those hard drives and any and all copies of any information on them, the bank won't file criminal charges against you. The official record will show you resigned for personal reasons. You'll be free to pursue other employment without any blemish on your record."

Brenda rolled her eyes. "For your information, those hard drives never left my cubicle. And Security searched everything I carried on the way out. So, there's your proof."

Harlan leaned forward. "Mike, I need to know what's going on."

Mike moved past Harlan and Brenda to open his office door. "We'll talk about it later. Brenda, I suggest you and Dennis trade phone numbers. My offer is good until tomorrow."

A security guard waited outside.

30.   Trial, Day One

Wednesday, August 1, 2018

From her kitchen table, Brenda dialed Dennis's number.

"Why'd you do it?" Brenda asked.

"Do what?"

"Install *Glimpse* on our computers?"

"I don't answer to you. You don't even work at the bank anymore."

"Mike must have told you to do it. But what I don't get is, why did he pick you?"

"When a top manager asks me to do something, I don't usually ask why."

"So, it was you. And maybe you should have asked why."

"The only reason I took this call is, Mike told you to call me and convince me you're giving back all the data you took. You were supposed to do that a long time ago."

"I told you in Mike's office. Those hard drives never left my cubicle. But what if I told you I can show you plenty of evidence Mike's a crook?"

"Everyone says the other guy is a crook."

"That's true. But, if I'm right, Mike will come after you next." Brenda paused. "I'll be at the Manitou Coffee in the Skyway near the bank tomorrow at 8 a.m. Mike wants you to talk to me anyway. You can do your due diligence right there."

"Bring every copy you made of everything."

"I told you –"

"I heard you in Mike's office. And I already checked those hard drives. You left a copy of a VM image on your computer. How did you get that out of the building?"

"It's the VM we used to buy credit cards for *Merchant Trace*. My friend Jerry says to check the event viewer."

"And what am I looking for?"

"Startup and shutdown events on the day they accused Jesse of stealing those credit card numbers."

"What will I find?"

"That it booted in the evening, when none of us were in the building."

"How do I know when you were in the building?"

"Check the badge reader logs. And check the event viewer on Jesse's and my computers. I'll bet you find somebody turned them on at night."

~

Jesse and everyone else in the courtroom stood when Hennepin County Judge James Earl Ford entered. "Ms. Bearheart, your opening statement."

The lead prosecutor stood. "May it please the court? Counsel. Ladies and gentlemen of the jury, good morning. My name is Marissa Bearheart and my goal in this trial is show how the defendant, Jesse Jonsen, took advantage of her position as a principal fraud analyst at Uncle Sam Bank to steal thousands of dollars in merchandise using stolen credit card numbers.

"Ms. Jonsen was in a unique position to commit this crime because a big part of her job was buying stolen credit card numbers from criminals."

A few jurors registered shock.

"Does that sound surprising? A bank buying back stolen credit card numbers and enriching criminals? Well, banks do it so they can trace how the fake cards were used to find a common retailer where the numbers first leaked. That's how the public finds out about data breaches. Welcome to the 21st century."

Jurors nodded. Jesse whispered to Dominic. "They get it. That's good, right?"

Dominic nodded. And wrote a note on his legal pad.

"Unfortunately, individuals might have different motives. It's as old as business. Even if it has a 21st century twist. Stealing is still stealing, even if over the internet in cahoots with people on the other side of the planet you've never met.

"Ms. Jonsen built an elaborate scheme to convince credit card thieves from around the world that she was a wannabe crook from Wisconsin. She knew them well. She knew their nicknames. She knew their histories. And she was good at bantering with them. She also knew many of them were from hostile countries. You'll see why that's relevant in a minute. But first, you need to know that she lied for a living. Routinely. She used lies and all kinds of deception to gather information. That was her job. Every day.

"Kind of ironic, isn't it, a fraud analyst as a master of deception. But as you'll see, that's a theme through her whole life, leading right up to when she stole all that money. You'll see video records documenting when and how she used the bank's money to buy credit cards. You'll see post office surveillance videos showing how she turned merchandise into money. And you'll see financial records documenting sizable bank deposits.

"And here's why it's important so many of those criminals she befriended were from hostile countries. Because she conspired with them. She used the bank's money to enrich hostile foreign agents, and she used their stolen credit cards she bought from them with the bank's money to enrich herself.

"Law school teaches us you need three things to commit a crime. You need a motive—a reason to do it. You need an opportunity to do it. And you need the means to do it. The defendant had all three. Motive is easy enough; everyone wants to get rich. The defendant has a history of trying to get rich illicitly. She had opportunity. Not even her defense will argue with that. And she certainly had the means. In fact, she was the most qualified person in the bank to carry out this crime.

"My colleague for the defense will acknowledge all these facts, but he'll offer alternative explanations. The defense will argue that motive, opportunity, and means aren't enough. We have to prove she actually committed the crime. And that's true. The defendant is innocent until proven guilty. And that's where the defendant's background becomes important. Because you have to decide whether or not her explanations are credible. So, how do you decide? Look at her past behavior and use it as a guide to interpret her present behavior.

"And when you do that, you'll decide she's guilty. Because she lies for a living, and she's lying today when she offers her alternate explanations.

"And it's a shame, because Jesse Jonsen really is one of the most intelligent and thoughtful people you'll ever meet. And it's also scary. But your job is not psychoanalysis. Your job is to answer one question—Is she guilty of this crime or not? And then maybe she can get some help during a rehabilitation period after you find her guilty. Thank you."

Dominic finished writing unintelligible notes on his legal pad. He squeezed Jesse's hand and then stood. He glanced at the prosecutor and nodded. "My colleague made a nice presentation. If I were in your shoes, after listening to that, I'd want to lock up my client and throw away the key.

"But her presentation has holes. Her 'alternative explanation' theory is a big one. We don't have any alternative explanations and we do dispute some of my colleague's so-called facts. When you see the video showing somebody using a computer to buy stolen credit cards from an overseas criminal, keep one thing in mind. That video does not prove my client did it. It proves *somebody* did it. Just not my client. And when you see the videos of people picking up merchandise from the post office? Remember, those videos only show somebody picking up merchandise.

"The prosecution will claim my client orchestrated all of it. Well, I can claim that winter is warm and summer is cold. That doesn't make it true. And so I'm asking you, be alert for claims from the prosecution without proof. I'll help you with that. I might even become more assertive than usual if she gets too egregious. I'll ask your forgiveness in advance if I say something, well, colorful, in the heat of the moment. But that's my job. I'll do it to get your attention, but I'll also do it because egregious claims genuinely make me mad. Especially when those claims might help send an innocent person to prison. And leave the truly guilty free to commit more crimes.

"When the prosecution finishes presenting their case, you'll have evidence that *somebody* used the bank's money to buy stolen credit cards, and that people really did pick up merchandise from the post office, bought with stolen credit cards. But you won't have *any* evidence my client was in the middle of it, or even involved, or even knew what was going on.

"Let's attack the elephant in the room. Why should you believe us and not them? After all, every defendant says they're innocent. But, if they're so innocent, why are they here, on trial? You've gotta be thinking about that. I would, if I were in your shoes. And here's how many of these cases go. First, the prosecution presents evidence that the defendant committed the crime. Then the defense plants doubt in the prosecution's arguments. And we'll plant plenty of doubt in their case. Because prosecutors have to prove beyond a reasonable doubt that the defendant is guilty. It's a high burden of proof because all we have to do is convince you to doubt them. Just a little bit. And that's why it's a classic prosecution technique to attack character. Because if they can attack character, that might help persuade you that the doubts we plant in their case aren't really doubts at all. And guess what? My client is a human being and she has made some mistakes in her life. I'm sure my colleague is eager to share them with you. But that puts you in a difficult position. Who do you believe?

"Fortunately, we can do better than 'our word against theirs.' We'll present evidence from computer event logs and badge reader logs that show Jesse Jonsen was not even in the building when somebody used her computer to buy those credit cards. What about remote access? Well, guess what? Major banks don't allow remote access other than for a few specialized situations. My client had no means to access those computers during the time the videos were taken. Remember the argument my colleague made about motive, opportunity, and means? The means component is missing here.

"You don't have to take our word for it that she's innocent. Just look at the evidence. She could not have done it. The logs and the evidence show otherwise.

"And all the rest, about her background and lying as part of her job? That's all a smokescreen. When prosecutors have a weak case, they set up smokescreens to hide their lack of evidence.

"Don't let their smokescreens cloud what's important. Focus on the evidence. The real evidence. Not the smokescreens. You only have to answer one question at this trial. Guilty or not guilty? That's it. After we're finished, we think 'not guilty' will be the only choice that makes sense.

And maybe that will encourage our justice system to go build a case against the real guilty parties. Thank you."

~

The prosecutor flipped the page on her legal pad and approached Mike Swanson in the witness box. "To summarize, you've told us about your credit card buyback initiative and why you need those samples to feed your *Merchant Trace* program. Thank you for that background. What made you suspect that the defendant was using this initiative to steal money from the bank?"

"This initiative really does put small amounts of money into criminals' pockets, but it's the only way we have to trace the source of data breaches. But, as you can imagine, there are many opportunities for abuse. And so, we instituted a system of approvals before anyone can access those funds. But then we found a few hundred dollars missing without the requisite approvals, and we noticed a fraud spike with our credit cards. The pattern was unusual, to say the least. And scary. That forced us, reluctantly, to monitor computer usage in our Fraud Department. Nobody was more surprised than me to find Jesse at the center of it."

The prosecutor turned to the jury. "By, Jesse, you mean the defendant, Jesse Jonsen?"

"Yes, that's right."

"Thank you. Now, I want to play a portion of a video you recorded with your *Glimpse* program. Would you tell the jury what we're about to see?"

"Of course. We use *Glimpse* to record keystrokes and mouse movements. It creates a video, so we can play back a Windows session. We usually use it for training. I don't like to install it on our employees' computers because our IT Department tells me it slows down the whole network. But mostly, I don't like it because it signals that we don't trust our people. And so we're very careful about where we install this program. What you'll see is what happened on the computer system Jesse, or the defendant, sorry, used. You'll see the screen she saw and you'll see what she did."

The prosecutor signaled and somebody started a video on a screen in the courtroom. It was a chat session.

The prosecutor glanced at the jury. "Tell us what's happening right now."

"She's chatting with a credit card thief using her Teena Fay from Green Bay persona." A few seconds later, "Here, they're haggling on the price. She wants a discount for buying a large quantity. They'll eventually settle on a price – yes – there it is – and now she'll send the money to a bitcoin wallet."

"So, at this point, she bought the credit cards."

"That's right. So far it's routine."

"Now what's happening?"

"Now she's going into her persona's email and opening the spreadsheet with the credit card numbers. As you can see, she bought fifty credit cards. Normally from here, she would copy the spreadsheet to a secure internal landing area, and then launch *Merchant Trace* to cancel the cards and find a merchant common to all of them. But that's not what she's doing."

"Looks like she's shopping online."

"That's exactly what she's doing. She'll spend around one thousand dollars with each credit card and have the merchandise delivered to different post office boxes."

"And then what?"

"And then she feeds the cards to *Merchant Trace*. But one transaction apiece first."

"Why just one transaction?"

"Our best guess is, to keep it under the radar. One fraudulent transaction and then cancel the card. And it would have worked too, if she hadn't made a mistake and forgotten to authorize the money for a credit card buy. That's what alerted us. We went back and checked as much history as we could, but there's no telling how many fraudulent transactions she did before we caught her."

"Thank you. Now, I want to call your attention to the lower-right corner of the screen. It shows the time at 9:07 p.m. My colleague suggests she could not have been the person doing this activity because she wasn't in the office. How do you reconcile that?"

"That computer is special because the Fraud Department used it to interact with criminals all over the world, but mostly in Eastern Europe. So we set its time zone for GMT."

"GMT?"

"Greenwich Mean Time. It's the time zone that runs through England. Six hours ahead of us here in US Central. Well, wait a minute, this was in the spring when we were on daylight savings time. So, the computer clock was five hours ahead of us. Spring forward, fall back."

"So, 9:07 p.m. on the computer was really, what, 4:07 p.m. in Minneapolis?"

"That's right. She was in the office. We checked the badge records."

Jesse whispered to Dominic. "That's not true. The time in that computer was the same as in the office. He's lying."

"Thank you, Mr. Swanson." The prosecutor turned toward Dominic. "No further questions at this time."

Dominic wrote more notes on his legal pad.

Judge Ford watched for a few seconds. "Mr. Levenson?"

"Yes, Your Honor. One second, please, I just need to capture some notes."

Dominic stood and faced Mike Swanson. "Just a couple of clarifying questions for now. I might have more later. But for now, Mr. Swanson, how do you know what time zone that computer is set for?"

"It's a setting."

"Can you show us?"

"Well, not right now, the computer isn't here."

"I see. So, we just take your word for it, is that right?"

"Your office requested a disk image of that computer, if I'm not mistaken. So, you could look it up if you want."

A few people in the jury chuckled.

Jesse's heart skipped a beat.

Dominic smiled. "I'm sure we'll revisit the time zone question. But for now, let's move on. How do you know my client was the one on that computer?"

"Because she was the only one who had the Teena Fay password."

"Ah. But you also had it, right?"

Mike blinked several times. "Um, no, I didn't."

"Well, didn't you install software to record her session?"

"Yes, that's what *Glimpse* does."

"And that includes her key strokes and mouse clicks, right?"

"Yes."

"Well, then you must have recorded her password when she logged in."

Mike rubbed his forehead. "Oh. Yes, now I see where you're going with this. And I apologize. I am not the technology expert. I'll have to get back to you on that."

Dominic turned to the jury. "I understand your technology expert is on the witness list. We may talk to him about that." Dominic turned back to Mike. "And I may have more questions for you later, too. But I'm finished for now."

~

Jesse tried to stay focused, but mundane question after question after question made her eyelids heavy. She flexed her fingers and toes. Anything to stay awake. At her own trial. She glanced at the jury. Some of their eyes looked droopy too.

"Your witness." It was the prosecutor. Dennis Waverly, somebody from the bank IT Department Jesse hadn't met, had just finished his testimony about installing *Glimpse* on the computers in the Fraud Department. Nothing exciting. Probably just a chain-of-custody thing. Nailing down the details for the jury.

Dominic finished a couple of notes and stood.

"So, Mr. Waverly I'd like to review what you told us about why Mr. Swanson bypassed the chain of command and asked you to install this software on Fraud Department computers. You said that Mr. Swanson just asked you to do it, and so you did, is that right?

"Yeah. That's pretty much it."

"Did he offer any reason?"

"Not really, no."

"What does 'not really' mean?"

"Well, he didn't tell me who he suspected or anything like that."

"I see. Well, what did he tell you?"

"He said he suspected somebody was stealing from the bank and he wanted me to install this software on the Fraud Department computers."

"Are you in charge of this software?"

Jesse straightened in her seat. Where's he going with this?

"No."

"Had you installed it before?"

"No."

"Then, why did Mr. Swanson pick you to install it?"

"I don't know."

"Do you have any experience with this particular piece of software?"

"No."

"Then, how did you know how to install it?"

"It was pretty easy. We had a GPOs ready to go."

"GPO?"

"Group Policy Object. It's automation in Windows to do this kind of stuff."

"How did you know about this, um, GPO?"

"I figured there had to be one."

"And so you searched for it?"

"Yeah."

"Why not just ask somebody with more experience?"

Jesse glanced at the jury. More attentive. And whoa, look at this Waverly guy. He's squirming.

"Isn't it common to ask for help from somebody more experienced than you when you're doing a task for the very first time?"

"I've used GPOs before. It's a standard system management practice."

"But they all have names, don't they? How did you know which GPO to use? And how did you know to which computers the new policies would apply?"

"As I said, I did some digging."

"On your own?"

"Yeah."

"How much time did it take for you to find what you needed?"

"About a half-day."

"Do you have other jobs besides installing software you've never seen before?"

"Sure. I take care of *Merchant Trace*. My latest project is getting it to work with open-source spreadsheets."

"But you had to take significant time away from that project to install this software, isn't that right?"

"Sure."

"So, why not just ask for help instead of spending so much time figuring it out on your own?"

"Normally, I would. But I couldn't this time."

"Why not?"

"Because Mike, um, Mr. Swanson, asked me not to tell anyone."

"Really. Define 'anyone' please."

"Well, anyone means just that – anyone."

"You didn't tell your immediate manager?"

"No."

"So, this was really a side deal between you and Mr. Swanson."

Waverly bowed his head and then looked up. "It wasn't a side deal. Mike told me to not tell anyone, because he suspected something bad was going on and it needed to stay quiet."

"And so, based on one manager's word, you installed software on these peoples' computers to spy on them?"

"Objection." The prosecutor stood. "Asking the witness to draw a conclusion."

"I'll rephrase the question. Did you find it unusual that one manager wanted to gather information from so many peoples' computers?"

"Well, um, yeah."

"So, why didn't you talk it over with anyone?"

"Objection. Relevance? Mr. Levenson is on a fishing expedition."

Judge Ford leaned forward. "Mr. Levenson, where are you going with this?"

"Your Honor, they're using data gathered from these computers to railroad my client. I'm trying to show two things. First, they improperly gathered the data. Two people conspired to plant spy software inside these computers, with no other input from anyone on the planet earth. And second, the data doesn't show my client did anything illegal. For all we know, Mr. Waverly could have been on that computer buying those credit cards."

Waverly stood. "Now, wait a minute."

Dominic smiled. "Sir, I am not accusing you of anything."

Judge Ford pounded his gavel. "Let's have some order here." He turned to Waverly. "Sir, please sit down." Now to

Dominic. "You know better than to act that way in my courtroom."

Waverly sat. The prosecutor smiled. Waverly's hands twitched. What's he so nervous about?

"Your Honor—" Dominic now looked humble.

"Hold your tongue. It's my turn." Judge Ford pointed his gavel at Dominic. "I'll allow this line of questioning as long as I believe you're not on a fishing expedition."

Dominic turned to Waverly in the witness booth. "First, I want to clear up a misunderstanding. Mr. Waverly, I am not suggesting you were on that computer buying stolen credit cards. I don't know if you're a crook or not, and frankly, I don't care. You're not the one on trial here. My client is on trial, and somebody made these videos implicating her."

The prosecutor stood. "Here we go again, Your Honor."

Dominic turned to face the prosecutor. His face was red.

Waverly spoke. "I didn't talk to anyone else about installing *Glimpse* because I couldn't."

Dominic turned back to Waverly. "What do you mean, 'you couldn't?'"

"I mean, I couldn't."

"Why not? Did somebody blackmail you? Did somebody hold you at gunpoint and threaten your life?"

Waverly opened his mouth, but then shut it. He bit his lip. "I can't talk about it. I'm sorry."

Judge Ford glared at both attorneys, and then at Waverly. "Just what in blazes is going on here?"

The prosecutor looked puzzled. "This is all a surprise to me, too."

Judge Ford turned to Waverly. "Why can't you talk about it?"

"I'm bound by a nondisclosure agreement. I don't want to go to prison."

Judge Ford nodded. "Whatever NDA you're under, it doesn't apply here in my courtroom. Answer the question.

You're under a judge's order, and that supersedes any NDA."

Waverly looked like death-warmed-over. He bowed his head and then looked up. "Because it was a secret FISA order. I was told that if I talk about it with anyone, I could go to jail."

Judge Ford's eyes went wide. "I see. Ms. Bearheart, care to shed some light on this?"

The prosecutor stood. "I promise, Your Honor, this is the first I've heard of it."

Dominic stood. "Wait a minute. You're telling us, you took it upon yourself to install that software because of some secret government order?"

Judge Ford glared at Dominic. "Just hold it, right there."

"Your Honor…"

"Don't 'your honor' me, Mr. Levenson. And, Ms. Bearheart, if I find out you knew about this alleged order and suppressed it, I'll have your legal license. Do I make myself clear to both of you?"

Dominic chuckled. "Yes, Your Honor."

The prosecutor gathered her composure. "Your Honor, I swear, I'm as surprised by this as you are. But whether or not there was a FISA order is irrelevant. The evidence still shows the defendant buying stolen credit card numbers and using those to buy merchandise."

Dominic's jaw dropped. "Oh, Marissa, the evidence shows no such thing. It shows somebody logging onto a computer and taking those actions, but nothing ties my client to it. And you know it. For all we know, Mr. Waverly or somebody used a fake order to justify installing spy software on these computers, stole the login credentials, and framed my client."

Marissa's face reddened. "That's preposterous. And *you* know it, Dom."

Judge Ford's voice boomed over the speakers. "Enough. Both of you, sit down. Now."

They both sat. But Dominic took his time.

"There's a reason why a FISA order has never been part of a criminal case. FISA orders are supposed to be secret, and the last thing we need is a national security crisis from this trial. If I see anything in the press about a FISA order related to this case, everyone in this room will feel the consequences. Do I make myself clear?"

Everyone agreed.

"Good. Now, this is what we're going to do. We'll recess until after lunch. Ms. Bearheart, if such an order exists, I want to see it. Today. I suggest you use the time to visit Uncle Sam Bank and get your hands on it. Mr. Levenson, if you can produce evidence showing this order is fake, I'll allow it. But regardless of any order, it's up to the jury to decide whether the evidence ties the defendant to the crime or not. We're in recess until 2 p.m."

"Your Honor, before we recess?" Dominic stood.

"What?"

"How am I supposed to prove an order is fake when I just now found out about it? We don't even know what this alleged order says or who supposedly issued it."

"Not my problem. I'll see you at 2 p.m." Judge Ford exited.

~

"How did you know?" Jesse took another bite of her sandwich in the basement cafeteria.

Dominic smiled. "I didn't. But it struck me as more than strange that nobody contacted HR or anyone else to install that software. I didn't know where it would lead."

Jesse nodded.

"All I know is, the deeper we get into this case, the more unanswered questions come up from your former employer."

~

Marissa Bearheart paced in the hallway, phone to her ear. "Mike, you told me you suspected fraud and that's why you had your guy install that software. And now I find out you had a FISA order? Get back over here this afternoon. I'm putting you back on the stand."

~

Mike Swanson ended his call with Marissa Bearheart. He leaned back in his office chair and rubbed his eyes. And then he dialed his phone. "We have a problem."

~

Judge Ford entered the courtroom. Everyone stood.

Judge Ford sat. So did everyone else. "Ms. Bearheart, I hope you were productive during our recess."

"Yes, sir, I was."

"Good. Mr. Levenson, do you have any further questions for the witness?"

"Not at this time. Although I may have questions later."

"I'm sure you will. Mr. Waverly, you're excused. See my clerk for a signed declaration that you answered your questions under my order. Ms. Bearheart, I have a hunch I know who you want to talk to next."

Waverly nodded and huddled with the court clerk.

"Yes, Your Honor. I'd like to recall Mike Swanson."

Judge Ford looked down on Swanson as he sat. "Sir, I remind you, you're still under oath. And the penalties for perjury can be severe."

The prosecutor approached him. "Mr. Swanson, first, thank you for coming back to help us clear up a surprise from this morning."

"You're welcome." Swanson smiled.

"Now, I need to ask you a delicate question. Mr. Waverly alleged this morning that he installed the software you mentioned, *Glimpse*, on peoples' computers because you were under a Foreign Intelligence Services Agency, or

FISA, government order. I remind you, you're in a court of law, under oath, and under a judge's order. And my question to you, sir, is, is that true? Did you order Mr. Waverly to install that software because you were under a secret FISA order?"

Everyone in the room leaned forward.

Swanson looked the prosecutor in the eye. "No. Of course not. Until you called over lunch, I had never even heard of FISA."

The prosecutor nodded. "So, just to be perfectly clear. This case is not about money laundering with foreign nationals or other illicit overseas financial transactions. It's a straightforward embezzlement case. Is that right?"

"That's right. Jesse used our bank's money to buy credit cards from, well, I guess we don't know who she bought them from, nor do we care."

"Objection." Dominic stood. "The witness says my client illegally purchased credit cards."

Swanson looked defiant. "She did."

"No. You claim that she did. You haven't proven anything. For all we know, you bought those credit cards."

Judge Ford's voice filled the room again. "This is your last warning, Mr. Levenson. The next outburst will cost you $200. Do make myself clear?"

Dominic rolled his eyes. "Yes, sir."

Judge Ford nodded. "No, I don't think I did. I'll sustain your objection because you're right. When the witness says the defendant took some action, it's up to the jury to decide whether or not that's credible. I'll ask the witness to use the word, alleged, when describing such action. Mr. Levenson, you owe the court $200. Now, do I make myself clear?"

"Yes, sir you do. And now, let me be clear. I expect you, as a judge, to keep any bias you may feel against me to yourself. If I find you're acting with bias toward the prosecution and against my defense, you can count on a swift and vigorous appeal. I am doing my job, sir, and you can fine me for eternity and I'll still do my job." Dominic strode to the court clerk and pulled two $100 bills from his wallet. "Here's your two hundred dollars. If you want to fine me some more, I'll have to find an ATM and get cash. Or you can throw me in jail."

Judge Ford leaned back in his chair and chuckled. "Nice performance. Are you done?"

"Yes, sir, that about covers it. I meant what I said."

The prosecutor shot Dominic a look and turned to the witness stand. "Okay, where were we? Mr. Swanson, it's your testimony then, that there was never a FISA order, and this whole case is a simple embezzlement against your bank. No secret agents, no government conspiracies, and" she turned to Dominic, "nothing dramatic." She turned back toward Swanson. "Is that right?"

"Yes, that's right."

"Thank you for clarifying that. No further questions."

Dominic stood and approached Swanson. "So, how do you account for Mr. Waverly thinking you showed him a FISA order?"

Swanson smiled. "I don't. I did ask him to keep it quiet. I mean, we suspected somebody in the Fraud Department, in a position of trust, used their position to steal not only from the bank, but also merchants. Frankly, that's not the kind of news I wanted blasting the airwaves and social media about our bank. So, I did ask him to be discreet. But I have no idea how that evolved into him believing there was a FISA order."

Dominic rolled his eyes. "No more questions at this time. I might have more later."

Jesse turned toward the back of the courtroom. Waverly's face was red. Every few seconds, he shook his head and mumbled, and clenched his fists and let go. Jesse gestured to Dominic. Dominic followed Jesse's gaze and then turned to Jesse and nodded.

The prosecutor stood. "The prosecution rests."

Judge Ford nodded. "Very well. Is the defense ready?"

"Yes, sir, we are. The defense calls Dennis Waverly back to the stand."

Dominic approached the witness stand. "Mr. Waverly, first, I want to apologize to you. I know we worked you over in our cross examination earlier, and I'm sorry we had to do that." Dominic paused. "I think we've beaten this whole fake FISA order issue to death, don't you? A senior manager convinced you a fake FISA order was real, and so you tried to proceed responsibly, right?"

"Objection." The prosecutor stood. "Calling for a conclusion."

"I'll rephrase the question. Mr. Waverly, you were trying to do your job to the best of your ability, right?"

The prosecutor sat.

"Yeah."

"And when you installed that software you had good reason to believe it needed to be secret, right?"

"Objection. Again." The prosecutor stood. "We've already covered this ground."

"Sustained. Mr. Levenson, why are you revisiting this?"

"Because I have one more question. Mr. Waverly, given what you've heard today in court, and knowing what you know now, do you still believe that secrecy was justified?"

Dennis squirmed.

"Objection. How many times do we need to cover this?"

"I'll withdraw the question. I'd like to cover one more small matter with you, Mr. Waverly. And I promise, this one should not be controversial. What is the bank's policy on remote access? Let's say somebody wants to work from home during the evening or on a weekend. Is that allowed?"

"A few people from the IT Department can do it to handle off-hours upgrades and emergencies, that sort of thing. It's all logged."

"Well, what if, say, somebody in the Fraud Department wanted to access a system remotely at night. Could they do it?"

"No."

~

Dominic approached the witness. "Ms. Hamilton, what is your position with the bank?"

"I'm the building security manager."

"You oversee the badge system, right?"

"Yes."

"How does it work?"

"Employees enter and exit the building through the front lobby and must use their badges to pass through a turnstile."

"And so, the bank has records of when everyone enters and leaves the building, right?"

"Yes."

"On the day in question, what do those badge records say about my client, Jesse Jonsen?"

"On that day, she entered around 8:30 a.m. and left at 5:30 p.m."

"Is there any possibility she could have, say, swiped her card into a badge reader, but stayed inside?"

"No. The only exit is through those turnstiles, and they have to pass through them to get their badge. We designed the system specifically to stop that sort of behavior. The badge records really do show when people enter and leave."

"Thanks. No further questions."

Judge Ford glanced at his watch. "Ms. Bearheart?"

"No questions, Your Honor."

"The defense calls Brenda Yang."

~

The prosecutor approached Brenda in the witness stand. "That was quite a story you spun in your testimony with Mr.

Levenson. You engaged somebody to teach you how to steal information from your employer, and you got caught with your hands in the cookie jar. Does that sum up what you said?"

"I was outraged, I wanted somebody objective to analyze those system images, and I trust Jerry Barkley. I tried to do the right thing and I lost my job because of it."

"Why do you trust Jerry Barkley? Doesn't the bank have a professional IT Department?"

"We, um, the bank, does. But Jerry helped us a few years ago in another difficult situation."

"The Bullseye Breach incident, right?"

"Yes."

"But nevertheless, what you did was illegal and against the policy that you, yourself wrote, right?"

"Not illegal. But against policy, yes."

The prosecutor turned to the jury. "And now tell us what you stole."

"I kept a copy of the system image for the system Jesse used to buy credit cards."

"And what did you do with that system image?"

"I gave it to Jerry Barkley. He made a copy and gave it to Dominic, I mean, Mr. Levenson, and I presume he gave it to you."

The prosecutor turned back to Brenda. "One more question. What were you trying to cover up?"

"Objection." Dominic stood.

"I'll withdraw the question. Two can play that game, Mr. Levenson. No further questions."

Judge Ford glanced at Dominic. "Redirect?"

"Nothing at this time."

"Very well. Let's all be back here by 9 a.m. tomorrow.

31.   Trial, Day Two

Thursday, August 2, 2018

Jesse took a bite of her Egg McMuffin in Dominic's office. "Dominic, I want to testify."

"I advise against it. They don't have a case and you don't need to take the risk."

"What risk?"

"You expose yourself to cross examination and Marissa will bring up every piece of dirt in your background. She'll twist everything you say to make you look like a crook."

"But I'm not a crook. And the jury needs to know that."

"No, all they need is reasonable doubt about this crime. The rest is irrelevant."

"No, it's not. Not guilty doesn't mean innocent. It just means they didn't prove it. How can I ever get a job or have a future with this cloud hanging over me the rest of my life?"

Dominic swallowed a bite of his breakfast sandwich and sipped his water. "Are you sure you want to do this?"

Jesse nodded. "Yeah, I am."

Dominic sighed. "Okay. I'll call you first."

~

Dominic approached Jesse in the witness stand. "Ms. Jonsen, why are you testifying this morning?"

"Because I don't have anything to hide and I didn't do what they accuse me of doing."

"Okay. Let's go through this. Where were you during the evening in question?"

"I spent some time with Gloria Warren at the Manitou Coffee that evening. And then I went to work on my house in Bloomington."

"Any witnesses?"

"Manitou has a video system, and I think I'm in there. And the neighbors in Bloomington would have seen my car."

"You live in a condominium near here, in downtown Minneapolis, is that right?"

"Yes."

"So, why the house in Bloomington?"

"I've always wanted to try a fixer-upper."

"But things aren't going as you planned, are they?"

"No. After I bought it, I found out it has a mold problem. And it needs all new mechanicals."

"What are you doing about it?"

"More than I bargained for. It's down to bare studs and I need to put in all new insulation and a vapor barrier."

"And is the city of Bloomington is pressuring you to finish the job?"

"Yes."

"So, it's fair to say, you were under some financial duress when the bank accused you of this crime."

"Yes, But I was working it out."

Dominic nodded. He turned to the jury. "Ms. Jonsen, why are you a fraud analyst?"

Jesse smiled. "It goes back to high school. I was a criminal, and a few good people helped me face the consequences. I found out that I had a knack for knowing how criminals think. And so, I decided to make a career out of stopping them."

Dominic turned back to Jesse. "But there's more to it, isn't there? Didn't you help a young woman trying to commit suicide?"

Jesse chuckled and nodded. "I did. But it wasn't like I was on some mission. I happened to see her on that bridge and I stopped to help. Anyone would have done that."

"I'm not so sure about that. Many people who practice compassion assume everyone does. It's unfortunate that's not always true."

Jesse nodded. "I guess."

"Ms. Jonsen, why do you think the bank is accusing you of this crime?"

"Objection. Calls for speculation." The prosecutor stood.

Judge Ford nodded. "Sustained. Mr. Levenson, you know better."

Dominic shook his head. "Very well. Is there anything else you want the jury to know before I turn Ms. Bearheart loose on you?"

Jesse shifted in her seat. "You asked why I think they're doing this. I think it's because I found myself involved with several college students who might be trapped in a human trafficking ring."

"Do you have any proof?"

"No, I don't. But they charged me with this crime shortly after I shared my concerns with them."

"Thank you, Ms. Jonsen. Your witness."

The prosecutor stood and stepped toward the witness box. "Ms. Jonsen, if somebody gave you fifty-thousand dollars, what would you do with it?"

"What kind of a question is that?"

"Just hypothetical. People talk about hypothetical situations all the time. What would you do with it?"

Jesse shook her head. "Well, okay, that would go a long way toward paying off the debt I accumulated with that house."

The prosecutor turned to the jury. "Sounds like motive to me."

Jesse's face flushed. "No, it's not. You asked a hypothetical question. I gave you a hypothetical answer."

"Ms. Jonsen, as a fraud analyst, what, specifically do, I mean, did—what did you do at work every day?"

"I did lots of things. I guess you could sum it up by saying, I tried to protect the bank from all kinds of fraud."

"How often did you buy credit cards?"

"All the time."

"Under your fictional persona, right?"

"Yes."

"So, you lied for a living. And from what I understand, you were pretty good at it."

"I couldn't very well tell them who I really was. It's part of the job, to infiltrate their forums and keep tabs on what they do."

"Did any of the criminals you associated with online ever suspect you weren't who you pretended to be?"

"Not that I know of. We went to great pains to make sure there wasn't a way to trace anything back to the bank."

"And so, not only did you lie for a living, you were so good at it that you fooled other people who lie and steal for a living."

"It's part of the job. We have to infiltrate those rings to protect the bank's customers."

"Yes, I'm sure it was all for a noble purpose. You brought up your background. Let's talk about that. As a teenager, you fooled your parents and quite a few other people into believing you had a job at, I think, Dairy Queen. But your real source of income was stealing, is that right?"

"Until I got caught. Not something I'm proud of. But I put it behind me."

"Are you sure? You lied as a teenager and got caught. And you lied for your job as an adult. And here you are, in court again. How do we know you're not lying to this jury right now?"

Jesse faced the jury. "You don't. The truth is, I was a delinquent in high school, until my senior year. If I hadn't gotten caught, I'd probably be in prison or worse today. But that was a long time ago, and since that time, I earned a college diploma and a master's degree. I tried my hand at rehabbing a house and that hasn't worked out well, so far. And now, especially after losing my job, I may have to sell it at a loss. And I might be in debt for a long time. But I did not use the bank's money to buy stolen credit cards for my own use, and I certainly did not use stolen credit cards to flip merchandise. Decide whether or not I'm telling the truth by comparing what I say against the facts. The facts are on my side because I'm telling the truth. Somebody is trying to railroad me."

The prosecutor softly clapped her hands. "Nice speech. I'll hold you to that criterion. I have one more question. Where were you during the afternoon on the day in question?"

"You mean, like during work hours?"

"Yes."

"I was at work."

"Inside the bank, right?"

"Yes."

The prosecutor nodded. "Thank you. No further questions for now."

~

Dominic approached Jerry Barkley in the witness stand.

"Refresh our memories. What time do the videos show somebody bought those credit cards?"

"Various times between 7 p.m. and 10 p.m."

"And so, to summarize, the videos we all saw from the prosecution happened between 7 p.m. and 10 p.m., there was no possibility to access that system remotely, and badge records show Jesse Jonsen wasn't in the building. Does that sum it up?

"Sure does."

"Okay. Thank you. And now, I want to turn your attention to Ms. Yang's testimony earlier about how she obtained the system image you examined. You heard why she did it and the consequences she suffered. Please tell us what you did with the system image she gave you."

"Sure. I set up a virtual machine based on that image—"

"Let me interrupt you right there. For the non-technical among us, what does that mean?"

"Oh, sorry." Jerry smiled and waved his hands. "A system image is a block for block copy of a hard drive, and a virtual machine is software pretending to be hardware. In this case, the system image Brenda gave me came from a virtual machine. The virtual machine thinks that system image is a hard drive, but it's really a file pretending to be a hard drive. Anyway, I made a new virtual machine in my lab and populated it with the disk image Brenda gave me."

"So, to summarize what you just taught us, you made a copy of that system in your lab, so you could analyze it, right?"

Jerry nodded. "Yes."

"I'm interested in couple of details. First, which system was this?"

"It was the one Jesse, um, I mean the defendant, used to buy credit card numbers."

"How do you know?"

"The hostname was just the word, Teena. It was set up to look like a home computer, probably in case somebody penetrated it."

"You can tell all that from a host name?"

"Well, no. But it wasn't part of any Active Directory domain. It didn't connect to any network shares. It had one local user named Teena. Other than *Glimpse*, no other software packages were on it. Overall, it just looked like a typical home computer but without the bloatware. And Brenda told me this was the system Jesse used."

"How do systems 'know' what time zone they're in?"

"Well, they don't 'know,' you set it."

"But as I understand technology, computers acquire an attribute called an IP Address and other attributes to fit into the environment to which they're connected. Is that right?"

"Yes, that's true. But not the time zone. You have to set it. With a fresh install, the time zone is US Pacific, probably because Microsoft is in Redmond, Washington, on the US West Coast. And then you set it to your local time zone."

"Okay. And so, that means the copy in your lab will have some attributes assigned specific to your lab. But its time zone is the same as the original at the bank, is that right?"

"Yes."

"Okay, thanks. What was the system's time zone?"

"US Central Daylight time."

"You're sure. Did that system have any evidence it was ever on a different time zone?"

"No. After the controversy about time zones came up, I went through all system events starting several days before the bank fired Jesse. The boot times were all during normal business hours. The Central Daylight Time offset is GMT minus five and so—"

"Wait. What's a time zone offset?"

"Oh, sorry. The time zone offset is the difference between our time and Greenwich Mean Time, which is the world's reference time in Greenwich, England. Here in Minnesota during daylight savings time, we're five hours earlier than GMT. That's what GMT minus five means."

"Okay, thanks. And now, please continue about your conclusion that nobody tampered with its time zone."

"The summary is, you'd see evidence of it in the Event Viewer. If somebody changed it from Central Daylight Time to GMT, you'd see an event that says the time zone offset went from three hundred minutes to zero. But the biggie is the log entries themselves. Nobody used that system at night, except for the night somebody bought those credit cards. That's the only night it shows activity. It booted around 7 p.m., US Central Daylight time, and shut down a little after 10 p.m., or around three hours later."

"And so, what does that mean when somebody claims the time on the video was 7 p.m. in England? Which would have been, what, 2 p.m. here in Minnesota?"

"No way. That's not what the evidence says. 7 p.m. on that system was 7 p.m. right here in Minnesota."

"Thanks for that lesson, Mr. Barkley." Dominic turned to the prosecutor. "Your witness."

The prosecutor took a breath and then stepped toward Jerry. "Why are you here?"

Jerry smiled. "Because Jesse, um, the defendant I mean, asked for my help."

"How much are they paying you?"

Jerry shook his head. "Nothing."

"Nothing? Are you sure? With the knowledge you have, I'd assume somebody would pay you a fortune as an expert witness."

Jerry chuckled. "Well, making money would be nice."

"I'm impressed. But I still don't know why you're here."

"I told you, because Jesse asked me."

"And she's not paying you. Do you owe her a debt?

"No. She's a friend. And somebody is railroading her and I don't like that."

"So, then, you're biased, right?"

Jerry nodded and grinned. "So, that's where you're going with this. Of course, I'm biased. But that doesn't change what I found. It's easy to verify everything I said."

"Yes, it is. It's also easy to verify things you didn't say. For example, you chose to examine the system image Brenda

Yang stole from the bank. Why didn't you examine the image the bank gave the defense team?"

"I did examine it."

"Interesting. You did examine it. But you chose not to talk about it under oath. I wonder why that is?"

Dominic stood. "Objection."

The prosecutor turned to Judge Ford. "I'll withdraw the question." She turned back to Jerry. "Since you examined it, but chose not to talk about it, what was its time zone?"

"GMT."

"And during daylight savings time, we're five hours earlier than GMT, is that right?"

"Yes."

"So, during daylight savings time, what time is it here, at 7 p.m. GMT?"

"Two o'clock in the afternoon."

"So, let me get this straight. The image Brenda Yang stole from the bank said the time zone was US Central, but the image the bank gave you said the time zone was GMT, or five hours later, is that right? And your theory is that somebody from the bank manipulated the time zone setting inside that system to make it look like 7 p.m. was really 2 p.m., is that right?"

"It seems likely."

"What, you don't know? Even if you go into what the defense team calls, 'professor mode?'"

Dominic stood, but Jerry waved him off.

"There's no way to know with the system image from the bank because it only has a few minutes of Event Viewer events before the bank shut down the system, presumably to copy it. Somebody must have cleared the events right before copying it."

"So, you say."

"Huh?"

"You're suggesting somebody at the bank altered that system image before providing it to the defense team, by removing the log information that could prove your theory, right?

"I'm not suggesting anything. I'm saying that's what was there."

"Okay. And now, I want you to go into your 'professor mode.' How would somebody manipulate those logs?"

"What kind of manipulating do you mean?"

"Make them show something that isn't true.

"Like what?"

"Somehow make the logs show something favorable to your theory, instead of a competing theory. How would you do it?"

"You mean like, insert bogus log entries, or maybe remove log entries that don't support you?"

"Yes. How would you do it?"

Jerry tilted his head and squinted. He spoke after a few seconds. "It's a lot easier to just zero the logs, which is what somebody did, than to plant or remove specific entries. I suppose it's theoretically possible. But those files are binary and you'd need some tooling to do it."

"But it's theoretically possible, right?"

"Sure."

"Then, how do we know you didn't manipulate the logs from the system Mrs. Yang stole from the bank?"

Dominic stood. "Objection. She's on a fishing expedition."

"I'll withdraw the question."

"Mr. Barkley, you said you're an independent contractor, right?"

"That's right."

"Who are your customers?"

"I'm sorry, that wouldn't be ethical for me to provide a list."

"No, that's not what I mean. What kinds of business do you target? What's your ideal customer?"

"Oh. My ideal customer probably has between one hundred to maybe a couple thousand employees. Any bigger, and the bureaucracy is a killer. Smaller ones don't usually do anything sophisticated enough to bother with."

"How many employees does Uncle Sam Bank have?"

"I don't know. Tens of thousands, I'm sure."

"So, aren't you really a little out of your league here?"

Jerry laughed. "Independent consultants like me have a marketing disadvantage with big organizations. But the computers and servers are all pretty much the same. Big organizations just have more of them."

"Why do you have a marketing disadvantage?"

"Because we have a credibility problem. Nobody believes us because there's no PR company pitching us."

"So, decision-makers have a hard time believing you?"

"Yeah."

"So, if you have trouble persuading experts to believe you, why should the jury believe you?"

Jerry smiled. "That's a great question." He turned to the jury. "You shouldn't believe me. Or anyone else. Not without verifying what I say. Everyone here probably has a Windows computer. Go change the time zone and then change it back, and then look at the events in your own Event Viewer. On Windows Ten, click 'Start,' and then 'Windows Administrative Tools,' and then 'Event Viewer.' You don't need an expert to see for yourself." Jerry turned back to the prosecutor. "Sorry. 'Professor mode' again. But it's not rocket science."

The prosecutor shook her head. "No further questions."

~

Somebody knocked on the conference room door. Dominic cracked it and spoke to somebody outside. He nodded and turned to Jesse. "They have a verdict. You ready?"

Jesse teared up. "Give me a sec. I need a tissue." She looked around the room. "Where'd they go?"

Dominic took her hand. "Jesse, the box is right here on the table."

"Oh." Jesse plopped in her chair and fought a losing battle to control her tears.

Dominic cracked the door and said something. He shut the door. "I told them we'll be right there."

"Thanks."

Dominic handed her another tissue. "Get it out of your system in here. Don't let them see you sweat."

Jesse wiped her eyes. "Right." She took another tissue and cleaned her face as best as she could. "I could use a mirror. Sorry. I didn't expect this."

Dominic nodded. "You look fine. Hold still." He wiped a corner of Jesse's eye. "You okay?"

Jesse took a breath. "Yeah."

"Okay, let's go." Dominic stood.

Jesse also stood. "Dominic, no matter what happens, thanks." She hugged him.

After a few seconds, Dominic broke the embrace. "You're welcome. And listen, your guy, Jerry, he killed them. Nobody in their right mind would find you guilty. Keep that in your head."

Jesse nodded and took another calming breath. "I'm ready."

They walked into the courtroom and took their places.

The jury entered.

Somebody had said jury members avoid eye contact when it's a guilty verdict. Jesse searched for clues in their faces.

"Please rise."

Everyone stood.

Judge Ford entered and took his seat. "Have you reached a verdict?"

"We have, your honor."

The jury foreman handed a piece of paper to the clerk. The clerk stepped to the bench and delivered it to the judge.

Judge Ford glanced at it, nodded, and returned it to the clerk. The clerk carried it back to the jury foreman. Just like in the movies.

Drawn-out insanity. Jesse pulled her arms in tight and made fists. Get on with it. She stared at her shoes and drew shaky breaths.

Judge Ford turned toward the jury. "Will the jury foreman please read the verdict?"

Jesse trembled and chewed her lip. She scanned the jury.

The jury foreman looked straight at Jesse and showed a hint of a nod and smile. "We find the defendant not guilty on all charges."

A million pounds lifted from Jesse's shoulders. She could breathe again. Tears flowed. But good tears this time.

Dominic beamed.

Jesse wiped her eyes and nose as best as she could.

The prosecutor asked to poll the jury.

Jesse savored every "not guilty."

The judge thanked the jury. And then it was over.

The prosecutor stepped to the defense table. She extended her arms. Jesse looked up and took a step back. The prosecutor and Dominic hugged.

Dominic laughed. "Dinner is on you tonight."

Jesse's jaw dropped. "What?"

Dominic stood back. "We used to be married."

The prosecutor, Marissa, smiled. "Whenever we face each other in court, the loser buys dinner. It's a tradition."

Marissa extended a hand.

Jesse's mind swirled. She extended hers.

Marissa shook it. "Jesse—may I call you Jesse—now that I'm no longer your prosecutor, I'm glad you won. I'll take my lumps for this case, but I never liked it and I'm glad it turned out the way it did."

"How long were you married?"

Marissa released her grip on Jesse's hand. "Not long. Only a couple of years. And Jesse—"

"Yes?"

"I hope you bring the traffickers you're onto to justice."

32.   FISA

Friday, August 3, 2018

Dennis Waverly smacked his desk. Again. The
cubicle wall shook. Every time he thought about how that
snake Mike Swanson threw him under a bus, he wanted to
erupt. Why tell Dennis about some secret FISA order but
then deny it in court? There were only two possibilities.
Either Mike Swanson was a liar, or this order was so secret
Mike could not reveal it, no matter what.

But Mike himself agreed that Jesse's case was just
embezzlement. No spy vs. spy or national security secrets.
And that meant Mike is a liar. But if he's a liar, did he lie
that the case was simple embezzlement? Was Jesse part of
some deeper crooked operation they couldn't talk about in
open court?

Why not go to HR? But how do you go to HR about
something like this? Why not just confront Mike? Yeah,
right. Maybe Mike was some kind of mastermind and HR
was in on it. If that were true, then they were probably
looking for a way to get rid of him, too.

And that conversation with Brenda Yang right before
the trial—she was right about the Event Viewer logs on that
VM Jesse used to buy credit cards. If Brenda hadn't made
her illegal copy, before somebody wiped the logs, nobody
would have known and Jesse would be serving time.

But Brenda didn't know anything about computers. How did she know about Event Viewer logs? That had to come from their expert witness, some guy off the street named Jerry Barkley. True, he knew his stuff, but what made him special? How did they find this guy? What made him think about checking time zones on that computer?

Maybe Jesse Jonsen really was a victim and not a perpetrator, even though Brenda broke protocol when she made those illegal disk image copies. He had to find out what was going on. If nothing else, to protect himself.

He pulled out his cell phone and stared at it. No. Not yet. He had to find that FISA order first. Mike had asked Karen, his assistant, to print the PDF, which meant it was online at the time, and Karen had access to it. Wait a minute. A government FISA order in a PDF? How did it come in? Did the government email it and Mike saved it somewhere? That doesn't add up. A super-secret FISA order as an email attachment? No way. Which means, Mike is a liar and I was a patsy.

Dennis put his cell phone down and dialed from his office phone.

"This is Karen."

"Hi Karen, Dennis Waverly. From IT. We met a few months ago. I need to do some updates on your computer. It should only take a few minutes. Can I come up?"

"I thought you guys did all those remotely."

"We usually do. But one of your updates had a problem and I need to do some troubleshooting to figure out why."

"Oh. That doesn't sound like only a few minutes. Can it wait?"

Dennis smiled. Lucky break. "Well, maybe I could stay late and work on it."

"You sure?"

"Yeah. As I think about it, that works out better for me anyway. I need to run some errands at home and I could do those in the morning and come in late."

"Sounds good."

"Hey Karen, as long as I'm staying late—" No. Don't push it.

"As long as you're staying late, what?"

"Well, Mike's computer also had a patching hiccup, but that would mean keeping his office unlocked so I can get in to look at it."

"Will you lock it back up when you're done?"

"You sure?"

"Yeah. His wife's in the hospital and if you can do it after hours, it's one less thing for him to worry about."

"Well, thanks. That would save me a ton of hassle." Dennis high-fived himself in his mind.

"Sounds like a win all around."

"I appreciate it. See you around four thirty."

"Listen, Dennis, let's keep this between us, okay?"

"Sure."

"He showed you that secret government order, so he must trust you, right?"

Dennis smiled. Sometimes things just work. "Sure. Thanks."

~

Dennis yawned. Almost done. It was dark outside. *Glimpse* was ready on Karen's computer and her computer's Event Viewer showed a failed Windows Update from yesterday and a manual update from two hours ago, so his cover story was auditor-proof. Keeping *Glimpse* auditor-proof was more challenging, but he solved it. The installation was easy because the program already hid from pesky scanners. The problem was controlling it. But he had come up with an elegant solution. Whenever Dennis placed a file in a special directory on the server, *Glimpse* would start recording activity. Another file stopped the recording. And still another file signaled *Glimpse* to remove itself.

Everything was going well. Even better than expected. Maybe he would submit his customizations to the *Glimpse* maintainers later. It was a nice feature. Just a couple more steps to go on Mike's computer, and then he could lock the door and leave.

"What are you doing in my office?"

It was Mike. Blood rushed to Dennis's ears. "Um, hi Mike."

"I asked you, what are you doing in my office?"

The bar graph showed the *Glimpse* installation was about ninety percent done. "I'm trying to fix an update problem."

"Are you sure that's all you're trying to do?" Mike stepped toward his desk.

Ninety five percent. Dennis stood and met Mike halfway across the office. "Look, Mike, I'm here to fix an update problem. Both Karen's computer and yours had the same problem and I asked Karen if I could fix both of these tonight. She wanted to get it done and not bother you. And I'm almost finished."

Mike nodded. "She tries to take care of me."

"But listen, I need to know. What's the deal with that FISA order? Why did you throw me under the bus at the trial?"

"How much more work do you have to do on my computer?"

"Just a few more minutes."

"Okay, sit back down. I'll tell you what's going on while you finish up, and then let's keep this between us. I owe you that much."

Dennis nodded and sat back behind Mike's desk. Ninety nine percent. He donned his best poker face.

Mike sat in front of the desk. "First, I had no idea they would grill you like they did."

"Well, they did, and it put me in a lousy position."

"And I'm sorry for putting you in that position. But there really is a bigger picture here."

Installation complete. Dennis clicked the OK box. Now to the last step. Apply the good update. He clicked mouse buttons. "So, what is this bigger picture?"

Mike stood and glanced outside his office.

Dennis followed Mike's gaze. The twentieth floor was still empty.

Mike sat again. "We suspect our former employees in that department were involved in a massive money laundering scheme with foreign nationals. The embezzlement was just a cover. Or maybe compensation to keep the money laundering under the radar. We're still looking into it with the feds. But I couldn't bring that up during the trial because it would have blown months of police work."

Dennis nodded. *He thinks I'm an idiot.* "So, were these foreigners depositing money somehow and then taking it back out again so it looked clean?"

"We're still unraveling details. But in general, yes, we think they shared a percentage with our Fraud Department former employees, and that's why it went on so long. I really can't go into any more detail."

Dennis fought to keep his poker face. *That's because you're making this up right here on the spot. If there were deposits, there would be a record.* "Wow. Okay."

Mike nodded. "Good. And now that I've shared that with you, I need you to do something for me."

"Sure, what is it?"

"I need you to keep this between us. Pretend like nothing happened. You do that and I'll see to it that it enhances your career."

Dennis nodded. "I don't see any reason to talk about this with anyone else."

"Good." Mike extended his hand. "No hard feelings?"

Dennis silently shivered and extended his hand. "No, no hard feelings."

They shook hands.

"How much is left?"

Dennis looked at the screen. "It's rebooting. When it comes up, why don't you login and make sure everything works while I'm still here." Dennis stood and gestured to Mike's chair. "I'll switch with you."

33.   1995—Missing

November, 1995. Itasca County Girls Group Home, Big Fork, Minnesota.

A staff member or Mrs. Adams herself always met the school bus at the edge of the property.

"Where's Nadine?" Mrs. Adams' voice had an edge.

"Didn't see her," one girl said.

Jesse looked down and hustled past.

"Jessica." It was Mrs. Adams' voice.

Jesse turned. The other girls walked past.

"Jessica, you're her roommate. Where is Nadine?"

"I, um, I, I don't know."

Mrs. Adams' eyes pierced Jesse's brain. "Come with me."

They walked into the building and into Mrs. Adams' office. "Jessica, please, sit."

Mrs. Adams sat behind her desk. Jesse sat in the same chair as when she first arrived.

"Jessica, it's a safety matter. If Nadine is out on the street somewhere, she could be in danger. We are responsible for her safety, and so if you know anything about where she is, I need to know what you know. Right now."

Jesse squirmed. "I'm sorry. I wish I could help."

"Very well. We need to search your room."

~

Mrs. Adams stood in the middle of Jesse's room. "Most of Nadine's clothes are missing. Jessica, what happened to them?"

"I don't know, I swear."

"I want you to think about every detail from today starting when you woke up this morning. Did anything stand out when you got ready for school?"

"No, nothing I can remember."

"What about during school. You two usually eat lunch together, is that right?"

Jesse stifled a gasp. How did she know?

"What happened at lunch today?"

Jesse swallowed. "Um, it was nothing. Really. She was telling me about some stuff with her family. That's all."

"What stuff?"

"She made me promise not to tell."

"Jessica, if there's anything you know about Nadine that can help us get her back, you need to tell me. She could be in mortal danger right now, and we don't know where she is."

"No, nothing." Jesse held her breath.

"Very well. If you think of anything, no matter how small, I want you to tell me about it, okay?"

Jesse nodded.

"And I'm calling an all-hands meeting in fifteen minutes in the living room." Mrs. Adams left.

Jesse exhaled and took a few breaths. All she had to do was keep quiet. She'd been in worse predicaments. That's why she was stuck here, two hundred miles from nowhere. Just keep quiet and everything will be fine. She took a few more deep breaths to calm the butterflies in her stomach.

~

The next morning. Saturday, the one day she could sleep in, somebody knocked on her door. "Meeting in the living room in twenty minutes."

"Another one? What for?"

"Just get dressed and be there."

Jesse rolled over. But the knocking didn't stop. Somebody was knocking on every door and the whole house was making noise. Jesse dressed and trudged to the living room.

A few girls were already there. A couple had a bowl of cereal in their laps. Mrs. Adams paced at the front of the room as more girls entered. Her eyes were red rimmed. Her hair, normally tidy and professional-looking, was disheveled.

After the last girl arrived, Mrs. Adams started. "Girls, I have an announcement." Tears filled her eyes. "Nadine Ladysmith died early this morning in a car accident near Grand Rapids." Mrs. Adams wiped her eyes. "She was in a car with a boy named Ethan Hendricks. I believe some of you might have known him. The police found two empty bottles of vodka in the car. If any of you know anything about why the two of them left from school yesterday and traveled to Grand Rapids, or how they came into possession of fake IDs, I need you to come talk to me in my office."

Jesse's heart stopped. Her stomach churned. She hurried back to her room, shut the door, and stared at Candy's bed. "Why?" She plopped on her bed and bawled.

This wasn't her fault. Yes, it was; she got the fake IDs. But she didn't buy the liquor, Candy and her boyfriend did. But she sold them the fake IDs. So what? Nobody forced them into a liquor store. But she knew that was what Candy planned. Big deal, why was that her fault? Because she sold them the way to do it. But if she hadn't, they would have found somebody else. Maybe. But *she* sold them the IDs.

"Candy, you weren't supposed to die. You were supposed to have a party and then be free." Jesse buried her head into her pillow and bawled harder.

~

At school the Wednesday before Thanksgiving break, Jesse's English teacher, Ms. Inglebertsen said, "Nadine's death affected us all, and I want to tell you a story today. Pay close attention because this leads to your final class assignment.

"I was a high school senior in 1975, just like you guys, and I lived in Superior, Wisconsin. One of our neighbors was a deckhand on an ore ship, and he used to give me tours. I loved watching those big ships go under the Duluth lift bridge, and I liked to imagine what it was like to work on one and sail all over the Great Lakes. Well, my neighbor gave me a chance to find out one day. It was a weekend run from Duluth to Detroit."

She pulled down a map of the Great Lakes. "This was the route." She traced across Lake Superior from the port of Duluth, through Whitefish Bay and Sault Ste. Marie, down Lake Huron to Sarnia, Michigan, and the St. Clair river to St. Clair Lake, and into Detroit.

"The plan was to drop me off at Sault Ste. Marie, and my parents bought a plane ticket to fly home. My parents told me it was an early graduation present. For me, it was the trip of a lifetime. I couldn't wait.

"Unfortunately, or so I thought at the time, I came down with acute appendicitis on Thursday. When that ship sailed early morning on Saturday, Nov. 9, 1975, I was in the hospital, recovering after they took out my appendix. We made arrangements for me to take another trip that spring. But I never went, because that was the last trip the Edmund Fitzgerald ever took. Our neighbor and my friend died in a horrible storm, right about here." She pointed to a spot on the map near Sault Ste. Marie.

"How many of you know about the song, *Wreck of the Edmund Fitzgerald* by Gordon Lightfoot?"

A couple students raised their hands.

"He wrote that song in 1976. It's a classic." She played the song. It was boring. Who cares about the 70s anyway? But Ms. Inglebertsen's friend died on that ship. Wow.

She turned her head toward Jesse. "I learned a lesson from that experience. None of us know how long we'll be alive, so we need to embrace life to the fullest. And that's your final project. I'm giving it to you now, so you have plenty of time to think about it. Before the last week of school, write about the most important lesson you learned this year in Bigfork, Minnesota. Have a great Thanksgiving break, think about your writing assignment, and we'll talk about it when you get back."

34.   Guilty Not Guilty

Friday, August 3, 2018

The court case was over. Jesse had won. But that was yesterday. Today, she needed an income. More than two months with no job had drained years of savings. And Dominic hadn't sent his bill.

Time to get serious about job hunting. Jesse kicked herself mentally for not keeping up with networking. But hey, everyone knows fraud analysts are busy. And she had presented at several conferences. How hard could it be?

Jesse launched LinkedIn on her computer. Her jaw dropped. Uncle Sam Bank Senior Vice President Mike Swanson had posted an announcement an hour ago. It already had hundreds of comments and thousands of views.

"The recent news stories are true. We've learned about numerous ethical lapses in our bank, especially in the Fraud Department. This tears at my heart because it happened on my watch. It's also frustrating because the Fraud Department is supposed to keep everyone honest, and if the Fraud Department fails in its duty, then it reflects badly on the whole bank. That's why we vigorously prosecuted the people responsible—to send a message. If you're in a position of trust and you violate that trust, expect consequences. The verdict didn't matter. What mattered was challenging the behavior.

"But now, we need to move forward. We're bringing in an independent consulting and audit team to root out any other unethical practices that may have happened and help us rebuild our reputation.

"Finally, on behalf of the thousands of hard-working people here at the bank, I want to apologize to all our customers and stakeholders. I ask one favor. Please don't let a few bad apples spoil a great institution. You have my word. I won't rest until we uncover and address every ethical lapse. And in the spirit of transparency, you'll read about our efforts right here."

Jesse flopped back in her chair. I should have expected this. She paced her apartment and pondered her next move. After a few minutes, she called Bremer Bank.

Her former mentee, Annette, answered. "I had a feeling you'd be calling."

Jesse didn't need body language to feel the tension. "Hi Annette. I was wondering if you need help on your fraud team."

"Jesse, it's great to hear from you, but the only reason I'm even talking to you is our history."

"What—why?"

"You know why. They wouldn't have charged you without good reason."

"Except I didn't do it."

"None of the crooks ever do it. Didn't you teach me that?"

"But the verdict was not guilty."

"Not guilty just means they didn't prove it."

"They didn't prove it because the whole thing was a setup."

"Jesse, I'm sorry, but I don't have time for this. I have a department to run."

"Listen, Annette, there's something bad going on at Uncle Sam Bank. It's big and it's ugly. And I got caught up in it. But I swear to you, I didn't do anything wrong."

"Jesse, even if I believed you, I couldn't bring you onto my team."

"Why not?"

"Do I really have to spell it out to you? Because nobody would trust you. Ever. On any fraud team. Anywhere."

Jesse took the phone away from her ear. She wiped tears. "Okay, Annette, thanks. I'm sorry I wasted your time."

Jesse collapsed at her desk and sobbed. Next month's lease payment was coming due. Nineteen-hundred dollars. And then utilities. And groceries. The downtown apartment made sense when she had a job downtown. But not anymore.

She could not put it off any longer. Maybe she could sell the house in Bloomington. The mold pit. For pennies on the dollar.

Jesse stared at her phone for an eternity before finally picking it up again. She dialed. "Dad, I need your help."

The next call was to the building owner. She left a voicemail. "Hi. This is Jesse Jonsen in unit twenty-two. I am sorry to do this to you, but I lost my job and won't be able to make next month's rent. Not even close. The lease still has nine months left, but I have to break it. I'll be out before the first of the month. I know this leaves you in a tough spot, but if you'll let me break this lease, I'll let you show the apartment to prospective renters any time you want. And I'll leave the place spotless, so you'll be able to rent it right away."

She terminated the call and cried.

But after a few minutes, she wiped her tears and started packing. Dad would be here soon with a rented truck.

~

"You have an impressive resume. Why do you want to work at Dairy Queen?"

Fair question. "I'm, um, taking a break from corporate America, but I need to keep busy. I know you hire high schoolers. I can work when they're in school. I also might want to operate my own franchise one day, and so the experience here will be helpful. And besides," she offered her most charming smile, "I can serve ice cream as well as anyone."

The store owner leaned back and grinned. He nodded. "I have one more question for you. When can you start?"

~

Jesse collapsed in her old bedroom. It hadn't changed since high school. But this time she smelled like grease, her career was dead, and, at almost forty years old, she was stuck living in her parents' house like a teenager again. Full circle.

She had never cared about advancing up any corporate ladder. Her mission was to take down criminals. More than a mission. That was her purpose. To the exclusion of all else. She had rarely even dated, because there was always somebody trying to hurt people she cared about and that kept her busy. And what did she have to show for all that dedication? Her high school bedroom. And a moldy house she couldn't live in and couldn't afford to fix.

All because not guilty doesn't mean innocent.

That thought invaded her consciousness again. Keep on seeking, and you will find. I am with you always, even to the end of the age. Touchy-feely mumbo-jumbo. That's the last thing I need.

Somebody knocked on her door. "Jesse, can I come in?" It was dad.

"Yeah." She wiped her eyes.

Dad walked in and sat next to her on the bed. He hadn't changed since high school, either. Well, other than the grey around the edges. And a few more lines in his face.

"I remember the last time I came in here and sat down next to you. You were worried."

Jesse shook her head. "Nah. More mad than worried."

Dad smiled. "Just like now. But you got through it."

The corners of Jesse's lips turned up. "Yeah."

"I was proud of you."

"Thanks."

"I'm proud of you now, too."

Jesse slumped. "Why?"

"Because from what you told me, you tried to help a bunch of victims. It's what you do."

"Look where it got me."

"Hey, if it were easy, everyone would do what you do."

Jesse chuckled. She fought tears. "I don't know what I'm going to do."

Dad opened his arms. Jesse leaned on his chest. He hugged her. "You'll figure it out."

They hugged for a few seconds. She pulled away. Dad had a twinkle in his eye.

"What?"

"Want some ice cream?"

~

"Hello, welcome to Dairy Queen. May I take your order?" As the only native English-speaker on the day crew, Jesse spent much of her time at the drive-up window. She made it her challenge to find out something about every customer because, somehow, it felt good. Maybe she could package it as soft skills training on her resume because, hey, why not? But there was more. She actually enjoyed the give and take.

A baby wailed over the speakers while Jesse took the order. A young mom pulled up to Jesse's window after a few seconds.

Jesse smiled at her. "How are things going today?"

"Getting ready for spring break." She handed Jesse a credit card.

"Oh. What do you have planned?" Jesse processed the card.

"We're going to visit my grandma in the nursing home before she dies."

Jesse swallowed. "Oh. I am so sorry."

"Don't be. Grandma lived a long life. Her grandma was a slave in Mississippi and they moved to Iowa after the Civil War. Her mom went to a one-room schoolhouse."

"Your great grandma, right?"

The mom took her card. "Yeah. They moved up here after the Korean war when my grandma was fifteen. She has all these amazing stories from her family, and she's been recording them for us, but the cancer is eating her up and she wants to record a few more while she still can."

Jesse wiped a tear. "Well, have a great visit. Your order will be ready in the next window up ahead."

"Thanks."

"Would you do me a favor?"

"Sure."

"Share some of those stories with me?"

The woman smiled. "Sure. Thanks for asking."

Jesse took off her headset. Amazing what people share with a total stranger at a drive-up window. I'm the ice-cream bartender.

Jesse swiveled in her chair in the window booth and surveyed her new workplace. Some of the crew smiled and nodded at her performance. She nodded back.

The day-shift crew was mostly recent high school graduates, some trying to make enough money for college, others starting adult life on their way to bigger and better things. All but Jesse, headed to bankruptcy and oblivion. No. Don't think like that. These kids barely speak English, but they all get along and the place works. And, so will I.

Jesse padded over to Asian An Li, who was tapping away on her phone as usual when business was slow. "Whatcha looking at?"

"Nothing."

It looked like a social media post. "New boyfriend?"

An Li turned away.

"C'mon. Give me something. I'm so bored, I might jump out that window." Fahad and Camila chuckled.

Another customer stopped at the drive-up window. Jesse used her best Arnold Schwarzenegger voice. "I'll be back."

An Li's eyes bored into Jesse's back as Jesse returned to the drive-up window. Jesse smiled. *I'll get her to talk to me.* She donned her headset. "Hello and welcome to Dairy Queen. What brings you here on this fine afternoon?"

"Huh?"

"I should probably take your order before I ask you a zillion questions about your day."

The whole crew watched her perform. *What can I say? It's a gift.*

After handling the customer's order, Jesse turned back to An Li. "So, tell me about this guy."

An Li smiled. "He's not a boyfriend. Not yet."

"Ohh. Is he charming his way into your life?"

"He calls me beautiful. He says I should go to work as a model."

Jesse's neck hairs stood on end. "May I see?"

An Li handed Jesse her phone. Jesse scrolled through some of the messages. Acid ate another hole in Jesse's stomach with every message. "Who is this guy?"

"He works for a university up north. He says he'll help pay for me go to college right now. I won't need to work here and save for it."

"And he brought you to a fancy dinner?"

"We had wonderful time."

Jesse's mouth went dry. *What are the odds?* "An Li, this guy is grooming you."

"What's grooming?"

"It means, he's recruiting you. He picks up on what you tell him and offers you what he thinks you want to hear."

An Li took back her phone. "How do you know?"

"Because I know this guy. I know, okay?"

"No. You don't. You can't." An Li walked away.

Another customer drove up. Jesse put on her headset. "Welcome to Dairy Queen. May I take your order?" Her heart wasn't in it.

Jesse finished the order and took off her headset. She stared at the wall.

"How do you know?" It was An Li.

Jesse turned to face her. "I know because those guys are the reason I have to work here instead of where I used to work. They own at least one senior bank vice-president and their operation must be huge. They've gotta be grooming on an industrial scale. I'll bet they have a whole assembly line to find the demographic they're looking for."

"What? How?"

Jesse told An Li about meeting Leilani, her trip to the NPU campus, her reverse-grooming attempt, that snake-in-the-grass Mike Swanson, her trial, and how she ended up working at Dairy Queen. "And this guy recruiting you. His name is Harold, right?"

"Yes."

"And his partner is Meaghan, right?"

"How do you know?"

"I told you. I met both of them. They're running a human trafficking ring and they're trying to lure you in."

Fahad and Camila wandered over.

"Wait, you know this guy?" Fahad's eyes widened.

"Yeah."

"He tried to recruit Camila. But me and Camila are tight and I didn't like her hanging out with that guy. We introduced him to An Li."

A customer walked up to the counter.

"Let's talk about this after work. I'll buy you guys ice cream. It's all I can afford."

The customer ordered and handed Jesse his credit card. His hand shook.

"Are you okay?"

"I'm fine." He forced a smile. Sweat beads formed around his temples.

Jesse put on her most sincere smile. "Nothing like a good soft ice cream cone, right? Give me just a second. I need to run this on my other machine. This one's on the fritz."

She strolled around the corner to her drive-up window booth, grabbed her cell phone and called Annette at Bremer Bank again.

"Hi Jesse, I told you, we aren't hiring."

"That's not why I'm calling. I need you to run a credit card number for me."

"What? What are you up to?"

"Maybe catching a crook. Just look up if this number is reported stolen, okay?"

"Jesse, what's going on?"

"This guy gave me a credit card and I think there's something wrong with it. It's from your bank."

"And so you called me to look it up?"

"That's right."

"You're taking advantage of our friendship."

"Yep. I am."

"Why should I trust you?"

"Because I need to know whether to call the police and I only have a few seconds to decide."

Annette sighed. "Give me the number."

Jesse read her the credit card number.

"Reported stolen two hours ago. Where are you?"

"Doing my job at Dairy Queen." Jesse gave her the store address. "Call the police. I'll try to stall this guy. We good?"

Annette sighed. "Yeah."

"I'll let you know how it turns out." Jesse terminated the call and gestured to Fahad.

Fahad strolled over.

"Fahad, I want you to grab a mop and mop around the entry door."

"Why?"

"Because that guy's a robber. I don't want him leaving before the police get here."

"How do you know?"

"Because he stole this credit card."

"How do you know?"

"Just pretend to clean up by the door. If he walks past you, get his license plate number off his car. And tell Camile and An Li to take their time with his order. The deep fryer has a problem."

"No, it doesn't."

"Do I really need to spell it out?"

Fahad looked puzzled. But then his eyes twinkled. "Oh. I get it now."

"Good. Go grab that mop. And be ready for anything. Tell them if I signal, to come running with anything they can use as a weapon."

Fahad said something to Camile and An Li. Both glanced back at Jesse and nodded.

Fahad wheeled the mop bucket toward the door.

Jesse nodded back. She took a breath and walked back to the counter. "Sir, I apologize, but the machine back there also went on the fritz. We have a backup number with our processor to straighten matters like this out. Give me just a minute to call them and run this by hand. Sorry again for the inconvenience." She grabbed a land-line phone and tapped phone keys. "Hi. This is Jesse at store number 1371. Our credit card machines are on the fritz and I have a Mastercard here I need to process." She sighed. "Yes, I'll hold." She shrugged at the customer. "They put me on hold and I'm listening to elevator music. Figures."

The man looked even more nervous.

Jesse made eye contact with Fahad.

The man reached for his pocket.

Jesse dropped the phone and raced toward the front counter. The man opened his coat. Jesse vaulted over the counter and knocked his arm away. "Fahad, grab his coat."

Fahad froze.

Jesse dropped to the floor and kicked the man's midsection. She scored. He doubled over.

She sprang to her feet. "Grab his coat. Now."

Fahad ran over and pulled the man's coat from his arms. A gun clattered to the floor.

"Camile, An Li – get up here. Bring some duct tape. Fahad, block the door."

Jesse picked up the gun, moved behind the man, and emptied the bullets into her shirt.

The man turned and staggered toward the door. Jesse jumped in front of him. She pointed the gun at him. "Don't make me use this."

The man stopped, dead in his tracks.

Fahad suppressed a smile.

An Li and Camile showed Jesse the duct tape.

"Put your arms behind you."

The man complied.

"An Li, Camile, wrap some duct tape around those arms. Tight."

The police arrived ten minutes later. The store owner arrived a few minutes after that.

~

They debriefed after the police left.

An Li asked, "How did you do that?"

Jesse smiled. "Brown belt in Kung Fu."

Fahad broke out laughing. "Jesse, why did you empty the bullets into your shirt?"

"Oh, I forgot." Jesse untucked her shirt. Bullets dropped to the floor. They sounded like rocks. "So he wouldn't hear that when I emptied the gun."

"But why empty the gun at all?"

"Because I didn't want anyone to die in case he took it away from me."

The store owner nodded. "How did you know?"

"I know how criminals think. Some people call it my superpower." Jesse turned to An Li. "Now, tell me about this fancy dinner you had with that predator, Harold."

"It's a resort named Norra lekplatsen. It means, Northern Playground. On Mille Lacs Lake."

"Wait – but the school's in Little Falls."

"He said they partner with Norra lekplatsen for work-study. You work there, study at school, they pay tuition."

Jesse's jaw dropped. "That scheme is even bigger than I thought."

The business owner shook his head. "Are you sure you're not an undercover cop?"

Jesse chuckled and shook her head. "Nope. I used to be a fraud analyst. Now I work at Dairy Queen."

~

Jesse tossed and turned in bed that night. The idea was preposterous. But she couldn't sleep in this bedroom forever. Can't hurt to ask. When life gives you lemons…

The next day, Jesse approached An Li on her break. "An Li, where do you live?"

"With my parents."

"Is it going well?"

An Li's face clouded. "No. We fight all the time. That's why I met Harry and Meaghan and almost turned into a prostitute."

"Well, maybe we can help each other out. I have a house full of mold I can't live in yet. Maybe we can go in together to fix it and move in. We could also bring in Fahad and Camile if they want. We share expenses and we all have a place to live."

35.   Deeper

Saturday, Sept. 8, 2018

"Welcome to Norra lekplatsen. Allow me to show you to your table." Ashley escorted the couple through the restaurant and sat them at a table in front of a floor-to-ceiling window overlooking the late summer northern woods.

"The leaves are just starting to turn. The peak colors are still about a month away. Do come back to enjoy it. In the meantime, watch through the greenery and mother nature might give you an unscripted show you'll never see anywhere else on earth." The couple sat. "Karlene will be your waitress."

Ashley made eye contact and Karlene approached. Ashley turned and headed back to her station. Several heads turned with her. Ashley blushed, smiled and acknowledged them. Of course, the dress was beautiful. But maybe the young woman inside was even more beautiful. It was a shame her parents couldn't see that. But Lake Nokomis and her parents and high school were a million miles behind her. In front was a future with amazing possibilities.

"Ashley, may I have a word at your earliest convenience?" It was Meaghan.

"Is everything okay?"

"Yes, my dear, you're doing a wonderful job. The guests compliment you every day."

"Thanks. So, what's going on?"

"Come with me, dear."

"But who will watch my station?"

"We have it covered."

Ashley followed Meaghan to Meaghan's office.

Meaghan walked behind her desk. Harold and another man she hadn't met were inside.

"Ashley Dunbar, meet Kyle Van Buren. We have an opportunity we think will suit you well."

Everyone sat.

"I have enjoyed watching you blossom these past few weeks." Meaghan's eyes drilled into Ashley, just like the first time back at Lake Nokomis. Only a month ago, but a lifetime away.

Ashley's heart raced.

Meaghan folded her hands on her desk and leaned forward. "Ashley, Norra lekplatsen started with a vision to attract people to enjoy the beauty of northern Minnesota, while also providing economic opportunities for those who live here. And I think we've done an admirable job at that. Important people are noticing."

"Well, that's good, right?" Ashley said.

Harold nodded. "Yes. That's very good."

Meaghan pursed her lips. "One of our investors noticed you, in particular."

Ashley scanned the room. Everyone smiled. Her cheeks were hot. "So, what does that mean?"

Harold's eyes danced. "Cut to the chase, Meaghan."

Meaghan nodded. "Ashley, one of our most important investors wants you to accompany him for a few days in Miami."

Ashley's mind exploded. Miami? On what, like, a business trip with a company president? She turned to Harold.

Harold smiled ear to ear and took her hand. "I think she's speechless."

Everyone laughed.

Meaghan leaned back. "My dear, it is truly an honor, both for you and for us. You will represent us in meetings with some of the most influential people in the world."

"But why me?"

"It's as I told you when we first met. You have a natural ability to represent yourself, and us, well."

"But I've never been farther away than Wisconsin. What would I do at some big business meeting?"

Meaghan nodded. "Kyle will accompany you and deal with the substantive business discussions. Your role will be to provide companionship for Congressman Catz. He is an influential man and an ally, and wishes to help build experiences in the Florida Everglades similar to what we offer here in northern Minnesota. You'll meet him in Miami and over the next five days as his companion, provide him a sense of what we have here, and act as a liaison with us. And of course, we will provide you with a wardrobe and a cash stipend."

~

Ashley lifted a shoe out of its tub at the end of the MSP airport security conveyer belt. "Why do they make us take off our shoes?"

"Stop asking questions," Kyle said, "and hurry up."

Ashley picked up her other shoe. "I've never flown before."

"Stop whining." Kyle grabbed her carryon bag as it slid down the conveyer belt. "Which of these are yours?" Tubs holding a hair dryer, a belt, phone, makeup bag, jacket, and other items piled at the end of the conveyer belt.

"All of them."

Kyle swore and disappeared into the crowd.

Ashley fought tears and finished repacking. What's Kyle's problem? She entered the concourse and made her way to the gate.

Where's Kyle?

She got in line to speak to a gate agent.

"May I help you?" The gate agent said.

Ashley's stomach eased. "Is this the only flight to Miami?"

The gate agent tapped some keys and looked at her computer monitor. "No, there are quite a few. Let me see your boarding pass." The agent smiled. "First time?"

"Yeah."

"Don't worry. You're at the right gate with plenty of time to spare."

"Thanks." Ashley wandered away. Where's Kyle?

Thirty minutes passed.

"Hey." Behind her.

Ashley jumped and turned around. It was Kyle. "Where were you?"

"Don't worry about it." He smelled like alcohol.

Ashley's stomach tightened. "I didn't know where you were. Why did you take off like that?"

"I said, don't worry about it. Just get on the plane."

~

The catered outdoor dining under the south Florida stars was different than Norra lekplatsen, but every bit as elegant. Men wearing business suits and women in low-cut dresses were everywhere. But something was wrong. It had gnawed at her since shortly after meeting Harold. Maybe because she was a million miles from home. Yeah, that was probably it.

Margaret, from Congressman Catz's staff, laid out the schedule for the next five days. Lots of appearances, where Congressman Catz would present the virtues of protecting the environment. Ashley's role seemed to be, just be there and look pretty. Kyle slammed down another drink.

As they stood to leave, Congressman Catz wandered to Ashley.

"Ashley, is it? I'm Matt Catz. Nice to meet you." He's young, confident. I like his dark hair.

"I'd like to go over a few details about what we want to accomplish this week. Can I stop by your hotel room in an hour?"

~

Ashley's hotel room was even more luxurious than her Norra lekplatsen room. She slipped out of her nice dress and put on her favorite sweats. Somebody knocked at the door.

"Wow. You look gorgeous."

Ashley blushed. "I'm sorry – my sweats are my comfortable clothes."

"No, you're fine. I like the look. Gonna let me in?"

"Sure." Ashley stepped aside. Catz strolled in. The door swung shut.

Ashley stepped back.

"Call me Matt." He moved closer.

She stepped back against a table.

Catz grabbed her and pulled her against him.

"No." She tried to push away.

His breath smelled like alcohol.

~

Near the end of another long shift, Marcia's desk phone rang. "Front desk. How may I help you?"

"Hi. We're in room 704. It sounds like a war zone in the room next door. Somebody is screaming and banging into walls."

"Thanks for letting us know. We'll investigate."

Marcia called her manager and filled him in.

"Who's in 706?" the manager asked.

Marcia looked it up. "An Ashley Dunbar with that group from Minnesota."

"Yeah, that's what I thought. We catered their dinner with Congressman Catz tonight. Offer the people in 704 a complimentary suite on the top floor. Get somebody to help and go move them right away. If anyone's on the other side in 708, find something nice and move them too. We'll give the congressman and this Ashley their privacy."

~

Ashley's eye hurt. The congressman had left a few minutes ago. Or maybe it was hours. She ran to the bathroom and vomited in the toilet. And then she stepped into the shower and turned the water on. As hot as she could stand it.

~

Carpenters. Pounding nails.

Ashley lifted her head. She had collapsed in the shower stall after turning the water off.

No. Not nails. Somebody pounded on the door. And now she was shivering.

She willed her legs to lift her body. She reached for a towel. Her hands shook. The mirror showed her bruised face and puffy left eye. Her hair was a tangled mess. Blood oozed from her lip.

More pounding. Louder. "Just a minute."

"Hurry up." It was Kyle.

"I, I need a few minutes."

"Figures, you overslept. Get up and get moving. I'll be back in fifteen minutes."

No. No. I can't face this today. "Kyle, I'm sick. I'm sorry."

"What do you mean, you're sick? Get over it. We went to a lot of trouble to set this up."

Ashley's stomach churned. She vomited. Again.

"Are you in there puking? What'd you do, get drunk and pass out last night?"

Ashley leaned over the toilet and cried.

Kyle swore. "Get cleaned up. I'll be back. Be ready. Or else."

Or else? Only a few minutes to get presentable.

~

Ashley found Kyle in the front lobby.

"What happened to you?"

"He raped me."

"No, he didn't. He paid for you."

"What?" Ashley stepped back.

"Why do you think you're here? You think we need a cheerleader?"

Ashley backed into a chair and slipped.

"Do you want to pay for college or not? Your job is to look good and satisfy customers and investors. You do that, we take care of you. Think you can handle it?"

Ashley whimpered, but her mind screamed. She nodded.

"Good. Now go fix your face. Here." Kyle pulled out one hundred dollars from his wallet. "Buy some makeup."

She wiped her eyes.

"And I'm gonna see to it that congressman never damages our goods again. Next time you see him—"

Ashley smirked. "He'll be wearing sunglasses. I bashed his nose and eye with my head."

Kyle looked her up and down. "So, you're a fighter, huh." He chuckled. "I like that. How about I get his other eye?"

"Yeah." Ashley set her jaw. Maybe this isn't so bad. Kyle's looking out for me. Maybe if I do this for just a little while, I'll make enough money... I just have to be more careful.

"Hurry up. Go fix your face. And get some sunglasses yourself. It's Florida."

36.   Endowment

The headline was on page two of the *Minneapolis Star/Tribune* Metro section. "North Prairie University Raises $10 Million Endowment." It read like a typical corporate press release, complete with a picture of Mike Swanson, Harold Rocklind, and Meaghan Maxwell smiling for the camera. Jesse slammed the newspaper down on her parents' kitchen table.

Dad finished pouring a glass of orange juice. "What's wrong?"

Jesse pointed to the picture. "This guy. He's the reason I eat here now."

Dad skimmed the article. "Ten-million-dollar endowment. Your Mike Swanson probably got a nice commission."

"And I got blackballed."

"Nobody said the world was fair. What are you doing about it?"

"Not a thing. There's nothing I can do."

"Yeah, there is."

"What?"

"You'll think of something."

"That's not helpful."

"Maybe not. But think of something soon. It'll improve your mood."

Jesse downed another bite of cereal. "I'm sorry, Dad. I don't know what to do."

He nodded. "Why don't you have some of your friends over and do some brainstorming?"

~

Mike Swanson stroked his wife's hair and kissed her. The monitor next to her hospital bed beeped faster. "That's how I know you're still inside there. I hope you can also hear me."

Mike sat next to the bed and watched her. Just like he'd done for the past two years since the accident. The heart monitor slowed to its normal pace of about 65 beeps per second.

"I'm supposed to talk to you because they say you can probably hear me. I know, you've heard that before. Because I've said it a couple hundred times by now. So, let's see, what's going on. I told you about that endowment with NPU. It closed yesterday. They got their ten million, we underwrote it, and I got a nice commission. We'll take a vacation when you get out of here." He wiped a tear. "So, get better and let's get you out of here."

His phone buzzed. He checked his text message. "Appt. set for 9 p.m. Pls confirm." He sent a confirming text.

"That was a work thing. I need to go to a meeting tonight. But I'll sit with you here for a few minutes."

Her eye may have fluttered. Or maybe it was the light.

~

Harold's goon Kyle met Mike in a conference room with a couple of other thugs. Kyle smiled. "You know the drill."

Mike handed Kyle his jacket and shoes. One of the thugs passed a wand up and down his body. "He's clean."

Harold strode in from the other room. "Good to see you, Mike. Can't be too careful."

"What happened to honor among thieves?"

"You watch too many movies." Harold handed Mike a USB memory stick.

"And that's it? That's the whole video?"

"Yep. That's your copy."

"But you said…"

"Doesn't matter what I said. We have a copy in case we need you again."

"What more could you possibly need from me? I got you ten million."

"And you earned a hefty commission. Maybe you'll spend some more of your money with us.'"

Mike looked down. "What do you want from me to make all this disappear?"

"I'm afraid we're not in a position to negotiate that point. But listen, you made a great video. I hope you enjoy it. Let me show you my favorite part. Kyle?"

Kyle handed Harold a laptop. Harold tapped some keyboard keys and brought up a copy of the video. Harold clicked on a time index about ten minutes in.

"How can I help you?"

"A man has needs. And my wife can't help."

"Don't worry, I'll take good care of you."

Harold paused the playback and laughed. "And she did. You were one satisfied customer."

Mike grabbed the laptop and slammed it to the floor.

Kyle and his goons moved toward him.

Harold gestured for them to stop.

"Mike, that was dumb. Now you owe us seven hundred dollars for that laptop. And you know the video wasn't inside it, right?"

Mike swore. "I'll kill you."

"No, you won't. But if you want to get out of this room alive, you'll give us an ATM card and we'll take eight hundred dollars. And every time I have to ask again, the price goes up by one hundred dollars. Oh, now it's nine hundred. Want to try for an even thousand?"

Mike dug his ATM card from his wallet and handed it to Harold.

"What's the number?"

Mike gave it to him.

"Kyle, would you run this please? Tell ya what. I'm in a good mood. Only take eight-fifty."

Mike shook his head.

"Don't worry, Mike. The video's online, but it's behind a TOR proxy. Nobody will find it unless they know where to look. And we're the only people in the world who know where to look. We don't intend to blackmail you. It's just an insurance policy."

Kyle returned with Mike's card.

"No hard feelings, okay?" Harold extended a hand.

Mike grabbed his jacket and shoes and stormed out.

37.   Beating

Friday, Sept. 28, 2018

"How can I help you?" Ashley had lost count of how many times over how many nights she had asked that question as they entered the hotel room where she worked night after night. Ten, twenty, a hundred—it never ended.

What was this fat old guy's story? Was he a judge? A politician? A rich businessman? Didn't matter. Here, he was just another customer. Her intuition alarm went off. This guy was trouble.

He slapped her across the face and swore at her.

Ashley saw stars. Her face went numb. She backed away. "Please. No."

He swore again and grabbed Ashley's arms. He pulled her close.

Ashley struggled. He kissed her. He smelled like alcohol, cigarettes, and sweat. She gagged.

Ashley kneed him in the groin. He pushed her down on the bed and came at her. He had murder in his eyes.

Ashley screamed. She kicked. He grabbed her feet. She grabbed a water glass from the night-stand and smashed his face with it. Broken glass and ice cubes spattered across the bed.

He put a hand on the gash in his face. It came away bloody. "You'll pay for that."

She wriggled free and scrambled off the bed. Heart pounding, she ran out into the hallway. He followed.

"Help!"

He advanced. She backed away. Shivering.

Kyle came out of the room next door. "What's going on?"

Ashley sobbed and pointed to the guy. She collapsed.

"Hey, I don't know what came over her. She went nuts in there and then ran outside."

Ashley brought her knees up to her chest and hugged them. What am I doing here?

Kyle swore. He hustled Ashley into his room and picked up his cell phone. "Meaghan, get up here." Kyle gave the guy a towel.

Meaghan showed up a few minutes later. "Kyle, get some people and a car and drop him off at the hospital. Ashley, come with me to my office."

~

Meaghan folded her hands into a bridge behind her desk. "Ashley, we simply cannot tolerate you attacking our customers. First, you attacked a congressional representative in Florida, and tonight you attacked another important client. You are single-handedly ruining our reputation."

"He tried to kill me."

Meaghan shook her head. "Discipline is important in our work and you failed to maintain it. Again. It is now a pattern. Each of our customers brings a unique set of desires, and it's your job to fulfill them. Injuring customers is never acceptable and we will not tolerate it."

"But..."

"Do I make myself clear?"

Tears formed in Ashley's eyes. "I want to go home."

"You are home. You left your parents and your old life last summer. We are your family now."

Ashley sobbed.

"Oh, stop it. We each have our jobs to perform. We've set up room 304 for you to work the rest of the night. Try not to destroy it."

Ashley's fingers tingled. Breathing came in gulps between sobs. "I want to talk to Harold."

"Of course, you do, my dear. But Harold is otherwise occupied at the moment."

Ashley wrapped her arms around herself. "Then I'm not doing this anymore." The words escaped on their own.

Meaghan stood and glared. "Yes, you are. I personally selected you because I sensed you offered a unique set of talents to contribute to our endeavors. We are trying to nurture you, but if you are not up to the task, then plenty of other girls will take your place. We keep you fed, clothed, and warm. If you wish to leave, you will live on the street, with no food, no clothing, and no shelter."

"Take me home."

Meaghan slapped her. "Stop this blubbering. You are home. Your parents made it clear. They do not want you back."

Ashley cowered.

"I simply cannot tolerate any more blubbering." Meaghan dialed her phone. "Kyle, have you delivered our client and his vehicle to the hospital yet?" She paused. "Excellent. When are you due to arrive back here?" Another pause. "Ten minutes? No, that's simply too long. Please call one of your security staff to escort Miss Dunbar to room 304, clean her up, and get her back to work." She terminated the call. "Go wait in the hallway. We are running a business and your blubbering gives me a headache."

Ashley trudged out of Meaghan's office, still sobbing and gulping for air. I need to get out of here. But how? No. I need to talk to Harold. Otherwise occupied? What does that mean? He loves me. Maybe he's in the restaurant.

Kyle's security people would be near the elevators. But the stairs should work. They can't be everywhere. She wiped her tears and headed toward the stairwell, each step more purposeful than the last. They would build a new life together, somewhere far away from all this. Harold was probably as trapped as she was.

She ducked into a restroom on the main floor and checked herself in the mirror. Makeup smeared everywhere. She cleaned it as best as she could. Her eyes were red-rimmed. Nothing she could do about that. But the restaurant was dark. He wouldn't notice. They could leave tonight. By morning, they would be far away from this place.

She walked into the restaurant. It was closed. But there was Harold with somebody at the same table in the back where they met that wonderful night last summer.

Maybe this isn't a good time to interrupt him. Ashley made her way around the edge of the room, in the dark. Harold had his phone out. He handed his phone to the woman he was sitting with. She giggled and handed the phone back. He scrolled with his finger—he was showing this woman pictures.

Ashley could hear snatches of conversation now. "Ohh, this is embarrassing. What if my parents find out?"

"Your parents won't mind. You're too beautiful to hide from the world. I love how the light accents your hair." Harold chuckled. "I can't believe we closed the restaurant down."

Ashley stopped. That was almost word for word what he said to me.

Harold and the woman stood.

"You can stay the night here if you like."

"I'd like that." She slid her hand into his.

They walked out into the lobby together, hand-in-hand.

Ashley fought tears. After a few seconds, she stumbled out and headed to the elevators. She rode the elevator up to the third floor.

One of Kyle's goons was there when the door opened. "Where were you?" He smelled like cigarettes.

"What do you care?"

He reached to slap her.

Ashley cowered.

He laughed. "I'm not gonna hit you. You got a customer waiting. You need to look good." He escorted Ashley to room 304 and gave her a key.

Ashley swiped the key over the door reader and trudged inside.

The customer was a regular. She closed the door and put on her smile. "How can I help you tonight?"

38. Help

Saturday, September 29, 2018

Somebody knocked on Ashley's door. She rolled over in bed. Noon. Memories from last night's nightmare flooded her head. Another knock. "Ashley, can I come in?"

Ashley padded to the door and peered through the peep hole. A girl. Dark hair. Native American maybe? Ashley had seen her before. Another "hostess." "What do you want?"

"Let me in. Please. Hurry."

"Why?"

"Please. I can't stay out here."

Ashley opened the door. The girl scooted into the room and shut the door behind her.

Ashley backed away.

"Ashley, no, I promise. I don't want to hurt anyone. I heard about that creep from last night."

'Who are you?"

"I'm Leilani. Leilani Berg."

"What do you want?"

"I want to get us out of here."

"Huh?

"That creep from last night. You put him in the hospital. I've also had a few creeps like that. Things didn't go so well for me. And the next one might not go so well for you."

"Meaghan says I need to find a way to deal with guys like that."

"I know. She told me the same thing. Do you really want to spend the rest of your life with stinky, fat drunks who want to beat you up?"

"It's not the rest of my life. It's just through college," Ashley said.

Leilani shook her head. "What will you be like after four years of this? I'm a senior, but I'm not sure if I'll ever graduate. I can't go home to my parents. And I can't stay here."

"So, leave."

"I will. I want you to come with me."

Ashley's jaw dropped. "Why?"

"Because you're a better fighter than me."

"Where would we go?"

"I met a lady a few months ago. Her name's Jesse. She'll help us. But we have to call her."

"So, how do we get a phone?"

"Kyle gets me Trazodone. It helps me sleep."

"So?"

"So, I'll mix some in a water glass. He'll drink the water; the pill knocks him right out. We'll leave tomorrow morning."

~

Jesse rolled over in bed. A ringtone. She answered.

"Hullo?"

"Jesse?"

"Yeah"

"This is Leilani. Remember me?"

Jesse shook her head. "It's six thirty on a Sunday morning. I lost my job because of you."

"Well, I'm sorry. But come get us. I'm at the Norra lekplatsen resort. It's where I work. On Mille Lacs Lake. Hurry. Please."

"Us?"

"Yeah. Ashley is coming too. Hurry. Please."

"Wait a minute. You blew me off when you first asked for help. You ran away and complained about me when I saw you at NPU. You helped set me up with that fake post office box. And now you call me at the crack of dawn to come get you? Who's Ashley?"

"She's a friend. Please hurry. Kyle's asleep. I snuck a sleeping pill in his water. But he'll wake up soon. And he'll kill me."

Jesse sat up. "Wait, this is real? This time, you mean it?"

"Yeah. A customer tried to kill Ashley last night. I can't stand it anymore. I want out. Please help."

Jesse rubbed her eyes. "Okay, let's meet in the parking lot."

"Sounds good."

"Okay. It'll take me three hours to get up there. I'll be driving a blue Honda Civic, license plate number LVL245. How big is the parking lot?"

"It's big."

"Okay. You probably don't want to be near the front door of the building. So, let's meet where you turn into the parking lot off the street."

"Okay. See you in three hours."

Jesse terminated the call and dialed another number.

Gloria answered after five rings. "Well, aren't you up early."

"I'm sorry. Remember Leilani? She just called. She's in this resort on Mille Lacs Lake. She wants me to come get her. Can you meet me here at my parents' house at noon?"

"Are you kidding?"

"I wish."

"Yeah. Let me rearrange my life today. And you'd better call your boss at Dairy Queen."

"Good idea. I also need to make a couple other calls."

Jesse finished her calls and then called her parents. "Mom, Dad, can I have a hundred dollars for gas and food? And I need to borrow the car."

39.   Abduction

Sunday, Sept. 30, 2018 6:45 a.m.

Leilani put Kyle's phone back where she found it. Maybe she should take it. But no, that would tip him off too soon that she was gone. She stared down at him, still sleeping soundly. Pangs tore through her heart. How could she still love this guy, knowing who he really was?

Everything about this place was a lie, and she knew too much. That was why she turned Jesse down last spring. Not because she wanted to stay, but because she knew better than anyone what these people were capable of doing. But no more. They had sucked Ashley in. And were working on some Asian girl she'd seen at the restaurant with Harold a few weeks ago. And when that creep attacked Ashley, it was like the last piece of a puzzle fit in place.

Ashley had no idea how dangerous these people could be. Hopefully, she would never find out. Jesse would know what to do. But first, Leilani had to engineer their getaway.

Leilani dressed and stuffed a few things into her backpack. She slipped out of her room and padded down the hallway to the elevator. I'll knock on Ashley's door, walk with her through the lobby and across the parking lot, and wait for Jesse. Piece of cake.

~

Jesse's phone rang. The caller-ID showed the same number as this morning. She pulled off the road and answered.

"Hello?"

"Jesse?" The voice sounded British.

Jesse's mind raced. "Who is this?"

"I assume I am speaking with Jesse Jonsen?"

"You can assume anything you want, I guess. Who are you and what do you want?"

"My name is Meaghan Maxwell, and I believe we met several months ago. I would like two things. First, I want to reassure you that we would never put any of our work-study associates in harm's way. We carefully select all our work-study associates because we believe they offer strong leadership qualities and we want to nurture that. But we also need the effort to make economic sense. And that's why we expect them to work in our Norra lekplatsen resort while we provide for tuition, room, and board. We believe it's a fair bargain, but we are always eager to discuss our ideas with interested parties.

"Second, I would like to invite you to tea when you arrive here, and if Leilani and Ashley want to withdraw from our program, they certainly may. However, I must insist that we cannot simply turn Ashley over to you. She is a minor and we can only release her to her parents."

Jesse's adrenaline pumped. She's lying. "Yes. I remember when we met. I've heard quite a lot about your operation, and I'd love to have some tea with you. Maybe there have been misunderstandings on all sides. If Ashley calls her parents and her parents give permission, then I'm happy to give them a ride to wherever they want. Or leave them in your care if that's what's best. Thank you for calling."

"Thank you for listening. When may we expect you?"

"I'm about an hour away."

"Fine. We'll see you when you arrive. Ask for us at the front desk and they'll direct you."

Jesse terminated the call. *This isn't good. I'm heading into a trap.* She put her phone down and forced herself to focus on the road.

~

The building looked like a Middle Age castle, with complex tan and brown brick walls, steeply sloped roofs, and long narrow windows reflecting bright sunlight. Carved on the left side was "Välkommen till vår norra lekplats, där det inte finns något som heter dåligt väder, bara fel kläder." On the right side, it said, "Welcome to our Northern Playground, where there's no such thing as bad weather, only the wrong clothes."

Jesse chuckled. *The place looks charming.* She took a deep breath and strode inside.

Jesse stopped to let her eyes adjust. A few people looked up from the front desk. A camera bubble stared at her from the ceiling.

Meaghan rose as Jesse approached her second-floor office. "Please. Come in. Ashley and Leilani are waiting."

Leilani looked away. A dark-haired young woman looked bruised.

Jesse forced a smile. "You must be Ashley."

The dark-haired girl nodded and also looked away.

Meaghan also offered a smile. "As you can see, it's been a stressful period for us. Ashley had to deal with a difficult customer, and Leilani, playing the role of older sister, quite-naturally over-reacted."

Leilani balled her hands into fists.

Jesse surveyed the scene. *There's more going on here. We need to get out. Now.* "Leilani, what happened?"

A tear ran down Leilani's eye. "I'm sorry."

"Sorry about what?"

"I'm sorry for all this. I'm sorry for everything that happened. And I'm sorry for what's going to happen."

"Don't be sorry. Let's just go. Ashley? Let's get up and walk out. They can't stop you."

Meaghan shook her head. "I'm afraid that's incorrect. I had hoped we could resolve this situation without a confrontation."

Harold, Kyle, and four other men appeared outside the office door.

Meaghan stood. "Harold, Kyle, please deal with this."

"I'd be careful if I were you." Jesse took out her phone. "I've been live-streaming." She showed her phone to everyone. "Looks like we have, what, only a couple of viewers so far. But the video will be there when the people who are watching call the police."

Meaghan nodded. "I see. Well, then, allow me to explain what is happening for your audience. Two of our employees want to terminate their association with us. Which is, of course, their right. However, one is a minor child, and neither you, nor her co-worker are her legal guardians. Absent permission from her legal guardians, I am legally bound to keep her here because her parents have entrusted us with her care. Further, we have a policy against audio and video recording in our establishment without written permission, because we must respect our guests' and employees' privacy. And, so I will ask you to turn off your livestream and delete any recording on any social media platform. If you refuse, then I must authorize our security staff to terminate your recording for you, and we will take every legal means at our disposal to remove the offending material from social media. Do I make myself clear?"

Jesse surveyed the room. Kyle had a glint in his eye. Harold stared at Jesse. So did Meaghan. Leilani and Ashley tried to make themselves small.

Jesse nodded. "Perfectly." Jesse spoke into the phone. "An Li, you know what to do." She turned her phone off. "Good luck taking down that video."

"Kyle, please confiscate her phone and search her for any other possible recording devices."

"I don't think so."

"My dear, nobody is coming to your aid." Meaghan strode out of her office. Harold followed. Leilani cowered. Ashley whimpered.

Kyle held out his hand. "Phone and purse."

"No."

"I was hoping you'd say that." Kyle punched Jesse's head. She flew across the room.

Jesse scrambled to her feet. "I promise, you will regret that. We're leaving."

Kyle blocked the door.

Kyle and his men forced Jesse, Leilani, and Ashley to the floor, zip-tied their arms behind their backs, stuffed rags into their mouths, and applied duct tape.

"Get the SUV," Kyle commanded. "These ladies are going for a ride."

~

"An Li, you know what to do." Jesse's livestream stopped. In the car just outside the resort parking lot, An Li shivered. Jesse was right. They really are monsters. And they almost got me. She dialed 911. And then the phone battery died.

~

Kyle's men carried Jesse, Leilani, and Ashley into a freight elevator to the basement and stuffed them into the back of an SUV. Kyle climbed behind the wheel.

Jesse scooted upright. Leilani and Ashley lay on their sides. Jesse tapped Leilani with her foot and signaled with her eyes to sit up. Leilani nodded.

Jesse nodded toward Ashley. Leilani tapped Ashley and Ashley also sat upright.

Great. Now what? Jesse scooted to the side and rubbed the duct tape covering her mouth against the carpet lining the SUV wall. Maybe she could peel it off.

Leilani and Ashley followed her lead.

The SUV turned out of the parking lot onto the road. Jesse craned her neck. An Li should be out there somewhere. And the police should be on their way. Forget the tape. Jesse slid to the back and kicked at the back glass as hard as she could. The others joined her. The glass shattered after a few kicks.

Kyle swore. "You'll pay for that." He fired. The bullet whizzed past Jesse's ear and out the back window. It glanced off the hood of the car behind them. Jesse squinted. It was a blue Honda Civic. Too far away to read the license plate number. But that had to be An Li. She would have seen the back glass shatter.

Now what? They couldn't jump out of a moving vehicle. Okay, wait until it stops. Jump out of the SUV, dive in with An Li, An Li floors it, everyone safe. Except, not everyone safe. Kyle shoots us.

We have to take out Kyle.

Jesse tapped Leilani and jerked her head toward Kyle. Next, she tapped Ashley and pointed with her eyes to the car following. Ashley acknowledged.

Jesse scooted up into the passenger section, behind Kyle on the driver's side. Leilani scooted into the passenger side.

Kyle raised his gun. Jesse kicked the driver's seat with everything she had. Kyle's chest flew forward. His head snapped back. The gun clattered between the seats.

Now it was Leilani's turn. She landed a kick to Kyle's head.

Kyle hit the brakes. Leilani and Jesse flew against the front seats while Ashley hurtled into the back seat.

With the SUV still rolling, Kyle reached for his gun. Jesse kicked his arm away. Leilani kicked him in the head again. Kyle's head jerked back and his chin lifted. Leilani kicked him in the chin. Kyle's left hand slipped off the steering wheel. The SUV careened off the road and into a ditch.

Bodies smashed into whatever was in front of them. Kyle's body smashed into the steering wheel. His head dented the windshield.

Leilani landed another blow. And another. Kyle's head bounced off the driver's side window. Leilani climbed into the front passenger seat. She kicked again. And again. And again. Kyle's head shattered the driver's side window and hung, limp. Leilani landed at least a dozen more kicks. Sweat drops spiraled from her head. Fire burned in her eyes.

The passenger door popped open. Leilani fell out on top of An Li.

An Li scrambled to her feet. "Jesse! Ohmygod. Let me get this off you guys!"

Jesse grunted and pointed her eyes at the gap around the center console between the seats."

"What?" An Li asked.

Jesse pointed harder with her eyes.

"Under the seat?"

Jesse nodded.

An Li fumbled under the passenger seat. "Ohmygod, what's this?" She pulled the gun out and up.

Jesse's eyes widened.

"Oh. Uh, what should I do with it." She placed it on the center console.

Jesse nodded.

An Li peeled a corner of tape from Jesse's face. "This will probably hurt." She yanked off the tape as fast as she could.

Jesse spit the rag from her mouth. "Watch out!"

An Li followed Jesse's eyes behind her. She grabbed the gun and turned. Kyle was almost on top of her. She fired.

Kyle's lifeless body fell on top of her. They crashed on top of Leilani, next to the passenger door.

An Li screamed and dropped the gun in front of the passenger seat. She pushed Kyle's body away and scrambled to her feet. Leilani pushed herself upright.

"An Li!" Jesse shouted.

"I killed him. Ohmygod, I killed him."

"An Li, you saved our lives."

An Li's eyes widened. Her hands shook. She collapsed.

"An Li, would you help get this stuff off of us? I think my dad might have a pair of pliers in the glove box." Jesse licked her lips. A faint taste of blood. "Where are the police?"

An Li rummaged through the glove box. "I found pliers."

"Good. Come get this tie wrap off me. Where are the police?"

An Li nodded. "Oh. They're not coming. My cell battery died. I couldn't call them." She sounded stoned. Probably shock.

"Oh." Jesse nodded.

An Li twisted the tie wrap from Jesse's wrist and handed the pliers to Jesse. Jesse released the other girls.

Jesse chuckled. "Your cell battery died. Don't ya hate it when that happens?"

An Li giggled. "Yeah. That's a bummer."

Jesse laughed harder. "Totally sucks."

"Murphy's law." An Li laughed even harder.

"Yep. At the worst possible time." Jesse guffawed.

Leilani and Ashley stared at Jesse and An Li, now both laughing so hard tears streamed down their eyes. Ashley tore the tape from her face.

The laughter subsided. Ashley looked up and down the empty road. "What do we do now?"

"Call 911. Kyle probably has a phone." Jesse surveyed the scene. An Li had blood all over her front. Leilani also looked disheveled and bloody. Ashley just looked disheveled. Nothing a hot shower couldn't fix. And maybe mental health counseling.

"Wait," Leilani said.

Ashley asked, "Why?"

"Because a lot of customers were cops. Maybe it's good your cell battery died. We call the cops, they find—this," Leilani waved her arm around the scene.

Ashley shrugged. "So what?"

"So, the cops arrest us."

Jesse nodded. "And finish what Kyle here started."

"So, what do we do?" An Li asked.

Jesse looked up and down the road. "We're in the middle of nowhere. Sooner or later, somebody will come looking for Kyle. Leilani's right. For our own safety, we need to disappear."

"What do we do with Kyle's body?" Leilani asked. "And the SUV?"

Jesse walked around the SUV. "Think we can get it out of this ditch?"

Leilani nodded. "Only one way to find out." She climbed into the driver's seat and started it. She put it in gear and gently nudged it onto the shoulder of the road. She climbed out and stared at Kyle's body. "Kyle's not his real name."

"I know," Jesse said.

"How do you know?"

"Because the real Kyle van Buren disappeared two years ago. This guy impersonated him. Another mystery."

A car appeared on the horizon.

"Follow my lead," Jesse said. "You guys get about 50 yards off the road and look out into those trees. You're looking for eagles. Leilani, take the gun."

It wasn't one car. It was three cars.

"Here we go." Jesse peered into the trees.

The cars slowed. The third one stopped. The driver was a man. Mid-thirties. Brown hair. "You guys okay?"

Jesse turned and smiled. "Oh—just fine. We saw some eagles and we're looking for the nest."

The driver nodded toward the SUV. "Something's leaking out of your SUV."

Jesse glanced at it. "Um. Oh." Greenish fluid dripped underneath.

"Here. Let me take a look. I'm a mechanic. Bill." He stepped out of his car.

"Nice to meet you, Bill. Je—um, Jilene."

"Who are your friends?"

"Um, Leila, Mary, and Margaret." The girls waved.

Bill swiped a finger through the fluid under the SUV. He smelled it. "Yep, that's antifreeze. Better get that thing into a shop before it overheats and dies."

"Oh. Good idea."

"Follow me. I have a shop just a few miles away, and we can take a look at it there."

"Thanks. That's okay. I think I'll try to get it home."

"Where's home?"

Oh crap. "Um, Little Falls?"

"That's forty miles away. You won't make it. Really, your best bet is my shop. Tell ya what. I won't even charge you for labor. But I can't just leave you stranded here like this."

Jesse nodded. "Okay, thanks. Let me tell my friends. They'll follow us in their car."

Jesse stepped toward the trees.

Bill followed a few steps behind.

Jesse turned. "Be right back. Just wait there."

"Where did you see those eagles?" Bill took a few more steps.

"Really. Just wait right there."

"Why?" The tire prints in the ditch came into view. Bill acknowledged Kyle's body, now visible next to the passenger side of the SUV. "Jilene? Want to tell me what's really going on?"

40.   Uncle Andy

Sitting in her office chair, Meaghan adjusted her telephone headset and squeezed her eyes shut. She swore silently.

"Anders, I assure you, we have the situation well under control."

"No, you do not. All our expansion efforts depend on you managing the property that I delegated to you. And your operation is far from smooth."

Meaghan cringed. "I acknowledge that we've had challenges beyond our control that none of us could have anticipated. But my staff and I are constantly recruiting new talent, and we expect today's uncomfortable situation to resolve itself very soon."

"By dumping more dead bodies in the Mississippi River to wash up against a dam? Are you aware of the science around decomposing bodies in river water?"

"I gave explicit instructions to dispose of these bodies below that dam. The next dam in Anoka is well over one hundred miles away and much larger. Decomposing bodies won't be an issue this time."

"Murdering more people and dumping their bodies in a river will not solve your problems. These bodies present enormous risk. And unlike your last victim, these people have families and friends. How will you respond when they start asking questions?"

Meaghan massaged her temples. "I will simply tell the truth. They left, never to be heard from again."

"This Jesse traveled in a car from the Twin Cities to the property, did she not?"

"Yes. I spoke to her in-route."

"So, presumably she left a vehicle in the parking lot. How will you dispose of it?"

"I've not had the opportunity yet to study the security footage. But surely, we can find her vehicle and implement appropriate measures."

"Countless variables. Your actions create too many decision-tree potential outcomes to properly model."

Meaghan stood. "Anders, what would you have me do? I could not let them simply leave."

"I hired you for your ability to persuade. Use it. We're trying to rescue a dying world from itself and we need to raise significant funds to accomplish that task. Therefore, we must show potential investors our economic value. You must constantly make your staff aware of our larger mission and of the education we provide in exchange for their labor. This is more than a fair bargain."

"I am well aware of all this, Anders, and I work tirelessly to implement your vision. A vision with which I whole-heartedly agree, by the way."

"But you've created a condition that increases the probability of a negative outcome. You must remedy that risk."

Meaghan sat. "How do you suggest I do that?"

"I leave those details in your capable hands. Obviously, individual sacrifice is necessary to enable the greater good, but further escalating this situation increases the risk to our mission."

Meaghan shivered. "Thank you for your counsel. I know how to proceed."

"You've made great strides. The world will one day thank us."

41.   Escape

Bill drew his weapon and flashed a police badge. "I'm a police officer. You ladies are not bird watching."

Jesse shook her head. "Bill, this is not what it looks like."

"Right now, I don't care what it looks like. I'm calling for help and then we'll straighten this all out. You will all sit tight."

Bill reached for a phone in his pocket.

Jesse stepped toward him.

Bill raised his gun. "Don't even think about it."

Ashley, An Li, and Leilani approached from the trees on Jesse's right. Jesse stepped to her left, toward the SUV. She just needed to distract him for a second. Timing would be critical.

Leilani's eyes widened. "I know you."

"You don't look familiar. Where do you know me from?"

"Last Friday. You were a customer at Norra lekplatsen.."

Bill's face changed color.

Jesse's jaw dropped. "Wait—this guy was your customer?"

"And a few of his friends too. Some kind of celebration."

"You're kidding me." Jesse glanced at Leilani.

Leilani nodded.

Jesse stepped closer to the SUV. "Hey Bill."

Bill turned his head toward Jesse. Leilani lifted Kyle's gun.

Jesse smiled. "Looks like we have a stalemate."

Bill's expression went cold. "Drop the gun or die."

Leilani aimed. "You'll also be dead. One scumbag is already dead."

Bill lifted his gun.

Jesse glanced at Leilani. "But we don't want any more dead people. Right?"

Leilani's hands shook. "Right."

Jesse moved toward Leilani. "Hand me the gun."

Leilani handed the gun to Jesse. Bill lunged. Leilani and Jesse sprang away in opposite directions.

Bill veered toward Jesse.

Jesse fired into the dirt in front of Bill's feet. Bill stopped.

Jesse raised the gun with both arms. "The next one goes inside you. You'd better hope it misses anything important."

Bill slowly lowered his weapon.

Jesse nodded. "Good. Nobody else needs to get hurt today. We did not murder this scumbag. He tried to kill us and we defended ourselves. And you know what? You paid this guy."

Bill gestured with his head toward Kyle's body. "If he's such a scumbag, why do you do what you do? I didn't see anyone holding a gun to your heads."

Leilani collapsed and bawled. Ashley and An Li comforted her.

Jesse shook her head. "Because these guys are master manipulators. They suck these girls in by offering whatever they want, and once they get sucked in, they're prisoners. You helped support a human trafficking ring."

"That's not the way I heard it. The way I heard it is, they get a college education in return for a little fun every weekend. Doesn't sound like a bad deal to me."

Ashley looked up. "Fun? Is that what you call it when some fat drunk beats me up and tries to kill me? And then they tell me it's my fault? And it's not just weekends. It's every night. Sometimes a dozen guys. Every single night."

Jesse cocked her head. "We want to leave now and report this to the state police. But we have a problem. What do we do about you?"

Bill's eyes narrowed. "Walk away. We both just walk away. I didn't see you. You didn't see me."

Jesse shook her head. "But maybe you already called somebody. Maybe they're on their way right now. Let's see your recent calls."

"You want my phone?"

"And your keys. And your gun.'

"That doesn't leave me in a good spot."

"You should have thought about that last Friday night."

Bill bowed his head.

"We can tie you up and bring you with us and drop you in the middle of nowhere if you want. Or we can shoot you. Maybe we'll write a message on your dead body about what happens to people who help human traffickers. Which do you like better?"

Bill shook his head and pulled out his phone.

"Bring up your recent calls and set your phone down on the ground. Set your keys and gun with it, and then step away."

Bill complied.

Jesse picked them up and handed them to Ashley. "Who did he call?"

"I see an area code two-one-eight number at 10:47 a.m. About fifteen minutes ago."

"Who does that number belong to?" Jesse said.

246

Bill nodded. "A repair shop. I called them when I saw your antifreeze dripping."

"You're lying. But it doesn't matter. We're running out of time." Jesse turned to Ashley. "Put everything in his car and lock it."

"Wait a minute." Bill stepped toward Ashley.

Jesse raised the gun. Bill stopped.

"Head back into those trees. Don't turn back until you can't see through the trees anymore. If you do, we'll let the air out of your tires."

Bill stared.

"Get moving. Jog, don't walk. Hurry up."

Bill turned toward the trees and jogged.

Jesse watched Bill jog away for a few seconds. "Lock his stuff in his car."

An Li asked, "Wait. What about his phone?"

"Somebody will stop. He'll flag them down and call for help."

"Do we really want somebody else to stop and see this?"

"What difference does it make? Somebody's gonna see all this sooner or later anyway."

"But if we give Bill a chance to use his own phone, he can get help and leave before anyone else sees this. Otherwise, he has to explain to somebody how he got into this mess."

Jesse nodded. "You have a point. Put his phone under his windshield wipers. Lock everything else in his car." Bill disappeared into the trees. "Let's go home."

They piled into Jesse's parents' Honda Civic. Jesse drove, leaving Kyle's body, the SUV, and Bill and his car behind.

42.   1995—Thanksgiving Break

November, 1995. Itasca County Girls Group Home, Big Fork, Minnesota.

Jesse's parents were waiting after school to bring her home for Thanksgiving. Dad must have taken time off his precious work.

Dad had his usual fake questions on the trip home. "How do you like your school?"

"It's fine."

"What are they teaching you?"

"Stuff."

"What stuff?"

"Just stuff, all right?" Why is he so nosy?

Mom started with her "you're my baby" speech Jesse had heard a million times. "Jesse, we care about you. Your father only asked about your schooling."

"My schooling was fine at home. You sent me away."

"But Jesse, the judge gave you a choice and we talked about it."

"You should have hired a better lawyer."

Jesse's bed felt wonderful. The sheets and stuffed animals were exactly where they belonged. But she needed to talk to Dylan. After midnight, she sneaked into the kitchen and dialed his number.

"I missed you."

"Me too. But listen, can you call me in a couple hours? I'm right in the middle of something right now."

"Dylan, I want to move in with you. I don't want to go back to Bigfork."

"Um, okay, that's cool. But let's talk about it in a couple hours, okay?"

"Okay, sure."

Something felt funny. Jesse padded to the kitchen and replaced the phone. Five minutes later, she was asleep. She woke up at 5 a.m. when the family cat jumped on her bed. She called Dylan.

He answered after several rings. "Oh, hey baby. I was asleep."

"I'm sorry, I fell asleep too. What do you think about me moving in with you?"

"Um, that might not be a good idea right now. You're not eighteen yet, are you?"

"You know when my birthday is."

"Oh, yeah. But listen, we could both get in big trouble. But I have something else we can work on together."

"What?"

"Well, tomorrow is Black Friday, and all the stores will be packed. What say you grab me some inventory tomorrow and maybe we'll celebrate tomorrow night. We never went to that movie the last time."

"I don't know if I can do that. My parents are watching me pretty closely. And if I get caught, I could go to jail."

"Yeah, okay. Well, maybe call me Saturday or Sunday before you go back."

"Dylan, my friend, Candy, and her boyfriend died. They used the IDs to buy vodka and they died in a car accident."

"Who's Candy?"

"You don't remember? Candy Smith. You made IDs for her and her friends a couple weeks ago. I don't know what to do. I sold those IDs to them."

"Don't worry about it. Who's gonna find out?"

"Nobody, I guess. But maybe not. Her boyfriend died with her, but his friends still have theirs."

"Think you could sell some more?"

"Dylan!"

"Baby, that's one of the things I like about you; you're resourceful."

"I can't sell more IDs up there. Ethan's dead and he had the cell phone."

"Listen, baby, I gotta go. Long day coming up and then it's Black Friday. I'm in kind of a jam myself and I have to pay back some investors. You know how it goes."

Jesse blinked back tears. "Okay. Bye Dylan." She replaced the phone and cried herself back to sleep.

~

Back in school in Bigfork Monday, Ms. Inglebertsen asked all the students to write an essay about their Thanksgiving breaks and what they were thankful for. Which was the last thing Jesse wanted to do. How could she be thankful for anything? Her roommate was dead, her boyfriend had turned into a jerk, her parents were idiots, and she was stuck in Big Butthole, Minnesota, in a special-ed class with a bunch of ditzy girl convicts.

Why does somebody live in the middle of nowhere and teach English to a bunch of special-ed girls anyway? Jesse finished her essay and turned it in.

Ms. Inglebertsen handed the essays back the next day. She asked Jesse to see her after class.

"You wanted to see me?"

"Yes, Jesse, why are you angry?"

"I'm not angry."

"Your writing suggests differently. I spoke with Mrs. Adams about your roommate, Nadine, and I want you to know, we all feel a sense of loss when somebody close to us passes."

Jesse laughed. "You think I'm mad because Candy died?"

"I can't give you credit for this essay, because you didn't address my question about what you're thankful for. But you're a good writer and I'll honor what you wrote. So, instead of giving me an essay full of BS, I want you to write an essay about your roommate and how her death affected you."

Jesse stepped back. "You're kidding, right?"

"No, I'm not. I think you have a story to tell, and I'm offering you an opportunity to tell it. What I don't know is, are you up to the challenge?"

Jesse smiled. "You're trying some psychology trick on me, aren't you?"

Ms. Inglebertsen shrugged. "Maybe. I also suspect you're angry about Candy's death, and maybe writing this essay will help you come to terms with it. Writing helped me when our neighbor died on the Edmund Fitzgerald."

"What makes you think I'm angry?"

"Your reaction to my assignment, for one. And anger is also one of the stages of grief."

Jesse looked down. "What about you?"

"What about me?"

"Why do you do this?"

"Do what?"

"Why do you teach special-ed English to the girls from Itasca Group home?"

Ms. Inglebertsen nodded. "That's a great question. After that ride on the Edmund Fitzgerald I never took, I made some choices I shouldn't have. Then God stepped in, and now I think He wants me here."

"I figured you might be one of those religious nuts."

Ms. Inglebertsen laughed. "Well, I've been called worse. But yes, I'm a walking, talking Christian and I believe everything in the Bible is true."

"So, why not just go hang out in a shopping mall and hand out feel-good stories?"

"There aren't any shopping malls in Bigfork."

"You know what I mean. You could do it on a street corner here."

"I don't need to. I can teach you to write your own feel-good stories."

Jesse smiled. "That's pretty good. You got me there."

"I want to see your essay tomorrow."

"All right. I'll do your essay. But only if you tell me more about why you're here."

"That's a good bargain."

Jesse worked that night in her room. Of course, she was mad. Candy was dead. Dylan was a snake. Her parents had sent her away. And she was stuck up here in North Butthole with a house full of misfits.

And how could Candy be dead? Jesse fought tears, but the tears won. She couldn't write why she was really mad. She'd have to make up something that sounded good. It was playing with fire, talking to Ms. Inglebertsen.

~

Ms. Inglebertsen made Jesse stay after class again. "Okay, you're mad about Candy's death. Why?"

"I wrote it down in my essay. I miss her, okay?"

"Why do you miss her?"

"Because she was my roommate."

"Were you two close?

"Not really."

"Well, then why do you miss her?"

"I just do, okay?"

"I think there's more."

"Well, there's not."

Ms. Inglebertsen cocked her head. "Jesse, where did she and Ethan get the fake IDs?"

"How should I know?"

"I think you do, and you're feeling guilty."

"Can I go now?"

"Yes. But I want you to think about how you feel. And dig really deep. Your own life might depend on it."

~

Mrs. Adams met her off the school bus. "Jesse, please come with me to my office."

A man was waiting. Mrs. Adams walked around behind her desk. "Jesse, this is Detective Higgins from the Grand Rapids police. Please, have a seat."

Detective Higgins started. "Jesse, Mrs. Adams and I have been talking about Nadine Ladysmith's death. You know we found fake IDs in the car. We just got Ethan's cell phone records, and they show several calls to a Minneapolis number. You were her roommate. We were wondering if this number was familiar to you."

It was Dylan's number. Jesse's heart raced. "Um, no."

Mrs. Adams and Detective Higgins exchanged glances.

Detective Higgins said, "Okay. Anything you can recall might be helpful. We need to get to the bottom of what happened for both of their families."

Jesse padded to her room and closed the door. She threw herself on her bed and bawled.

Somebody knocked on her door. It was Mrs. Adams. "May I come in?"

"I need to be alone for a while."

"Jesse, please unlock this door and let me in. Or I'll unlock it myself."

Jesse trudged to the door and unlocked it. "Can't you just leave me alone?"

Mrs. Adams walked in and sat on Candy's bed. "Jesse, two people are dead and we need your help to figure out why. You're not in trouble, but if you know something, then you need to share it. If you don't share what you know, and the police find out another way, you could be in big trouble. I don't want to see that. You might not think so right now, but you have a lot to offer the world. I want to see you blossom and offer it. That's why you're here and not in a juvenile detention center."

"I don't know anything, okay!"

"I think you do."

"Will everyone please just leave me alone?"

Mrs. Adams stood. "You know how to find my office. Or if you want to talk to Ms. Inglebertsen this week, that's okay too." She left.

43.   On the Run

Sunday, Sept. 30, 2018, afternoon

A hammer pounded inside Jesse's head.

Leilani's voice from the passenger seat. "Jesse?"

Jesse jumped.

"Pull over. You don't look good."

"My head hurts. I feel woozy."

"You probably have a concussion," Ashley said from the back seat.

"Pull over. I can drive," An Li said.

Jesse pulled over. She leaned back in her seat and put her hands to her head.

An Li opened the driver's side door. "Let me help you."

Jesse staggered to her feet. The world spun. She dry-heaved and collapsed into An Li's arms.

Somebody placed Jesse onto the back seat. "Ashley, keep her awake." An Li's voice was in a tunnel.

Ashley closed her fingers around Jesse's hand.

"Jesse, you look white," Leilani said.

Jesse giggled. "I am white. You look red."

Leilani laughed. "Very funny. And it's brown. We need a doctor."

An Li pulled back onto the road.

"Um, Jesse, where did you go to high school?" Ashley said.

"A couple of places."

"Did you move or what?"

"Why are you asking me this?"

"I'm supposed to keep you awake. What's your favorite color?"

"Dunno."

"Well, okay, what's your favorite food?"

"You're not very good at this, are you?" Jesse said.

"Shut up. And stay awake."

Jesse laughed. A sledgehammer pounded her brain.

"Turn here," Leilani said.

"That's not the way home," An Li said.

"I know. I might know somebody who can help."

Ashley shook Jesse. "Wake up." Jesse's eyes popped open.

"Listen," Leilani said. "My family lives near here. Let's go to them for help."

Jesse nodded. Another hammer pounded right above her eyes. She rubbed her eyes.

"Hang on Jesse." Ashley's voice grated in Jesse's ear.

44.   Cover

With one arm to the phone in her ear, Meaghan gestured to Harold with her other arm. "Officer Rasmussen, thank you for bringing this to our attention. Have you called anyone else?"

"No. I called you first."

"Excellent. I must emphasize, that given our unique relationship, discretion is the best choice in this matter. The man you describe was one of our own."

"But—"

"Officer Rasmussen, we gladly extended our hospitality to you and members of your department last Friday. And now, one of our valued staff members lies dead in a field and you are locked out of your car. For your protection and ours, I strongly urge you to not publicize this situation."

"Yeah, I see your point."

"We're gathering a team right now to help you. They should arrive at your location shortly."

Meaghan muted her phone and turned to Harold. "Handle this personally."

"You'll have to give me a ride out there."

Meaghan nodded and unmuted her phone. "Stay on with me until we arrive."

~

The man was an incessant chatterbox. How does somebody this mentally deficient become a law enforcement officer? They crested a hill and she pointed to him about a quarter-mile away.

Harold acknowledged her.

Harold parked behind the SUV, retrieved his tools, and exited.

The officer shook Harold's hand. Decent of him.

"What happened?" Harold asked.

"It's embarrassing. At first, I didn't know there were three of them. One trained a gun on me. And then they took my gun and locked it in the car."

"Yeah, that is embarrassing," Harold said. "Help me get this body in the truck."

They hefted Kyle's body up and into the truck bed and moved to the officer's car.

Harold glanced inside. "Is that your gun on the passenger seat?"

"Yeah, it is." The officer looked embarrassed. Understandable, since somehow three women who couldn't lift anything but their dresses somehow took it away from him.

"Give me just a minute." Harold put on rubber gloves.

"What are those for?"

"I don't want to scratch your car." Harold inserted his air wedge between the passenger door and car frame, pumped it full of air, and slid his tool inside. He made quick work of the lock, let the air out of the wedge, and opened the door.

"Thanks, man. I really appreciate this."

Meaghan smiled. "As we discussed—"

The officer turned his attention to Meaghan.

"—we'll keep this embarrassing incident to ourselves. And you say, one of them had their hands on your gun?"

"Yeah. And you're right, I sure don't need anyone—"

"Bill," Harold called.

The officer turned toward Harold. "Huh?"

Harold fired the officer's gun.

A clean shot through his heart. The officer dropped. The fool. Such a waste. But it had to be done.

"You'll dispose of Kyle's body?"

"Yeah. Let me get the tarp over the truck bed."

"Below the Little Falls Dam this time."

"Of course."

"I'll bring the SUV back to Norra lekplatsen. We need to inform Anders."

45. Concussion

The Onamia, MN. ER doctor lifted her finger in front of Jesse's eyes. "Follow my finger." She drew an X.

Jesse followed with her eyes. "That gives me a headache."

"Okay, now spell world backwards."

Jesse focused on the doctor's face. "You have brown eyes."

The doctor smiled. "Yes, I do. But spell world backwards for me."

Jesse blinked a few times. "Um, worl—D—it starts, I mean ends, with a D. Um, R, EL, um, wa, um W. Right?"

Ashley, An Li, and Leilani exchanged glances with the doctor.

"What?"

"Jesse, you have a concussion. Do you feel like you're in a brain fog?"

"Yeah. That's a good way to describe it. Like something ground my thoughts together in a blender."

The doctor nodded. "You said that guy knocked you across a room?"

Ashley said, "Like a rag doll. I thought he'd killed her for a second."

Jesse yawned. "Can I go to sleep?"

Leilani shook her head. "No."

The doctor also shook her head. "No, it's okay. People with concussions can sleep. If that's what your body tells you it needs, then listen. Get some quiet rest. Preferably in a dark room so you don't aggravate that headache. We call it relative rest, which means no heavy exertion for at least a few days. And quiet is good. Take naps when you need them. Don't drive until your headaches get better."

~

An Li parked in front of a small, white, stucco house. Somebody inside peeked around the closed curtain in the front window.

Leilani exited the car and trudged up the driveway. Grass grew through cracks in the concrete. She stepped up to a concrete porch that may have been level fifty years ago. She knocked on the outside door. The inside door opened a crack. A pair of eyes peered out. The eyes focused on the car and then moved back to Leilani.

The door opened wider. An older Native American woman stood behind the glass storm door. She opened it and stepped outside. Leilani hugged her. She wrapped her arms around Leilani and sobbed.

They broke their embrace and spoke. Leilani motioned for them to come up.

"Jesse, An Li, Ashley, this is my mother, Dyani. May we come in?"

~

Dyani looked over Jesse, An Li, and Ashley. "That's quite a story. Have you reported it yet?"

Jesse put her hand over her eyes. "The only phone we have needs to charge. So, no."

An Li nodded. "Is it okay if I charge my phone? And do you have a cable and charging brick?"

Dyani nodded. "Right over there. I haven't seen you in four years, and now you and your new friends show up here,

261

covered in blood, with a wild story about why you killed somebody. Maybe I should report you."

Another knife stabbed behind Jesse's eyes. She grimaced. "Mrs. Berg—"

"Berg is our White name. Our Anishinaabe name is Bravebird."

Leilani shook her head. "Nimama, they don't know our words." She turned to Jesse. "We are the Mille Lacs band of Ojibwe, part of the Anishinaabe."

Dyani stood. "You left your people and your home for that White resort. I told you no good would come of it."

"I had no choice. And you know it."

"I would not have allowed anyone to harm you."

"Is Wematin still alive?"

"No."

"How did he die?"

"He was drunk. He had a car accident with a train."

"But his family still owns this house."

"Yes."

"Then, harm to me is not what you should worry about."

Jesse's head throbbed. "Wait. I'm confused."

Leilani nodded. She looked down and wiped her eyes. She focused on Dyani. "They deserve to know. We risked our lives together. And we killed to save ourselves from being killed."

Dyani nodded.

Leilani turned to Jesse. "Wematin and I grew up together. His family is powerful in our community. But he found whiskey and when we were sixteen, he became a drunken fool. His father covered for him. I wanted us to go to college together, to make something of ourselves. But he wouldn't listen. And then he raped me."

"Oh, Leilani, I am so sorry," Ashley said.

Leilani took a breath. "Do not be sorry. You helped me escape. You fought your attacker. I didn't. I should apologize to you. You made me realize I don't need to be anyone's slave. After Wematin raped me, his family turned me into an outcast."

"No they did not," Dyani said. "All you had to do was apologize for putting Wematin into that position. And then all would have been forgotten."

"What?" An Li said. "In your culture, is rape the woman's fault?"

"It's not the woman's fault in any culture." Jesse said.

Dyani shook her head. "It is the woman's fault when she prances around and lures him and then calls it rape."

"Nimama, I don't want to fight. It makes no difference whose fault it was. I knew I had to leave before Wematin's family made life miserable for you."

"What?"

"Wematin's father threatened to evict you unless I publicly apologized to Wematin. Instead, I offered to leave. I filled out an application to attend NPU. Landon approached me and offered to help me pay for college with the NPU work study program. He was charming. He took me to dinner. He bought me gifts. And he took me to his bed. And then later, after the real Professor Kyle Van Buren left, he told me his new name was Kyle. I didn't know why until I realized, he probably took Professor Van Buren's life."

Jesse grimaced. "Wait a minute. Who's Landon?"

"Landon is, was, Kyle's real name."

Ashley's jaw dropped. "Wait a minute. Kyle, the guy who went to Florida with me and got drunk? The guy who tried to kill us? That's not his real name?"

"No. His real name is Landon Miller. And I loved him because I thought he rescued me from Wematin and the situation here. And then I hated him when I realized I only traded one form of slavery for a worse form. And then I helped kill him before he could kill me." Leilani tried to cover her shaking hands. "Nimama, I did not lure Wematin. He was drunk and I tried to help him into his bed. He attacked me with a knife to my throat."

Leilani sobbed.

Dyani stood. "Indaanis, I am so sorry. My heart ached for you when you were gone. I love you more than life itself."

Leilani stood. They embraced.

Jesse's head throbbed. She covered her eyes. "But why did Landon Miller kill Kyle Van Buren and then take his name?"

Leilani and Dyani broke their embrace. Leilani wiped her eyes. "Because of me."

"How?"

"Professor Van Buren asked us to write essays about something in our lives we wanted to change."

"And so, you—"

"I wrote about my life. I said I wanted to be normal."

"So, how did Landon find out about it?"

"I don't know. I wrote the paper on my school laptop and then emailed it. Landon confronted me, and then Professor Van Buren disappeared at the end of the semester."

Jesse nodded. "He was inside your email. And probably also inside your laptop."

"They can do that?"

"I have a friend who could make your head spin with all the technology things they can do. So, why take Professor Van Buren's name?"

"To taunt me. He said he wanted to remind me about what happens to people who cross them."

"That guy was sick."

Ashley nodded. "He gave me the creeps."

"And we killed him," An Li said. "What do we do now?"

"By now, Bill probably has the police looking for us. We need to wait until after dark to go home," Jesse said. "Mrs. Berg, or, sorry, Mrs. Bravebird, is there someplace we can hide the car until dark while we charge An Li's phone? And may we use your phone?"

"You have to report this," Dyani said.

"I know. And we will. But first, I'm calling Dominic Levenson."

"Who is Dominic Levenson?" Dyani asked.

"My attorney. Dominic and another guy I know are going to help us expose this whole operation."

~

In the car on the way home, An Li's phone rang. Ashley answered. It was for Jesse. Ashley handed her the phone.

Jesse averted her eyes from oncoming headlights. Even the glow from An Li's phone made her head hurt. "Hello?"

It was Jesse's mother. "Jesse, don't come home. Somebody murdered that police officer you told us about and the police are here to arrest you."

"What?"

"I can't stay on much longer. I'm upstairs. They think I'm looking for your picture. They don't know you moved out but it won't take them long to figure it out."

"They?"

"The police are here, looking for you."

"But wait. Bill's dead?"

"Officer William Rasmussen. They say your fingerprints are on the gun."

"Mom, we locked him out of his car and made him walk back to the woods to give us time to drive away."

"I believe you, honey. Listen, I have to go."

"I love you, Mom. And Dad too."

"We love you too."

Jesse terminated the call.

"What?" Ashley asked.

"Somebody murdered Bill."

"I'll bet it was Meaghan or Harold," Leilani said.

Jesse nodded. "Yep." She took a couple of deep breaths and then dialed again.

"Hello, this is Jerry Barkley."

46. Hiding

From inside Jerry Barkley's house on a cul-de-sac, a dog sounded like it wanted to eat them as its next meal.

"Are you sure about this?" Ashley asked.

Jesse smiled. And grimaced. "Jerry's family likes animals. I'm sure it's harmless."

An Li stepped out of the car. The front door to the house opened and a large black Labrador bounded out. An Li jumped back into the car. The dog lifted its paws to the car window and panted.

"Um, nice doggy?" An Li said.

The dog woofed. Slobber drops smacked the car window in front of An Li's face.

Jerry Barkley made his way out to the car. "Maddie, get down." He chuckled. "Just let her smell you and she'll be fine. She loves humans. I heard you guys had quite the adventure. I'm Jerry."

An Li, Ashley, and Leilani introduced themselves.

Jerry gestured to the open garage. "Put the car inside and I'll close the door. You're safe here. If you like dog kisses, Maddie has the fastest tongue in the Midwest." He paused. "Oh—I should have asked this before. Is anyone allergic to cats?"

They all glanced at Jerry and then back at each other. "No."

"Okay, good. Put your car away and I'll help you unload."

~

Lynn Barkley collected cups from everyone seated in the living room.

"Here, let me help you with that." Jesse stood and a cat jumped off her lap. Scissors stabbed the inside of her head. She grimaced.

Lynn set a handful of dirty cups on the kitchen counter. "I've got it. But I have to be at work at 6:30 in the morning and I need to get some sleep. Jerry, I need your help with something upstairs."

Jerry nodded. "I'll be right back. Help yourself to whatever's in the refrigerator. Or the pantry. Or whatever." He trudged up the stairs behind Lynn.

"What do you think she wants?" Leilani asked.

"She's probably worried. His daughter and two grandsons also live here," Jesse said.

Jerry returned a few minutes later.

Jesse lifted her head. "Jerry, I'm sorry we're doing this to you. I wouldn't have called if there was any other option."

"Can Gloria help?"

"She'll be back from her trip tomorrow."

"Jesse, you know I'll do what I can to help you. And Lynn is onboard too. But you're wanted for murdering a police officer. You can't run. And you can't stay here forever."

"I know. We all know. Jerry, we didn't murder anyone. Let me tell you about my day."

Jesse brought Jerry up to speed. An Li, Ashley, and Leilani filled in details.

Jerry intertwined his fingers behind his head. "So, how did the police officer—Bill? How did he die?"

"We don't know. My mom called and said the police are looking for us. That's how we found out he died."

"Do they think you did it?"

"Probably."

"I wonder if anything's online." Jerry took out his phone and searched for articles. "Here's one from WCCO TV. It says they want you as a person of interest."

"They don't go to your parents' house to find you if you're a person of interest. Jerry, they think I did it."

Jerry nodded. "Yeah, you're right."

Leilani leaned forward. "Meaghan and Harold probably did it."

Ashley shook her head. "I'd believe Meaghan. But not Harold. He's not a killer."

Leilani rubbed her eyes. "Yes, he is, Ashley. He groomed you the same as Landon groomed me. He was there when Kyle and his guys kidnapped us."

"But he left."

"So did Meaghan. Did he try to stop them?"

"No. But how could he? He wasn't there."

"Meaghan told Kyle and his goons to kidnap us. And then Harold left with her. If he loved you so much, why didn't he protest? Ashley, he's part of it."

Ashley flopped back in her chair. "No. He loves me." Tears formed in her eyes. She put her head in her hands.

"Wait a minute," Jesse said. "Ashley, you said earlier that you went to Florida with Kyle. Or Landon. Or whatever his name was. What happened on that trip?"

Ashley lifted her head. "They were by the Everglades. They had a nice restaurant and hotel, just like Norra lekplatsen. And some Congressman hurt me. I gave him a black eye. And then we came home. Why?"

"Are you thinking, there's more than one resort?" Jerry asked.

Jesse nodded. "Yeah. It makes sense, doesn't it? Why else would they fly Ashley down there?"

Ashley folded her arms against her stomach. "You're saying I was a piece of meat?"

Leilani nodded. "Yeah."

More tears formed in Ashley's eyes. "I was so stupid. Harold probably doesn't know. Meaghan's probably keeping it from him."

Leilani shook her head. "We all were stupid. And Harold worked on you the same way Kyle worked on me."

An Li shook her head. "They almost got me. I was stupid too."

"Jerry, we have to stop them. Nobody else is gonna do it," Jesse said.

Jerry strummed his knee. "I wonder what their revenue stream looks like. Ashley, how full was that restaurant every night?"

"There were never many people there. But the last few weeks, I didn't see much of the restaurant. I was always in a hotel room. Harold kept telling me we needed to make sacrifices for our future."

Leilani sighed. "Yeah, I heard that from Landon, too, at first. But after he took Kyle's name, he didn't even bother with that. He just beat me every time he didn't like something."

"Maybe there's more online." Jerry continued searching.

Jesse grimaced again. "Why would they think I did it?"

An Li's eyes widened. "Your fingerprints. You held the gun."

Jerry nodded. "And they have your fingerprints on file from the embezzlement case."

"They'll want all of us," Jesse said.

Jerry looked up after a few minutes. "Here's something. It's a PBS video about Earth Day and a guy named Anders Nordqvist. He's big into ecology and he operates a bunch of resorts with a Swedish brand name, Lekplats, that means, playground. The transcript says he gave away a bunch of tree saplings. I'll play the video."

The video opened with a female narrator. "In honor of Earth Day, we're here, somewhere in northern Minnesota, talking to Anders, 'Uncle Andy' Nordqvist about the Marceau experimental forest."

She waved her arm and the camera followed to a sea of pine and birch trees. The camera panned back to Anders, standing next to the interviewer in front of a large, round glass structure.

"Anders—", she started.

"Please, call me Andy. Or 'Uncle Andy' if you prefer."

"Pause it." Ashley pointed to Anders's image. "I know that guy."

Leilani nodded. "I do too. Landon told me he's an investor."

"I saw him in Florida in one of the crowds," Ashley said. "He eyeballed me. Gave me the creeps."

"Let's see what we can find out about this guy." Jerry searched more websites. "Graduated from MIT, made a fortune on Wall Street, and started his eco-tourism business a few years ago."

"So, he's rich and smart," Jesse said.

Jerry nodded. "The video mentions a website." He opened another browser tab. "Bingo. Resorts in Minnesota, Florida, and Arizona, with more coming in Iceland, Denmark, Sweden, and Italy. And more in Asia. He's gotta have partners to grow that fast."

"And they all like to sample the goods," Ashley said.

"How do we fight this?" An Li asked. "Especially from jail?"

Jesse turned to Jerry. "Remember Project Lemonade with Bullseye Stores?"

Jerry smiled. "Yeah. I still have the scripts."

"Project Lemonade?" An Li asked.

Jesse nodded. "Bullseye Stores was sending stolen credit card numbers to Russia. After Jerry figured out what was going on, I suggested sending fake numbers for a few days."

Jerry chuckled. "We poisoned the lemonade. Because when life gives you lemons—"

"How does that help us here?" Leilani asked.

Jerry's eyes twinkled. "We need to find out what their lemonade looks like, so we can poison it."

Jesse rubbed her forehead. "And we need to do it from jail because bail will probably be more money than any of us have."

An Li stood. "So, the five of us are going to stop this whole operation from jail?"

"I might know somebody who can help with the jail part," Jerry said. "The FBI owes me a favor."

"I don't get it," Leilani said.

Jesse nodded. And grimaced another time. "Jerry stopped a terrorist group from infecting the whole country with Ebola a couple years ago."

Jerry shook his head. "I didn't do it alone. And that's not for public consumption. They didn't catch everyone from that group. But maybe the FBI will return my phone calls now."

47.   Cop Killer

Monday, October 1, 2018

Jesse and the others finished their breakfast at Jerry Barkley's dining room table.

Jesse finished her eggs. "Jerry, when was the last time you guys talked?"

"It's been a while."

"And now you're just gonna call him right out of the blue?"

"He'll talk to me."

"This is a longshot, Jerry. And it's risky."

Jerry nodded. "I know. You want me to not call him?"

"No. We need to try."

Jerry put his phone on speaker and dialed.

FBI Supervisory Special Agent Jake Channing answered. "Jerry Barkley. Been a long time."

"Agent Channing. I see they promoted you. How are you?"

"Jake. I told you back then, after what we went through together, call me Jake."

"Right—Jake. I'm still sorry about what happened."

"It wasn't your fault."

"I'm still sorry."

"Jerry, a lot of people are alive because of what you did. Focus on that. You aren't getting weird thoughts in your head, are you?

Ashley, Leilani, and An Li glanced at each other. Jesse nodded.

Jerry chuckled. "I still have PTSD episodes, if that's what you mean. But I'm not calling for therapy about the past. I need your help with something new today."

"Trouble seems to find you, doesn't it?"

"Yeah, something like that. But this time it's not for me, it's for a friend. She uncovered a human trafficking ring, somebody murdered a Mille Lacs County cop, and they think she did it. But this cop died a few days after he and a bunch of others in his department spent Friday night partying at the Norra lekplatsen resort up on Mille Lacs Lake. She didn't do it.

"By, partying, you mean—"

"Yeah. My friend and her friend rescued two of them."

"Sometimes hookers do it because they want to. You got any evidence?"

"I have their stories. And Jesse and I go back a long time."

"Oh, yeah?"

"Not like that. She brought me in as a contractor when we put a dent in that credit card ring that stole those 40 million credit cards from Bullseye Stores back in 2013."

"You're talking about Jesse Jonsen?"

"Do you know her?"

"She's wanted for killing a cop. It's probably going out on the TV News today. If you know where she is, you need to tell me right now."

Jerry swallowed hard. "Um, that's the thing. I was hoping the FBI could take her into custody instead of Mille Lacs County and keep her safe."

"Do you know where she is?"

Jerry glanced at Jesse and the others. "That's not relevant. I think the Mille Lacs County police are corrupt and her life could be in danger if they take her."

"You didn't answer my question."

"And I'm not going to until you answer my question."

Jake sighed. "Jerry, you've proven yourself and so I'll give you this advice. If you have evidence of a corrupt police department, the FBI would consider protecting a witness with valuable information. But all you've given me is that a suspected cop killer says she didn't do it. From where I sit, this suspect would say anything to protect herself. And if you're trying to help her, then you're obstructing justice. Now, I'll ask you one more time. Do you know where she is?"

Jerry bit his lip. "Thanks for taking my call, Jake. I'll talk to you later and I'll show you hard evidence."

"Jerry—"

"Thanks Jake. I'll let you go now." Jerry terminated the call.

Jerry stared at his phone for a few seconds. "I'm sorry, Jesse."

Jesse nodded. "We need to leave. The police will be here in a minute."

"Where will you go?"

"You don't know, remember?"

~

Dennis Waverly stared at his phone. Again. He put it away and sipped on a beer in his living room. Brenda was right. Mike Swanson was a crook. But she didn't know half of it. By now, he knew Mike's login credentials. He knew Mike's other email addresses. He knew that FISA order was fake. He knew why. And he had proof. He turned his phone over and over. What are you waiting for? He dialed.

"Hi Brenda. We need to talk."

48.   Milaca

Tuesday, October 2, 2018

Gloria sat a cup of coffee on her dining room table in front of Jesse and sat facing her. An Li, Ashley, and Leilani looked on.

Jesse rubbed her eyes and squeezed An Li's phone. "Dominic, I just need a couple days."

"For what?"

"For time to prove the NPU work-study program with that resort, Norra lekplatsen is really a sweetheart human trafficking ring."

"And how will you gather this proof?"

"I don't know. I need a couple days to figure it out."

"Every day that goes by gets you into more trouble. If you don't turn yourself in and they find you, you'll make my job extremely difficult."

"I didn't kill anyone."

"I know that."

"How am I supposed to prove it from jail? And what happens if they deny bail this time?"

"Let me work on that. It's my job. For now, come meet me in my office and turn yourself in today."

"What about Ashley, An Li, and Leilani?"

"Nothing ties them to the murder and the police don't know about them. Let's keep it that way."

Jesse finished the call. She sipped her coffee and looked at An Li, Ashley, and Leilani. "After what we've been through, I feel like you guys are my sisters. You too, Gloria. What do we do with them?"

Gloria touched Jesse's hand. "Leave that to me. We'll figure it out."

~

Jesse stared out the window of the police van along Highway 169 North toward Milaca, Minnesota and the Mille Lacs County jail. Memories from a 1995 trip north in a police van flooded her mind. How do I make lemonade out of this one, Candy?

The police officer in the passenger seat tilted his head back. "I hope you find the accommodations to your liking. We reserve our best rooms for cop killers."

Mile marker after mile marker whizzed by. Jesse closed her eyes. Keep on seeking, and you will find. I am with you always, even to the end of the age. The sentences scrolled like a message on the bottom of a TV screen. She squeezed her eyes harder.

The van stopped in front of the courthouse building. A mob of reporters and TV cameras waited on the sidewalk. A police officer slid into the seat next to Jesse. "Hold out your wrists. Don't even think about putting on a show."

Jesse gestured toward the crowd. "And you're not?"

"You might run and then we'd have to shoot you in front of this crowd, cop killer."

"I didn't kill anyone."

The officer finished applying handcuffs.

"Look, I'm sorry. I know you're doing your job. I'm not a criminal, I didn't kill anyone, and I don't plan on making a spectacle of myself. I hope you find who really did this."

"Bill Rasmussen was my friend."

Jesse nodded. "I only met him once. He died because he spent last Friday with a few of his friends and some girls at a resort hotel."

"What?" The color drained from the officer's face.

"You were there with him, at that same party, weren't you? I can see it in your eyes. I know some people who might recognize you."

He shook his head. "Anything you say can and will be used against you in a court of law."

"If we're quoting famous quotes, how about, 'the truth will set you free?'"

"Give me your ankles."

"I didn't do this. But I might be able to help you find who did. And nobody will care about your party last Friday."

The officer finished applying the ankle cuffs. "Welcome to your new home. You'll be staying in the Tango wing, our luxury suite for women. Most of the toilets work."

A few other officers from inside the building assembled on the street side of the van and escorted her around the van and inside. Questions from the press came from everywhere.

"Why'd you do it?" The question floated in above all the noise, as clear as a sunny day.

Jesse froze. She turned, and a million microphones flew into her face like bugs to a light. The officers tried to hustle her away but she shook them off. One officer spoke into a radio.

She would only get a few seconds. "I didn't kill anyone. I hope they find who did, but it wasn't me. And I hope you help me stay alive in there. You got that? Did you record it?"

A few reporters nodded.

The officers whisked her inside, removed her cuffs, and then guided her into a packed courtroom.

Somebody whispered to the judge as police officers brought Jesse in. People stood and watched as they escorted her to a table and left her there.

The Honorable Judge Galen Lundgren glared down at Jesse from his bench. "Ms. Jonsen, I presume?"

"Um, yes."

"I understand you did some grandstanding on the way into my court."

"Huh?"

"Is it your intention to try your case in the court of public opinion? Don't you have an attorney? Where is he?"

"I don't know. I turned myself in in Minneapolis and he was going to meet me here. We didn't know your court would already be in session and waiting."

"Well, while my clerk tries to find your attorney, why don't you fill me in on your grandstanding play with the press outside."

Jesse swallowed. "I didn't grandstand. I just want to come out of this alive."

"And what is that supposed to mean?"

"It means I didn't kill Officer Rasmussen. I don't know if you or others in the police department here are in league with a human trafficking ring, and I would rather not die in your jail. So, if the press is watching, maybe I'll stay alive."

The courtroom stirred.

Dominic made his way to the defense table. "Dominic Levenson, Your Honor. And I apologize for being late. I had to park a million miles away because there's no place to park near the courthouse."

"It seems you're popular with the press, Ms. Jonsen. Mr. Levenson, your client and I were passing the time, having a conversation about grandstanding with the press."

"Ah, I see. May we confer for a minute?" Dominic turned to Jesse and whispered. "What happened?"

"I did just what we talked about. I grabbed a mic and made an impromptu statement."

"That's it?"

"Yeah."

"And the ride up was fine?"

"One of the officers said Bill Rasmussen was his friend."

"I can use that. Anything else?"

"Yeah. He was at that same party."

Dominic nodded. "Your Honor, thank you. My client informed me that one of the officers escorting her to this courtroom told her that deceased Officer Bill Rasmussen was his friend."

"So what?"

"My client further believes this officer, and possibly others, were at a party Friday night with Officer Rasmussen, and something happened at that party that led to his death."

"Mr. Levenson, you are licensed in the state of Minnesota, right?"

"Yes, sir."

"Well, maybe they do things differently in Hennepin County. But here in Mille Lacs County, we follow state law, which means you'll get your chance to present your case at trial, which is not now."

"Yes, sir, I am fully aware of that procedure. I bring up the matter now because this friendship presents a prejudice against my client, and, frankly, we fear for her life. And so, I respectfully ask for a change in venue to move this to Hennepin County in Minneapolis."

Judge Lundgren leaned back in his chair. "I see. Well, I'm going to deny that request. We will run this trial right here, in Mille Lacs County, which is where it should be. I suggest you familiarize yourself with highway 169." He turned to the prosecutor. "Kelly, any objections?"

The prosecutor stood. "No, sir, no objections."

"Good. What's your bail recommendation?"

"Five hundred thousand dollars, your honor."

Dominic's eyes flashed. "Your honor, my client is not a flight risk. She has ties here and we believe we will win any trial. We all want to find who really did this."

"But you just told me she lives in Hennepin County. So, by definition, she is not part of any community here. And she has friends with money, which makes her a flight risk. I'm accepting the prosecution's recommendation of a five hundred-thousand-dollar bail. All cash."

"Your honor—"

"I want to see everyone back here in two weeks, on Tuesday, October 16, where I'll accept a plea and we'll cover any motions from either side. Unless, Mr. Levenson, your client wishes to save us the trouble and plead guilty right now."

Jesse started to speak.

Dominic raised his hand in front of her. "No, Your Honor. We intend to plead not guilty and vigorously contest this charge. I also intend to contact the Minnesota bar about any prejudice I see here."

The judge glared at Dominic. "We're adjourned." He rose and hustled out his door behind the bench.

Jesse turned to Dominic. "What just happened?"

Three officers approached Jesse. "Hold out your hands," one said.

"What? Why?"

"We need to cuff you again."

Jesse shook her head. "It takes three of you for that?"

Dominic pursed his lips. "They're trying to railroad you. I'll appeal his bail amount, but it will take longer than two weeks to get a court date. So, for now, sit tight. I'll be in touch."

One officer applied cuffs to Jesse's wrists.

"Where am I gonna find five hundred thousand dollars?"

The officer who cuffed Jesse gestured toward a chair. "Now, your feet. Please sit."

"You've got to be kidding me. Worried I'll kick somebody?"

"Some of us hope you'll try."

Jesse sat and held her feet up. An officer applied cuffs around her ankles.

Dominic sighed. "We can always use a bonding company. We pay them ten percent, they put up the full amount, but they keep your money."

"Legal robbery?"

"Yeah, something like that."

49.   Ashley

Ashley sat next to Gloria on the couch in her parents' living room. As always, the house looked like a layout for a home magazine cover. She glanced at the glass curio cabinet. Its shelves were full of abstract art, quartz chess pieces, ancient artifacts, and something new that looked like it was part tree root, part octopus.

"Daddy, what's that?"

Daddy smiled. "I picked that up from a friend who just returned from China. He bought it from some locals. It's a root from a ginseng plant. The Chinese say they enhance pleasures of the flesh, but nobody has been able to grow them commercially."

"Pleasures of the flesh. You mean, like sex?"

"We don't need to descend into the gutter here. The Bible teaches to only trust God, and so I keep this as an example of the world's depravity."

Mom smiled her plastic smile.

Ashley turned to Gloria. "Everything in that cabinet has a story."

Gloria nodded. "Thank you for seeing us."

Mom also nodded. "Ashley, your message said this work study program was different than you expected, and now you want to return home, is that right?"

"Yeah. It, um, it didn't work out."

Daddy sighed. "That presents us with certain logistical difficulties. Re-enrolling you in school, for example. You've missed at least six weeks of your senior year and I'm just not sure how we would explain that to everyone."

Ashley looked back and forth to Mom and Daddy. "Don't you want to know what happened?"

Gloria took Ashley's hand. "This is a difficult story to tell."

"I can see that," Daddy said. "But before we proceed, I'd appreciate it if you would tell me who you are and your relationship to my daughter. Are you associated with that British woman who recruited her into this work study program?"

"No. Not at all. I've heard about her but never met her. My name is Gloria Warren, and I own a Manitou Coffee franchise in the Minneapolis Skyway. I'm friends with Jesse Jonsen and Jesse rescued Ashley and another girl."

"And so, why isn't this Jesse here to speak with us?"

Gloria grimaced. "Well, because she's in jail, charged with murdering a police officer."

"What?"

Gloria held her palms out. "Why don't we tell you the story, start to finish."

Daddy turned to Mom. "A coffee waitress who's friends with a murderer is bringing our daughter home."

Mom said, "We should pray first."

Daddy nodded. "Yes, that seems appropriate. Dear Lord, please bless this time together. Protect this home from all the evil out there. Amen."

Mom smiled her Stepford Wife smile again. "Amen."

Ashley mumbled, "Amen."

Daddy said, "Okay, Ashley, let's hear it."

Ashley sighed. "You know how Meaghan recruited me. And at first, it was wonderful. They did a photo shoot, and I met a man and fell in love. I started pre-college classes and worked in the resort. But then we took a trip to Florida and one of their investors raped me."

"You told us you were a hostess at that resort on Mille Lacs Lake."

"I was. But they're opening resorts around the country and they brought me to Florida to meet with an important investor."

"But, you were a hostess."

"Daddy, I was more than a hostess. Men paid the resort for sex with me."

Mom's smile faded.

Daddy flopped back in his chair.

"Why did you go to Florida?"

"They told me it would be a weekend fun trip to help the resort."

"And, so after somebody in Florida raped you, then what happened? I assume somebody called the police?"

Tears fell from Ashley's eyes. "I don't want to talk about it."

"Well, you'd better talk about it, young lady. My daughter, a whore?"

Ashley looked down and sobbed.

Gloria said, "Mr. Dunbar, maybe the details aren't important right now. Maybe what's more important for now, is helping Ashley get through this."

His head turned red. "I did not raise my daughter to be a whore. I taught you right from wrong and dedicated my life to your future. And look what you did to me."

Mom put a hand on his shoulder. "Ted—"

"No. Get out. Both of you. A coffee waitress and a whore. Go strut your stuff on Hennepin Avenue. You belong together."

Mom's smile disappeared. She looked away.

Daddy stood. "Get out. Now."

Ashley stood. "But, Daddy—"

"Get out now or I'm calling the police."

"But Daddy, I'm your daughter."

"You're no daughter of mine."

Gloria's face reddened. "Mr. Dunbar, please, for your daughter—"

Ashley stepped toward the guy who used to be her dad. "And you're no father of mine. You never were. You hypocrite." She turned to Mom. "Mom, did you know I caught him in bed with Aunt Sydnee?"

Mom's ears turned red. "What?"

"Yeah, it was last year. You were with Grandma. I was spending the night with Carissa and I came home to get a nightgown and there they were. In your bed. Naked." She stepped into her former dad's face. "You call me a whore? You were probably a regular of some of the girls I worked with. What would you have done if you'd gone into a room and it was me in there?"

She stormed out the door.

Gloria followed.

Muffled shouts came from the house.

In the car, Gloria took a minute to compose herself. She fumbled with the car keys and drove away.

At the next stoplight, Gloria loosened her grip on the steering wheel, "That went well."

Ashley laughed through tears.

"Kiddo, you can stay with me for a while. We need to pick up Leilani and drive her home."

50.   Leilani

Leilani and Nimama waved at Gloria and Ashley in Nimama's driveway and walked inside. Gloria and Ashley drove away.

Leilani's father was on the couch.

Leilani stopped. "Nipapa? Nimama, why is he here?"

Nimama closed the door. "Please. Sit. And I'll explain."

Leilani backed up against the door. "You're not Nipapa. You're just an old man named Mukwoh. But your name mocks all bears everywhere. You should change your name to Ininiikaazo."

"I deserve that. And more. When I wasn't in jail, I was drunk. Or worse." Mukwoh wiped his eyes. "Leilaini, I am sorry for what I did to you and your mother. I can't change the past. But now, all I want to do is earn your forgiveness. And your respect."

Leilani stared at him. "Let me smell your breath."

Mukwoh stood. "Come here."

Leilani stepped a few feet closer. "Breathe."

He exhaled.

She inhaled. "No alcohol. What did you cover it with?"

"You know nothing really covers it. Believe me, I spent many years trying."

"I still smell cigarettes."

"Yes. My AA sponsor tells me I need to get rid of those next. And I will. Starting tonight."

"What about weed?"

"Cigarettes are all that's left."

"Nimama, do you believe him?"

"Time will tell. But he is my husband and I agreed to give him another chance. If you approve."

"You're putting this on me? What happens if I say no?"

Mukwoh glanced toward the door. "Then I will leave and try to earn your trust from afar."

"And what if I never want anything to do with you?"

"That is your choice. In my mind, you have always been my daughter, and you always will. What I am in your mind is up to you."

"Do you intend to help pay rent and other bills?"

"I have a job at the Mille Lacs Clinic doing cleaning and janitorial work. And they might let me do building maintenance in a few months after I prove I want to stay clean."

"Then, why aren't you at work?"

"I clean at night and get the building ready for patients the next day."

"How long have you had this job?"

"Three months. And I've been sober for six months. I approached your mother yesterday. She told me your story and I offered to help in any way I can. When she told me you were coming home today, I wanted to see you."

"Nimama?"

Dyani smiled. "I told you my thoughts. All I know is, first you came home. And then your father came home. My family is back." Her eyes watered.

Leilani sighed. "Old man, do not hurt Nimama. And know this. You can't push me around anymore. And you can't fool me with your lies. If you come here drunk, I'll smell it. And if you hurt Nimama, I'll feel it and I'll make you feel it worse."

"I want nothing more than to earn your trust. The day you decide to call me Nipapa again will be the greatest day of my life."

"Words are cheap. You taught me that."

51.   An Li

An Li fired. Kyle kept coming. She fired again. And again. But Kyle kept coming. He reached for her throat. She screamed and woke, sweating.

Fahad and Camile burst through the bedroom door.

Fahad brandished a softball bat. He scanned the room. "What happened?"

An Li sat up. "Nothing."

Camile sat next to her. "An Li, this is the third time this week. Please tell us what's going on."

"Just a bad dream. That's all." An Li's hands shook.

Camile took her hands. "An Li?"

An Li's heart felt wrong. Her mouth was dry. The room spun. "Am I having a heart attack?"

Fahad said, "Maybe we should call 911."

~

The paramedic put the last of his gear away. "You had a panic attack. They're common and they're scary. But you're okay. Your heart is fine."

"You're saying this is all in my head?"

"No. It starts in your head, but your body responds as if it were real danger. It's the same post-traumatic stress disorder that many war veterans experience."

"I was never a soldier."

"But I'll bet you've been in a war."

An Li nodded. "How do I live with it?"

"There are techniques to manage it. Work on breathing exercises. Eat healthy. Get plenty of sleep. Talk over whatever it is with somebody you trust. Sometimes they go away with time."

The paramedics left.

Fahad sipped a cup of water. "I'm glad it wasn't a heart-attack."

Camile sat next to An Li. "What happened on that trip with Jesse? You were going to bring two girls home from that resort, and now Jesse's in jail and you wake up screaming for three nights this week with panic attacks. And they're getting worse. What happened?"

An Li's dizziness returned. She gulped for air.

Camile took her hands. "Just breathe, An Li. In and out. In and out."

Fahad sat on An Li's other side. "Whatever it was, it was bad. But maybe telling us about it will help."

An Li panted. "They…tried…kill…us." Her panting got worse. Tears spilled from her eyes. "Kyle."

"What about Kyle?" Camile asked.

"Who's Kyle?" Fahad asked.

An Li gulped a few deep breaths. Her breathing slowed. "He drove the SUV. We got free. He came around the other side. I shot him. He died on top of me. We washed the blood off my clothes at Leilani's Mom's house."

52. Ashley

Gloria took Ashley's breakfast dishes away and wiped her kitchen table. "I am so sorry about your parents. We need to figure out a living situation for you."

Ashley sipped her orange juice. "Where's your husband?"

"He died last year."

"Oh. Sorry."

"That's okay. I have my business and the Chamber. I stay busy."

"Do you have any kids?"

"No. We tried, but it never worked out."

"Do you miss your husband?"

"Yes. Very much."

"I know this probably sounds weird, but I miss Harry."

"Hmm. If somebody tried to kill me, I don't think I'd miss them after I got away."

"But Harry loved me. I can't live here forever. My parents don't want me. Maybe we can have a life together."

Gloria dropped a plate. "What? Are you kidding me?" She picked up the plate and flopped it in the sink. "After what they put you and Jesse and the other girls through, now you want to go back to that place?"

"No. Not back there. I was thinking, I could contact Harry and we'd build a life together somewhere else. He's really smart. He doesn't need that place."

Gloria shook her head. "Ashley, he tried to murder you."

"No. That was Kyle. Or Landon. Or whatever his name was. Meaghan ordered Kyle to do it. Harry left before any of that happened. He probably doesn't know how evil she is."

Gloria sat across from her and took Ashley's hand. "Honey, that guy, Harry, Harold. He's in the middle of it."

"But he never saw what was really going on. He always tried to take care of me, but Meaghan had him wrapped around her finger."

"How did you get involved with that place?"

"Meaghan found Carissa and me and brought me up there to take some pictures."

"What kind of pictures."

"Of me in a bed. She said they wanted to use them to help sell rooms."

"In a bed?"

"It wasn't like I was naked. They gave me a nightgown"

"They?"

"Yeah. Harry and Meaghan."

"Harold was also there when you posed for those pictures?"

"Yeah. He took them. With his phone."

"So, you were in a nightgown, posing in bed, and Harold took pictures of you. And they told you it was to help sell rooms."

"You make it sound like it was dirty or something."

"Well?"

"Well, nothing. Harry and I fell in love that night. We had something special."

"If it was so special, then why did he make you sell sex every night?"

"He didn't. Meaghan did."

"But they were partners, right?"

"No, I think he worked for her. He might not have known what was going on."

"How could he not know?"

"Do the people who work for you at your business know everything that goes on?"

"No. Of course not. But that's different."

"How?"

"They're employees, not partners. Some things aren't relevant to them."

"Well, maybe Harry was an employee and not a partner. And Meaghan wouldn't tell him how badly she treated me. That might make him mad and then he'd want to leave."

Gloria shook her head. "Because he loves you, right?"

Ashley nodded.

Gloria sipped her coffee. "You said Harold was a partner, but then you said maybe he was an employee instead."

"I guess I don't know which he was."

"You were an employee too, right?"

"Yeah."

"Well, maybe you didn't know everything that went on. If you don't know whether Harold is an employee or a partner, then maybe you didn't know other things."

"I know Harry loves me. I know if I were to call him right now and meet him someplace, we could leave and build a life together. And then I wouldn't need you or Jesse or Mom or Dad or anyone."

Gloria took another sip. "Okay. I disagree with you. But I see you're serious. But it's a big step and it will put your life at risk. And mine. And Jesse's. And your friends'. Tell ya what. Why don't we talk it over with Leilani and An Li before you do anything you'll regret. They were with you that whole day and night, weren't they?"

"Leilani was. An Li was behind us in a car."

A new thought flew into Gloria's head. "How did you guys decide to leave?"

"Leilani came the morning after that drunk tried to beat me up and Meaghan brushed me off."

293

"Why did Leilani want to leave?"

"She said she couldn't take it anymore, but she was afraid to leave until she saw me fight back."

"So, why didn't you guys just leave?"

"We were going to meet Jesse in the parking lot. But the security guys stopped us and brought us back to the office. That was when Meaghan called Jesse."

"Was Harold with her?"

"Yeah."

"Why didn't he let you leave? Or leave with you if he knew Jesse was coming?"

"He couldn't. Meaghan's security guys would have stopped him, just like they stopped us."

Gloria shook her head. "Okay. Just promise me we'll talk to Leilani and An Li and maybe even Jesse if we can before you run back to this guy."

Ashley sipped her orange juice. "But where will I stay?"

"You can stay here for a while. I have plenty of room. We'll even work on getting you back in school if you want."

53.   Leilani

A car door slammed outside. Leilani sat up in her bed.

Voices. One was her father, Mukwoh. The other— Leilani strained her ears. A voice she hadn't heard in almost four years. Wematin's father, Ishkode.

Her heart exploded. How could I have been afraid of that worm? But that was long ago and I was a coward. She shook her head and took in a breath. Wematin was where it all started. First, Wematin, then his father with his money and power, and then Landon/Kyle. But Kyle is dead. And so is Wematin. Isn't three goals in hockey a hat trick? Maybe it's time for a rapist hat trick.

The voices continued from the kitchen. Friendly words. "Let's fix this." And "Maybe a night out will be good." The refrigerator opened and shut. Bottles clinked. Or maybe cups. So, Mukwoh wants me to call him nipapa? But he's friendly with the filthy piece of trash who wanted me to apologize when his son raped me?

Her hands trembled. She took another breath to tame the fire burning inside her. No, not to tame it, not this time. To master it. To use it. Send Wematin's father to the same hell as his son. Maybe Mukwoh can join them. What do they call four goals in hockey?

She slipped on clothes and shoes and held out her hands. Still shaking. She needed a weapon. And a plan.

Nimama used to keep tools in the shed. A garden shovel could work.

She slipped the screen off her bedroom window, opened the window and climbed outside. Just like when she was younger. She gently slid the window back down. She raced around the other side of the house opposite the kitchen and ducked into the shed in back.

Nimama's shovel leaned against a wall. She grabbed it and held it up. No more hands shaking. It must be true, what they say. Plans really do help calm nerves. Her body felt like ice. Not ice cold, but ice calm. Preparing for war with Wematin's father, Ishkode. My ice will kill the man named after fire.

She needed a way to get them outside. Not enough room to swing in the kitchen. And Nimama didn't need to clean all that blood. She stepped outside and everything came into place. Right in front of the shed, and partially shielded from the road.

She lifted the shovel and screamed the loudest war scream in the history of war screams. She ran at Ishkode's truck, brought the shovel up, and slammed it against his windshield. The glass splintered. She lifted and screamed and swung it again. And again. The glass shattered. She stepped toward the headlights and smashed those. And then the passenger window.

The driver's window was too close to the house for a good swing. But no matter. She stepped on the rear bumper, hopped into the truckbed, and smashed the rear window. And then the top, over and over, screaming and swinging and smashing and denting.

Mukwoh and Ishkode ran outside. Nimama followed. Leilani stared at Ishkode for a few seconds with ice in her eyes and caught her breath. She screamed and swung the shovel into the truck top again. The shovel pierced the metal and caught.

Ishkode ran to the truck and hopped into the truck bed. Leilani pulled on the shovel with all her strength. Ishkode wrapped his arms around her from behind. She kicked and screamed and swung her arms around, trying to smash anything she could contact. She pushed off from the back of the truck. Ishkode staggered, bobbed and weaved and ducked and held on.

Mukwoh jumped into the back of the truck bed. Ishkode swung Leilani around to face Mukwoh. Leilani lost her grip on the shovel.

"Leilani," Mukwoh thundered.

Leilani kicked him in the groin.

Mukwoh buckled and backed away. Ishkode pulled Leilani toward the back window.

Leilani kicked into the air.

Ishkode slipped his arms under Leilani's armpits. Leilani raised her arms and tried to slide down. Iskkode squeezed tighter.

Mukwoh stood and advanced a step.

Leilani caught her breath and lifted a leg. She stared at Mukwoh. Sweat dripped from her eyebrow.

Mukwoh stepped toward Leilani.

Leilani kicked.

Mukwoh grabbed the leg and held tight.

Leilani swung her other leg up and kicked Mukwoh's arms.

Mukwoh pulled Leilani's foot under an armpit, grabbed the other leg and foot, and pulled it under his other armpit.

Leilani struggled with all her strength. She screamed and spit at Mukwoh. Saliva stuck to his face and hair. She tried to bend her knees and kick again and push Ishkode off balance.

Mukwoh held tight. "Dyani, open the tailgate."

Tears flowed from Nimama's eyes. Why? She floated to the back of the truck, opened the tailgate, and backed away.

Mukwoh stepped toward the tailgate. Ishkode stepped forward. Mukwoh nodded at him.

"How do we get her down?" Ishkode asked. "Can you jump and hold on to her?"

Mukwoh glanced over his shoulder. "I don't think so."

"Well, we can't stay like this forever. I'm getting tired."

Mukwoh nodded. "She's probably tired, too. Are you tired, Leilani?"

She screamed and spit at Mukwoh.

Ishkode laughed. "I don't know why I'm laughing. I liked this truck. Who's gonna pay for this?"

Leilani screamed and flailed. She pulled and pushed with her legs. Mukwoh stumbled, but caught himself.

"How about we turn sideways. We'll sit on the wheel wells until she calms down."

"Good idea."

They rotated.

Leilani kicked and pushed, but Ishkode and Mukwoh held firm. They sat on the wheel wells.

"Mukwoh, I can't hold her forever like this. You have her feet but she's getting heavy for me."

"Can you slip your knees underneath her?"

"I'm trying. But she needs more support."

Leilani swung her arm backward and smashed Ishkode's ear.

"And every time she does that, I have to duck, and it messes up the balance."

"Yeah, I see what you mean. Dyani, can you get a kitchen chair and climb up here and set it underneath her?"

Tears streamed from Nimama's eyes "Stop it. All of you. Leilani, look what you've done." She turned to Mukwoh. "And you. Making light after what your daughter has gone through." She turned to Ishkode. "Because of you. Leilani, come down off that truck bed. Right now."

Leilani screamed. "No. Don't you know what these men did to us?"

"Yes. I do. And that's why Ishkode is here. To ask for our forgiveness."

The ice in Leilani's veins melted. Tears flowed. Her arms and legs went limp, so sore she could barely lift them.

Mukwoh loosened his grip on her feet. They dropped to the truck bed.

Ishkode stood. She let him guide her to her feet and toward the tailgate.

Mukwoh jumped down and helped Leilani to the ground.

Nimama took Leilani's hand. Leilani collapsed into Nimama's arms.

54.   Reconcile

Nimama finally let go of her embrace. She wiped her eyes and then brushed Leilani's hair and tears away from her face. "Come." She put her arm around Leilani's shoulder, turned to the street, and guided Leilani with her.

"Where?"

Nimama turned onto the street, still guiding Leilani. She looked over her shoulder to Mukwoh and Ishkode. "You too."

Ishkode stopped. "I didn't come here to have my truck destroyed."

Nimama let go of Leilani and invaded Ishkode's personal space. "Come with me and don't argue." She reached up for his ear and directed him toward the road.

"Ouch. You don't have to do that."

"Then come." Nimama let go of his ear.

Mukwoh and Ishkode shrugged and followed.

"Nimama, where are we going?"

Nimama put her arm around Leilani. "To get help."

"How far?"

"Not far."

They stopped at a gravel driveway leading to a spartan white church building with a van parked in front. Nimama led them inside.

A grizzled bear of a man wearing coveralls and boots met them at the door. Dirt filled the space under his fingernails. Black outlines accented his finger and hand prints. He reached for Nimama's hand. "Good to see you again, Dyani."

Nimama took his hand. "Thank you for meeting us here."

He nodded. "You must be Leilani, Mukwoh, and Ishkode. I'm Arik Williamson." He led them into an office. Everyone sat.

Ishkode said, "I recognize you. Where have we met?"

Arik smiled. "Probably at an AA meeting. Why don't I tell you my story and why I said yes when Dyani asked for my help."

Ishkode and Mukwoh nodded.

"But—"

"Leilani, please," Nimama said. "Arik has kept my old car running and made sure the house has heat for the past four years. If not for Arik, I probably would not have been alive to greet you when you showed up with your friends. You told me what happened to you and I sensed more trouble coming. After Gloria dropped you off, I called Arik and asked him to meet with all of us this morning. That's why Ishkode is here. We need to reconcile."

Leilani stood. "You want me to reconcile with the man who demanded I apologize after his son raped me?" She took a step toward Ishkode.

Ishkode stood. "She destroyed my truck. She wanted to kill me with that shovel."

"That shows even more why we need to reconcile," Nimama said.

"Dyani, I already told you, I'm sorry I threatened to evict you. I was mad at my son and took it out on you. And now my son is dead." Ishkode wiped his eye. "But your daughter went off the deep end this morning." He stepped toward Leilani.

Leilani closed her fists. Her heart pumped.

Arik stepped between Leilani and Ishkode. "I don't have many rules, but one is, there will be no violence here. Both of you. Please, sit down. If you want to leave, then leave. You can even kill each other if you want, just not on this church's property."

Ishkode slowly backed down and sat.

"Agreed?"

Leilani trained her eyes on Ishkode. She nodded.

"I want to hear 'yes.' From both of you."

"Yes," Ishkode said. "Leilani, I'm sorry for what I said and did to you. And for what my son did to you."

Arik nodded. "Leilani?"

"Yes. I won't kill you on this church's property." She sat. But ready to spring at the first sign of trouble.

Arik chuckled. "Well, that's a start." He returned to his chair. "I'll give you the brief version. I'm stronger than just about every man in this county. I don't say that to brag. I say that because I've come to realize that was the gift God gave me. I don't deserve it and I abused it. Badly. I killed a man with my bare hands thirty years ago because I thought he cheated me. But the police fouled up the investigation and the judge threw the case out. And then God told me that was a gift because He had plans for me. I should have listened. I don't remember much from the next ten years because I was drunk or stoned most of it. And then the Lord finally brought me to my senses. And now, I'm here. I help maintain the building, and in return, the church helps me live. And along the way, I've taken a few classes. I'll graduate from Seminary next year, Lord willing."

Mukwoh asked, "So now, what, you do good deeds so you can score points upstairs?"

"I don't know why the Lord called me here, I just know this is where I want to be and what I want to do. You don't earn your way into Heaven."

Mukwoh leaned back. "Okay."

Arik nodded. "That's enough about me. I'm a big, dumb Swede. Dyani, what happened this morning?"

Nimama glanced toward Leilani. "She used my shovel to destroy Ishkode's truck. Both Mukwoh and Ishkode had to hold her to stop her from doing more damage. I think she would have bashed Ishkode's head in if they hadn't stopped her."

Arik nodded again. "Is this true, Leilani?"

"Yes."

Arik shrugged. "I don't blame you."

"What?" Ishkode stood.

Arik stared at Ishkode.

Ishkode slowly sat.

"Dyani said your son raped her and then you wanted her to apologize. Is that true?"

Ishkode looked down. "Yes."

"And then you threatened to evict her family unless she left her home. True?"

"Yes."

"And Leilani chose to spend the past four years as a prisoner because of you. She barely escaped last week."

"I didn't know that."

"Well, now you do. I'd be mad if I were in her shoes."

Leilani's hands shook. "Well, then, why don't I get the shovel and finish the job?"

Arik's eyes pierced her. "Because you're better than that."

"No, I'm not. I'm just a whore. Ask him."

"It doesn't matter what Ishkode thinks or Mukwoh thinks, or even what Dyani thinks. It matters what God thinks, and God thinks you're better than that."

"How do you know?"

"Because I asked Him and He told me."

Mukwoh laughed. "Here we go again with superstition."

Arik turned to Mukwoh. "What's the second AA step?"

Mukwoh rolled his eyes. "Believe that a Power greater than ourselves could restore us to sanity."

"And the third step?"

"Make a decision to turn our will and our lives over to the care of God as we understand Him."

"And both of you are working on the ninth step, trying to make amends to the people you harmed. Right?"

"Yeah. I am," Mukwoh said.

Ishkode shook his head. "That's why I visited this morning. Dyani asked me to come and my truck paid the price."

Arik nodded again. "I'm working on those same steps. If we make a decision to turn our will and our lives over to the care of God, then why is it a stretch to believe God says we're better than that?"

Leilani rolled her eyes. "I'm not a drunk and I don't need your twelve steps."

"Leilani, you want to kill Ishkode, and you're mad enough to really do it, but I did kill another human being. Trust me when I tell you, it doesn't solve your problems. It only makes them worse, and if you choose that path, you'll probably end up dead or stoned to blot it out. You *are* better than that. And your life is worth more than that. Work on yourself now instead of putting yourself through what we did to ourselves."

The ice infused Leilani's body again. But this time she shivered. Her arms hurt.

Arik must have noticed her arms shaking. "Do you want a blanket?"

"No."

Arik took a breath. "Can I tell you a story from the Bible?"

Leilani tried to relax her arms. "Sure. Why not."

"It's about a guy named Joseph."

Ishkode laughed. "Isn't that supposed to be a Christmas story?"

Arik's eyes danced. "No. Wrong Joseph. This Joseph lived about seventeen hundred years before Jesus was born. He was Jacob's youngest son."

"Okay."

"Long story short, Joseph's brothers didn't like him and so they sold him as a slave to some traders on their way to Egypt. The details are in the last few chapters of Genesis."

"Why didn't they like him?"

"They were jealous. Jacob loved Joseph more than his older brothers."

Leilani's shivering slowed. "What does this have to do with me?"

"The details are different, but the important piece of the story is, Joseph's brothers treated him badly and he had good reason to be mad at them."

Leilani nodded. "Okay, so then what?"

"Well, Joseph spent the next several years in Egypt, many of them in prison."

"Why?"

"A powerful person's wife accused him of trying to rape her. He didn't do it, but the husband threw him in prison anyway."

"But he got out?"

"Yeah. He did, and eventually, he became the second most powerful person in Egypt. And that's when his father and brothers showed up. There was a famine and they needed food. And so, they met with Joseph. Long story short, he forgave them and they had a big party."

"I still don't see how that applies to me. Nobody loved me more than anyone else and I don't have any power. Nobody accused me of raping anyone." Leilani pointed to Ishkode. "His son raped me."

"Maybe you have more power than you think. The rest of your story isn't written yet. I think you'll influence many people, so maybe future generations don't go through what you went through."

Leilani pointed at Ishkode. "I don't care about influencing future generations. I want him dead."

"You're better than that."

"Here we go again."

"You're better than that because God has a bigger mission for you, but your anger gets in the way."

"Yeah, right."

"Let me ask all three of you something. What do you think about this trafficking ring Leilani escaped from? There are still people trapped there, you know."

Leilani shook her head. "I can't do anything for them."

"From what Dyani told me, you helped another girl get away. Ashley? Was that her name?"

Dyani nodded. "Yes. She was frightened."

"What if you could help more people escape?"

"I can't."

"What if you could?"

"How?"

"By showing the world what that place is really like."

"But who would listen to us?"

"I would," Ishkode said.

"Me too," Mukwoh said.

Arik nodded. "I'm here because Dyani told me your story."

"And I'm here too," Dyani said. "I listened."

Arik's eyes twinkled. "Seems we have a common enemy."

55.   Team

Gloria parked her car in front of Jesse's house. "Here we are."

Ashley scanned her social media messages again. The ones from Harry. "I love you." And "You're so beautiful." And "We'll build a life together." And "I can't wait to see you again," right after they snuck away and spent a Sunday evening under the moon. How could he not love her? Her heart ached.

Gloria glanced at her. "You ready?"

"Yeah. Ashley put her phone away.

An Li waited in front of the door. She introduced Gloria and Ashley to Camile and Fahad. They entered and sat.

An Li started. "Ashley, I heard you wanted to go back to that guy."

"I didn't say that."

"You're thinking about it."

"He loves me. I still have the texts he sent."

"He was grooming you, Ashley," Camile said. "Just like he tried to do with An Li."

"What's grooming?"

"That's where they tell you whatever you want to hear so you'll do what they want. They get into your head and you do crazy stuff," An Li said. "Except, you don't think it's crazy. I know because I almost did what you did."

"Huh?"

"We never met officially. Why do you think I was there with you when we killed that guy, Kyle, who kidnapped us?"

"I don't know. You followed us in Jesse's car. She must have brought you."

"Now I have panic attacks about it."

"Oh. I'm sorry."

"Here, let me show you something. Look at these messages." An Li handed Ashley her phone. "I'll bet you've seen these before."

Ashley scrolled through them. "It's a great program," and "I can't wait to see you," and "I love your passion," and "I love you." And more.

"Harold sent an audio clip. Did he want you to call him Harry even though everyone else called him Harold? Go ahead, play it."

Ashley scrolled and found it. She tapped it.

"Hi An Li." It was Harry's voice. "I'm sorry to hear your parents are so regimented. I can't wait to enroll you in our work study program. It's amazing what we're doing here and I can't wait for you to be part of it. And, selfishly, I also want to get to know you better. You're special, An Li. And special to me"

The recording stopped. Ashley stared at the phone. She wiped away a tear. "Why didn't you go?"

"Because Jesse wouldn't let her," Fahad said."

An Li nodded. "They all recognized he was grooming me. But I thought he loved me. I was an Asian girl just out of high school, I wanted to break away from my parents, and this sophisticated businessman made me feel special. If Jesse and Camile and Fahad hadn't stopped me, I would have been you. And that's why I helped Jesse get you out of there."

"So the whole thing—"

"It was all a lie. All of it. We were pieces of meat."

Ashley looked down.

Gloria knelt in front of Ashley and took her hands. "Ashley, if you try to go back to Harold, you'll put all these girls at risk and they'll kill you. You know too much and you tried to leave."

Ashley sobbed.

An Li's phone rang. "It's Leilani." She answered. "Hi Leilani... Yeah, she's here... Okay. Let me put you on speaker."

Ashley looked up and wiped her eyes.

"Hey Ashley, you there?" Leilani's voice echoed from An Li's phone speaker.

"Yeah."

"I know Jesse's trying to stop Harold and Meaghan's operation. I want to help. My mother and a couple other people here also want to help. Ashley, I was thinking, maybe you and An Li might also want to help."

"Yeah. Count me in," An Li said. "Maybe it'll help with my panic attacks."

"You have panic attacks? I almost murdered Wematin's father."

"What?" Gloria asked. "Who's Wematin?"

"We grew up together. He raped me four years ago."

Gloria's eyes widened. "Why'd you try to kill his father?"

"Long story. But we're past that now. Ashley, want to help stop Harold and Meaghan?"

"I thought Harry loved me."

"I know how you feel. I thought Landon loved me. That worked out badly for Landon."

Ashley wiped her eyes again. "It's gonna work out badly for Harold, too. Count me in."

"We'll help too," Camile said. "Right, Fahad?"

Fahad nodded. "Yeah."

"I don't recognize that voice. Who's Fahad?" Lelani asked.

"Camile and Fahad, our roommates," An Li said. "We met Jesse at Dairy Queen and now we all live here with her."

Gloria smiled. "Jesse will be glad for the help. So will I. We need to raise five hundred thousand dollars for her bail."

"Dairy Queen," Camile said. "The owner owes Jesse a favor. She stopped a robbery."

Gloria nodded. "That's our first order of business. Get Jesse out on bail. Then we go after the traffickers. Welcome to the team."

56.   1992—Eighth Grade

Spring, 1992

Youth pastor Donato Alcaraz gazed deep into eighth grader Jesse Jonsen's eyes. He moved in for a kiss. Her heart raced.

She woke up. Smiling. The clock beside her bed said 6 am. Hey, it's only a harmless fantasy. Just a little secret between parts of her brain. Nobody outside needs to know. She drifted back to sleep.

~

Donato had been sneaking glances at her all evening. Which made Jesse's skin tingle.

Donato strode across the youth room. "Jesse, can I see you for a minute?"

Jesse blushed

He gestured through the door toward a chair. He followed her in, shut the door and sat opposite her.

"Jesse, you seemed a little distracted tonight. Is everything okay?"

Oh, if he only knew. "Um, yeah, just fine."

"You're blushing."

Jesse giggled. "Well, I did have kind of a strange dream this morning, and I guess it affected me more than I thought."

Donato nodded. "Ohhh." He took her hands in his. "Entiendo."

"Huh?"

"It means, I understand."

"Oh. It sounds kind of romantic when you say it in Spanish. Entiendo." She giggled.

Donato smiled. "Jesse, I want you to know, I like you very much. And I was thinking, maybe we could have, you know, kind of a special relationship."

Jesse's heart jumped into her throat. "Special? How?"

"I don't know. Just special, I guess. You have a boyfriend?"

"No."

"That's a shame. Any young man would be privileged to have you for his girl."

Heat rose in her face. "Thanks."

He chuckled. "You're blushing again."

Jesse looked down. "Donato, you know that dream?"

"Yeah."

"Well, it was about you."

Donato looked deep into her eyes. "Well, I have a confession for you, too."

"What?"

"I also had a dream."

Where is he going with this? "Really?"

"Yeah. About you."

Can he hear my heart beating?

"Your hands are sweaty."

"Sorry."

"I like it." He stroked Jesse's hair. "Keep on seeking, and you will find." He kissed one hand. "I am with you always, even to the end of the age." He kissed her other hand. "Let's keep this our little secret."

57.   1995—Guilt

December, 1995. Itasca County Girls Group Home, Big Fork, Minnesota.

Jesse felt sick Wednesday and missed school. She was worse Thursday. Mrs. Adams set up a doctor appointment on Friday, but the doctor could not find anything wrong.

Saturday morning, somebody knocked on Jesse's door.

"May we come in?" It was Mrs. Adams and Ms. Inglebertsen. They entered and sat on Candy's old bed.

Jesse sat up in her bed. "Ms. Inglebertsen, why are you here?"

"We're worried about you, and Karen and I thought you might find this story helpful. Well, two stories actually."

Jesse rubbed her eyes. "Whatever."

"Jessica," Mrs. Adams said, "The doctor said there's nothing physically wrong with you. And that means your problem is mental. We want to help, but we can't do it without you. You and Janet have a bond, and so I asked if she wouldn't mind visiting for a few minutes. She's taking time away from her own family to help you. I'd appreciate it if you gave her the courtesy of your attention."

"Janet?"

Ms. Inglegertsen smiled. "I do have a first name you know. In school, call me Ms. Inglebertsen. But here, this morning, you can call me Janet."

"Why are you doing this?"

"Karen just told you. We want you to succeed. We care about you."

Jesse pulled her legs up. "Okay, I'm listening."

Ms. Inglebertsen pursed her lips. "I want to tell you about two people. One was named Judas Iscariot. The other was named Peter. We don't know Peter's last name."

"You mean, like Bible stories?"

"Yeah. But with an interpretation you may not have considered. And they're relevant to your situation. You know Judas and Peter were two of Jesus's disciples, right?"

"Yeah."

"And you know what a disciple is, right?"

"A helper maybe? Kind of a student?"

"Yeah, kind of like that. And you know how Judas betrayed Jesus. We see reenactments every Easter. The religious leaders offered Judas money to betray his leader, Jesus. Judas took the money before they ate their Passover meal, betrayed Jesus, and the Romans eventually crucified Jesus. It's a horrible way to die."

"I've heard all this. What's it got to do with me?"

"I'm getting to that. Is it okay to keep going?"

"Sure."

"Okay. At that last supper, Jesus told Peter that Peter would deny ever knowing Jesus three times that very night, before the rooster crowed the next morning."

"Yeah, I remember that story. So what?"

"Move forward a few hours. Judas betrayed his leader, the Romans are dragging Jesus away, and it's pandemonium. Everyone's scared. Peter and the other disciples think they're about to get strung up themselves. Peter is standing by a fire and somebody says, 'Hey, I know you. You're part of that guy's entourage.' And Peter says, 'No, I'm not.' 'Yes, you are.' 'No way.' 'Yeah, you are. I saw you with him.' 'Look, I don't know who you're talking about, okay?' And right about then, probably close to dawn, a rooster crows and Peter realizes what he just did."

"So?"

"So, how do you think he felt?"

Jesse thought about it for a second. "Bad, I guess."

"Maybe guilty?"

Jesse nodded. "Yeah, I suppose. He probably felt guilty."

"Why?"

Jesse thought about it for another second. "Maybe because he let everyone down?"

Ms. Inglebertsen smiled. "Yeah, that sums it up. A few hours earlier, he swore he'd stand by his master's side and defend Him, no matter what. But then the situation got hairy and Peter choked. The Gospels say he wept bitterly. I think he might have even gotten physically sick."

"Okay."

"Well, the rest of Peter's story is, he had a heart-to-heart talk with Jesus a few days later and he recovered. And he went on to become one of the most famous and powerful people ever in history."

"How could he have a talk with Jesus when Jesus was dead?"

"He was resurrected. We'll do details on that later. Or you can read about it. For now, I want you to see that Peter messed up. Badly. But he recovered."

"What about the other guy, Judas?"

"His story is different. He also felt guilty. He tried to give the money back to the people who paid him off. But they laughed at him. Then he killed himself."

Jesse fidgeted.

Mrs. Adams took Jesse's hand. "Jesse, Janet and I have seen what guilt can do to people. You can let it ruin you or you ask for forgiveness and learn from it. Something's eating at you about Nadine's death, and Nadine's parents have a hole in their heart. Sooner or later, the police will piece together what happened. For your own sake, and for Nadine's parents, but mostly for you, you need to tell us what you know."

Jesse closed her eyes and tried to blink back tears.

"I can't."

Mrs. Adams asked, "Why not?"

"Candy made me promise not to tell anyone."

Janet took Jesse's other hand. "Under the circumstances, I think Candy would be okay with you telling us."

Jesse looked down. Tears dripped from her cheeks. "It was her uncle."

"What about her uncle?"

"She was afraid to go back home because of her uncle."

"Did she tell you why?"

"No. Just that she couldn't go home. She said her uncle always told her after, 'We have to be a good little girl for school in the morning.'"

"After what?"

"She wouldn't say."

"And, so that's why she left from school and drove to Grand Rapids with that boy?"

"Yeah. She was gonna start out on her own."

"How did she get the fake IDs?"

"I don't know." Jesse pursed her lips and crossed her toes.

"Okay," Mrs. Adams said, "Thanks for sharing that. It's important. If you can think of anything else—"

They left.

I need to tell them about the fake IDs. No. I'll go to prison. But if they find out anyway, it'll be worse. But they won't find out. Dylan isn't stupid. But how much of a boyfriend is he, anyway? Why couldn't he see me over Thanksgiving? I did everything he wanted. And now, I'm stuck up here and he's still free. But I can't tell anyone about the fake IDs. I have to. No, I don't.

Jesse lay on her pillow.

How many other kids my age have three thousand dollars in the bank? What happens to my money if I tell? But wait a minute. Dylan paid me five dollars for every item. What did he sell them for? Some of those things retailed for more than a hundred dollars. Dylan probably sold them for half that. And he paid me five dollars? And I'm here and he's still making money.

She tossed and turned.

What will I go back to? Working for Dylan forever?

It had seemed so easy three years ago. The secret rides home from school, the ice-cream dates, the fun, the plans. They wouldn't have to go to a job every day like dad. They were going to be smarter. It was easy money. They were going to live on a South Pacific island after she finished high school. They'd planned it all out.

Or had they? "Whatever you say, baby." That was Dylan's line. Or, "sounds good." I made all the plans. All he did was say yes. And he kept most of the money. Some partnership. What did he do while I was in school or out stealing? Who was he with?

Okay, maybe I don't need Dylan. I can sell the stuff myself. But he knows all the buyers. Or, so he says. Maybe I do need Dylan to introduce me to his buyers.

She'd seen his gun. He carried it with him all the time. "Just in case," he'd always said. In case of what? If I start selling what I steal myself, do I need to start carrying a gun? Who buys this stuff? Probably the kind of people you need a gun to be around.

I can't go back to the way it was. And I can't tell them about the fake IDs. What do I do?

~

Home for Christmas break, Jesse dialed a phone at her parents' house. It was midnight. "Dylan, I'm home for Christmas and I don't want to go back."

"Good to hear from you, baby. Listen, want to get back in the saddle again?"

"I was hoping you'd say that. I figure I have a score to settle. I'm gonna hit every Bullseye Store in town. And then I want us to run away together."

"I like that. When do you want to get started?"

"Today. I already have one dress. My parents didn't even know I took it."

"Oh, baby, you're fantastic. I missed you. Bring it over. If it's nice, maybe I'll have you keep it and you can grab another one."

~

Dylan opened his door and his face lit up. "Come in. Great to see you, baby!"

They kissed.

"Now show me that dress you picked up today."

Jesse took it out of her bag and displayed it in front of her.

"Mighty fine. Mighty fine. You still got a knack for this stuff. You got a good eye too."

"Thanks. But I'm trying to figure out how they caught me last summer. You still got your camcorder?"

"Yeah."

"Okay, good. I want you to video me." She walked into his kitchen and found salt and pepper shakers. She walked back into the living room and set them on a shelf. "These are about the same size as lipstick tubes. I practiced this over and over and over again, but somehow, they saw it."

"Baby, can't that wait? Let's take care of some other business."

"We will. But this has been bugging me. Let me practice and you watch. Just like before."

Dylan chuckled. "Whatever you say." Dylan retrieved his camcorder.

Jesse went through the motions. "Okay, now let's play it back."

Dylan stopped in the middle of the playback. "You slippin' girl. Look at that." He pointed to the screen. "Your hands are in the wrong place. They should be on this side of the camera. Your left hand needs to block the camera while you palm the second one with your right hand and put it in your sleeve. Or drop it in your bag if your body's blocking the bag. But it's better to put it in your long sleeve and then drop it in the bag later. The camera never sees you take it, nobody knows it's gone."

"Oh man, you gotta be kidding me. That's probably how I got caught." Jesse slapped her forehead.

"Don't worry about it girl. Everyone slips up." Dylan reached to massage her shoulders.

Jesse shook her head. "I'm tired. I gotta go. Keep that tape, okay? I'll want to watch it again later."

"Well, do you want to practice some more?"

"No, not tonight. I can't believe I did that."

~

The lights were on at Jesse's parents' house when she arrived. She parked, took a deep breath, and walked inside. Detective Higgins and several other police officers met her at the door.

Jesse stopped and looked at each one. After a few seconds, Detective Higgins smiled. "You did good, kid. The Minneapolis guys are taking Dylan into custody as we speak."

"I was a little worried he'd find it when he kissed you," the sound technician said.

"I had it covered. He wasn't getting anywhere near your transmitter. Are we good?"

"We'll keep our end of the bargain. We'll still need you in court."

Jesse's dad was front and center. "I'm proud of you."

Tears formed in Jesse's eyes. Candy, we made lemonade today. I miss you.

58.   Tango Wing

Monday, October 8, 2018

Jesse stretched on her cot in her cell in the women's Tango wing of the Mille Lacs County jail. Her home for at least the next two weeks. *How do I make lemonade this time, Candy?*

Why does Mom keep bugging me about church? Seriously? The church question pops into my head now, when I'm stuck here and somebody out there wants to murder me?

Alone in a jail cell in an almost empty cell block, ninety miles from home. At least, for now, she could be alone with her thoughts. Let them flow. Periodically take stock of yourself. Isn't that what the therapist said?

After eighth grade, the therapist told her that her experience would have a profound influence on her life. That's what everyone called it—her experience. Because nobody could say the word. A pastor who violated her parents' trust, and Jesse's virginity. There was a scandal and he went to jail, and then it was over, but it never ended, because it replayed in her mind every time she saw that building. *Why Mom wants me to go back to church is beyond insane. If God cares about me so much, why did he let his buddy abuse me?*

Looking back, the therapist was right. That was the real reason she hooked up with Dylan in high school, which led to her senior year at the Itasca Group Home for Girls, which led to her career, which led to Leilani, which led here. Full circle. Again.

But a phrase fought its way to her mind's surface. "Even though I walk through the valley of the shadow of death, I will fear no evil, for you are with me; your rod and your staff, they comfort me." Psalm twenty-three, verse four.

How do I even remember that?

Why this verse? Why today? Well, with at least one murderer on the loose, plenty of evil waited outside her cell. And the dim light did make it shadowy.

Wonderful. I'm in the valley of the shadow of death, but I'm not supposed to be afraid of somebody who wants to murder me. Well, whatever. Okay, God, if you're out there, maybe you'll let me in on your little secret.

Somebody tapped on her cell door. It opened. An officer who looked like Xena the Warrior Princess stood with a tray of food.

"Jessica Jonsen?"

"No, I'm the pope. The person you want is in the cell next door."

She stepped toward Jesse. "I'm Anita Rasmussen."

Jesse stood. This isn't right. Corrections officers don't introduce themselves. "Um, nice to meet you, Anita. What can I do for you?"

The officer took another step. "I told Alicia I'd deliver your meal. I wanted to meet you. It's against the rules but I don't care. Bill Rasmussen was my husband."

Jesse stepped along her bed. Nowhere to hide. "I'm sorry for what happened. But I didn't do it."

"Your fingerprints on the gun that killed him say you did."

"No. We locked his keys in his car to give us a chance to drive away."

"That's the best you got?"

"He agreed to let us go. We needed time. We had leverage."

"You keep saying, 'we.' What leverage?"

"He spent last Friday at a party at a resort named Norra leklatsen."

"How do you know that?"

"Some of the people I was with recognized him. That was our leverage."

"That he spent Friday at a retirement party for a thirty-year veteran?"

"No. That he spent at least some time Friday with one of the people with me. I had his gun. I made him jog back into the trees and out of sight. We locked his keys in the car and left."

"Now I know you're lying." She tossed the tray and pulled a knife. Food and dishes clattered across the floor. "I wanted to meet the person who murdered my husband. You died trying to stab me while I brought you food."

She raised the knife and moved toward Jesse.

Jesse slid under Anita's legs, spun, came up behind her, kicked the knife out of her hand, and then barrel-rolled away and grabbed the knife off the floor.

Jesse raised the knife and stepped into Anita.

Anita backed away.

Jesse landed a kick into Anita's chest. Anita stumbled backward and fell.

Jesse jumped behind Anita's head and swung the knife against Anita's neck.

"Make one move and this knife will slit your throat." Jesse grabbed a hunk of Anita's hair, brought the knife up, and chopped off the hunk of hair. She tossed the knife through the cell door into the empty common area. "I did not kill your husband."

Jesse released Anita and took a fighting position, still holding Anita's hair. "You want your hair back?"

Anita stood. Her face was white. "You let me live."

"I'm not a murderer. And you aren't either. Want your hair back?"

"Where'd you learn how to do that?"

"Kung Fu training. I'll test for my black belt in a few months."

Some of Anita's color returned.

Jesse reached toward Anita with the hunk of hair. "Take this. It's yours. I don't want it."

Anita took the handful of hair as if in a trance.

"You're gonna need a haircut. Use that as a reminder that you didn't murder me and I didn't disable you. I think I know who murdered your husband, and I want to get them as badly as you do."

59.   Investors

Anders Nordqvist swallowed a sip of water from the bottle at his podium and faced an international investor group. He smiled and held the bottle up. "This is a perfect example of what I am trying to address. This plastic bottle represents what is wrong with society today. We need to redouble our efforts to eliminate pollution and leave a better world for future generations. And we will do it by showing the raw beauty of this planet to premium customers."

Congressman Catz stood. "Cut the BS, Anders. You're not in front of any cameras in here. Your revenue is not meeting projections and your quality needs work."

Anders gestured to the video conference camera above the row of large screen monitors in the back of the room. "Congressman, I must take exception to your statement. Today, we are always in front of cameras."

People chuckled.

"Congressman, I understand you had an altercation with one of my employees in Florida."

"Yeah, she attacked me."

One investor on the video link with a British accent said, "Attack? Is that what they call it these days?"

Another in the room said, "Matt, I heard you like it rough. Anders, maybe you should offer a premium package with girls trained in martial arts and cater to that market."

A few chuckled. Catz shook his head and sat.

A Middle-Eastern man wearing a white robe with headgear spoke next from inside one of the large monitors in the back of the room. "Congressman Catz brings up a valid point. Your promised profitability date is fast approaching. But your financial reports show a widening gap between revenue and spending. We deserve an explanation."

Anders nodded. "Yes, and I shall provide it. As you know, and especially Congressman Catz, we are supplementing our revenue stream by offering various companionship services. This area of business faces tremendous local competition in every market we serve. To overcome this competition, we need to operate on a large scale, so we can offer our customers all the choices they desire. Our wide array of choices, even including bringing in service providers from other areas for customers with specific needs, will overwhelm the competition. As a proof of concept, and a gesture of appreciation one of our valued investors, we matched Congressman Catz with a recent recruit from our Norra lekplatsen resort in northern Minnesota. We learned from that encounter, and we will take more precautions in the future. And if any of you are interested in a similar gesture of appreciation, please contact me and we will arrange it.

"We must also invest heavily in security because, as you know, this facet of our business operations must remain discreet. And so, we continuously recruit security professionals to help us maintain your anonymity. We cannot and will not scrimp in our investments in this area. I hope all of you appreciate that. Our highest duty is to keep your identities as our valued investors safe."

Another investor spoke. "On the topic of security, I understand you terminated your relationship with two of your recruits in your northern Minnesota resort. What is your plan to discourage them from discussing our activities?"

Anders took a breath. "One of our security specialists is addressing that situation as we speak. It should not present a problem."

"That's not what I heard. I heard you have a dead police officer on your hands."

"Yes. A police officer, unfortunately, did inadvertently lose his life during our operation. But his death will serve a greater purpose because his killer, a woman hostile to our business, is in jail awaiting trial for his murder."

The Middle-Eastern man said, "All well and good, but when do you anticipate profitability? Our generosity has limits, no matter what non-financial benefits you offer."

"I anticipate profitability within six months."

The Middle-Eastern man said, "We will hold you to that promise. I expect to see progress at our next meeting."

60.   Bail

Tuesday, October 16, 2018

Somebody pounded on Jesse's cell door. The door popped open. Gloria, Anita, and Dominic smiled.

Jesse stood. "Am I going home?"

Gloria nodded. "Yep. All cash, just like they ordered. But ten dollar bills this time."

Jesse laughed. "How did you raise it?"

"Your parents kicked in some. I did some. So did your boss at Dairy Queen. Brenda helped out. And a few others."

"Wow. Thanks."

Dominic nodded. "But first, the prelim. We're pleading not guilty while they count the cash."

~

Judge Lundergan tapped his gavel and stared down over his bench at Jesse and Dominic. "I see your attorney graced us today with his presence."

"Yes, sir, Dominic Levenson, representing Jesse Jonsen."

The judge nodded. "First, the matter of bail. The clerks counted the money your friend brought. I'm afraid you're one hundred dollars short. We rejected your bail submission and your friend can pick up her cash on the way out. See my clerk for details. And I don't want any more wheelbarrows in my court building."

Gloria stood from the seats in the back of the courtroom. "Wait a minute. The bank counted that money and wrapped them in hundred-dollar wrappers."

Judge Lundergan smacked his gavel. "I will have order in this court. Any further outbursts and I'll have you removed."

Dominic's face turned red. "Your Honor, the bank double and triple-counted that money before we brought it here. There must be some mistake."

"Are you accusing our clerks of corruption?"

"No, I'm suggesting somebody must have miscounted or made some other mistake, and I respectfully request that you count it again, this time in my presence as a representative of the defendant. I also request that you provide me with a receipt."

Judge Lundergan nodded. "Of course, Mr. Levenson. I believe we count bail submissions every morning at 8:30 a.m. I'm sure our clerk will be happy to accommodate you in the morning."

"Uh, huh."

"What was that, Mr. Levenson?"

Dominic took a deep breath. "I said, thank you, Your Honor."

"Your Honor?" Heads turned. It was Anita in the back of the courtroom, in uniform. "Just so you know, I'll contribute that last hundred dollars. And last time I checked, I was still an officer in this court, and I'd appreciate it if you would put energy into bringing my husband's murderer to justice instead of trying to railroad this prisoner."

Judge Lundergan leaned back in his chair. "Well now, that's a surprise, Mrs. Rasmussen.

"Very well. It seems, your client has a friend with influence in this court, Mr. Levenson. And since you have a friend willing to help your cause, I'll ask my clerk to make a procedural exception and re-count your bail submission, this time including Mrs. Rasmussen's contribution. If the total is five hundred thousand dollars, then, Ms. Jonsen, you'll be free to leave on bail."

"Thanks, Your Honor." Anita rushed toward the door.

"You're welcome. And, Anita—"

Anita stopped and turned. "Yeah, Dad, um, sorry, Your Honor?"

"We'll discuss it later. Be back here in five minutes." Judge Lundergan turned to Dominic. "I assume your client still wishes to plead not guilty?"

"That's right, Your Honor. My client pleads not guilty."

"Very well. Let's set a trial date for six months from now."

61.   Emails

Dennis Waverly sat across from Jesse and Brenda at a table at the Minneapolis Skyway Manitou Coffee. He handed Jesse a USB stick. "You didn't get this from me. It has a PST file with all of Mike Swanson's emails at work."

"What's a PST file?" Brenda asked.

"It has all of Mike's work emails. Your tech consultant, the guy who testified at your trial, Jerry? He'll know what to do with it. Or, he can call me."

Jesse smiled. "I thought we didn't get this from you."

"I'll talk to Jerry. At the trial, he looked like he knows what he's doing."

Jesse nodded. "He does."

"There's one email you'll be most interested in. I printed a copy." He handed a hard copy to Jesse. "Mike sent this from his home email to work. It has contact info for a couple people from North Prairie University."

"We already know who they are," Brenda said.

"That's not what's important. What's important is, from that email, we know Mike's home email address. I didn't see anything else that looked personal from his work email. So, he probably communicated with them from his home email, and these are probably the people he communicated with."

Jesse skimmed the hard copy. "Yep. Harold Rocklind and Meaghan Maxwell. If those are even their real names."

"Your guy Jerry needs to figure out how to get inside Mike's home email." Dennis looked down and then back up. "Brenda, Jesse, I am so sorry I did this to you. I had no idea Mike was a crook. I thought you guys were the crooks."

Brenda nodded. "Seems you violated a few policies yourself to get us this information."

"I did. But I didn't get caught. But if I'd known then what I know now, I would never have installed *Glimpse* on any of your computers, and you would both still have your jobs."

Jesse tapped Dennis's hand "If you hadn't done it, Mike would have found somebody else. It wasn't your fault."

"Thanks. One other thing. I copied the fake FISA order Mike showed me. I want to be there when you nail him for that."

62.   2FA

Monday, October 22, 2018, 6:00 p.m.

Jesse, Gloria, and Jerry Barkley sat around a temporary card table in Jerry's basement.

Jesse scribbled doodles. Her fingers tingled. Must be an adrenaline rush.

"Everyone ready?" Jerry asked.

They all nodded.

"Okay. Showtime."

Gloria pressed the speaker button on her phone. She dialed a few digits and then dialed Mike Swanson's phone.

Gloria assumed her professional mode. "Mr. Swanson?"

"Yeah, this is Mike Swanson. Why is Google calling me?"

"We're sorry to bother you this evening, but I'm glad you noticed our caller-ID. We've detected what might be fraudulent activity with your email and we need to verify your identity."

"Is this some kind of scam?"

"I can assure you, it's not. The process is really quite simple. We're sending a text message to your cell phone. Just read back the code we send, and that will verify that you possess the phone our records say you possess."

"What kind of fraudulent activity?"

"It appears somebody unauthorized has been trying to change your password. As a precaution, we've disabled the account. When you give us the code, we'll re-enable it. You'll need to go through the forgot-password process. And again, we apologize for the inconvenience, but we need to take these steps to protect our customers."

"You disabled the account, huh?"

"Yes, that's right."

"Well, I'm looking at my Gmail inbox right now. So, how is it disabled?"

Gloria glared at Jerry.

The whites of Jerry's eyes grew until they looked ready to pop out of his head.

Jesse tumbled her hands over and over and pointed at Gloria, as if to say, "keep talking."

Gloria swallowed. "Um, I do apologize for this. I'm not technical, but my support people are in the next row of cubicles. Would you give me just a few seconds to ask them and get back to you? I was under the impression that you wouldn't be able to access your Gmail at all. But obviously, if you're already using it, the system must not log you out immediately. But I believe you'll have trouble getting back in later. Let me check with my team to find out. And again, I apologize. May I ask you to hold for just a few seconds?"

Gloria muted her phone. She glared at Jerry again. "Got any brilliant ideas?"

Jerry's eyes lit up. "Okay, here's what you tell him. Tell him to look for an email from Google about all this. We just now disabled the account, and so people don't normally see the confirming email until after we re-enable the account. That's why we call."

"Okay. But wait," Jesse said. "Then why isn't it in his inbox yet?"

Jerry shook both his hands. "Oh—right—because we haven't sent it yet. Sometimes it takes a couple hours for the system to send it."

Jesse pursed her lips. "Okay. So, how does Google send a confirming email?"

Jerry smiled. "Because anyone can impersonate anyone else in an email. I'll send it. He'll think it came from Google."

Gloria nodded. "Okay, I think I get it.

Gloria unmuted her phone. "Thank you so much for your patience. My support team tells me the system disabled your account just a few minutes ago, and you should see a confirming email soon. But you wouldn't have a way to access that email unless you were already in your account. That's why we also reach out by phone in these cases, so our customers know what's happening with their email accounts." She paused. "Um, anyway, may we send you that code? And again, we apologize for the inconvenience."

Mike sighed. "Okay, fine. Send me the code."

Jerry clicked buttons on his laptop and navigated through the GMail "forgot password" page. He nodded at Gloria.

"The code should be coming any second. Just read it back to us and we thank you for your time."

"Yeah. It just came in. Five-six-four-two-seven-one."

"Thank you, sir."

Jesse wrote the numbers on a piece of scratch paper. Just in case.

Jerry entered the code and gave Gloria the thumbs-up signal.

"Yes, that matches. Thank you for helping us protect your account."

"You're welcome. Are we done?"

"Yes, sir, and thank you again."

Jerry's fingers flew over the keyboard.

Gloria terminated the call.

Jerry exhaled. "Great ad-lib. Our church drama team could use you."

Jesse high-fived Gloria and Jerry. "What's his new password?"

Jerry chuckled. "I was thinking about something colorful, but I just went with 'MyGuyMik3.' It won't last long. He's probably changing it as we speak. The download will take a few minutes, and then let's see what we've got."

63.   Plan B

Wednesday, October 24, 2018, 2:00 a.m.

In his basement office, Jerry Barkley's jaw dropped. He clicked on the link again. The same video played. He fumbled for his cell phone.

"Jesse, you're not going to believe this video. They blackmailed Mike Swanson."

~

After sunrise, Jesse sipped coffee across from Jerry in a conference room in Dominic's office.

Gloria sipped her coffee. She nodded at Jerry's glass of water. "I don't know how you survive without coffee."

Jerry chuckled. "Coffee might be the grossest drink ever invented. I never acquired a taste for it. Ashley, don't let them hook you on that stuff."

Gloria feigned shock.

Jerry put his phone on speaker and dialed.

Supervisory Special Agent Jake Channing answered. "Well, Jerry Barkley. I'll give you this, you have nerve calling me back."

"Jake, first, I'm sorry our last call didn't end well. I shouldn't have called you at all. I put you in a tough position. It was my fault."

"You didn't put me in any position at all. But out of respect for you and what you did for us earlier, you'll notice I didn't send the police to your house. Because I promise, this time you'd still be locked up if I would have."

Jerry smiled. "And you'll notice Jesse turned herself in and now she's legally out on bail."

"I noticed."

"Good. I didn't lie to you, Jake. I told you I'd call back with solid evidence and that's why I'm calling right now."

"I'm listening."

"Okay. There's a senior manager at Uncle Sam Bank named Mike Swanson. He was a couple layers above Jesse Jonsen in the food chain."

"Okay."

"You can look him up on the internet. He's the guy who oversaw a ten-million-dollar endowment campaign at North Prairie University. He probably earned a fat commission from that."

"Nothing illegal about commissions."

"I know. But he raised a lot of money for those guys. Keep that in mind when I tell you about the X-rated video I found with him in it."

"Nothing illegal about making sex videos, either."

"I know. But this video came from that same Norra lekplatsen resort I told you about earlier. He was soliciting prostitutes, and they videoed it and emailed a link to Swanson. They're using it to blackmail him."

"Got proof?"

"I have the video and the email. It's behind a TOR proxy. I made a copy."

"So, you have a link to a kinky video in an email. Got any proof they're using it to blackmail him?"

"Just look at the chain of events. He framed Jesse for embezzlement, she went to trial and won, the traffickers tried to murder her, and now they've framed her for killing that police officer."

"Great theory. No facts."

"Aren't you guys the Federal Bureau of *Investigation*?"

"We are. And we need probable cause to *investigate*. Because, as you know, we aren't a police state."

"Okay. So, what do you need for probable cause?"

"Let me ask you a question. You said that video was behind a TOR proxy. How did you find it?"

"I have ways."

"Uh huh. And so, you want me to start a federal investigation into, I-don't-know-what, because you illegally obtained a sex video with a guy you don't like."

"Jake, he was part of a group that tried to murder three people. And they probably also murdered that police officer."

"Maybe. But you have a credibility problem."

"So, what do you need to see?"

"Facts. Go look up what facts are. That's what I need to see."

Jerry sighed. "I'll get back to you."

"You do that, Jerry."

Jerry terminated the call. "I'm sorry, Jesse. We're on our own. Again."

Jesse sighed. "Looks like plan B."

From Dominic's speakerphone, Leilani said, "We'll be ready."

Jesse nodded. "Arik, Mukwoh, Ishkode, I look forward to meeting you guys in person."

64.   Blackmail

Saturday, October 27, 2018, noon

Jesse waited at Gloria's Manitou Coffee.

Mike Swanson made his way to Jesse's table. He sat. "Here I am. What do you want?"

Jesse eyeballed him.

"Yeah. That's what I thought." Mike stood.

"'A man has needs?' And, 'My wife can't help?' I didn't believe you really said that until I watched it with my own eyes. I mean, Mike, that's gotta be the worst line ever."

Mike returned to his chair. "What do you want?"

"First things first." She slid a piece of paper across the table. "You'll recognize this link to your little porno video. My IT friends tell me it's behind something called a TOR proxy, so you have to know where to look. Naturally, I have a few copies tucked away in case your friends get rid of the original. If anything happens to me, well, you've seen it in the movies. Your little video will become public. But to answer your question, after what you did to me, to Brenda, to the whole Fraud department, and the girls you helped lure into slavery, I want to beat your brains in."

"Good luck with that." Mike stood again and turned.

"Walk away and your little video goes viral. I have something else in mind for you."

He stopped.

"Sit down."

Mike sat.

"First, you're going to send an email to the bank CEO and board of directors. You're going to tell them about your little video and how you framed me and you're going to ask them to keep it quiet for now. And then you're going to find contact information for all the investors in Harold and Meaghan's trafficking scheme. And then, maybe the FBI won't send you to prison."

Mike grinned and nodded. "You'd better watch over your shoulder the rest of your life."

Jesse laughed. "Or what, they'll stuff me into an SUV and try to murder me and dump my body somewhere? They already tried that. You'll notice, their security guy, Kyle, or Landon, or whatever his name is—he's not around anymore."

"Tough talk."

"Mike, see that big guy at the table next to us? His name is Arik." Jesse nodded at Arik.

Arik stood and towered over Mike. "Nice to make your acquaintance." He turned a chair backwards and sat, facing Mike.

Jesse smiled. "See those two guys on the other side? Ishkode and Mukwoh." They wandered over.

Mukwoh reached for Mike's hair. "Nice scalp."

Jesse stifled a laugh. "Just a few of my friends." She pointed at the camera bubble in the ceiling. "We have some technology watching us too. I know the guy who set that system up. He helped the bank a few years ago and he punched holes in your little frame job back at my trial." Jesse nodded again.

Leilani wandered over and sat next to Jesse. "Yeah, I think I recognize you. You made a video where I used to work."

Jesse leaned forward. "So, Mike, you might want to think about looking over your own shoulder. Because you're between a rock and a hard place."

Jesse nodded at Ishkode and Mukwoh. They returned to their tables.

"So, this is what you're going to do right now. You're going to login to your bank email from my laptop so I can send an email from you to a recipient list I compiled."

Mike chuckled. "Nice intimidation job. Who am I supposed to send this to?"

"The bank CEO, board of directors, a guy we know at the FBI, and a few others."

"Really. And, what am I sending?"

"I'll show you after you log in."

"Jesse, you of all people should know we don't allow remote access into bank email."

"Except for director-level managers and above. Which you are. They'll probably fire you after they read your confession."

"I can't send it from your laptop."

"Why not?"

"I don't know the password."

"Oh, Mike. You should come up with something better than that."

"I don't know how to login to my remote mail. It's set up on my laptop, but not yours. I don't know how to do it."

Jesse shrugged. "Okay. Never mind then. Let me show you the other email I composed. I was just putting the final touches on it when you showed up." She tapped some keyboard keys and then turned her laptop around to show Mike. "You'll recognize the recipient list. Skim it if you want. This one has more details and a wider distribution list than the one I want you to send. Notice I copied the *Star Tribune* and *Pioneer Press*. And *USA Today*. And the *New York Times*. And a few other newspapers. I also copied your buddies, Meaghan Maxwell and Harold Rocklind. And the local TV channels. Maybe the media won't pick it up. But Harold and Meaghan? They'll care. Maybe their goons will give you a ride in the back of an SUV. And all these managers at the bank? I imagine a few will care."

Mike skimmed Jesse's laptop screen.

"Maybe that will help your memory."

"I'm a dead man if I do this."

"Don't worry. I want you to send a different email to a smaller audience. But if I send this email, yeah, the odds are decent you won't live past next week."

"And how am I supposed to find all their investors?"

"First things first. Login and send the email I want you to send. Then we'll be on the same side. Or walk away." Jesse stared at Mike's eyes.

After a few seconds, Mike looked away. "Okay. How do I log in?"

Jesse took back her laptop and tapped a few keys. She turned it back around facing Mike. "Here's your login screen. Just type your password. You'll also need your one-time-code generator."

Mike finished logging in. He turned the laptop back around to Jesse.

"Good. Now, give me just a second." She tapped keys and swiped the touchpad. "Want to read what you're sending? Maybe check it for grammar and typos?" She turned the laptop to face Mike.

Subject: Coming clean

I, Mike Swanson, solicited services from a human trafficking ring in late 2017 or early 2018. Unknown to me, the traffickers recorded a video of me soliciting and of one of their workers delivering their service. They posted the video online on the dark web.

```
The video link is

http://fivlsyxjh0gg39zkbp72x3sjasoworaf
bgcvmfimafty7twagswzczad.onion/

They used that video to blackmail me
into supporting their efforts,
including framing Jesse Jonsen for
embezzlement, firing her supervisor,
Brenda Yang, and destroying the bank's
Fraud Department.

I also oversaw the bank's efforts to
underwrite a $10 million endowment
campaign involving North Prairie
University and this group, for which I
collected a large commission.

I now wish to help remedy this
situation and I will accept any
consequences the bank or law
enforcement sees fit.
```

Mike turned the laptop back around. His eyes looked red-rimmed.

"Any grammar changes, Mike? Typos?"

Mike shook his head.

"Good." Jesse tapped the Send key. "It's on its way to their inboxes."

Mike stared off into space.

"Now, here's what you're going to do next. Ask Harold or Meaghan to call a meeting. You raised ten million for them. Tell them that now you have a way to raise one hundred million, but you need to talk directly to their investors about it. Get their contact information and give it to me. You do that and I'll put a good word into the FBI friend of my friend, Jerry. Who knows, Mike, you might get out of this without going to prison."

65.   Goodbye

Saturday, November 10, 2018

Mike stroked his wife's hair and kissed her. The heart monitor next to her hospital bed beeped faster.

"Amanda, I need to tell you some things you won't like." He grabbed a tissue and wiped his eyes. "I am so sorry. I've fallen as low as a man can fall, and I hurt you because I was selfish."

Mike took Amanda's hand and sobbed for a minute. He wiped his face again and took a deep breath. "I enlisted services I should not have enlisted. And some people recorded it all on video and blackmailed me. And now an ex-employee of the bank is also blackmailing me."

He took another jagged breath. "I created this situation. I can't go to the police. I'm the only one who can fix it."

He wiped his eyes again. "And I have a plan. You'll get the best medical care there is. Money won't be a problem. And when you get better, you can reconnect with Jamie and Marcy. I left a note with their addresses and phone numbers. They'll be happy to hear from their mom. But it means I won't be coming back."

He put both hands on hers. "Just know that I love you. And I miss you. More than words can express. And I'm sorry. I came today to say goodbye."

He stood and wiped his eyes again. He looked down at Amanda one last time, and listened to the monitors. The heart monitor showed ninety beats per minute. Amanda's eyes glistened. A tear drained along her nose. The monitor went to ninety-three.

He sat again and took her hand. The monitor slowed to seventy-five. He wiped the tears from her eyes. "I'm sorry. I have to go. It's the only way." The monitor went to 107. He strode out the door.

~

At home that evening, Mike scrutinized the signed non-disclosure agreement one more time. In exchange for a $200,000 cash payment, he agreed not to disclose why he and the bank separated. The bank had doubled its offer, thanks to his negotiating skills. Apparently, a major bank underwriting an endowment campaign for human traffickers creates a liability problem for people who serve on a board of directors. Who says crime doesn't pay? He chuckled. Of course, one-twenty-five-k after taxes won't last long, but so what? He'd be dead in a few days after tying up loose ends.

After turning in the leased Ford Expedition, selling the fully furnished house, cashing in his retirement savings, and after taxes and penalties, he should have about $2 million to show for his life. Which should be enough to buy a decent annuity and pay for Amanda's care for the rest of her life.

His career was over. Which was really all he ever cared about. Which was the real reason his adult daughters Jamie and Marcy both married the right husbands and lived in the right neighborhoods and drove the right cars, but rarely visited anymore.

He downed another sip of his drink. For the first time ever, the world was clear. He had been a fool his whole life. He should never have ridiculed Ecclesiastes. And now, his life was over. Meaningless.

But maybe not.

~

Mike parked his new, rusted 2007 Toyota Camry in a space under the Ikea Store near the Mall of America. A guy wearing a grey sweatshirt eyeballed him. Mike climbed out of the car and stepped toward sweatshirt-guy.

"Got the money?"

"Five hundred cash, right?"

"Yeah."

The seller looked around. Just cars, no people. He pulled out the handgun.

Mike pulled out the cash.

66.   Revenge

Monday, November 19, 2018, 8:30 a.m.

Mike positioned his car facing north across from the power substation at the intersection of Minnesota State Highway 27 and 295th Avenue, about one half mile West of a one-stop-sign-town named Lastrup. Harold and Meaghan should pass by westbound in a gold Cadillac Escalade SUV in the next thirty minutes on their way from Norra lepkpatsen to North Prairie University.

Mike knew that because he had watched them follow this routine for the past week. And he had scoped the whole route. This was the ideal spot.

The car would appear over the crest, about twenty-five-hundred feet East, in front of a driveway leading to a house on the North side of Highway 27. Mike would have about twenty seconds to react. Trees would block the view for anyone near the house, but they would probably hear a noise that sounded like a thunderclap. Which would be unusual on a clear morning, but it was an unavoidable risk.

After Harold and Meaghan passed by, it would probably be at least five minutes before the next car. Which should allow plenty of time to clean up.

Mike slipped on plastic medical gloves and waited in his car. He rolled down the passenger window and stared east with binoculars.

A car crested the hill. Red. Wrong color. It passed by. Nothing unusual to see here. Just an old Toyota sitting behind the stop-sign on a dirt road, facing north.

A few minutes later, the next car crested. Gold. This was it. Mike's heart pumped. He coasted into the intersection, blocking both lanes, with just enough room for the westbound Escalade to squeeze between the street sign on the North side and Mike's Toyota.

Mike grabbed his gun and ducked around the driver's side of his car.

Mike watched from under his car. The Escalade slowed and drifted right. Good. He took the bait.

The Escalade slowed to a crawl and veered right, now onto the cross street.

Mike crouched behind his left front wheel.

The Escalade bumper passed in front of Mike's car.

Mike popped up.

The driver was Harold. Meaghan in the passenger seat.

Mike fired.

Glass shattered.

Mike fired again. Harold slumped.

Meaghan grabbed something next to Harold. A gun. She raised it.

Mike fired again. Missed.

She fired.

Mike's shoulder burned. He swore and fired again. Hit her arm. He stepped toward her.

They both fired. Point blank through the shattered window.

She slumped. His right shoulder burned again.

The Escalade coasted through the intersection and hit the stop-sign.

Mike couldn't raise his right arm. He switched hands and ran to the Escalade.

Meaghan still had the gun. She tried to lift her arm. Mike fired, lefthanded. She slumped.

Mike opened the door and pushed Harold's body over. A blood pool formed on the seat.

Mike slipped in and shifted to reverse. He backed the car onto the road and maneuvered into the parking area in front of the substation, front bumper now facing east so the shattered driver's side would not be easily visible from the highway. He shut the Escalade off and left the keys in the ignition.

Mike pulled Harold's body back behind the wheel and wrapped the fingers of Harold's right hand around Mike's gun. He lifted Meaghan's gun arm and fired another bullet into Harold from her side. He put Meaghan's arm back down and then grabbed his gun from Harold's hand and wrapped her fingers around it. Who knows. It might fool somebody. They killed each other.

He jumped out, closed the Escalade driver's door, and ran to his car. He backed it onto the road and turned west.

Safely through Lastrup, he turned his attention to his wounded right shoulder. He felt light headed.

After a few miles, he turned onto a side road. One more task and then he could die. He dialed Jesse's cell number with his left hand and put the phone on speaker.

"Mike?"

"Just wanted to let you know. I did you one better than what you wanted."

"Mike, what did you do? You're slurring your words. Are you drunk?"

"Probably loss of blood. Listen, Harold and Meaghan are dead. You don't have to shay, um, say, thanks."

"Loss of blood? From what?"

"A couple shangs didn't go as planned. Don't worry about it. I'm shorry I got you fired."

"Mike, do you need a doctor?"

Mike coughed. "Couldn't hurt. Got one out here in the middle of nowhere?"

"Where are you?"

"Good question. Uh, highway 27, a little South of Lastrup."

"I might know somebody. Think you can get to Onamia?"

"Maybe."

"Well, head that way. Don't hang up. Maybe I'll help save your life."

67. Rescue

Jesse put Mike on hold and dialed Leilani.

"Jesse, hi!"

"Shut up and listen. I need your help. Remember that guy I told you about who tried to frame me?"

"Mike, right?"

"Yeah. Mike Swanson. I think he killed Harold and Meaghan."

"What?"

"He's on hold on my phone; says he's lost a lot of blood. He's probably been shot. Do you think your doctor friend can help?"

"Where is he?"

"On highway 27 south of Lastrup. Just a minute, I'll bring him into the call."

Jesse tapped call phone keys. "Mike?"

"Yeah, I'm still here."

"Leilani?"

"Yeah."

"Okay. Mike, where are you?"

"At the stop-sign in Lastrup. Back on the way to Onamia."

"Okay. Leilani, can you call your doctor friend?"

"Yeah. I'll put you guys on hold."

Leilani came back on a minute later. "Jesse?"

"Yeah."

"Doctor Sutton?"

"I'm here."

"Doctor Sutton, I'm Jesse Jonsen. You worked on my concussion a few weeks ago."

"Ah, yes, I remember."

"We need your help again. A man named Mike Swanson is heading toward Onamia and I think he has a bullet wound."

"And you want me to patch him up?"

"Something like that, yeah. I think he's maybe an hour away from you. Mike, you still with us?"

"Yeah. The road'sh gettin' blurry."

"Hang in there. We have a doctor waiting for you in Onamia."

"Um, Jesse. And Mike. Working on a concussion is one thing. But bullet wounds bring on lots of questions. Like, how did you get shot?"

"We think he killed a couple of human traffickers. And he probably has information the FBI could use," Jesse said.

Leilani's voice. "Jesse, do you want me to go find him and bring him in?"

"Doctor Sutton, what do you think?"

"Call me Lydia. Bringing him in is a good idea. If he's losing blood, he might lose consciousness, and that tends to work out badly with driving. But I'm not a surgeon. Let me call an ambulance."

"I'll try to stay awake," Mike said.

"Nimama is right here," Leilani said. "She says Arik is visiting the Lutheran Church, right on Highway 27 and 213th street, so he should be close. Maybe they can help."

"Mike, did you hear that? Look for that Lutheran church," Jesse said. "I'm bringing it up right now on Google Maps. She tapped buttons. "Look for it on your left, where the road curves to your left."

"I shee it," Mike said.

"Nimama, tell Arik he's right there," Leilani said.

A few minutes later, Mike said, "I'm parking."

Muffled voices.

"Hi everyone. I've got Mike's phone," Arik said. "We have some people here getting him inside."

"Are you Arik?" Lydia asked.

"Yeah. Dyani called me a couple minutes ago."

"Okay. I'm Doctor Lydia Sutton. What does he look like?"

"Well, he's white."

"I don't mean his race. His condition."

"White as a ghost. Bleeding pretty bad."

"Where?"

"His right shoulder."

"Is there an exit wound?"

"Let me check. Yeah. Bleeding pretty bad back there too."

"Okay. Sit him upright. The wound is above his heart, so let's use gravity."

Arik relayed to people in the room. "Okay. He's in a chair, sitting upright."

"Good. Next thing, get his clothing away from both wounds. Cut it, tear it, whatever you have to do. Find the wounds and with the cleanest towels or rags you can find, put pressure on them. Do what you have to do to stop the blood flow.

"Okay."

"All right. You work on that. I'm putting this phone down and calling an ambulance from a different phone. I'll be right back. Keep pressure on those wounds."

"Okay."

Lydia came back a minute later. "Ambulance on the way. How are we doing?"

"We've got people squeezing him pretty good. He's not bleeding as much."

"Good. The ambulance is about fifteen minutes away from you."

"I think he's gonna make it."

Jesse exhaled. "Leilani, Lydia, I'll meet you up there."

"I'm not a surgeon. The ambulance will take him to the ER. Meet him there."

"Okay. Thanks. I'm hanging up and heading up there." Jesse terminated the call and then called Jerry Barkley. "Hey Jerry. You're not gonna believe this. You gotta call your friend with the FBI. And then meet me in Onamia."

68.　　ER

Supervisory Special Agent Jake Channing put his hands behind his head and stared at Jesse across a hospital emergency room waiting area in Onamia, Minnesota. "So let me see if I've got all this. Before the victims died, they videoed your ex-boss's boss's boss soliciting prostitutes and blackmailed him into raising money for North Prairie University and its work-study program. But that program was really a front for a sex trafficking operation at the Norra lekplatsen resort. You found out about the video and confronted your guy. He apparently got mad and got into a gunfight with the victims. And that's why I drove eighty miles to meet you today. Does that about cover it?"

Jesse nodded. "Yeah. But don't forget that your so-called victims murdered a police officer and framed me for it. Hopefully you can help get to the bottom that, too."

Jake leaned forward. "You know that murder and prostitution are state crimes, right?"

Jerry Barkley, sitting next to Jesse, shook his head. "And I know that you know this operation is part of something bigger because I've told you at least a couple times. And you might also have a corrupt local police department. Who knows, Jake, this case might get you another promotion."

Jake chuckled. "You don't have to sell me, Jerry. I drove up here, didn't I? I'll talk to this Mike Swanson and we'll see where it leads. Okay?"

Jerry grinned. "Okay. Thanks for coming."

Somebody in a white lab coat approached them. "I'm Doctor Maravich. Are you family?"

"No. I called for the ambulance," Jesse said.

Doctor Maravich's furrowed his brow. "Wait. I thought Doctor Sutton called the ambulance."

"She did. I called Leilani, who called Doctor Sutton. Doctor Sutton helped with first aid over the phone, and then she called the ambulance. I'm, um, a friend." Jesse extended her hand. "Jesse Jonsen."

"And the rest of you are?"

Leilani and Jerry introduced themselves.

Jake stood. "I'm Jake Channing with the FBI. How's he doing, doc? And when can I talk to him?"

"Give him a couple hours in recovery. The surgery went well. He'd lost a lot of blood. Jesse, if you hadn't made those calls, he wouldn't have made it."

Jesse blinked away tears. Why do I care if this guy lives? She shook the doctor's hand. "Thank you."

~

Jesse looked down at Mike Swanson in his hospital bed. A sea of monitors and oscilloscopes monitored him. Mike opened his eyes.

Jesse shook her head. "Looks like you lived."

Mike struggled to speak. "My car. Phones. You said you wanted contact information."

"You got their phones?"

Mike nodded. "In my car. At that church."

"Got keys?"

"The big guy who helped me has them."

"Okay. FBI Agent Jake Channing has some questions for you."

Mike took a shallow breath.

Jake stepped forward. "I'll start with a few yes or no questions. If it's too difficult to talk, you can just nod or shake your head. Okay?"

Mike nodded.

"Okay. First, from what we can piece together, you had a gunfight with Harold Rocklind and Meaghan Maxwell this morning. That's how you got injured. Is that right?"

Mike nodded.

"Okay. And the reason for your gunfight is, they blackmailed you with a video, right?"

Mike nodded.

Jake also nodded. "Okay. That's it for now. Do you have an attorney?"

Jesse waived her arms. "What do you mean, that's it?"

Jake glared back at her. "I'm doing my job. Don't get in my way."

"Ask him if he's a murderer. Ask him if he framed me."

"I'm only going to say this once—" Jake said.

"Hang on a second," Jerry said. He got in Jesse's face. "Listen. He can't ask any more right now. Read the room. Mike's not a witness. He's a suspect. Jake has to do this by the book."

Jesse fumed. She turned and sat in a chair against a wall away from Mike's bed.

Jerry took a seat next to her.

Jake nodded at Jerry and then took a card from his pocket and turned to Mike. "I'm going to read this to you now. And I'll read it again tomorrow when you're more alert. You have the right to remain silent. Anything you say can and will be used against you in a court of law. You have the right to an attorney and to have that attorney present during questioning. If you cannot afford an attorney, the court will appoint one for you. Do you understand these rights as I have explained them to you?"

Mike nodded and then whispered, "Yes."

"Okay. One more question for now. Where did this gunfight take place?"

"Power substation." Mike took a breath. "H...highway twenty-seven and," Mike took another breath. "295th Avenue. Before Lastrup. Car parked," Mike took another breath. "In front of the substation."

Jesse stood. "Jerry, I have an idea. You need to support me."

"Huh?"

"Just—trust me." She turned to Jake. "Jake, I'm sorry. You're right. I'm mad. My whole life is on the line here."

Jake finished putting his Miranda card away and nodded. "Apology accepted." He strode into the hallway.

Jesse followed. "And so, now I need you to listen to me. I think we can get the guy in charge of all this."

"And this guy is?" Jake asked.

From behind Jesse, now also in the hallway, Jerry said, "His name is Anders Nordqvist. He's a Swedish guy with lots of money. We looked him up a while ago. Jesse, what's your plan?"

Jake put his palms out. "Hold on, guys. I appreciate the enthusiasm, but you know the rules."

Jerry chuckled. "Jake, do you notice a pattern here? We come to you guys, you blow us off, then we prove we were right, you try to take over, but you still need us? At least listen. We've saved the world a couple times, you know."

Jake grunted. "I already don't like it."

"Not here," Jesse said. "In private."

They made their way into a meeting room adjacent to the waiting area. They all sat.

"I'm listening," Jake said.

Jesse pursed her lips. "First, you're right. I'm mad. And everyone knows why. Including Nordqvist. He'll also know. He knows I'm out to get him. Heck, I rescued two of his workers. He's gotta know who I am and that I'm a threat."

"Okay..."

359

"Okay, so we use that. I'm also greedy. I know about the video. I know who made it and why and I want a piece of the action."

Jake leaned back and narrowed his eyes.

"Are you nuts?" Jerry asked. "You want to go meet this guy and pretend to be his partner?"

Jesse nodded. "Or maybe his blackmailer. I'd wear a wire. I've done it before."

Jerry's ears turned red. "Wait a minute. No. I'm saying no. This stuff never works right. Trust me. I know."

Jesse grinned. "Read the room, Jerry. He's thinking about it. We could take down this whole operation. All of it. And you don't get to vote."

Jerry stood. "Jake, don't let her do this. You know what happened when I tried it." And to Jesse, "Wear a wire? You *are* nuts. This isn't some two-bit hustler making fake IDs. This guy and his buddies will strip-search you before he ever lets you in. If he doesn't kill you first."

Jake nodded. "Jesse, I like your thinking. But Jerry's right. It's risky."

"I know. But otherwise, I go on trial for murdering a police officer and the organization that set me up keeps operating. I'm the right person to do this and you know it."

Jake nodded. "I'll talk it over with my supervisor and get back to you."

Jerry hissed. "You guys are nuts."

They all stood to leave.

Jesse raised her eyebrows. "So, Jerry, you in?"

Jerry sighed. "Yeah."

Jesse smiled. "Good. Why don't you go pick up those phones Mike told me about?"

"No," Jake said.

"What do you mean, no?" Jerry said.

"I said, no. You're not analyzing those phones in your basement. Our team will pick them up. The FBI will analyze them in our lab. Chain of custody."

"But—"

"Jesse, don't give me buts. This is now a federal investigation and we need to play by the rules. This is what you wanted, right?"

"Okay."

69.   Strategy

From a conference room in the Minneapolis FBI field office in Brooklyn Center, Minnesota, Jake handed Jesse a temporary cell phone. "Here. Call from this phone."

Jesse took a few calming breaths.

"Consider yourself privileged," Jerry said. "The first time I was in this building, they wouldn't let me near a phone. They practically strip-searched me."

Jake chuckled. "The security guys still talk about the nutcase who came in here that day."

Jerry turned to Jesse. "You ready?"

Jesse nodded. "Let's go." She launched the recording app and then dialed Norra lekplatsen.

"Welcome to Norra lekplatsen, where there's no such thing as bad weather, only the wrong clothes. How may I direct your call?"

"Hi. I'm Jesse Jonsen, and I know that your bosses, Harold Rocklind and Meaghan Maxwell, are missing."

"Um, I'm sorry, but neither Harold or Meaghan are available at the moment. May I send you to voicemail?"

Jesse grunted. "No. No voicemail. I just told you they're missing. I know where they are. I want to talk to your boss's boss, Anders Nordqvist."

After a pause, "Um, I'm sorry, I'm not familiar with that name."

"Well, you should be. Your bosses are missing, I know why, and your operation is in big trouble. Why don't you connect me with a supervisor."

"Please hold. I'll transfer you."

Elevator music. A phone rang. "Hi. This is Melinda Wright. How may I help you?"

"Melinda, you're not going to help me, I'm gonna help you. We both know that Harold Rocklind and Meaghan Maxwell are missing. You're looking for them. You won't find them. But I know where they are. I want to talk to Anders Nordqvist."

"Your name is Jesse, is that right?"

"Yep. Turn on your recorder if you want. Call the police if you want. I'm not hiding. But if you involve the police, you might not see Harry or Meaghan again. I want to talk to Anders Nordqvist."

"How do I know you're on the level?"

"You don't. But I just told you Harry and Meaghan are missing. You and I both know that information is not public. They left this morning as usual. They were supposed to be back by early evening. It's now past 7 p.m. and they haven't arrived yet. And they won't arrive tonight."

"How could you possibly know that?"

"Not your concern." Jesse paused. "Now, connect me to your big boss.

"I can't."

"Do you care about your bosses?

"It's not a matter of caring. He's not here. I don't have a way to connect you."

"What's his cell number?"

"I can't give that out."

"Given the circumstances, you should reconsider."

Melinda waited a beat. "Okay." She gave Jesse the number.

Jesse terminated the call and dialed Anders Nordqvist's number. It went to voicemail. She left a text message.

This is Jesse Jonsen. You
know who I am and I know who
you are. I also have a copy
of the blackmail video your
missing managers Harold and
Meaghan made. And I know
where they are. We both know
they killed that Mille Lacs
County cop and why. Tell the
police. Say they went rogue
if you want. I want $1
million to disappear and
start a new life since you
ruined this one. Call or text
for transaction details. Meet
me at the Manitou Coffee in
the Minneapolis Skyway
tomorrow, Tuesday, November
20, 2018, at noon.

The reply message came back five minutes later.

I accept your proposal to meet
in person, but I am afraid I am
out of the country at the moment
with no possibility of getting
to Minneapolis by noon tomorrow.
May I suggest Wednesday,
November 21 at noon instead? I
will provide lunch at Norra
lekplatsen. Or I can bring you
here to Belize to meet tomorrow
if you wish. Surely, as a
reasonable person, you can offer
some flexibility on the time and
place of our meeting, given the
sudden nature of our situation.

Jesse smiled and showed the reply to Jake and Jerry. And then she composed her next message.

> The last time I met on your property, things did not go well for me or your team. Especially your security chief, Kyle. I agree to Wednesday noon at the Manitou Coffee in the Minneapolis Skyway near eighth and Nicollet. It's a neutral site. Don't be late.

70.   Meeting

Wednesday, November 21, 2018, 9:00 a.m.

In a room deep inside the Minneapolis FBI field office, Jake gestured to a man wearing a white lab coat. "Jesse, meet Gunnar Friedrich."

Gunnar gestured for Jesse to sit in what looked like a dentist's chair, but with a cushion on the side.

Jesse surveyed the room. "This looks right out of a James Bond movie."

Jake chuckled. "Yeah, we've never heard that before."

Gunnar nodded. "No exploding pens or cigarette lighters today, I'm afraid. We're going to inject a temporary cochlear transmitter into your ear canal. It senses vibrations in your ear drum, translates those into Bluetooth network packets, and sends them to a device integrated with an undergarment you'll be wearing, which will both record the conversation and transmit to our team."

"What if they have equipment to detect it?"

"They might. But you'll transmit over the 2.4 gigahertz frequency band, and so it's likely any detection equipment will mistake it for a public WiFi."

Jesse nodded. "But what if they want me to drive somewhere with them?"

Gunnar and Jake exchanged glances. "The transmitter range is only about 200 meters," Gunnar said. "The video claims the same range, but it's more limited as a practical matter."

"The video?"

"Yes." Gunnar showed Jesse a few devices that looked like shirt buttons. "Miniature video cameras. Bluetooth wireless again, with electronics integrated with that same undergarment."

Jesse nodded. "So, don't leave with those guys."

Jake smiled. "Yeah, pretty much. But listen. Unexpected things happen, so be on your toes."

"I know. Jerry told me about what happened with his meeting."

Jake's face clouded. "I lost a dozen good people that day." He sighed. "Well anyway, this situation is different. There's only one way in and out and the restaurant and skyway are public."

Jesse chuckled. "And no airplane parked at the back door."

Gunnar approached Jesse, carrying a small electronic device, a garment that looked like an undershirt, and a pair of tweezers. "Tilt your head, please."

Jesse leaned her head on the cushion.

Gunnar dropped the transmitter into Jesse's ear and handed her the shirt. "Why don't you put it on in the bathroom and then we'll mount the video camera and test everything."

~

11:30 a.m.

Jesse strode into the Manitou Coffee and ordered her usual latte. She made eye contact with Gloria and sat at her designated table. As planned, Gloria pretended to ignore her. Jesse scanned the room. Like Jake said, he probably has people here. She sipped her latte.

~

11:59 a.m.

Jesse finished her latte. Just stick to the plan the way we practiced. I'm mad because you guys tried to murder me and then you set me up. I want a million dollars or I tell the cops everything I know. She clenched and unclenched her fists. What was I thinking? I'm a fraud analyst, not a secret agent. Well, I was a fraud analyst. Now I work at Dairy Queen.

~

12:10 p.m.

Jesse fidgeted. He's late. Gloria glanced at her. People walked in and placed their orders. Others left. And now I look conspicuous. She fiddled with her phone.

~

12:32 p.m.

A man in a business suit, wearing a baseball cap and carrying a briefcase approached Jesse's table and sat across from her. "Jesse?"

"Yeah."

"I need you to come with me."

"Who are you?"

"Agent Channing asked me to come get you. Anders isn't coming."

"Why not?"

"You need to come with me."

Jesse's phone rang. Jake.

The man stood. "Don't answer that. Come with me. Now." He moved to Jesse's side of the table.

Jesse answered and put the phone to her ear. "Yeah?"

"Both the audio and video died when that guy walked in. I don't know who he is. Nordqvist is dead. Get out of there."

The guy reached for Jesse's arm. She pulled away.

He grabbed her by the shirt.

Jesse knocked his baseball cap off his head. Brown hair. Almost a buzz cut. Greying on the sides.

He pulled her close. He needed a shave. "We were hoping to do this in a more civilized manner. We have a message for you. We handled your murder rap. Now, you back off or you'll see worse trouble."

"Tell your bosses I said no."

"That would be a mistake."

He let go, grabbed his briefcase and hat, and hustled back into the Skyway.

Over the phone, Jake said, "Wait a minute, now it's clearing up. What's going on?"

Jesse followed, trotting with the phone in her ear. "That guy. With the briefcase. He's in the Skyway. I'm trying to find him." She put the phone in her pocket and broke into a run.

His hat. On the escalator, going down.

Jesse bobbed and weaved around people. She ran down the stairs between the escalators.

He walked outside.

She hit the first floor and followed out the door.

He climbed into a car. It took off.

She ran behind it on the sidewalk. Minnesota license plate. The car rolled away. She grabbed the phone from her pocket. "Jake, you still there? He got in a car on eighth street. Minnesota plates. MNV305."

"Which direction?"

"It's one way. East."

"Okay. Meet me back at Manitou. I'll see if I can get the local PD to grab him."

~

Gunnar and Jake were waiting. Jake was on his phone.

He flooded you with noise." Gunnar looked angry. "That's why we lost audio and video."

Jesse nodded. "He was carrying a briefcase. He probably hid something inside."

"Yes. But it was directional. He only flooded you. WiFi continued uninterrupted for other customers."

Jake finished his call. "The police got the driver. It was an Uber. Your guy wasn't there. He walked away on foot a couple blocks away."

"But he paid with a credit card. You can follow that, right?"

"We're working on it."

Jesse sighed. "If I were him, I'd use a gift card tied to a fake ID. I'd have a car parked in a ramp and I'd hop out of the Uber, walk to my car, and drive away. Probably a rental, but with a different credit card. If he's from out of town, he's on his way home. But he won't use the airport because he knows you'll be watching. He'll drive somewhere else, return the car, and catch a flight home. If he did this right, you won't find him."

Jake and Gunnar stared at Jesse.

"What? I know how criminals think. It's what I do. How did Anders die?"

"We don't know yet. He collapsed yesterday at a layover at DFW on the way here. Apparently, it was on the news this morning," Jake said.

Jesse smirked. "Am I the only one suspicious?"

Jake shook his head. "No. You're not."

Jesse nodded. "Good. Maybe we can find out more about the guy here. Hey Gunnar, I knocked that guy's hat off his head. Think you can help us figure out who he is?" She gestured to the camera bubble in the ceiling. "Jerry Barkley put in that camera. I'll bet he can get us some images. Got any fancy government image databases?"

Gunnar smiled. "Maybe."

Jesse dialed Jerry Barkley.

Jerry answered. "Hey Jesse, I thought you were in your big meeting."

"I was. But it didn't go like we planned."

"What a surprise. You're not in an airplane are you?"

Jesse laughed. "No. You're still the champ on that one. Listen, Anders is dead. Another guy showed up and apparently, he had a jammer. So, the FBI doesn't have any audio or video. Can you help us get some images off of Gloria's DVR?"

"Our tax dollars at work, huh?"

Jesse glanced at Jake. "Right. I'll tell Jake you said hi."

Jerry chuckled. "Okay, I'll work on the snark for now. Give me a second. I can grab video off that DVR from here and save it. For you guys there, Gloria has an app on her phone to play it back. And I think she can freeze frames. Get me a time index and I can get you a full-sized screen grab with a still image. You can look at it on Gloria's computer in her office."

~

Ten minutes later, the group stared at a still image from above the man's head on Gloria's computer monitor in her office.

Gunnar squinted over Jesse's shoulder. "Can you zoom in on the briefcase?"

From Jesse's phone, now on speaker, Jerry said, "Sure. Give me a sec." Keyboard keys tapped over the speaker. "Okay, refresh your display and open the new image."

Jesse opened the new image and looked up at Gunnar.

Gunnar's face went white. "The antenna is integrated with the decorative trim in the top front corner of that briefcase. Just point it and set the decibel level. I helped design that jammer. The design team is in Florida."

Jesse's jaw dropped. "Catz?"

"Who?" Jake asked.

"The investor in Florida Ashley told me about. That guy who beat her up. Congressman Catz."

"Wait a minute," Jerry said over the speakerphone. "You're telling us the FBI built that jammer and then somebody used it on you?"

Gunnar looked sick.

Jesse shook her head. "Apparently so."

"Well, I'll just say it out loud. Our tax dollars at work."

"Not now, Jerry."

"What do you mean, not now? That sex ring you uncovered has people in the FBI. Which means they probably have people in high places all over."

Jesse glanced at Jake. He looked stricken.

"I think they know, Jerry."

Jake's eyes hardened. "Jesse, who knew about this operation?

"Jerry, you, me, my parents, Gloria, An Li, Ashley, Leilani. Leilani might have told her mom and a couple friends in Onamia who helped save Mike Swanson. I trust all of them." Jesse paused. "Jake, who knew from your side?"

Jake turned red. "We had to go through an approval process to get your surveillance equipment. So, a few." He nodded. "Somebody above me is dirty."

"Duh!" Jerry thundered over the phone.

"Maybe," Jesse said. "But a few people in Anders' group knew too."

"But how did they get the jammer?" Jerry asked.

Jesse's phone beeped. "Hang on Jerry. It's Dominic." She put Jerry on hold and answered.

"Great news, Jesse. I just got off the phone with the Mille Lacs County prosecutor. They dropped all the charges."

"Why?"

"When the prosecutor says they're dropping all charges, good defense attorneys do not ask why. We accept our good fortune."

"Thanks Dominic. Let me merge your call with Jerry. We have kind of a situation here and we might need your help."

"There's worse trouble than being framed for murder?"

She added Jerry back to the call and filled Dominic in. "So, is Mille Lacs County dirty too?"

Jake nodded slowly. "Maybe. Or maybe somebody showed them evidence that clears you."

"Right. And I shouldn't look a gift horse in the mouth."

Over the speakerphone, Dominic said, "I'll find out what persuaded them to drop the charges."

Jake's eyes bored into Jesse. "So now, you're off the hook. The guy who framed you for embezzlement is disgraced. You rescued your friends. The people who murdered the police officer and framed you are dead. And now their boss is dead. For you, it's over. You can walk away right now."

Jesse shook her head. "No. It's not. They know who I am and how to find me."

"We can hide you."

"I don't want to hide. And no, you can't. You said it yourself. Your bosses might be in on all this. You could be a target too. And what about An Li? And Ashley? And Leilani and her family?"

Jake sighed. "Looks like we're a team. Who do we trust?"

"I have a few friends." Jesse chuckled. "Jake, you know you won't have the full resources of the United States Federal Government behind you anymore, right? But don't worry. We know how to get creative."

Jerry laughed over the speakerphone. "I still have nightmares from the last time I got creative."

Gunnar nodded. "If you're talking about another mission to rescue humanity, I'd like to help. That was my jammer."

"If you need legal services, you know how to find me," Dominic said over the speaker.

Gloria joined the group. "Count me in, too."

Jesse and Gloria hugged.

After a few seconds, Jerry asked over the speaker, "Are you guys having another hugfest?"

Jesse wiped away tears and laughed. "Shut up, Jerry."

Jerry laughed over the speaker. "Thanks to Jake, I know a good PTSD doc. After this is all over, I'll fix you guys up. Maybe we can finagle a group discount."

71.   Earl

Friday, December 7, 2018, 2:45 p.m.

Jesse entered Niigaanii Hall on the North Prairie University campus and searched the directory again. Earl Townsend, English Department Chair. Still in the same office, room B426. She trudged up the stairs again and approached his office.

The door was shut. But she was early. Maybe she'd find a coffee machine.

Muffled voices behind the door. A girl, crying. Familiar voice.

Jesse glanced around the hallway. She was alone. She stood close to the door.

"How am I supposed to study and spend three nights every week at that hotel?"

Jesse shivered. Something was wrong. She wracked her brain. Where had she heard that voice?

"Young lady," Earl's voice sneered. "We rescued you and your so-called boyfriend and enrolled you both in the Norra lekplatsen work study program. Instead of hustling on the streets in Minneapolis, now you spend three nights per week in a luxury hotel, all expenses paid. Your day has the same twenty-four hours as mine. I suggest you find a way to use them wisely."

Jesse's mind raced. How is that place still operating? The girl's voice—Maribel? Yeah. From the Hennepin County Jail. The girl with the great singing voice. Earl must have recruited her. Which means, he's the missing link. He oversees it all from this side.

Jesse's fingers tingled. Fight or flight. She stepped away from the door and glanced left and right. Nobody. She closed her eyes. Inhale—exhale. Inhale—exhale. Just a couple more calming breaths. Breathe. And think. Fight or flight, huh? Use it, so it doesn't use you.

She opened her eyes and scanned the hallway again. Only two ways out—the elevator or the stairs. Both led to the first floor. She backtracked down the stairs and positioned herself midway between the stairwell and elevator. Maribel would have to cross here.

Ten minutes later, the elevator dinged. Jesse pretended to study the directory, her back partially turned away from the elevator.

The elevator door opened. Maribel stepped out. Earl followed, holding one of Maribel's arms.

Jesse jumped in front of them. "Maribel?"

"How do you know me?"

"We met over Memorial weekend. In Minneapolis."

"No, we didn't, I was in—wait—Jesse?"

Jesse smiled. "Yeah. I still remember your beautiful singing voice."

Earl looked uncomfortable.

"Professor Townsend, nice to see you again. Jesse Jonsen. We had a 10 a.m. appointment, remember?" Jesse reached to shake his hand.

"Oh, yes. Um, I'm afraid something has come up and I'll need to reschedule." Earl pulled Maribel tighter.

Maribel's eyes pleaded.

Jesse spread her legs, one leg slightly behind the other. Better balance that way. Just in case. "I don't think so. Last time we met, you didn't tell me you're the school's work study coordinator."

Earl smiled. "You didn't ask."

"Uh huh. And is Maribel one of your workers?"

"That's none of your business."

"Maribel, you don't have to go with him. You can walk away with me. Right now. He's going to prison."

Earl laughed. "Aren't you presumptuous. And why am I going to prison?"

"Because you're the missing link. Somebody had to help Landon Miller take Kyle Van Buren's name after he murdered the real Kyle Van Buren. When you said Kyle went missing, your story didn't add up. Remember the news story from fourteen months ago about the dead body at the Little Falls dam? After I rescued two other people from that place, the FBI compared that body's DNA with Kyle's sister in North Dakota. It matched. That was the real Kyle Van Buren. But you told me he didn't have any family, remember? That's what I came here to see you about."

"Nice theory. Too bad you don't have any proof."

"I don't need any. You're gonna help the FBI take the whole operation down. Not just Norra lekplatsen, but the whole thing. All the resorts. Everywhere. Maribel, c'mon. We're walking out of here, right now."

Earl tightened his grip on Maribel's arm. "No, she's not. And you're also coming with me."

"Oh, really? Or what, you'll shoot me right here in the lobby?"

Earl showed his gun. "Silencer. Nobody will hear it."

"How do you plan to clean up the blood?"

"The lobby is empty. Everyone is in class. I'll exit the back door, stash the gun, and come around to the front and report a horrible murder."

Jesse nodded. "Good plan. What are you waiting for?"

Earl raised his weapon.

Maribel cowered.

Jesse slid and swept her legs under Maribel's feet.

Maribel fell.

Earl lost his grip on her arm.

"Lower your weapon. Now." Jake's voice.

Several FBI agents poured into the building, guns drawn. They grabbed Earl's gun and handcuffed him.

Jesse stood and dusted herself off. She glared at Jake. "What took you guys so long?"

Jake chuckled. "You were on a roll."

Gunnar walked in.

Jesse turned her glare to him. "Did you get it all?"

"Yes," Gunnar said. "The audio fidelity was excellent. The video was a little wavy, especially when you performed that, whatever-it-was."

Jesse shook her head. "Want me to stand still next time, so you can watch the bullet hit me in the heart? Maybe play it back in slow motion?"

"Jesse, I'm sorry." Jake looked stricken. His eyes said it was more than just professional.

Jesse's heart beat a little faster. But it wasn't fear this time. She hinted at a smile. "I'll bet you say that to everyone who helps save the world for you, right?"

"No. It's just, well, I just didn't want to see you get hurt. That's all."

Jesse broke into a smile. "You're cute when you stammer. Makes you vulnerable."

Jake actually blushed. Mr. tough FBI guy.

Jesse laughed.

Maribel's eyes looked ready to pop out of her head.

Jesse reached for Maribel's hands. "Maribel, meet Jake Channing and Gunnar Friedrich, with the FBI. Maribel and I met inside the Hennepin County Jail, last Memorial Day weekend. Maribel, you never told me your last name."

"Martinez. Maribel Martinez. How did you know I would be here?"

"We didn't. I suspected Earl knew more about Kyle Van Buren's death and I wanted to ask him about it."

"Who?"

"I'll tell you all about it later. And I want to hear your story."

72.   Morning After

Saturday, December 8, 2018

Jake leaned in for a kiss. Jesse closed her eyes. The first since Dylan. But this time, it felt clean. A helicopter flew overhead. Dust washed everywhere. What was that noise?

Jesse sat up in bed and turned her 5:30 a.m. alarm off. Why did she set up a drywall party for so early Saturday morning that it was still late Friday night? But who could have predicted yesterday? They nailed the missing Norra lekplatsen link, and then the FBI, well, mostly Jake, invited her to celebrate the win. Jake dropped her off here after midnight.

With the mold finally cleaned from inside the walls, it was time for real walls again. Leilani and her handyman family friend Arik were coming down from Onamia to help. Jerry and his wife, Lynn, were coming. Jake even said he might show up.

Somebody knocked on her bedroom door.

"Come on in. I'm awake."

Camile opened the door with a cup of coffee. "Late night saving the world?"

Jesse chuckled. "Something like that. Thanks." She took the coffee and sipped it. Her new friends would all be fine. Ashley was with Gloria and finishing her senior year in high school. Leilani was with her mom and her friends from that church in Onamia. Maribel was in a women's shelter, at least for now. Maribel's family had disowned her, and so she would need somewhere more permanent. Maybe a halfway house or something like that.

Jesse took another sip. Her Dairy Queen companions, An Li and Camile and Fahad, were working out well here with her, coming up on four months. She was the only one still in a mess.

She swallowed one last sip. Sitting in a Dairy Queen driveup window and talking to people who want ice cream. That's the reward for saving the world. No good deed goes unpunished.

Keep on seeking, and you will find. I am with you always, even to the end of the age. The thoughts bubbled into her head. Again. She sighed. What do those phrases even mean anyway? She picked up her phone and looked them up. The first one was from Luke 11, verse 9. The second was from Mathew 28, verse 20. Both just fragments out of context. From that creep back in eighth grade. That's why they were familiar. Or, maybe she was supposed to become a TV preacher and dispense fake wisdom for money.

Spiritual mumbo-jumbo. I wonder how many other perverts use Bible verses to lure middle-schoolers. But what the heck. Nothing to lose. She whispered, "Hey God, if you're really there and you're supposedly looking out for me, how about throwing a real job my way? Or am I supposed to sling ice cream at Dairy Queen the rest of my life?"

~

The doorbell rang at 6:30 a.m. Arik and Leilani came inside. Jerry and Lynn Barkley were right behind. Jerry carried a crockpot full of Lynn's sloppy joe.

Lynn and Jesse hugged. "Where should Jerry plug this in?"

Jesse directed Jerry to the kitchen.

The doorbell rang again. It was Jake.

Jesse smiled ear to ear.

Lynn smiled and nodded. "I want all the details."

Jerry returned from the kitchen. "Huh? Details about what?"

Lynn's eyes gleamed. "Nothing, Jerry."

~

Arik lifted the next drywall sheet in place. Jake drove two screws to hold it, while Jerry cut the next sheet. Fahad, Camile, and Leilani drove the rest of the screws.

Jesse and Lynn shuttled between the kitchen and cleaning.

Jesse tossed another scrap away. "Can I ask you guys a question?" She nodded toward Jerry and Lynn.

Jerry chuckled. "I heard the answer to everything is forty-two."

Lynn thumped Jerry. "Shut up, Jerry. She's serious."

Jesse looked down and then back up. "Okay. It's no secret I'm mad about what happened to me at Uncle Sam Bank. But I'm grateful for my job at Dairy Queen. And for you guys." She looked around the room. "I know you had better things to do than hang drywall at my house on a Saturday morning."

Arik's eyes twinkled. "De nada, seniorita."

Jesse nodded. "But something is missing. These thoughts keep bubbling into my head, and they did again this morning. 'Keep on seeking, and you will find.' And then, 'I am with you always, even to the end of the age.' I looked them up. They're parts of Bible verses. You guys are, well, religious. I was hoping you'd have some ideas."

Arik lifted the next sheet. "Sounds like God's tryin' to get your attention."

Jake drove two screws near the top.

Jesse nodded "That's what my mom says all the time. But how do you know?"

Jerry marked the next piece. "God talked to me under a tree in a park one time."

Lynn's eyes sparkled.

Jesse noticed. "This must be good."

Jerry slid his drywall knife along the straightedge. "The short version is, I was alone in a park near a bunch of trees by our house with our dogs, and I figured I could challenge God."

Arik chuckled. "Pretty heady stuff. Next piece ready?"

Jerry nodded. "Well, yeah, IT people, we think we're pretty smart, ya know. Anyway, I said, 'Hey, God, if you're really everywhere all the time, then just show yourself. Right here, right now. There's nobody else here but me, nobody needs to know. So, how about it? Just show up. Carry some rocks. Say something important.'"

"You said that?" Jesse laughed.

Arik lifted the next piece and Jake drove the two screws to hold it.

Jerry nodded. "Well, I was the only one there. But yeah, I pretty much made a fool of myself."

"That's Jerry." Lynn smiled.

Jerry chuckled. "Anyway, nothing happened. So, then I said, 'Okay, God, are you gonna show up, or is all this stuff I keep hearing about you just a bunch of BS?'"

"So, let me guess." Jesse spread her hands. "Nothing happened?"

Jerry shook his head. "No. This is where it gets weird. I heard a voice in my right ear, as if somebody stood right next to me. The voice said, 'You're not ready yet.'"

"But nobody else was there, right?"

"Right. Just me with the dogs, alone in the park."

"So, then what happened?"

"I tried to argue, but that voice made me afraid of ghosts and goblins under the trees. I ran home."

Everyone laughed.

"Is that how you became a Christian?"

Jerry shook his head. "No. That was in 1993. I became a Christian in October, 1994."

"What did it?"

"Some people taught me a history lesson. Those New Testament Gospels? Matthew, Mark, Luke, and John? And Acts? They're not just stories. They're real history. The Romans really did crucify Jesus and Jesus really did come back from the dead, three days later. When you piece together all the motivations and what we know from other sources, the only conclusion that makes any sense is that events happened the way those books say they happened."

"How do you know that stuff is true?"

"A couple tests. First, does today's Bible accurately reproduce what the original authors said? The answer is yes, there's tons of science and scholarship around it, and the translations footnote a couple places where we still aren't sure of the original wording."

"Okay, so we reproduced what they said. How do we know they told the truth? Everyone has an agenda."

Jerry measured for the next piece. "Right. That's the next test. Look at the politics of the day and everyone's incentives. That area, near Jerusalem, was a Roman backwater. The Jews wanted the Romans gone and they revolted pretty much all the time. So, why would the Romans let an outrageous story about Jesus spread so far and wide so fast? Even if it was fiction. Why not squash it? Well, they tried for a while, until they embraced it a couple hundred years later."

Jerry cut the piece to length. "But then, if you're going to write fiction about a conquering hero, why would you have him spend three years shocking everyone, then kill him and bring him back three days later, and then send him away to Heaven a few days after that? And without conquering anyone? And why would your supporting characters all have obvious flaws? The good guys are supposed to like Mom and apple pie, and ride white horses, right?"

Jesse chuckled. "You have a way with words, Jerry."

"Well, you know what I mean. The good guys are supposed to be heroes. Role models. Pillars of the community. But in the Gospels, Matthew was a tax collector, Peter was a fisherman who could barely read, Simon the Zealot might have been an assassin, Judas was a traitor, and later on, Paul was a reformed murderer. Somebody killed every one of them except John, and the Romans exiled him offshore."

Camile, Fahad, and Leilani continued driving screws.

Jesse shook her head. "Okay, but what about the inconsistencies? How do you explain those?"

Jerry nodded. "I don't. Some details are mutually exclusive. They can't both be true."

"So, how do you trust it?"

"For me, it's like people reporting on a car accident from different points of view. If everyone is honest, they'll never agree on all the details. And there's no reconciling the differences."

"Okay. Let's say all that is true. Just the way you explained it. So what?"

"That's the best question of all. The way I answer it is probably different than anything you've read. You know how Christians keep saying 'Jesus died for our sins?'"

"Yeah."

Jerry put down his knife and went into professor mode. "What does it mean?"

"Adam and Eve sinned and we're all bad people, right?"

"Yeah, pretty much. And so we all deserve to die. The wages of sin is death, and all that."

"Yeah, I have a hard time with that."

"You should. I do, too. This hit me inside a McDonalds a few years ago. It's the fundamental assumption behind Christianity. We all deserve to die, Jesus died in our place, and now we have an opportunity to live forever. It's an assumption. It comes from the Bible. We believe it because everything else in the Bible is credible. But there is no proof. If you don't buy the assumption, the conclusion doesn't make sense. We have a hard time with it because, well, it's just creepy. It violates everything we want to think about ourselves."

Jesse swept a pile of scraps into a dustpan. "So, do you get this feeling of inner peace I keep hearing about?"

Jerry and Lynn exchanged glances.

Jerry chuckled. "No. Not even close. Do I look like somebody who spends a lot of time getting in touch with my feelings?"

"Wait a minute. I thought your religion was a feel-good thing for you guys."

"It makes me feel good." Lynn said. "I know there's a savior and no matter what happens, I'm saved and I'll spend eternity in Heaven."

Arik picked up the next piece and held it in place. "Yep. If Jesus saved me, He can save anyone. You need to do one more thing."

Jake drove the top two screws. Fahad, Camile, and Leilani started on the rest.

Jesse dumped her dustpan into the trash. "What's that?"

Arik turned and faced Jesse. "Accept Christ as your savior."

"You mean, like right now?"

"Yeah. Why not?"

"How?"

"Just ask God to forgive you and tell Him you want to join His kingdom. There are all kinds of suggested prayers, but it's not like there's a secret handshake or anything."

"Forgive me for what?"

"All your sins. Everything. I had to inventory mine. It's a long list. Still workin' on it."

"Yeah, I've heard this before. What about the people who sinned against me? What about Donato Alcaraz?"

"Who?"

"The youth pastor who groomed me back in eighth grade. I was in a youth group until we started having sex in his office. I was fourteen. He was in his twenties. What does God do about him?"

Arik nodded. "That's a tough one. Sooner or later, you'll have to forgive him."

"Poof, just like that? Forgive and forget? Pretend it never happened? That guy manipulated me into things that still make me sick. They told me back then I needed to forgive him. I never did. He's a scumbag who needed to go to jail."

"Sounds like he was. Maybe still is. Have you heard anything about him?"

"No. He went to prison, my parents got me a bunch of counselling, and I went on with my life. But then, I got involved with another guy who taught me how to be a thief. I helped put him in prison too. And then I became a fraud analyst. I've taken a lot of scumbags out of circulation since then. But now, I work at Dairy Queen."

Arik offered one of those wisdom smiles. "No good deed goes unpunished, huh?"

"Yeah, something like that. And so now, to save my eternal soul, I'm supposed to just, what, forget all that and don't worry, be happy?"

"No. In fact, if you accept Jesus as your savior, your life will probably get even more complicated. You're still you, and scumbags are still scumbags. Jesse, at my core, I'm still a scumbag. And I'll pay for it for the rest of my life. I had to tell a man's family I was sorry for murdering him, fifteen years after I did it. You know what they did?" Arik teared up. "They broke down and cried and forgave me. I didn't deserve it. But they forgave me anyway." Arik wiped his eyes. "Sorry. That still gets me and it was fifteen years ago."

Jesse fought tears. "But nobody told me they were sorry."

"Right. But that family—they forgave me years before I came to them. I just didn't know it until I finally worked up enough guts to talk to them. You don't think God helped out with that? Before I talked to them, I thought somebody on every street corner was out to kill me. That fear went away after that. It was five years after I finally accepted Jesus."

"And so, if I forgive Donato Alcaraz, he'll show up out of the blue in a couple years and apologize?"

"Probably not. But who knows? God has a plan for everyone. I sense he has a big plan for you. But you have to be ready."

"So, what's the big plan?"

"I don't know. I don't have ESP."

"Well, then how do you know?"

"You said it, yourself. You said, something is missing. You used to be a fraud analyst. Now you work at Dairy Queen. Do you want to keep working at Dairy Queen the rest of your life?"

"No."

"Do you want to go back and be a fraud analyst?"

Jesse tilted her head. All eyes bored into her. She set the broom down and leaned against a door frame "I don't know. I hadn't thought about it. Maybe not. So then, what?"

"Maybe, try to listen to God. See what he wants you to do."

"How?"

"Just watch for clues."

"What does that even mean?"

"It's different for everyone. All I can tell you is, you'll recognize it."

Jesse picked up the broom again and puttered with sweeping.

Jerry worked on setting up the next sheet.

Fahad, Camile, and Leilani continued driving screws. Jake also drove a few screws.

Arik strolled behind them. "You guys are gettin' pretty good at this."

They chuckled.

Jesse took in the whole scene. Friends hanging drywall for her, just because they're friends. And already more than halfway done. She wiped her eyes and smeared drywall dust on her face. "So, what do I have to do?"

Arik smiled. His eyes lit up. "Just ask Jesus to forgive you, tell Him you accept Him as your lord and savior. You'll work out details over the rest of your life."

"That's it?"

Jerry shook his head. "Wait a minute. No. There's more."

"What?" Arik's eyes went wide.

"There's more. There's a catch and we need to tell her."

Jesse's stomach churned. "What's the catch?"

Jerry looked more serious than Jesse had ever seen him. "It's a biggie. You have to mean it. You can't BS God. Don't even try."

Arik chuckled. "Yeah. Jerry's right. I was wonderin' where you were goin' with that."

Jerry nodded. "I tried to BS God. Didn't work out well."

Arik's eyes bored into Jesse's soul. "You ready?"

"I guess."

"Okay. So just repeat this after me. Jesus, I ask you to forgive me for all my sins, and I accept you as my lord and savior. Amen."

"Do I need to kneel or anything?"

"If you want to."

"No, that's okay. Jesus, I ask you to forgive me for all my sins, and I accept you as my lord and savior. Amen."

"Welcome to the club." Lynn teared up and hugged Jesse. "How about you, Jake?"

Jake smiled. "I've been listening. And thinking."

"So, what are you thinking?" Jerry's eyes danced.

Jake chuckled. "Just thinking, that's all."

Jerry nodded. "Which is fine. I like to razz you. But don't sit on the fence forever."

Lynn smiled. "Jesse, why don't you go to church with your mom tomorrow?"

"I might." Jesse turned to Jake. "Want to come with me?"

Jake found a tissue and wiped the drywall dust from Jesse's face. "To church?"

"Yeah. With my mom and dad. You'll need to meet my parents sooner or later."

Jake's ears turned red. "Uh, well, uh, I guess. Been a long time."

Jerry chuckled. "Mr. tough FBI guy."

Jesse laughed. "You're cute when your ears turn red."

Jake shook his head and grinned. His ears turned even more red. "Okay, I'll go with you."

Jerry's eyes turned mischievous. "So, does that mean you guys are a couple?"

Jesse and Jake exchanged glances. Jake looked embarrassed.

Lynn tossed a drywall scrap at Jerry.

Jerry grabbed his rib. "Ow."

Lynn turned to Jake. "You don't have to say anything. Jerry likes to embarrass people."

Jake nodded. "Yeah. I know." He turned to Jesse. "But I think I'd like that. If you would."

Jesse's lips turned up on their own, into the biggest smile she could remember. "Yeah. I'd like it too." She moved next to Jake. Jake put his arm around her. She leaned against him. It felt good. Really good. And right.

Arik chuckled. "Guys, I really like this, but we still have a bunch of hangin' and tapin' and muddin' to do."

"Right," Jerry said. He finished cutting the next piece of drywall.

"I'll check on the sloppy joe," Lynn said. She headed into the kitchen.

Arik lifted the next piece of drywall, Jake drove the first two screws, and Camile and Fahad followed.

Jesse smiled again and wiped a tear. Thanks God. Hey, as long as you're listening, how about that job?

73.   Henri

Monday, December 10, 2018

Another car in an endless stream of cars pulled up to the drive-up station. Jesse put on her headset. "Welcome to Dairy Queen. May I take your order?"

Her phone rang. The caller ID said Henri Carpentier. The guy on the Uncle Sam Bank board who shut down her plan to catch predators. But that was a different lifetime. She rejected the call. "I'm sorry—did you say only ketchup on that burger or no ketchup?"

She straightened out the order and waited on the next car. And the next car. And the next one after that. And before long, the lunch rush was over.

Three new voicemails waited. All from Henri Carpentier, with his thick French accent. She dialed and listened. He asked for a call back and said it was important.

Her shift ended at 6 p.m. She checked her phone again. This time, it was a text message.

```
Hello, this is Henri Carpentier again.
I recently became aware of certain
events and on behalf of both the bank
and myself, I apologize to you several
times. First, for my lack of text
messaging skills, but I endure this
```

```
tiny keyboard to gain your attention.
Next, for what the bank did to you
earlier this year. I assure you that we
will do our best to deliver justice to
Mike Swanson. Today, I wish to propose
a role for which you might be uniquely
qualified to fill. Please call me to
discuss it.
```

Nothing to lose. She called.

"Bonsoir, Jesse, Merci for returning my call."

"Hi Henri. You know I don't work for the bank anymore. What do you want?"

"Ah. Yes. Down to business as they say. Very well. You are no doubt very upset with your former employer, and I do not blame you. But please indulge me. I only recently learned about your separation from the bank. I read your trial transcript. Mike Swanson was a long-time family friend. My wife and I were devastated when we heard about his wife's accident. But what he did to you was unconscionable and I apologize to you for it. We will find him and bring him to justice. Hopefully that action will also help vindicate you."

"Well, thanks. But lots of things have happened since you shut me down in your boardroom."

"I was thinking that perhaps, as I recall you like to say, we can make a lemonade from this lemon. Did I say that correctly?"

Jesse chuckled. "It was close.'"

"Ah. Even after all these years, English still evades me. Parlez-vous Français?"

"Sorry, I'm afraid I only speak English."

"Ah. A pity. Such a beautiful language, Français. But I shall muddle through in English."

"Okay."

"We are in a similar predicament, you and me. Both of us have had our reputation tarnished and we seek vindication, yes?"

"Yeah, sure. Vindication. You guys tried to send me to prison and ruined my career. So now, the only place I can work is Dairy Queen, for minimum wage. So, you work on your vindication. I need to pay bills."

"Oui, the consequences you felt through no fault of your own were more devastating than mine. If the bank were to reimburse your legal expenses and offer you a job to rebuild the Fraud Department, at a higher salary than before, would that interest you?"

"Are you guys worried about lawsuits?"

"It is my fiduciary duty to worry about liability issues, oui."

"Well, if you want to buy me off, the legal expenses are only the start. How about apologizing in public and paying my back wages from the time you fired me? And making Brenda whole? Plus, a little bit extra for the trouble you put us though."

"I am willing to discuss that, but I had something more, how do you say, substantial, in mind."

"I'm listening."

"Merci. It occurs to me that you enjoy taking on causes you believe are just. Yes?"

"I suppose. But I won't be doing any of that because, thanks to you, I'm broke. I can't help anyone when I can't afford to even pay my own rent."

"I wish to help remedy your financial situation. I also wish to understand more deeply how trafficking rings like the one involving Mike Swanson use banking services to further their goals. And your proposal from earlier this year to impersonate, how you say, Johns, continues to intrigue me."

"Oh. Now it intrigues you. Too bad it didn't intrigue you when I presented it. Things might have turned out differently"

"Oui. I still do not believe it is the bank's proper role to pursue these predators. But perhaps a nonprofit organization dedicated to this task, possibly affiliated with the bank, might do an effective job. Do you have thoughts around that?"

"Right now, no. Victims all have issues, that's how traffickers groom them, so if you're going to attack traffickers, you also need resources to undo their grooming and help get victims back on their feet."

"Sounds like a big job."

"Yes. It is."

"Why don't you think about how you would contribute to that job, and what kind of resources it would require. Come to our next board meeting as my guest on Thursday, December 20, and present what you would do and what you need."

"What? Why are you doing this?"

"As I said, this incident tarnished all our reputations. I wish to propose to the board that the bank underwrite an effort to fight trafficking. You are a logical choice to lead such an effort, both because of your recent experience, and from your career as an accomplished fraud analyst. I also wish to propose that the bank fund it from the marketing budget and use it as an example of how we care about the world around us. You will help the bank restore its reputation. The bank will help you accomplish a worthy goal. We would, of course, also encourage other institutions to help us fund this effort."

"So, was the job offer just hypothetical?"

"Do you want a job?"

Jesse thought about if for a second. "I suppose not."

"Well, then, perhaps this opportunity would be better than a job, no?"

"It might. How about compensation for what the bank did to me?"

"I will propose it. I cannot guarantee a positive answer."

"Tell them the lawsuit will cost even more."

"Oui. I will ask them to think rationally instead of with their egos."

"Okay. What's the next step?"

"The next step is difficult. We, but mostly you, need to persuade the board that supporting this endeavor is a good use of funds. I will work on that to prepare for the meeting next Thursday before everyone leaves for the Christmas holidays. The quality of your presentation will plant seeds, and then I will work to win them over."

74.   Boardroom

Thursday, December 20, 2018

Other than a few Christmas decorations, the Uncle Sam Bank boardroom looked the same as the last time Jesse was here, eleven months ago.

At the front of the room, Henri Carpentier called Jesse up and introduced her. He shook her hand and returned to his spot around the long table. This time, no company laptop, no A/V team to connect it, no impressive job title, no department heads in the room with her. Just five-foot, one inch Jesse, with her dark hair and blue jeans.

Jesse looked around the room and mouthed a silent prayer. "A lot's happened since the last time I was in this room eleven months ago. After we hosted the Superbowl, you guys fired me and tried to send me to prison, you fired Brenda Yang, I liberated two sex trafficking victims, a guy who called himself Kyle kidnapped and tried to murder us, somebody murdered a Mille Lacs County police officer and tried to frame me, somebody else murdered two of the traffickers, the FBI finally got involved, somebody murdered the traffickers' boss, and now I work at the drive-up window at a Dairy Queen. And that's just the stuff I can talk about in public. Henri tells me you're looking for Mike Swanson. Which I appreciate because he led the effort to railroad me. I'm authorized to tell you that you'll never find

Mike Swanson, but Henri, I promise you, he experienced justice. So, you guys can take prosecuting Mike Swanson off your to-do list. Do I have your attention yet?"

Puzzled looks.

Jesse nodded. "Henri asked me to talk about what this bank can do to fight sex trafficking. And I'll get to that, but first I thought you should meet some people I've met over the past few months." She gestured.

An Li, Ashley, Leilani, and Maribel made their way up front.

"This is An Li. We work together at Dairy Queen. She helped get Ashley and Leilani out of Norra lekplatsen after the traffickers there tried to groom her. They came this close." She held her thumb and forefinger close together. "An Li saved our lives when she stopped Kyle from murdering us. Kyle died on top of her and she crawled out from under his dead body. He called himself Kyle, after he murdered the real Professor Kyle Van Buren and stole his name. His real name was Landon."

Jesse gestured to Ashley. "This is Ashley. A scumbag who's now dead convinced her she was part of a growing business, and if she worked hard, she would earn an early college degree and enjoy a great life. Guess what? They lied. And then at least two men assaulted her, she fought back, and the people she worked for told her the assaults were her fault.

"This is Leilani. Leilani and I met a couple weeks after the last time I was in this room. She spent four years in hell because traffickers convinced her she could never have anything better. But when Ashley fought back, she inspired Leilani to get out and bring Ashley with her. Leilani kicked Kyle's brains out. And then Kyle tried to murder us, but An Li got him first."

Finally, Jesse gestured to Maribel. "This is Maribel. You guys gave me an all-expenses-paid trip to the Hennepin County Jail over Memorial Day weekend to meet her. She has an amazing singing voice. After the original Norra lekplatsen gang died, whoever replaced them still tried to get their hooks into her."

Jesse looked over the group. Definitely had their attention now. "I introduced these women to you because sex trafficking is not just statistics. Real, flesh and blood people get caught up in it, and the consequences reach everywhere. And the people who perpetrate these crimes use our financial system to move money. This bank underwrote at least ten million dollars of it.

"So, if you're serious about setting up a nonprofit to fight this evil, here's what you'll need. First, full scholarships for Ashley, Leilani, and any other Norra lekplatsen victims. And tutoring for Ashley and any other high school students caught up in that mess to graduate with her high school class this spring. North Prairie University promised these women and others an education and this bank underwrote a ten-million-dollar endowment campaign. If you want to restore your good name, start there.

"Next, make Brenda Yang whole. You fired her for violating company policy, but then you put her in a position where she had no choice. You owe her a big debt because if she hadn't copied that computer, you would be in bed right now with some very nasty people, and sooner or later, it would have cost you. Personally. So, make things right with her.

"Next, Henri said you want me to run this nonprofit. I like that idea, but I can't afford it. After losing my job and paying to defend myself in court, I'm broke. If you're serious, then pay my legal expenses, pay my salary from the time you fired me until now, add two years of severance so I can focus on getting this new nonprofit off the ground without taking a salary from it, fund it with at least ten million dollars in startup money and ten million per year, and give me complete access to the predictive analytics program I helped this bank build. I'll use the data to continue improving the analytics. I'll use the money to pay for equipment and expertise, set up scholarship programs for other victims, and to gather intelligence and operate reverse-grooming operations to infiltrate these outfits and work with law enforcement to take them down."

Henri nodded. "What you request is within reason. The bank could wrap a marketing campaign around it and develop ROI measures. What would your specific mission be?"

Jesse smiled and unfolded a piece of paper from her pocket. "I wrote it down. We would do five things. First, continue to refine the analytics I started developing at Uncle Sam Bank, and share those with other financial institutions. In return, I would ask them to share anonymized versions of their transaction databases with our nonprofit, so we can continuously refine our transaction pattern profiles.

"Second, we would role-play as potential victims or potential customers using social media, telephone, or other means of contact. We would use this effort to gather intelligence and keep ongoing profiles on sex trafficking operations.

"Third, we would share our intelligence with law enforcement agencies and assist them going after trafficking organizations.

"Fourth, we would assist trafficking victims' physical, mental, and spiritual recovery. We would use a variety of tools, including counselling, college scholarships when appropriate, and physical and mental health care.

"And fifth, we would coordinate our efforts with other agencies around the world dedicated to fighting human trafficking."

Henri nodded. "What would you name this organization?"

"I'm thinking about 'The Nadine Ladysmith Foundation,' in honor of the first sexual predator victim I met a long time ago. But I'm open to other ideas."

"Wait a minute," one board member said. "Henri, I recognize what you're doing here. I've seen you engineer too many of these feel-good shows. We're a bank, not a social services agency, and while I can empathize with this woman's cause, and I might even donate to it privately, I cannot support our bank underwriting it. And Henri, you know better than me that granting an outside organization access to the bank's most private analytics data is a recipe for disaster. How do you support this when you're usually the one who thunders about cybersecurity?"

"Oui," Henri said, "we would need to work out significant details around sharing data. Some of it may involve legislation. Perhaps we only share transaction information about account-holders convicted of sex trafficking offenses. Or perhaps we anonymize all of it. I am not suggesting we lower our cybersecurity standards, only that we work within the banking industry to adopt a proper method of sharing information for the common good. Jesse, your thoughts?"

Jesse nodded. "If I do this, I don't want to violate anyone's privacy. I'm willing to work out with the board what makes sense. I need transaction histories, but I don't need names or personal information. In return, I'll give you better analytics about patterns to look for."

"But still," Henri said, "my colleague brings up a valid point. You will hold sensitive information and you will be a cyberattack target. How will you protect yourself and your organization?"

This time, Jesse's face smiled ear to ear on its own. "I would probably ask a quirky bald guy we both know to lead the cybersecurity effort. I met Jerry Barkley five years ago when we handled the Bullseye Breach incident, and we've stayed in touch. Henri, you also know Jerry. He's the reason I'm standing here in front of you talking about the next phase of my life, instead of inside a prison for embezzlement, because he punched holes in your case against me."

The board member said, "I read your trial transcript after Henri prodded me. And I agree, the bank's case was weak. But that only means the bank had insufficient evidence to prove your guilt. How do we ensure you—as you claim—were, in fact innocent and unjustly accused? By your own admission, you lied routinely as part of your job. Who's to say you didn't steal those credit cards some other way?"

Jesse was primed for this one. Henri had said somebody would bring it up. But it still stung. Her face flushed. She paused for a few seconds. Do I really want to do this? Yeah. Meet it head-on. "Are you married?"

"What?"

"It's a simple question. Are you married, yes or no?"

"I've been married since before you were born, young lady."

"Well, do you still beat your wife?"

"What? How dare you."

"How dare I what? Hit you with a question that no matter how you answer, you incriminate yourself? Accuse you of something out of the blue with nothing to back it up? You just did that to me. How dare *you*. If you want to prosecute me with speculation, then let's end this meeting right now and stop wasting each other's time. And for the record, I did not steal any credit cards."

Henri stood, with that typical gleam in his eye. "Might I suggest we discuss privately the proposal we just heard?"

Nods all around.

"Excellent. Jesse, I'll ask you and your friends to wait in the lobby for a few minutes."

Jesse nodded and followed An Li, Ashley, Leilani, and Maribel out to the lobby. Henri closed the door behind them.

Jesse and the group sat in plush chairs around a coffee table in the lobby.

Ashley looked down. She wiped her eyes.

"Ashley, what's wrong?" Jesse knelt in front of her and took her hand.

"I'm sorry. What you said – how Meaghan and Harold lied. I loved him, you know. I was ready to spend the rest of my life with him."

Jesse nodded. "I know. I felt that way about a youth pastor when I was in eighth grade."

Leilani also wiped a tear. "I felt the same way about Landon at first. But in the end, I hated him."

Ashley wiped her eyes. "And I hate Harold. And Meaghan. I miss my friend, Carissa. And my parents. I wish I could go back in time and tell myself not to get in that car with Meaghan when she spotted us at Lake Nokomis."

"Would you have listened?" Jesse asked.

Ashley nodded. "Maybe. I'd see me, but a few months older. My older me would tell my younger me what's coming. I might listen."

Jesse stood. "That's what I want you guys to do from now on. Tell everyone in the same position as you before the traffickers got their hooks into you not to believe the promises and look past all the glitz to the ugliness behind it. Tell them about what their future will look like if they fall for the grooming. Pass the wisdom you've gained to others. You've earned the right. And maybe the responsibility."

"How?" Maribel asked. "We're just four girls."

Jesse smiled. "You'll be part of a nonprofit with lots of backing. This time, your hard work really will make a difference. You'll help stop girls just like you from falling into a trap. You'll turn the lemons you were dealt into lemonade."

"What if this board says no?" Leilani asked.

"They'll say yes. And then we'll save the world."

"How do you know?" Maribel asked.

"I just do." Maybe this is how God talks to me.

The boardroom door opened. Henri smiled from ear to ear.

Jesse looked at the women with her. "See. What'd I tell ya?"

"Congratulations," Henri said.

The hostile board member made his way around Henri. "Jesse, for the record, none of us believe you stole those credit cards. Henri nominated me to challenge you because we needed to see how you react under stress."

He extended his hand.

Jesse gaped at Henri.

Henri's eyes twinkled. "Oui. We needed to see how you, how you say, fight? When you are in an interview with a hostile press, you need to handle yourself assertively. You did well. We will coach you on finer details."

Jesse chuckled. She shook the board member's hand. "Thanks. Now the hard work starts."

75.   Ashley

Monday, December 24, 2018

Jesse rang Ashley's parents' doorbell. Ashley's mother answered.

"Mrs. Dunbar, thank you for seeing us. May we come in?"

Mrs. Dunbar let Jesse, Ashley, An Li, Leilani, and Maribel in. Her eyes looked tired.

Everyone sat.

"Where's Gloria?" Mrs. Dunbar asked.

"She thought it would be best if she didn't come this time," Jesse said. "She said your last meeting didn't go well."

Mrs. Dunbar shook her head. "It wasn't Gloria's fault. Or Ashley's." She looked down.

Ashley stared at indentations in the carpet. "The curio cabinet is gone."

Mrs. Dunbar nodded. "Your father took it with him. I didn't want it here."

"Where?" Ashley asked.

"I asked him to leave. We're separated."

Ashley covered her mouth.

Jesse also looked down. "Gloria told me what happened at the end of your last meeting. Is that why you separated?"

"Partly. Mostly, maybe."

"Mom, I'm so sorry."

"For what? For showing us we'd been living a lie all this time? You were right about your father. And me. I suspected, but didn't want to believe it. And I realize now that he put you in an impossible position. Ashley, I am so sorry for judging you. I'm sorry for putting appearances ahead of everything. I'm sorry for living like a hypocrite. I don't want to live that way anymore."

"Mom, I just want us to be a family. A real family. Not a fake one."

"I do too."

Ashley and her mom squeezed each other tight. Both cried.

An Li, Leilani, and Maribel shifted in their chairs.

After several seconds, Jesse asked, "Are you and your husband trying to work things out?"

Mrs. Dunbar let go of the embrace. "We're seeing a counsellor. I don't know how it will turn out. But you didn't come visit on Christmas eve to talk about my marriage."

Jesse nodded. "We're starting up a nonprofit to fight sex trafficking. I wanted to introduce you to An Li, Leilani, and Maribel on our core team. I'd also like Ashley on the team. And I wanted to tell you that Uncle Sam Bank is offering her tutoring to catch up in high school and a college scholarship if she wants it."

Mrs. Dunbar's eyes widened. "That's amazing. Really?"

Ashley nodded. "Yeah. I'm thinking about pre-law. Mom, this group is going to do amazing things. I want to be part of it. And I want to live here, with you and Dad, and be a family."

Jesse pursed her lips. "Gloria wanted you to know that Ashley is welcome to stay with her for as long as she wants. But nothing can substitute for your family."

Mrs. Dunbar nodded. "I'd like that. What are you all doing for Christmas tomorrow?"

Jesse chuckled. "I don't know. I guess none of us have thought that far ahead."

Mrs. Dunbar smiled. "Why don't you guys spend Christmas here. You're all invited. Ashley, I'll call your father. I can't promise what he'll do." She dabbed a tear. "Jesse, I never got the chance to say thank you for rescuing our daughter. The things we said that night when Gloria and Ashley visited were horrible and I'm sorry. As far as I'm concerned, you're all family and all welcome here anytime."

It was Jesse's turn to fight tears. "Thanks."

76.   First Ave

Saturday, May 25, 2019

Jesse, Brenda, and Maribel peeked out at the audience from backstage at the First Avenue nightclub in downtown Minneapolis. Jesse waved to a group of tables on the balcony level. Leilani with her group, Ashley with her parents and Carissa, An Li, Gloria, Jerry, and Jake waved back.

The emcee's voice boomed. "And now, for a special segment of our Nadine Ladysmith Human Freedom Foundation Fundraiser, I can't wait to introduce a fresh new voice from right here in Minneapolis. Give it up for Maribel Martinez."

Maribel and Jesse hugged. Maribel exchanged glances with Brenda and glided onstage.

The emcee gestured to the mic.

Maribel stepped up and gazed at the crowd.

The room quieted.

Maribel wiped a tear. "Before I start, I just wanted to say thank you for allowing me to sing for you. Could I ask a favor?" She turned toward Jesse. "Jesse, would you come out with me for a minute, please?"

Jesse's jaw dropped. She turned to Brenda. "Did you set this up?"

Brenda nodded. She mouthed, "yep," and gestured toward the stage.

From onstage, Meribel said, "Please? I promise, I won't make you sing."

Jesse shook her head and made her way to Maribel in the spotlight at the mic.

"I'm embarrassing Jesse because I wanted to publicly thank her. We first met a year ago in jail. I was supposed to be there, she wasn't. But now, I think maybe God put her there. Because she met me that day, and then a few months later, she rescued me from slavery. So, I just wanted to say thanks."

Maribel hugged Jesse.

Jesse embraced Maribel back, laughing and crying. She wiped tears with one arm. "I'll get you for this." Jesse's voice boomed over the hot mic. "Oh, great, now I'll really get you for this."

The crowd roared.

Jesse shook her head. "Can I go backstage now?"

"Thanks Jesse. Yes."

A few minutes after the show, Jesse's phone chirped. It was a text message from an offshore country code.

```
We know how to find you. And
your friends. Leave us alone and
we'll leave you alone.
```

An attached picture showed the First Avenue front facade.

Jesse tapped a reply.

```
            Take your best shot. The last
            scumbags who threatened me
            are dead.
```

77.   Acknowledgements and a Note to readers

Back in 2019, I searched for a reformed trafficker willing to talk to me and I found John Turnipseed. John was a notorious Minneapolis gang leader, pimp, and drug dealer until 1994, when he turned his life around and accepted Jesus. He became one of the first participants in Minneapolis Urban Ventures' Center for Fathering, eventually running the center. Later, he served as Urban Ventures' Executive Vice President and Campus Pastor. He mentored hundreds of men to become better fathers before meeting the Lord on Nov. 22, 2022.

John told me that when he was pimping, he found women to work for him by charming them, learning what they wanted, and offering it. They all were vulnerable because of issues with their fathers, and they always wanted another father figure. John said pimps are masters at exploiting that vulnerability. That was why he worked tirelessly at Urban Venture's Center for Fathering after he put his life together. John, thanks for talking to me. I'm sorry it took me too long to finish a manuscript draft.

Thanks to the real-world St. Paul Hotel for letting me use its lobby and hallway as a stand-in for the fictional Norra lekplatsen to snap pictures. And to Joan, Nicole, and Caleb for posing for pictures I used on the book website page. That's Joan and Nicole in the back cover picture, playing Leilani and Ashley escaping.

Thanks to beta readers, Gemma, Gloria, Hannah, Kayla, Jon, Darolyn, PJ, Jan, Mike, and others who want to stay anonymous. You guys helped make the characters better. I am in your debt.

Thanks to pastor Kevin with the real-world Onamia, MN. Alliance Church for reading the manuscript and offering feedback.

Thanks to all the writers in the Jerry Jenkins Your Novel Blueprint group. And to Jerry himself. Jerry's mentorship and the critiques everyone in the group offers back and forth are priceless.

Thanks to Cynthia Hickey and the team with Winged Publications for saying yes, and for sticking with it when my over-eager spam filter hid their emails.

Thanks to copy editor Kathryn Eckert, who fixed my grammar, spelling, and typos. And thanks to beta reader Jan who pointed out the difference between "discreet" and "discrete." I hope that was the last copy edit problem, but the odds are still good that I missed a few. If you find such problems, let me know. We're distributing this as an ebook with Print on Demand (POD) for paperback copies, so we should be able to fix typos on an ongoing basis.

Finally, thanks to you for reading my book. Readers are the reason writers write.

For more about safety on the Internet, see my earlier novels, *Virus Bomb* and *Bullseye Breach: Anatomy of an Electronic Break-In*. And keep an eye on my website, https://www.dgregscott.com, for future novels. Enjoy the fiction. Use the education.

Liars, cheats, manipulators, predators, and perverts all use the internet to ensnare vulnerable people. Keep an eye on https://www.dgregscott.com/social-media-online-abuse-resources/ for resources to fight back. I'll add more links over time.

-        Greg Scott, March 8, 2024

Author D. Greg Scott spends nights and weekends researching ways to hijack trucks, blow up buildings, launch cyberattacks, groom vulnerable people, and improve his writing. During the 1990s, he wrote a popular back-page column with IT industry publication, ENT Magazine. He was also a pioneer ferreting out online grooming. In 1994, he accepted Jesus as his Lord and savior. He published "Bullseye Breach" in 2015 and "Virus Bomb" in 2019.

Made in the USA
Monee, IL
16 April 2024

56664337R00233